SPOTLESS

SPOTLESS

CAMILLA MONK

Montlake
Romance

Text copyright © 2015 Camilla Monk
All rights reserved.

Published by Montlake Romance, Seattle

www.apub.com

Amazon, the Amazon logo, and Montlake Romance are trademarks of Amazon.com, Inc., or its affiliates.

ISBN-13: 9781477829714
ISBN-10: 1477829717

Cover design by M.S. Corley

Library of Congress Control Number: 2014958511

Printed in the United States of America

This book is dedicated to B. who wasn't even allowed to read it, M., M.J. & M.S. who know a thing or two about cleaning, P., whose trips to Africa certainly inspired me, and A. who knows just how special she is to me.

Table of Contents

Author's note:

All quotes introducing this book's chapters are—thank God—fictional.

Well, except for chapter 31: I give back to Caesar what belongs to Caesar.

ONE

The Visit

"The icy professional they called 'the Nazi' was the cruelest, most dangerous assassin in the world, a heartless madman whose sadistic fantasies could only be fulfilled by the darkest hobbies."

—Jayna Devile, *From Russia with Lust*

I could start by explaining why my parents called me Island, or even dissert on the many reasons why being the daughter of a Frenchwoman and an American curmudgeon can traumatize a child for life . . . but I suspect no one really cares. So let's start with the day my apartment got cleaned—I promise this is more interesting than it sounds.

It was a Friday in late October, and much like the rest of my colleagues in EM Tech's R&D department, I had spent the entire day looking for a way to fix a major bug in our latest banking app. Around 5:20, I finished the floor's last Dr Pepper, pressed Enter, and announced to my colleagues that our software was back on track. I then proceeded to call them losers—in a common display of virile superiority over fellow engineers—and, for once, left early.

I can still see myself walking up Amsterdam Avenue that evening. I kept combing my auburn bob with my fingers and checking my reflection in store windows because I was particularly proud of my new duffle coat. Joy said it was too long, though, that it didn't flatter a petite figure like mine, and that I needed to show some leg if I ever wanted to get laid. As my roommate and best friend, she had grown to feel it was her responsibility to ensure that I would lose my virginity before my lady-bits crumbled to dust, thus she spared me no amount of encouragement to update both my wardrobe and my profile on Yaycupid.

I mostly ignored her advice, because at twenty-five, all I had ever accomplished with men was some silent stalking and a few awkward dates. I blamed it on the combination of round hazel eyes and a childish gap-toothed grin that still occasionally got me carded for cocktails, but in truth, I feared it had more to do with . . . well, *me*. I wish I had been a blonde and blue-eyed hurricane like Joy. Surely that would have helped a little.

To be fair, this was a nonissue, since I had tons of romance books to occupy my Saturday nights with, whose heroes were much more exciting than any of my dates had ever been. Billionaires, vampires, werewolves, cowboys . . . you name it. And they all came wrapped up in super-passionate love stories where the heroine is not only smart but also beautiful, and no one ever tells her that real adults don't use the Japanese restaurant's chopsticks to pretend they possess antennae—this particular piece of advice is from my stepmom, Janice, by the way. She keeps a pic of Jimmy Kimmel in her wallet all the time, so you bet she knows what it means to be a real adult.

———

It wasn't long before I entered our old building on West Eighty-First Street. I liked that place: the paint in the hallway was chipping something awful, but I've always had a thing for early prewar, and the neighborhood was pretty quiet. Joy and I had moved into a comfy little two-bedroom nest on the second floor after her epic breakup with Clown-dick—aka David-the-senior-accountant, who had publicly threatened to marry her and put babies in her vagina; dreadful stuff. I could tell Joy was grateful for the change of air after eleven months spent with an overly demonstrative creep, and I, on the other hand, enjoyed her joyful presence— no pun intended—as well as the privilege of more space for less money.

I climbed the stairs because the elevator was broken, as usual—kept telling myself I'd bitch to the super about it, never got around to doing so. It was only six fifteen; I rarely left my desk before seven thirty, and there was no doubt in my mind that I was going to make the most of this evening and, at long last, do some cleaning in our grotto.

Yeah.

Okay, I was probably lying to myself. Joy and I shared rather liberal views on housekeeping, making the jungle of poorly assembled Ikea furniture we called home a complete war zone. Heaps of clothes and books littered our respective bedrooms, three days' worth of dishes snoozed in the sink, and a delicate sheen of dust covered our vacuum cleaner, which I believe speaks eloquently of just how many shits were given in this house.

At any rate, when I turned the key in the lock, I was confident that tonight was going to be different and that those Oreo crumbs between our couch's cushions were going to meet their match. I was right about that specific point, by the way, but I'm getting ahead of myself. I closed the door behind me, entered the living room, and . . . nearly had a heart attack.

A huge, dark figure stood there, back turned to me.

Maybe I'm overdoing it a bit because of the initial shock. I suppose it wasn't unlike those times when you wake up in the middle of the night and you mistake that coat hanging from the wall for a ghost. Past that second when I felt the blood thrum in my ears, I realized that while the creature before me was indeed tall—likely topping my regal five-foot-three stature by a foot—and broad shouldered, the rest of him suggested a regular male rather than a Nazgûl.

Short chestnut hair, a well-cut navy-blue jacket . . . I allowed air to escape my lungs in a long sigh: I had obviously just run into one of Joy's conquests. She didn't give them keys that often, but when she did, I could be sure that I'd eventually come home to some hunky asswipe helping himself to my granola bars.

In this particular case, the latest addition to her ever growing collection of "Joy toys" didn't seem to have registered my presence yet. And I was more than a little pissed that she had once again failed to issue a proper notice regarding the arrival of a new model. Wasn't she supposed to still be dating her Pilates instructor? That being said, I wasn't going to bite the poor guy's head off just because she had forgotten to warn me of his presence.

I examined the faint movement of his shoulders as he stood in front of the long black sideboard resting between the living room's windows. In his hands I caught sight of a few papers.

Change of plan. I *was* going to bite his head off.

"*Excuse me*, those are my tax returns. Can I ask you not to touch anything here? And maybe to introduce yourself?" I had meant to sound collected, but I ended up snapping at him.

My guest didn't bother to turn around, and kept reading my tax returns as if he hadn't heard me.

He had, though.

"Good evening, Miss Chaptal. Please make yourself comfortable while I finish this."

The nerve of that guy . . . Concise, precise, courteous. *Totally unfazed.* I registered a faint accent. Been here for quite a while, but not American. British, maybe? I didn't like his little game. "I'm glad Joy warned you that I live here too. Care to explain why you're snooping into my papers?"

That jerk just ignored me.

Now fully pissed, I crossed the room and tried to pull at his arm to stop him. "Hey, I'm talking to you!"

When he finally turned to look at me, I registered just how thick his arm was: my grip loosened and I felt my pulse quicken a little. I was no longer merely irked by the guy's blatant disrespect; he was starting to scare me.

A cold blue gaze met mine, and the smile he gave me didn't quite reach his eyes. "I believe I just asked you to wait until I'm finished. Why don't you take a seat?"

My throat went dry. I let go of his arm and took a step back. "A-Are you Joy's . . . Is she the one who gave you the keys?"

"No. I'm here for you, Island."

My heart rate sped up brutally, and I registered a heaving sensation in my stomach, like the room around us was spinning. I think my legs moved before I even made the conscious decision to escape: I bolted and tried to make a break for the apartment's door, shrieking at the top of my lungs in hopes that Mrs. Josefsky, our neighbor, would have turned on her hearing aids for once. "Stay away, don't come near me! I'm calling the police!"

A viselike grip around my shoulders hauled me backward before I could reach the door, and a chill of absolute terror spread through my body, from the center of my chest to the very tips of my fingers. My black tote bag slid off from my shoulder and landed on the floor with a soft thud, its contents scattering at our feet. A black-gloved hand released my right shoulder to clamp onto my mouth, squeezing my cheeks almost painfully. I struggled against him and let out a series of muffled howls. Tears started building at the corners of my eyes when I realized that my vocalizations were growing weaker: my throat was too raw, my breath too short.

After twenty seconds or so, all my vocal cords were able to produce were weak croaking sounds in between short pants. I felt like I was drowning. As my voice died, the grip around my mouth progressively lessened, and I registered his breath against my hair. "Can I trust you not to scream again?"

I nodded shakily. He released my mouth. The hand holding my shoulder never let go, however, as he turned me around to face him like a limp ragdoll. He didn't seem angry, or even flustered in any way. He just brought a gloved index finger to his lips with a warning look.

We spent a good minute like that, both standing still near the apartment's entrance door, waiting for someone, anyone, to respond to my screams. It felt like time had thickened, slowed down and trapped me: Every single muscle in my body was paralyzed; my breathing had nearly stopped. The fingers resting on my shoulder splayed and traveled down my arm, until they lingered around my wrist in a near-caress. I shivered. Blood was drumming in my ears, and in that moment, my universe shrank until it was contained entirely in this stranger's dark blue eyes. Call it a reverse big bang if you will.

Outside the apartment, nothing came. Only silence.

The soulless smile he had greeted me with returned, and he waved a scolding finger at me. "Please don't do that again. Why don't you make us some coffee instead?"

I blinked. "I . . . What?"

His lips twitched and he tilted his head, amusement filling his once icy irises. "Coffee. You know? Ground roasted beans, water, cup . . . coffee."

I can only assume that his joke was meant to ease the atmosphere a bit and make sure I wouldn't scream again while he did whatever he had come here to do. It didn't work. All his faint smile reminded me of was Jack Nicholson smiling at Shelley Duvall before trying to cut her to pieces with an axe in *The Shining*. The beads of sweat that had formed on my temples earlier now felt cold. I gave a timid nod. Anything to get away from him.

I stepped back with slow, controlled movements, my eyes never leaving his, watching for any sign that he might try to grab me again.

I noticed my tote bag, which was still on the floor, a few feet away. A couple of crumpled candy wrappers had escaped during its fall, and they were now lying near the couch; his gaze focused on them as well, his smile faltering for a second.

Focusing on my phone, I forced my lips into what I hoped was a friendly and submissive rictus. "Sorry about that, I'll pick it all up."

The smile he gave me seemed just as sincere as mine. "No, don't worry. I'll take care of it. Remove your coat and go prepare that coffee, please."

He knelt down and reached for my phone first. Watching him slide it in his jeans pocket rather than back into my bag, I gulped softly. With some effort, I tore my eyes away from his hands gathering my tampons, shrugged off my coat, and flung it on the couch. As soon as he saw this, his hands stopped working, his eyes narrowed, and he gave me a long, disapproving gaze.

I felt myself shrink under his stern scrutiny. Was it maybe a fashion faux pas? As my mind raced in search for an explanation, my eyes darted to the coat stand a few feet away.

He saw this, and his smile returned. "That would be more indicated."

Picking up the garment warily, I went to hang it, before scurrying toward the kitchen. His voice stopped me before I could make it in; my hand froze on the doorknob.

"Island, I usually try to make things like this go well, but I suppose they can also go terribly wrong." I turned to look at him. From this angle the front of his jacket gaped slightly, revealing a gun in a black holster.

Oh God. What things, exactly?

I thought it would be better to know right away just how wrong "things" were going to be. "A-are you a mobster?"

He seemed genuinely puzzled. "I don't know how to answer this. What's your definition of a mobster?"

"Um, it's someone who works for the Mafia and kills people," I offered.

"I only kill people."

That one turned my spine into a Popsicle.

I took a quivering breath and entered the kitchen.

As soon as the door had closed behind me, I lunged at the cutlery drawer, searching it with shaking hands. I didn't have much of a plan, though, and when I found myself holding a flashy pink vegetable knife—the only object that came close to fitting the definition of a weapon in our apartment—I started entertaining doubts. It wouldn't do, not against a gun. My eyes fell on the kettle. Boiling water, straight in his face. Plus knife. That could work . . .

"Do you need any help, Island?"

I jumped so badly at the sound of his voice that I nearly dropped the knife. My left hand gripped the counter for support while my heart slowed down. Forget the kettle. I needed to make that coffee, or else he'd come in, see me plotting his assassination with my pink knife, and cut me in half like a baby carrot.

"No . . . I-I'm good," I yelled through the door.

I froze for a couple of seconds, listening to the noises coming from living room, trying to assess whether he'd come in or not. Nope. Thank you, Raptor Jesus. I searched the wooden cupboards and retrieved two long boxes, half-filled with colorful capsules. Decaf imposed itself: No need to give a self-admitted killer a caffeine rush. While the coffee machine spat drop after drop of *Whatevero decaffeinatto* into a small white cup, I glanced at the microwave's clock: 7:10. Joy wouldn't be back from Pilates before nine thirty, and Leatherface back there had taken my phone. There was the landline, though. Maybe I could distract him long enough to reach it and call 911? I stared back and forth between the pink knife, still lying on the counter, and the dark liquid now filling the cup.

Strange how the rich, smoky aroma floating in the air was almost comforting.

I made up my mind and returned to the living room with a stiff back and wobbly legs. He was still there, of course. Everything had been placed back in my bag, which was now resting near the couch and well out of reach. He seemed to be done inspecting my tax returns, but before he placed them back on the sideboard, I saw him stop to fiddle with them some more. I didn't understand, until I focused my eyes on each sheet of paper.

2013.

2012.

2011.

That sicko was sorting them back in chronological order.

No wonder I hadn't suspected anything when first entering the apartment: the place actually looked better than when I had left in the morning, as if he had been putting each object he touched back in its rightful place while he searched our stuff.

Which was in all likelihood what he had done.

I heard a clatter. In my trembling hands, the cup of coffee was rattling against the small saucer. I gritted my teeth and exhaled. I had to collect myself if I was going to spend the evening with some neat freak home invader and survive.

He turned to look at me with that cold and disarming smile of his. "Thank you. You can leave it on the coffee table."

I complied, searching his eyes. "Who are you? What do you want from me?"

"People call me March," he said, picking up the fuming cup. "And I think you know why I'm here, Island."

No, I didn't, and it felt very strange to realize that having a name to put on this man's face didn't change anything. After all, no one remembered Jack Torrance's name; his face, however, smiling maniacally through a jagged hole in a door, axe in hand, had become the incarnation of terror and entrapment. And so, my visitor's name was "March." First name? Last name? What did it matter? To me, he was merely the shape fear had molded itself into. I blocked from my mind the innumerable possibilities and tried to keep my tone neutral. "You don't seem like a burglar. What do you want, March? What do I have to do to make you go?"

At first he didn't reply. He just took several slow sips of coffee, appraising me. I seized the opportunity to do the same, trying to memorize every detail. At least I would be able to provide the cops with a precise description, should I live to do so.

His neat and ordinary looks clearly belied his brawny build—and the extent of his civility, as I had already found out. Shaved closely, no black mobster suit or anything terribly formal: just a pair of jeans, an immaculate white shirt, that blue jacket, and well-polished brown oxfords hinting at a spit-shining fetish. Scanning his chiseled features and deep-set blue eyes, I found his physical appearance sort of deceptive, especially since he kept such a relaxed, half-smiling expression that high-lighted two dimples. The faintest crow's-feet suggested he had passed the thirty-year mark. My eyes lingered on his light chestnut hair. Here again, no crazy middle-parted hairdo that might have hinted he was a maniac. Just your basic short cut that probably got wavy when it grew.

He seemed to notice I was staring, and something shifted in his expression, a twitch of his brow, a slight hardening of his features. He placed the cup back on the table and took a few steps toward me, moving with predatory grace.

"I'm looking for two billion dollars. Any idea where I can find something worth that, Island?"

Well . . . I sure hadn't expected that one. I know it's going to sound stupid, but my mind suddenly started reeling with dozens of positive-outcome scenarios. March had the wrong person; he was clearly hunting for much bigger fish than me. Granted, he wasn't exactly a gentleman, but so far he hadn't shot me, right? Maybe he'd leave if I swore never to mention our encounter to anyone? Choosing to ignore the obvious alternative—that his routine might include eliminating witnesses—I crossed the room to retrieve a stack of crumpled sheets from the top shelf of the bookcase standing near our couch. I walked back to him, handing him my pay stubs with a pleading look. "Look, I have no idea what you're talking about, but I swear I won't press charges if you just leave." His eyes widened, and what might have passed as a genuine smile deepened his dimples. "You have a remarkable sense of humor, Island. Right now, however, your priority shouldn't be to make me laugh but to tell me where that stone is and how you plan on returning it."

What the . . . ?

I took a step back, letting the pay stubs fall from my hands. I had wanted to believe I could rule over my fear long enough to face him. But it was back with a vengeance, squeezing my lungs.

Oddly enough, I looked up to see that March's expression appeared to mirror mine. His throat constricted at the sight of the dozens of papers scattered at my feet. "Please pick them up and place them back on your shelf."

All right, the guy completely had a cleaning disorder.

I figured it wasn't worth testing him further to discover just how many wires hung loose in that brain of his: I quickly knelt down to pick up my pay stubs, as I had been instructed. Before I could complete the movement, though, a sharp pain at the base of my spine stopped me. I jerked up reflexively and panic exploded in my chest.

Oh God. Nonononono!

Above me, I heard a deep, long sigh. He had seen it. Or maybe guessed. It was all the same: March knew about the vegetable knife, the one I had clumsily tucked in my tights' waistline under my little wool dress, and which had just—quite literally—stabbed me in the back when I'd bent down.

Performing a rigid ballet, I picked the papers up anyway, aware of the warm blade brushing again my spine with each movement, wondering if it showed that well through my dress. Once I was done gathering them in a neat stack, I got up slowly and handed them to March, my eyes downcast. He took the pay stubs wordlessly and extended an arm to place them back on the shelf without leaving me any room for escape.

I found the strength to sustain his gaze, and when my eyes met his, I physically felt myself blanch. I couldn't see it, of course, but there was this prickling sensation, like a thousand shards of ice biting my cheeks, cooling the sweat there, and I knew blood was draining from my face.

He held out his hand without a word, pinning me in place with his intense, knowing stare. Tears built fast, blurring the edges of my vision, and my own hands were shaking so badly that it took me ages to reach behind me and fumble with the hem of my dress. It's a little pathetic, but I tried not to lift it too much because I didn't want to undress in front of this guy.

I finally managed to extract the flashy pink blade from under the gray wool. He remained silent, the muscles in his jaw tightening as the knife came in sight. It crossed my mind that I could try to use the knife: I mentally pictured myself taking a wild swing in his direction to wound him.

I can only assume March read my thoughts, since he . . . Well, he judoed me, for lack of a better word. In a split second, I felt a painful grip on my wrist that made me drop the knife, and one of his legs swiped mine, causing me to lose my balance. His free arm locked around my waist to catch my fall, before he hauled me like a bag and flung me over his shoulder caveman style. That day, I discovered that all those ninety-nine-cent romance novels had lied to me.

There was *nothing* even remotely pleasant about being swept off your feet.

TWO

The First Time

"Shouldn't she feel guilty that she was allowing this huge werewolf to force himself on her? But he was so perfect and well-muscled! Cindee's body reacted instantly."

—Gilda Sapphire, *Scorching Passion of the Billionaire Werewolf*

My memories after the whole judo attack are a bit blurry, but I know I struggled and cried hysterically all the way to my bedroom. Of all the outcomes I had envisioned, rape had been the least likely until now, because the guy appeared to be looking for something specific, and let's be honest, that smooth bastard and his dimples didn't look like they needed to resort to coercion in order to get laid.

Needless to say, when he dropped me face-first on my flowery comforter, I was quickly reconsidering my earlier assessment of the situation. I tried to bat his hands away as he leaned toward me, resting one knee on the mattress.

"Don't touch me! Don't touch me or I'll—"

"Or what, Island?"

I couldn't come up with any satisfying answer to this rather rhetorical question, and I guess that's more or less when what little backbone I had been holding on to until then deserted me. He locked my arms against my back, his hold both inescapable and unexpectedly controlled. My heart raced and pounded against my rib cage until it hurt. Common sense screamed for me to call for help or to try to struggle again, but March clearly overpowered me, and I had no idea what he might do if he so much as saw me open my mouth. This time, the call remained stuck in my vocal cords as he shifted to sit on the edge of the bed.

"Y-You're going to rape me?"

"No. I'm going to interrogate you."

Whatever relief his initial denial had caused me promptly vanished, replaced by horrifying visions of movie spies getting their fingers cut off with pruners. An unpleasant pressure started building in my skull, and my thoughts scattered like pieces of a broken mirror: I could picture myself reacting in hundreds of different ways, but my body remained paralyzed. I just froze and tried to block what was happening—the slight warmth elicited by the contact of his hand on my arm and his faint scent of coffee and mint. He brought my wrists closer together, and I heard a metallic sound behind my back. Somewhere in the maze of my mind, a little chunk of gray matter that wasn't pissing itself in terror connected this sound with the cold sensation around my wrists.

He had handcuffed me.

My arms jerked in an instinctive response, and I think that the realization I was physically restrained triggered something primal within me. It was way too late, but I fought back for real this time, Bruce-Lee style and all.

Pumped up with adrenaline, I tried to roll away from him. My legs flailed and kicked in all directions, and I thought I had landed one good hit against his stomach with my right heel, but all my foot met were hard muscles under the fabric of his shirt; he didn't even flinch. My little loafers went flying around us, one landing near the bed, the other hitting the wall. I howled in rage and tried to kick him again. This time, he stopped my heel effortlessly, rewarding the initiative by a strong grip on my neck and a cool warning.

"Don't push your luck, Island."

What luck? The battle cry died in my throat, along with my offensive. There was a beat, a floating couple of seconds during which I released a trembling breath. I heard him exhale as well, and I felt his fingers tapping gently twice against the nape of my neck, as if he had just come to a decision regarding my fate.

Lightning-quick, one of his hands sprang to reach under my gray sweater dress and grab the hem of my tights. He pulled down, and my panties threatened to roll down my thighs along with them. I couldn't process this: hadn't he said that he wouldn't . . . ? I let out a panicked sob, begging him not to rape me, and squeezed my legs together. I felt his fingers untangle themselves from my underwear, though, to focus solely on the tights. A swift tug nearly tore the black cotton, and they came down.

I was in all likelihood being assaulted by a former cowboy, since March had just lassoed me with my own fricking tights. I whimpered in fear at the realization that my ankles were now locked together by the stretchy material.

A little part of me still wanted to be strong, but all I did was bury my face in the pillow, hot tears wetting its red peonies pattern. His fingers threaded in my hair, caressing it in a surprisingly gentle manner, considering the way he had treated me until now.

"This doesn't have to be difficult. Tell me where it is, and I'll let you go." His voice had turned soft, coaxing.

It only made me weep harder. "I swear I have no idea what you're talking about . . . please don't kill me!"

He was about to speak when a faint noise coming from the apartment's entrance door caught his attention and mine. We both heard the lock at the same time, and my chest swelled with a mixture of dread and hope when I heard Joy's despondent voice in the living room.

"It's me . . . I need a hug, and an Irish cocoa . . . 'cause right now I wanna die."

Well, that could be arranged on short notice.

I registered March's short huff of aggravation. Mr. Clean actually seemed surprised. Scratch that, he *was* surprised. As I'd learn later, our phones had been tapped, and our respective schedules diligently tracked. My working hours and Tuesday yoga, Joy's Friday Pilates followed by hot sex. He already knew it all. The only thing March couldn't have guessed was that I would call it a day at five instead of seven, while, somewhere in SoHo, Joy was getting dumped over a kale and banana juice by her Pilates instructor.

All that crying had broken my voice. I barely heard myself croak against the pillow. "Joy! Call the p—"

March didn't need to cover my mouth this time. He pressed his hand against my neck again and I shut up instantly, deciphering the unspoken message on the tip of his fingers.

"Please, don't hurt Joy—" I whispered my plea, afraid that a mere decibel too much might cost Joy her life.

"Then tell her to leave us alone."

I said the first thing that came to my mind, hoping she would buy it, but I had a feeling this wouldn't end well. "Joy, I thought you'd be with Dan . . . Don't come in. I-I'm with someone—"

It didn't end well.

There was a slight rustling sound that I assumed was her coat landing where it belonged—on the couch, mind you—and high heels clanked on the wooden floor as she rushed to my bedroom. March stood up, ready to deal with her, and I gave him a desperate look when I saw him adjusting his black gloves over his knuckles. I remember grinding my teeth in tune with the faint squeak of the leather.

Joy burst in the doorway, her long golden locks falling over her shoulders, her eyes wide.

Silence sometimes speaks louder than words. The ten seconds of absolute peace, the wordless intensity filling the room as she took in the scene before her, those were worth a thousand oratorios rising to the firmament to celebrate an event of biblical proportions. I was lying on my bed facedown, handcuffed, my legs tied with my own tights, my panties showing; a handsome guy stood near me, and I thought Joy was going to cry.

She didn't. But it was a close call: when she recovered the ability to speak, her tone was reverent. "Oh my God . . . Finally. Finally!"

Her eyes then met March's; I winced as a suggestive smile stirred her lips. "Mmm . . . which is it? Sir . . . ? Daddy, maybe?"

Seriously? Daddy?

Joy would probably be safe, since she had no clue what was going on. I, on the other hand, would die, and all people would remember about me was how my life had ended at the tender age of twenty-five, in a miscalculated BDSM scene.

I returned to nuzzling my pillow in shame and defeat. "Joy, can you leave us—"

"Oh. Sure . . . I guess I can go see a movie. Do you guys have everything you need? Booze, toys, *protection?*"

"Yes, thank you, Joy." March seemed to know exactly how to make his voice sound deep and sexy when needed. Had I not known any better, I almost could have believed he was about to perform.

She wiggled her hips with a provocative grin and turned to leave, sending a last wink in our direction. "Losing your V-card *Fifty Shades of Grey* style. I respect you, girl. You're gonna have to tell me e-very-thing!"

And with this, she was gone.

After the apartment's door had slammed, March focused his attention back to me, and there was a sympathetic smile on his face. "Good thing it's not what we're here for. I can't think of a worse scenario for a first time."

I won't lie. For a second there, when I heard his meditative tone, devoid of the threatening edge it previously held, I thought Joy's intervention had defused the whole situation and that March had fallen prey to her innate ability to lighten the mood wherever she went.

I was wrong.

As soon as he had said this, he switched back to inquisitor mode, grabbing my right elbow and twisting it against the cuffs with controlled pressure. "Island, my employer has been hunting that diamond for more than a decade. So tell me where it is, or I'll break your limbs one after another until you talk. Do you understand?"

I was far beyond rational thinking, and all I could do in response was wail and pant. The discomfort slowly grew in intensity, my joint fighting its unnatural position, and when I thought things couldn't get any worse, it started.

I knew the signs: the dull thudding against my temples had been present for half an hour or so. I had been prone to occasional but violent bouts of migraines since the age of fifteen, a permanent souvenir of the car accident that had killed my mother in Tokyo and left me in a coma for two weeks. The strain in my arm increased; I could no longer move, no longer breathe. My entire skull exploded with white-hot pain. I slammed my head against the pillow and hissed in agony.

Of course he didn't buy it, no doubt filing me as a wimp. "I haven't even started . . . Wait at least until it hurts."

There was the slightest hint of mockery in his voice, and I hated him even more for that, especially since I was going to have to beg. My mouth was watering already, and the unpleasant sensation in my esophagus told me this was going to be a large migraine with a side of nausea.

"I need to go to the bathroom."

My plea fell into deaf ears. "I'm sorry to inform you that it can and will wait."

Giving up all control, I screamed, "March, I'm going to throw up!"

I felt his grip loosen, as if he were pondering the authenticity of my plea.

My entire body shook in urgency as I begged again, my voice cracking. "Please! Please!"

I suppose that the prospect of vomit all over the sheets carried a peculiar sense of threat for a guy who loved order so much. Strong hands hauled my body and carried me to the small bathroom, setting me in front of the toilet. I bent forward and waited for a few torturous seconds, soon rewarding us both with a series of awful gurgles as my stomach heaved and poured its contents in the bowl. Once I was done, the nausea itself was momentarily relieved, but the waves crashing inside my skull wouldn't stop. I let myself fall on the old blue tiling and rubbed my forehead against the cool surface in despair.

I think it was the head rubbing that gave him a hint. Kneeling beside me, March turned me over, cradling my face in his right hand with unreadable eyes. "You have a migraine."

I nodded haphazardly, sweating, unable to talk. The ceiling light was setting my eyeballs on fire, and my surroundings were getting blurry.

He remained perfectly Zen, as if all his victims always collapsed in a similar fashion. "Do you have any medication?"

I managed to raise my chin at the mirror cabinet resting above the sink, prompting him to get up and open it. As he examined the jungle of beauty products crammed onto the shelves, I rasped two mangled syllables that he was able to connect with the box of Zomig resting in front of him. When he pried my mouth open, I gladly welcomed the tablet, letting it dissolve under my tongue.

I felt the cuffs around my wrists and the tights squeezing my ankles come undone before he carried me into the tub. I still had my clothes on, but I was so out of it I didn't care. Warm water started pouring on my head and neck, and when his hands moved to cup my cheeks, I registered he had removed his gloves at some point. I progressively went limp as large thumbs pressed on my temples, massaging the pain away in slow circles.

The motion was familiar. Like a gentle swell rocking me. I remembered the sun peeking behind clouds, kissing a long teak deck. The turquoise sea. A boat in Antigua that belonged to a man. A friend of my mother, or maybe a work acquaintance, I wasn't sure. My mind wandered to her long auburn curls and vibrant green eyes. I thought of those fifteen years spent wandering the world with her, of happy times . . . until the descent into darkness, and at the end of the rabbit's hole, the white light of the hospital room. I had come to live with my father in New York afterward and tried my best to ease into a new lifestyle made of regular school attendance, friends, or concerns about finding a suitable prom dress . . . Stupid, foreign notions that had made me feel trapped.

Trapped like in that burning car.

Trapped in March's arms.

I tried to shake his touch away, but I was getting increasingly drowsy and my movements seemed slowed, as if I had been struggling at the bottom of some warm, viscous lake. The last thing I heard was the shower stopping and March's voice as he answered a phone call. "No . . . nothing significant at this point . . . I understand . . . I won't interfere again unless there's a need to."

I begged my brain to stick with me and make sense of all this, but it declined, and everything went black.

THREE

The Cherries

"Her sweet lips tasted like an entire basket of fresh cherries, and her supple body was soft and pliant in his strong arms. 'Oh, Jed,' she gasped. 'Your embrace is a dream I never want to wake up from!'"

—Sidney Rush, *Hearts Colliding in Applebarnville*

According to my alarm clock, I slept for seventeen hours. When I woke up, it was Saturday afternoon, I was tucked in bed, wearing my Mortal Wombat nightshirt, and I could smell my own breath. Rubbing my eyes, I looked around before getting up on unsteady legs.

March . . . Where was March?

Had he even been real? There was no trace of the man, and my room didn't look like it had been searched. It looked . . . Well, it looked like some cleaning had taken place, but I had no idea when. I sure as hell never put my clothes in the laundry basket, and I was pretty certain those books were supposed to cover the floor rather than stand neatly aligned on my bookshelf. I couldn't hear Joy. Perhaps she would help me clarify the fudge of incoherent memories filling my head. She had been part of my dream, after all.

As I wobbled my way to the living room and inspected my surroundings, my eyes narrowed to slits. Something was *wrong* in there. Raising my right foot to look at its sole, my heart skipped a beat—it was clean. There was no dust, nothing on the floor. I checked the furniture with trembling fingertips. Where had all our dust gone?

All around me, countless subtle changes betrayed the horrifying truth. Someone had cleaned our apartment. Someone with issues. A trickle of sweat ran down my back at the sight of the perfectly arranged cushions on the couch. My gaze stopped on the sideboard, and I opened all its drawers frantically, searching for my tax returns.

They were sorted in chronological order.

Holy Macanoli!

I barged into the kitchen to finish my inspection, only to bite back a scream at the sight of our sparkling clean, dish-free sink. Spotting a note stuck to the fridge, I read its contents, my gaze still somewhat unfocused. Joy had left me a message:

> In Southampton with Holly for the weekend.
> BTW, no man ever did that to me . . .
>
> Marry him.
> XOJ.

Yeah well, no man had ever tied me up either before March, and I sure as hell wasn't going to marry one who'd be into that sort of stuff—I made a mental note to ask upfront, next time I went on a date.

Once in the bathroom, I took what was possibly the quickest shower of my life before hunting for the first clothes I could get my hands on. My knees buckled when I opened my underwear drawer— neatly folded and sorted by fricking color. *March.* I made damn sure I messed my stuff back into complete chaos while I fished for a bra and a pair of panties. This was a question of honor.

The rest of my room would have to wait since I had more urgent matters to attend to. I jumped into a pair of jeans and an old gray hoodie, slipped on a pair of ballet flats, and barged back into the living room to take my tote bag. It was still sitting in the exact same place March had left it the previous night, near the couch. The guy was definitely not a burglar: My phone was back in the front pocket, the only tidbits missing were my SIM and SD cards. Nothing crucial, really. *Asshole.* I tucked my bag over my shoulder with a grunt. There was no time to waste: I needed to go to the precinct as soon as possible. Now that the evening's fog had dissipated, I was starting to realize how lucky I was that this malevolent fruitcake had somehow left—maybe gangsters had their shifts too. Still, he could come back anytime, perhaps with some friends . . .

I flew down the stairs and across the lobby, running all the way to Broadway, only to freeze when I reached the avenue. Around me, the trees were turning a coppery hue as autumn progressed, my favorite bookstore had received an entire box of Aquaman comics that they were selling by the weight; all shops looked the same as usual . . . Yet I suddenly felt lost. There, standing in the pale afternoon light, surrounded by the hum of the city, I got scared. Of cars, of passersby, of everything. My heart started racing, my head spinning; long story short, I was freaking out in front of Staples.

I took a series of deep breaths to calm myself. All I needed to do was take the 1 line to Columbus Circle, and I'd be at the Midtown North Precinct in less than fifteen minutes.

I was shaken out of my stupor by a strong smell of industrial cherry, and the feeling of a hand on my shoulder. I jerked and turned to see a red-haired girl with tired, puffy eyes, a little too much makeup, and a shabby beige fur coat. My eyes focused on her thin pink lips; she seemed to be chewing something—candy, no doubt.

She swallowed before speaking. "Hey, you okay?"

"Uhm. I think so. Thank you."

"You were like . . . freaking out . . . and you look like shit." She grinned, revealing oddly decayed, almost translucent teeth.

I returned her smile nervously. She was nice to have noticed that I was having some sort of panic attack, but right now, the only help I wanted was that of a cop. I glanced at the subway station's entrance, a little farther down the avenue. I realized I couldn't do it. The idea of being alone among all these people, any of whom could be March, the noise, the crowd . . . I couldn't.

She seemed to read my mind. "Wanna get a cab?"

I nodded and gazed at the traffic on Broadway; a couple of cabs seemed available. I stretched my right arm to hail one, but my newly appointed guardian angel acted before I could.

Damn, that girl had a strong whistle. My ears rang from the shrill echo, and a yellow Ford instantly stopped a few feet away from us, tires screeching on the asphalt. Inside the vehicle a young black guy with a shaven skull and a short beard greeted me with a smile. I opened the passenger door and stepped in.

I smelled the cherry before I fully figured what was going on, and discovered that the girl had climbed inside the cab with me. She flashed me that odd, ravaged smile again. I sighed. "You want a ride, right?" No wonder she had been so nice.

Her eyes darted to the cab driver. She took a quivering breath. Any other day I would have laughed at myself for ending up stuck in a cab with a potential junkie, but I wasn't exactly feeling peachy, and her weird, invasive manners were now creeping me out. Fighting the slight buzz under my temples, I fumbled in my bag until my fingers met the leather of my wallet. "Look, I'll give you some money for a cab, but I need to be alone, I—"

I saw her arm move from the corner of my eye, and yelped when the pain registered in my thigh. The buzzing in my ears became louder; I looked down where she had just stabbed me with some sort of needle. I think it took me a couple of seconds to start screaming and shield

myself while my legs kicked at her in a fit of panic. I have vague memories of her exiting the car with equally panicked shrieks and crying
to someone that she just wanted her money. My vision was becoming
blurry, my body felt heavy, and to be honest, I think the memory I have
of reaching for the cab's door to try to open it is fabricated. I'm pretty
sure I was in fact sprawled on the backseat, hallucinating and seeing
myself escaping in the street, but my body wouldn't move. In the front
seat, the driver had remained perfectly calm, his head turned to better
watch me sink.

My thoughts melted in a confused treacle in which swirled safety
instructions regarding used needles, and a few verses from a song Joy
loved.

I'm paralyzed and you are still alive.

FOUR

The Woods

"Ramirez laughed evilly. 'Ha, ha! Rica, your luscious body will surrender to my sensual torture; no one will ever come to rescue you!'"

—Kerry-Lee Storm, *The Cost of Rica*

When I regained consciousness, the first thing I felt was something cold against my right cheek. I cracked an eye open. Glass. I was in a sitting position, and my face was squished against a window. My tongue felt strange. Dry, aching. Scratch that: my entire face felt like that. Brownish-green, ocher, red. Trees were flying past me, trees everywhere. I was in a car speeding through unidentified woods, in gray weather. I gathered it had to be an SUV since I felt high up on the road. A few minutes passed before I was fully awake, but as soon as my senses had cleared, a surge of panic rushed through me.

I tried to swallow the drool pooling at the corners of my mouth, only to connect the cramps in my jaw and the dryness of my tongue with a gag, made of some dubious rag. A series of high-pitched pants rose from my throat, spasms shaking my rib cage with each intake of air. My eyes darted around frantically. I recognized the driver first. Shaven

Spotless

skull. Black beard. I jerked my shoulders, which made me aware of the fact that I couldn't move my arms. I looked down at my hands resting on my lap; handcuffs circled my wrists and angry red marks were already forming on my skin where the steel had rubbed against it.

Fighting a rising pain in my skull, I breathed through my nose and tried to focus. Those few hours spent with March had taught me a valuable lesson about not thrashing or screaming in the face of danger because, really, it only made things worse. Summoning every single bit of self-control I possessed, I tried to calmly assess the extent of my predicament.

There were three men with me in the vehicle, including the driver.

Sitting to my left, and watching me, was a big guy with unsavory black hair slicked back in a short ponytail, and which looked suspiciously like it had been dyed. Examining the roots, I came to the conclusion that it indeed had. His nose had been broken at least once, and that detail made me cringe. My eyes met his for a second; I looked away, frightened by the unspoken threat in those murky brown depths.

Occupying the passenger seat was a much older guy, wearing an elegant dark coat and an old-fashioned black homburg hat. I got the impression that he smelled of something medical, like a dentist's office.

None of them seemed to be interested in talking to me for the time being, so I swallowed through the rag and just kept as still as I could. One thing worried me more than those guys' looks, though: I wasn't blindfolded. So either they didn't care that I might identify them, the car, or even the place we were headed to, or they were confident this would be a one-way trip for me. Noticing the outline of what seemed to be a gun in the half-open leather jacket of the giant sitting beside me, I prayed it wasn't the latter.

I couldn't tell how long the ride through the woods lasted; all I know is that with the pungent smell of grease and cigarettes emanating from the big guy's leather jacket, it felt like forever. The car eventually stopped in a large glade, on an alley that led to what looked like an old farm. A

27

wooden barn stood nearby, and overall, it seemed whoever owned the place sucked even worse than Joy and I did at housekeeping.

The one I had now forever dubbed as "Greasy-jacket" nodded, grabbed my shoulder, and hauled me out of the car. Once in the open, cold air greeted me, along with the earthy scent of woods and wet grass. I heard the double beeps of the car locking. The driver had exited as well, joined by the creepy older man with the hat. "Creepy-hat" walked up to me, his angular features contorting in a warm smile. I noticed for the first time a long, pale scar on his left cheek, which started underneath his eye and went all the way down to his mouth. He spoke in a soft, fatherly voice. "Follow us, my dear."

Like I had a choice.

Perhaps I should mention that there was another important thing I had learned from my encounter with March: the toxicity factor of a gangster is a real number that can be expressed as: $\left(\frac{w}{f}\right)$ - $\mathbf{g}$, where f would be how gentle he sounds on a scale of one to ten, $\mathbf{w}$ the number of wrinkles on his shirt, and $\mathbf{g}$ the number of black leather gloves. The lower the score, the higher the toxicity factor, -1.9 being the worst possible scenario. A quick mental calculation told me that while March had scored a remarkable -1.25, Creepy-hat was dangerously close to . . . *-1.86*.

I was making tremendous efforts to rationalize the situation and stay cool as a cucumber in order not to displease my captors any further—Greasy-jacket seemed pretty pissed already. My cucumber-act didn't last long: When the guy tugged at my hand with a growl, everything became more real. My fear, which I had kept at bay until now, became more real. Sounds were sharper, the browning woods seemed darker, the air colder. I was choking on the gag again, and my feet wouldn't carry me into that barn.

From the corner of my eye I saw Creepy-hat wave impatiently at Greasy-jacket, who tugged harder, making me trip forward. His huge frame hovered above me, and he was bending down: I realized that if I didn't walk, that gorilla was going to pick me up caveman-style the

same way March had. I managed a step, and another, until I was saun-
tering behind him on wobbly legs, struggling to keep up with his long
strides. Twenty feet away from the barn's doors, Greasy-jacket and the
driver stopped, allowing Creepy-hat to enter the building alone while
the three of us waited outside.

The rag in my mouth now soggy with saliva, I let out a series of
inarticulate grunts in hope that my new tour guides would get the hint
and take the gag off. I guess hopping up and down helped, since the
driver eventually gave a rough tug on the cloth and freed my lips.

I coughed and gasped. "Who are you? Do you work with March?
I already told him I know nothing! I—"

"Don't waste your time," the driver said curtly while Greasy-jacket
glared down at me.

This answer did little to alleviate my concern that I might have
signed on with one of the worst travel agencies in the area. "What is
this place? What is he doing in there?"

"Preparing his stuff. He doesn't like to have people in there while
he does that. We'll bring you in a moment."

I didn't like his tone. It sounded like he felt sorry for me. I looked
away. I could feel tears building again, and I didn't want to look like a
chicken, even if it was precisely what I happened to be. Perhaps sensing
my distress, the driver went on, offering what sounded like a pity-ridden
piece of advice. "Look, once you're in there, *talk*. Whatever you're hiding, it ain't worth it."

"You mean to that guy with the hat? Who is he?"

Greasy-jacket grunted in warning, and the driver shook his head.
"Can't tell. Trust me, just tell him everything and spare yourself the mess."

All right, now I was chickening out. "Look, I swear you're making
a terrible mistake. I have no idea—"

Greasy-jacket casually slapped me with the back of one huge paw.
"Shut up."

Stunned as much by the gesture as by the stinging pain on my left cheek, I cowered, once again thinking of March. What if he had been the bad cop they sent first before handing you to the really bad cops? I figured it wouldn't have made much of a difference. I knew nothing about the diamond he had been rambling about, and he had left anyway, likely aggravated by the lack of meaningful answers, or maybe the uncontrolled barfing.

This time I couldn't hold back; hot tears started to roll down my cheeks. The driver saw this and opened his mouth to speak again, his expression softening. He was interrupted by a muffled bang coming from the woods, and Greasy-jacket fell to the ground with a blood-chilling howl.

It took me a couple of seconds to put the pieces together. There was blood everywhere on his right leg, and his friend had pulled out a gun that he was now frantically aiming at nothing in particular. Someone was shooting at us. For real.

I freaked out at the realization that I wouldn't be able to go far with the handcuffs and hopped behind the driver to use him as a shield. It was useless. A second detonation resounded, and the guy fell in turn, knee-capped in the same fashion his friend had been. I stood frozen, fighting the urge to wet myself and unable to decide whether to run or lie on the ground. More experienced than I was with these sort of things—or perhaps less indecisive—Greasy-jacket struggled with what must have been a considerable amount of pain and took out his gun to point it at me. Albeit no expert at criminal protocols, I believe the message he was trying to convey was "keep shooting and no one gets her."

In retrospect, I now understand that this strategy was completely stupid. The sniper shot him again, except this time it was his wrist that got ruined, and his long black gun landed at my feet. My legs were shaking, my eyes were wide with terror, but my bladder was still holding on, so things were good, I guess. Or not, since Creepy-hat finally decided to come out of the barn, strolling toward me with one hand tucked in his coat pocket.

Barely glancing at the two men panting in agony at our feet, he looked in the direction the gunshots had come from and yelled cheerfully, "You make a compelling point, partner! Why don't we try to discuss this change in our arrangement?"

His invitation was met by a deep silence in the surrounding woods, occasionally troubled by shrill bird calls, until faint steps echoed in the distance, crushing twigs and dry leaves. A tall silhouette appeared between two trees—broad shoulders, long gray coat, a scary sniper rifle, nothing like the old Remington my grandpa hunted squirrels with . . .

I didn't want to look at his face. I already knew.

March covered the distance between us with a tranquil stride, his gentle smile belying the way his gloved index finger still rested on the weapon's trigger. Creepy-hat seemed to be about to greet him, but before he could open his mouth, March glanced at the two men curled on the ground behind us and spoke in a cold voice. "Leave your weapons and drag yourselves to the car."

I think the driver and Greasy-jacket wanted to comply, but there are things you can't do so well with a bullet in your leg, or in your wrist for that matter. Each movement tore groans of pain from them, and I couldn't see this working. How would they get up to climb inside the SUV? Call me selfish: I chose to ignore such practicalities and scurried away from Creepy-hat to hide behind March, the handcuffs that locked my arms threatening my balance with every step.

Creepy-hat caressed his scar absently, his right hand still inside his coat's pocket. "March, what sort of game are you playing? Since when do you take investigative jobs?"

"I'm taking care of the client myself. I don't think your services will be needed any longer," came his "partner's" curt reply.

Creepy-hat's grin turned almost maniacal. "Says who? The Queen? Somehow, I doubt that!"

"I'm merely seeing to my employer's best interest. Don't test me. You know better," March retorted flatly.

"You're seeing to your own grave, my friend."

This particular remark made me wonder what sort of history these two had, because there was no trace of concern in Creepy-hat's voice, but rather a barely contained joy. Glancing at his men resting near the SUV, neither of them able to get up due to the extent of their injuries, he let out an exasperated sigh. "Very well . . . have it your way. This silly dispute is only a minor setback. I'll inform the Queen of the incident, and expect to recover my client soon."

I wanted to snicker at the way Creepy-hat made it sound like he was indulging March, when it was clear that he didn't have the balls to face him alone and was, in fact, retreating. I didn't, because when I heard March's voice, any fleeting relief, any amusement I had felt died right away. "Island. Close your eyes."

I obeyed, inching closer to him, until I was almost brushing his back, smelling rain and cedar on his wool coat. I did register the noise, like two firecrackers bursting one after another, but I didn't understand immediately. Until I opened my eyes again.

Creepy-hat was still standing in front of us. The hand that had been resting in his pocket all this time was now visible, holding a small brown pistol equipped with a long black suppressor. There was a little smoke, a smell I identified as powder, and his men were no longer moving. The driver had collapsed face-first in the muddy ground, whereas Greasy-jacket lay on his back, a bloody wound visible on his left temple.

For a few seconds, my mind couldn't process that Creepy-hat had just killed his own men. All I could focus on was the sound of the gunshots, so different from the movies. He put the gun back inside his coat and knelt beside the driver's body to retrieve the SUV's keys from the guy's jacket. I watched, paralyzed, as he unlocked the car and turned one last time, silently tipping his hat to bid us good-bye. I think I closed my eyes at that point because I don't remember seeing him climb into the vehicle. The engine hummed to life, and when I peeked again, he was gone.

I thought of horses with broken legs, and I cried.

March turned to face me, his expression blank. Without saying a word, he produced a tissue from one of his pockets to wipe my nose and cheeks; I let him proceed without reacting, in a daze. Once he was done, he meticulously folded the dirty piece of paper until all that was left was a compact little square, which he wrapped several times into a second, clean tissue before tucking it back in the same pocket. My shoulders were still shaking, and he waited patiently until I was more or less in a state to form coherent sentences.

"Now . . . I believe we have some unfinished business, Island."

I took a few steps backward, my eyes traveling back and forth between his indecipherable expression and the rifle, and I blurted out the question I needed answered the most. "Who were they? Are they looking for that diamond too?"

"Yes."

"He called you his partner. Why would your boss hire competing forces?"

He appeared to hesitate, and what came out was a masterpiece of vague non-explanation. "My employers had second thoughts about their primary choice of professionals."

"Why? Aren't you both the same, with the guns and—" My eyes darted to the two bodies on the ground, but the words wouldn't come out.

Something a little dark flashed in March's eyes. "That man doesn't work like me. He has his . . . kinks."

I swallowed hard. March had rescued me from whatever Creepy-hat had been planning to do with me, but at what cost? From the looks of it, I had merely traded one soulless asshole for another. I suddenly felt terribly alone, half-incapacitated and trapped in front of him in the middle of nowhere. I figured it would be preferable if I kept asking the questions, given his track record with interrogation, so I shot first before he could threaten to break my arms again.

"I don't get it. You had me! Why did you let them take me?"

A little frown creased his brow. "You were very unresponsive after you threw up in your bathroom, so I decided to let him make his move and tenderize you for me. Also, your apartment was messy. I thought you deserved a little chastening."

"T-tenderize me?"

"Yes, I planned on rescuing you after you were on the table."

"The table?"

He dismissed my concerns with a quick flick of his left wrist. "No need to elaborate on that."

"What changed your mind?"

"You're a bit scrawny. I realized that if he wasn't careful enough, you might die before either of us had a chance to learn anything." As he said this, a little disappointed sigh escaped him, which I found somewhat euphemistic considering the implications of his words.

I tried to breathe my rising panic out. "What makes you think I know anything about that diamond?"

He shook his head in disbelief and placed a menacing index finger on the rifle's trigger. "This is getting ridiculous. I could shoot you in the knees, and you'd tell me everything you know."

Said knees buckled at the prospect.

"Wouldn't that cause permanent injuries?"

"Undoubtedly."

I laid anxious eyes on the long suppressor extending the rifle's barrel. "March . . . I don't understand any of this. Please . . . at least explain—"

An expression of doubt appeared on his features, like he wasn't sure what to do with me. "I assume you know what the Cullinan is?"

"The big diamond? The one they made the crown jewels from? You're aware that those are in London and not in my bedroom, right?"

"Don't play with me. I'm talking about the Ghost Cullinan, the one your mother stole from my employer."

His words hit me like a slap in the face, dissipating my fear in favor of white-hot anger. "What? How dare you? My mom never stole anything from anyone!"

"I can assure you, she did. My employer has spent the past decade looking for it, until they learned from one of your mother's former associates that she had entrusted it to you."

"What are you rambling about? She was a diplomat! How would she have ended up involved in a diamond heist? March, I really think that you and those guys have the wrong person—"

March's eyes hardened. "Are you Island Chaptal?"

"Yes, but—"

"Born on September 20, 1989? Daughter of Léa Chaptal and Simon Halder?"

"You're not listening—"

He placed his index finger on my forehead and pressed gently, as if to force his words directly inside my brain. "*You* listen. Island, your mother was *never* a diplomat. Her position as a consular officer was one of many covers. Your mother worked for a criminal organization called the Board; she was a spy and a remarkably gifted thief . . . And believe me when I say that the CIA could fill an entire room with the classified files her name appears in."

CIA? Spy? My knees were shaking again, and I was tempted to hold on to something. I think March saw it: he took a step forward, and his left hand moved as if to catch me. I staggered back, holding my handcuffed hands in front of me in attempt to keep him at a safe distance; I'd sooner drink the milk from a thousand cereal bowls than collapse in his arms.

"You people are all insane!" I shouted. "You . . . you broke into my house, and then you kidnapped me, and I keep telling you that I have nothing to do with this, and . . . and—" I had to stop. My eyes were watering, and I could feel my voice crack.

"You're a smart girl, Island. I doubt she fooled you entirely," March said, his tone softer.

She had.

Maybe.

I wasn't sure anymore. I needed air. Yet the air wasn't coming. My lungs were contracting rapidly, struggling to find oxygen for my brain. I thought of my mother, of the little I knew about her career as a diplomat, of the car accident in Tokyo.

Had I unconsciously refused to see certain things?

I racked my brain for memories that might have served to back March's claims, but I couldn't find anything conclusive. True, during my first fifteen years spent with her, we had more or less lived from a suitcase, always gliding from one place to another too quickly to form any ties to the people around us. As a result, I had been homeschooled—make that self-schooled—which *might* have been the reason why I had blossomed into a socially inept adult. She had probably been aware that ten hours of Internet a day were detrimental to my development, but she'd always say that since we relocated so often, it would have been frustrating for me to change schools all the time; better not go at all.

So, yes, my mom had been weird, maybe even a tiny bit irresponsible at times. Yet, being a free spirit doesn't make you a criminal. She had raised me as best she could, and with her I had visited many countries and become fluent in several languages. How many kids can say that?

My hands bunched into fists. I couldn't accept this. Couldn't stand the way March's words were already worming their way inside my head. "This doesn't make any sense! And I swear to you she didn't leave me a diamond or anything like that. All I ever received was some cash that had been sleeping in a bank account. I got six thousand dollars and nothing else. They didn't—" My voice faltered as I recalled this episode. "They didn't even give me her things. My dad disposed of them while I was still in the hospital, and I had *nothing* left from her."

An emotion that looked closely like fake sorrow shadowed March's features. "Didn't you ever wonder why he would do that? Erase her like that?"

A cold, prickling sensation radiated from my spine throughout my body. Of course I had. My father and I weren't big on drama or personal discussions, though. Months after my relocation to New York, I had timidly brought up the issue and expressed regrets that I had no actual souvenir left from my mother, only memories. Knowing myself though, it probably sounded like I had dropped my toast on the peanut-buttered side or missed an episode of *MythBusters*. I could still remember that lunch at the Russian Tea Room, during which I had stared down at my blinis while my father vaguely apologized, claiming he had no idea I wanted to keep her things, and that no one even knew if I'd ever wake up, back then.

One thing hadn't changed after all these years: I was still a champion at looking down and shunning people when I didn't want to listen to what they had to say. My gaze focused on the tips of my ballet flats, covered in mud and glistening grass blades; I blocked March's voice, his very existence. What did my father know? *Really know?*

"Island? Island?"

I felt March's hand on my shoulder, bursting through my bubble, and looked up to see a line of worry on his brow. "Are you still with me?"

"I . . . Yes . . . I am. Go on."

He nodded. "As I was saying, in 2004, the Board sent her to Pretoria to steal the Ghost Cullinan, but she betrayed them and disappeared with the stone. She fled to Japan, where—"

He stopped there, perhaps out of some shred of decency. I didn't need to hear again that my mom had burned inside her car, and that the only reason I was still alive was that a passerby had extracted me from the wreckage that day.

"Even if any of this was true, I know nothing about that damn stone," I mumbled.

"Didn't she leave any sort of hint? Try to remember."

"How would I know? That notary was a good-for-nothing anyway. We never received any paperwork, *nothing*!"

A spark lit in March's eyes. "Notary?"

"Yes, I know he contacted my dad once, months after her death. But we never heard from him again. My dad said he had no way to reach the guy." I shrugged. "Maybe it was better this way: the estate was negative anyway."

"Did your father say that? That your mother's net worth was negative?"

"Yes. Look, I was fifteen . . . I don't really know . . . I dropped the issue, okay? It was just a bunch of bad memories." I looked away, fighting a mixture of anger and shame. I had given up on my mother's will so I could forget, be strong like my father and act like she had never existed. Only now that I was confessing it out loud did I realize how ugly, how cowardly that decision had been.

Of course, Mr. Clean didn't care about my feelings; he cared about the facts. "What was the notary's name?"

"Mr. Étienne. He was calling from Paris. Don't waste your time with the yellow pages. I checked once, years ago. My dad was right: found no trace of him."

March appraised me for a few seconds, his face blank, and it dawned on me that now that he was done squeezing out what little intel I could provide, he was probably going to kill me. When he finally opened his mouth to talk, I was busy addressing a silent prayer to Raptor Jesus for the sake of my poor wretched soul.

"Well, that's settled then. First we're going to question this Mr. Étienne."

"*We?* You mean . . . in Paris?"

He gave me a candid look—the first since I had met him. "Where else? Your mother was no rookie. I doubt she left the Ghost Cullinan in the hands of her notary, but if she did leave a will, it might contain indications as to where the diamond is. I'm sorry, but we're not done. I still need you."

I gauged him suspiciously. One could hardly trust a professional killer, but then again, *he* was the one carrying the rifle, so my options were limited—and by limited I mean: "March or Creepy-hat, pick your favorite Saturday night date." That being said, the guy seemed in no hurry to get rid of me, despite his claim that it was his specialty. There'd been several occasions for him to maim or kill me in the past twenty-four hours, and he hadn't acted on any of them. No, March was a consummate sociopath, but I had a feeling he wasn't actual psycho-killer material.

And at the moment, he was the only door to my mother's past. A past that was quickly catching up with me and might swallow me whole if I didn't find a way to either escape, or help March find the Ghost Cullinan and give it back to its (il)legitimate owner.

I gave him a decided nod. "I get it. I'll go with you."

He cocked an eyebrow.

"I don't want to go back with that guy," I muttered, in guise of an explanation.

Lowering his weapon, he stepped forward, closing the distance between us, and raised my chin with a gloved index finger. His eyes plunged into mine in a way that made me pray I had been right about him not being psycho-killer material. His low, dangerous voice sent an unpleasant chill all the way down to my knees. "Let's be clear. I'm a little old-fashioned. I usually try not to hurt women too much. But if you hide anything from me, Island, I'll make an exception . . . and all the crying in the world won't help."

I nodded hastily, and when he let go of me, breathed a shivering sigh of relief. Placing a firm hand on my back, March steered me toward the woods and away from that sinister glade. As he did so, I turned my head to look at the two bodies still resting on the humid ground. When my nose caught the scent of fresh blood mingling with wet leaves, I fought a wave of nausea. "March, what about—"

He checked a black chronograph on his wrist without looking back. "Rislow doesn't leave loose ends. A cleaning team should be here for them soon . . . which is why we need to leave now."

So that was Creepy-hat's name: Rislow. I thought of asking March if he might be waiting for us already with a rifle of his own, somewhere in the vicinity, but I figured it was unlikely, since March didn't look particularly worried. He led us through the desolate woods, and I tried my best to keep up with his pace without falling face-first on the ground, steadied by his hand on my shoulder.

"Are you scared of the cleaning team?" I murmured as we reached his own car, a black Lexus that lay hidden a quarter mile down the small road I had arrived on.

"No."

"Oh. Have you ever . . . cleaned a cleaning team before?" I insisted.

"Yes," he sighed as he helped me into the passenger seat.

I didn't ask him for the specifics, but I do recall wondering if I would get lasting PTSD over all this.

FIVE

The Road Rules

"Let's be real. If you purchased this book and are currently riding alone with a man, he's, in all likelihood, one of the following: a relative / a taxi driver / a kidnapper.

—Aurelia Nichols & Jillie Bean, *101 Tips to Lose Your Virginity after 25*

If what you listen to says something about who you are, then March's musical tastes confirmed my earlier impression that, even if he wasn't a psycho killer, he *was* a terrible human being. Old country? Really? We were in New England, somewhere near a place called Barnstable, and a cold drizzle covered the windshield while Bobby Bare's drawl filled the car, asking Jesus to drop-kick him through the goal posts of life. Oh well, at least March had been kind enough to free me from the handcuffs, thanks to some sort of universal key—I had no idea they even made these.

As we drove through miles and miles of pine woods, though, I did start to mentally fill a scorching review of March's chauffeur service. I had no choice but to give him a one-star rating, because this simply wasn't how you drive when you carry guns and rifles in your car. As a teen, I had been used to my father's boorish driving and constant challenging of speed limits. March was nothing like him: his driving was smooth, slow, mindful of other drivers and cute animals crossing, and, to sum it up, completely lame. I mean, stopping on the side of the road to text? *Who* does that anymore? I refrained from huffing every time we paused in front of a red light waiting for no one to cross, rubbing my feet against the floor mat in impatience.

I caught him glancing at my muddy shoes and rolled my eyes. So what if I got a little mud on his carpet? No big deal.

Okay, maybe big deal.

"I'm sorry for being a little tense, Island. I suppose I'm not used to having guests in the front seat. My clients usually ride in the trunk, you know."

Wow. He was the first person I'd met who could turn the gentlest apology into an ominous threat. Squirming uncomfortably, I peeked at his profile while he drove. Could you read noses like you read the lines of a hand? Were men with nice aquiline noses more prone to pursuing criminal careers than others? If so, where did Hitler's and Al Capone's bulbous appendages fit into my newly established table of criminal noses? I spent several minutes lost in my classification efforts, until my thoughts drifted to my mother's own "criminal career."

"March, that diamond . . . how big is it? Is it really worth two billion?"

The usual poker smile swiftly fell in place, and I was beginning to understand that the man smiled whenever he needed to conceal his hand. For all his skills, March was actually a shitty bluffer. "Approximately 4,137 carats."

My jaw went slack. "Sweet Jesus, that's like"—I did the math in my head—"almost two pounds! It's bigger than the Cullinan, right? Why does your boss call it the Ghost Cullinan?"

He tapped his fingers against the wheel while we waited at a red light. "When the Cullinan was discovered near Pretoria in 1905, one of its sides was perfectly smooth, likely the product of a split. The experts concluded that the stone was actually half of a bigger diamond and that the remaining part might still await in the Premier Mine."

"The Ghost Cullinan?"

"Precisely. It was eventually found in early 2004. Tests confirmed its purity equaled the Cullinan's and that it topped its sibling as the biggest natural diamond ever found."

"So the Board decided to dig in—"

"Excellent choice of words. They charged Léa Chaptal with the task of stealing the stone from the Premier Mine before its discovery was made public," he went on. It felt strange, almost painful, to hear my mother's name in his mouth.

"Why didn't she deliver it to them? What happened?"

He shrugged as the car restarted. "I'd be tempted to ask *you*."

"Hilarious."

"Thank you." He smirked. "To answer your question, your mother's motives are unknown. What we do know is that she had two accomplices. The first one was eventually identified by the Board. He went into hiding, and it took them ten years to catch him. His name was Victor Koerand. Ever heard of him?"

I shook my head. "You say 'was' . . . so he's dead? Is he the guy who said my mother left me the Ghost Cullinan?"

"Yes. The Board found him in Tenerife a few weeks ago, and they sent someone to discuss the matter with him," March confirmed.

A little chill made my scalp prickle. "You."

"No."

Reflecting on this laconic answer for a second, I gave it another try. "Creepy-hat?"

It seemed to take him a few seconds to figure out whom I was talking about, and when he did, a chuckle escaped his lips. "Yes. As much as I dislike his methods, he did bring results. Koerand confirmed the existence of a second accomplice, likely the one who convinced Léa to double play the Board and keep the diamond. Koerand helped Léa and that man access the vault in which the Cullinan was kept . . . and that's when your name came up. "

"I never had anything to do with that guy! I don't even know him!" I nearly yelled.

March's lips pressed together in a thoughtful expression. "Koerand's tale was quite interesting: according to him, Léa became wary of her mysterious partner and tried to back away from their deal."

"How so?"

"He claimed that Léa had been planning to give the Cullinan back to the Board after all. There's no evidence of this being true, though. Léa made no attempt to contact the Board during the three months she spent in Tokyo."

The more March spoke, the more I wondered how the hell my mother had been able to swim among such sharks. So far, every player in this game seemed to be either a gangster, a pathological liar, a corpse, or a combination of the three. "What do I have to do with this? Did the Board threaten to hurt me? Maybe this is why she was so afraid to go to them and waited instead."

March went on. "Koerand said that Léa knew she was in danger; she was convinced that she didn't have much time left to live."

"Because either the Board or that second accomplice would have killed her as soon they got the diamond anyway?" I completed. That, at least, made sense.

He leaned back in his seat with a meditative sigh. "Possibly. Koerand wasn't very clear about this point. He suggested that Léa hadn't escaped to survive; she had merely wanted to scrape a little more time 'to play her last card right' before the inevitable."

Survive.

I hadn't paid much attention until now, but the sky around us had started to darken. I saw my own reflection in the windshield, the dark circles under my eyes, only accentuated by the pallor of my face, my messy hair, and to my left, March, as cold and collected as ever. In that moment, I wondered if I was really seeing myself . . . or my mother.

"March. You're not answering my question. How did the Board end up thinking that I had the diamond?"

"Because according to Koerand, *you* were that card. He told the Board to look for the only person Léa would have trusted with the entire truth, the only person her second accomplice wouldn't kill. *You.*"

What came out of my mouth was almost a snort, but believe me, I wasn't amused. Just so damn bitter that laughing was all I could do not to cry. "She didn't even trust me enough to tell me about her real job . . . Those guys from the Board are complete idiots for buying that kind of crap. Even I can see that Koerand was probably trying to feed them a name to escape getting tortured to death, and I'm not even a mobster to begin with!"

March ignored my remarks. "The only thing Koerand couldn't reveal was the name of Léa's second accomplice, who presumably helped her leave South Africa after the theft."

The memory of a shadow and quiet footsteps on the parquet floor of our house in Pretoria filled my mind. *The tall shadow.* Could he be that second accomplice March was talking about? He had been my mother's lover, this much I knew. She had never mentioned him in front of me, perhaps choosing to believe I wouldn't hear his car park in the alley under the old Jacaranda tree when he visited her at night.

Even years after our brief stay in South Africa, my sleep was still sometimes haunted by memories of the way he whispered her name, of his silent, feline stride, or how they would sometimes open my bedroom door when they thought I was asleep and stand together in the doorway for a few seconds. I had often wanted to ask her if she loved him. Was he nice to her? Would I ever meet him in daylight, see what he looked like? We had left Pretoria in a hurry—I now understood why—and my questions had been left unanswered, an occasional flicker of sadness in my mother's eyes the only evidence he had ever existed.

Maybe my inner turmoil showed in my face, or maybe my ears turned a little red like they always do when I'm embarrassed. Whatever it was, March saw it, and he detached his gaze from the road for a second, icy-blue eyes daring me to try and lie to him. "What is it? Do you know the person who helped her escape?"

I averted my eyes. "My mother was seeing someone in Pretoria. I don't know what he looked like, or his name. All I know is he had a car, and he was tall."

March seemed skeptical. "How come you've never seen his face? What about his voice? What did he sound like?"

"He would only come at night. I think he was an Afrikaner. He had this slight accent when he spoke English. Well educated, I guess; kinda like you."

His lips twitched in a derisive smile. "Island, *you* are well educated. I didn't even go to high school."

My face scrunched as I considered this bit of information. "Oh, sorry . . . Do you regret it, not finishing school?"

"Are you trying to analyze me?"

"Of course not!" I remembered my father's lectures about displaying tact at all times, and never asking people if the way they yelled at their kid in the middle of a crowded train stemmed from a personal history of abuse. "I'm just curious from . . . say, a sociological point of view. I've never met anyone like you. Have you ever been to jail?"

He chuckled, shaking his head in a way suggesting that, despite my best efforts, I had said something weird and inappropriate again. "Yes, when I was young, but I believe you're changing the subject. What else can you tell me about your mother's lover?"

"Like I said, nothing. Maybe it's not even related."

His fingers resumed their drumming against the wheel. "You haven't given me much so far."

I didn't like the way he said this. It sounded like people who couldn't provide anything useful belonged in the trunk. Fighting a shudder, I slumped in my seat and stared at the road ahead of us.

———

We rode in silence for a little while, no doubt both reflecting on our bizarre arrangement, until I felt a low rumble in my stomach. I hadn't eaten in nearly twenty-four hours, and hunger was starting to kick in badly. Looking through the window, I noticed we had passed a small gas station with a large sign advertising a burger joint a few miles down the road. My stomach wrenched in anticipation. "Can we stop to buy food? It's a drive-through. It will only take a few minutes."

The corners of his mouth turned up, which didn't mean he was happy in any way—I now fully understood that. "I'm afraid this is not an option."

I frowned and leaned my forehead against the cold glass of the window, moping and wondering why he would deny me such a basic request. Then it hit me. "Don't tell me it's forbidden to eat in your car!"

He didn't reply.

It was forbidden to eat in his fricking car! Aggravated, I turned my attention to the contents of the passenger door's little storage compartment. Several travel maps of the USA and a bunch of Latin American countries rested there. He was a cautious driver: GPS could indeed let you down. They all appeared to belong to the same collection and were therefore of equal size, which had allowed him to press them together in two perfectly rectangular stacks of paper, standing parallel to each other in the compartment. Of course they were sorted by country and according to their respective number in the collection, in increasing order.

I moved the Mexico one, disrupting the left stack's shape and order. March cast me an anxious sidelong glance but said nothing otherwise, focusing on the road. Empowered by his lack of reaction, I set my sights on New Jersey, pulling the map until it stuck out an inch or so from the right stack.

He smacked his tongue in annoyance. "Could you *please* stop that?"

I stifled a laugh. Waiting for him to relax a bit, I fiddled with his maps again and this time did the unthinkable: I moved a New Jersey map into the Latin countries stack.

The Lexus came to a screeching halt on the side of the road.

March wasn't looking at me. His gaze was straight, locked on the twilight horizon line. "Fix this. Now."

I stammered the closest thing to a sincere apology. "I'll put them back in place . . . You're not gonna kill me, right?"

"Not if you fix it."

My heart racing, I worked on putting those damn maps the way they had been minutes ago. Once I was done, I crossed my arms and waited for him to start the car again. He didn't. I looked back and forth between his stern gaze and the door storage until it hit me. The New Jersey map was still sticking out from the stack, its yellow cover glaring at me. I pushed it carefully and smoothed the compact stack until all sides felt even again. At last, the engine started.

Granted, he hadn't shot me, but I couldn't look at him for a while after the incident. The sun was setting, and as we drove, I mulled over his excessive reaction to such an insignificant stimulus. What if he had *really* gotten mad? Replaying the scene over and over again in my mind, I was desperately trying to find the right words to voice my concern.

"March, have you seen a shrink about this?" I cringed as soon as the words left my mouth. It had sounded so much subtler in my head.

"No, Island. I don't need counseling. I need you not to touch anything in my car."

I pursed my lips. "You know, I can give you the number of one of my dad's friends. His office is on Beach Street, and he's a great listener—"

His smile finally returned, as a small airport came in view. "Do you think I'm crazy?"

"March, you are the single most damaged person I've ever met, and I include myself in that statement."

"You're not damaged, Island."

"I'm making small talk with a hit man."

He knew I had a point. Ducking his chin, he seemed to fight a laugh, and for the first time since we had met, I thought March could sometimes be charming.

SIX

The Trunk

"He had given up on love to lose himself in the never-ending night of crime. Only she could save his dark soul with the purity of her innocence."

—Tracey Hurricane, *Hit On by a Hit Man*

My previous assessment had been wrong. What we reached wasn't even an airport. It was rather a small private aerodrome. A staggering three planes waited outside a long hangar for potential passengers, and only one of them looked big enough for a flight all the way to France.

I had never seen a private jet up close before but assumed it was one, since it was larger than the two small Cessna-like planes and looked more like a tiny version of an airliner. Watching it from a distance, I have to say it was a bit underwhelming. I liked the paintwork, though, which appeared to represent blue waves of water engulfing the tail and threatening to swallow the white hull as it crashed into the ocean. Nice touch, especially for those afraid of flying. Squinting at the words painted in white on the tail's stabilizer, I wondered if "Legacy" was the name of the company or the aircraft's brand.

Lost as I was in my musings, I didn't notice the fat bearded guy in a gray suit coming our way with a huge smile on his face. It was almost dark, but his teeth were so white he looked like *Alice in Wonderland*'s Cheshire Cat. March exited the car, locking me inside, and I watched as the man gave him a hug—which he welcomed rather stiffly. They chatted for a while before disappearing into the hangar. My eyes locked on the large metal door while I waited for them to return.

It's crazy the way every noise sounds louder and sharper when you're alone—or when you're not listening to country for that matter. I hadn't noticed that faint tapping until now. I looked around, puzzled. The sound seemed to be coming from the backseats, or maybe the trunk, like something unsecured was moving around while the car . . .

Wait.

The car wasn't moving.

I swore under my breath and loosened my seat belt with shaking hands. Thank God I was a midget; I managed to slide easily between the front seats to reach the backseat.

I whispered against the black leather, "Is there anyone here?"

A muffled groan answered me, and I jerked back in panic. I hadn't been offered the passenger seat because March was nice to the ladies; I had because the trunk was already taken! Cold sweat dampened my skin as I frantically looked for a way to fold the seats, pulling with all my strength. I'm not sure what I did, but at some point the left seat clicked and gave way, revealing a black-haired man swaddled in some kind of body bag with straps everywhere. March had left the man's head outside of the bag, but a large band of duct tape covered his mouth. I stared for a few seconds at the tattooed tears and numbers on his face, his angry brown eyes, and poked the duct tape with a trembling finger. A growl welcomed this first contact, prompting me to tug at the silvery tape gingerly. More loud grunts followed as I worked on removing the damn thing, and I discovered he had a thin mustache—most of which remained stuck to the tape.

Once I was done, he swallowed a big gulp of air and hissed at me with a strong Spanish accent. "Get the hell out, *pequeña*! You are in great danger!"

Blood froze in my veins and I recoiled instinctively. "Oh my God! He told me he wouldn't kill me! But you . . . Was he going to—"

"What do you think? Somoza sent that fucking *psicópato* after my ass!" He snarled, revealing a row of white teeth with sharp incisors.

Okay. So that Somoza person had hired March to kill my co-hostage. Logic and some modicum of social prejudice therefore suggested that Somoza was a bad person.

That guy in the trunk might be a bad person too.

March was a bad—just kidding, that had already been thoroughly established.

I tried the left rear door, but the handle moved in vain. I shook my head and cast a desperate look to the man. "He's locked the car—"

"I'll tell you what to do. Get behind the wheel!"

Call me the Stockholm syndrome poster girl: for a second or so, I hesitated. March had after all agreed to keep me alive, and our deal might lead me to learn more about my mother. Not to mention that betraying him meant losing whatever protection he could offer me from Creepy-hat. Did I really want to do this? What would happen once I was alone with that tattooed guy in the trunk? Weighing my options, I stared at my co-hostage. Tattoos or not, he didn't look like he had benefitted from the same type of arrangement I had.

"What are you waiting for?"

His urgent voice startled me back into reality. If I wasn't going to do this for me, I had to do it for this guy. Nodding fearfully, I crawled into the driver's seat. Dammit, the seat adjustment was all wrong. I could barely reach the pedals!

It's a pity March chose that moment to come back with the fat man, because otherwise, with a little help from my new friend, I would have unveiled the second biggest mystery in the world after the Voynich manuscript's code: How to steal a Lexus with your bare hands.

The fat veneers guy scratched his black beard and cracked up, roaring with an Italian Brooklyn accent. "Fuck me! The lil' countess is trying to jack your car!"

March, however, wasn't cracking up much as he took in the scene before him. He fished for a small key fob in his pocket and unlocked the driver's door, eyes narrowed in a menacing glare. When he opened the door, I first shrank away, not daring to look up at him. I could understand his perspective: I had enthusiastically promised not to stab him in the back lest I wanted to die a painful death, and there I was, sitting in the driver's seat, hands on the wheel, ready to steal his car and elope with the gangster he kept in his trunk. Said guy was now silent, perhaps wondering which of us would die first.

March handed me the Lexus's keys, nostrils flaring. "I believe you will need *this*."

Of course. Very funny.

"It's . . . it's okay. I wasn't actually going anywhere," I blurted.

"Indeed. Get out of the car."

I complied, peeking up at his face through my lashes.

"March, I—"

He stared down at me and placed his index finger on the tip of my nose, tapping it delicately twice. "Don't talk; don't move."

I gritted my teeth, expecting the worst, but he walked away from me and toward the rear of the car to open the trunk. A string of curses flew out of the cramped space.

"Chinga tu madre!"

My accomplice clearly had unresolved issues with March, because he was encouraging him to satisfy his own mother. (Just so you know, I practice Spanish watching *Dora the Explorer* and playing *GTA*, so I know how to say backpack, whore, and weed. I hope you're impressed.)

I had no idea if March understood Spanish and whether that played a role in his decision to pull out his gun and aim it at the guy's head.

A vision of the way Creepy-hat had coldly executed his men flashed before my eyes, and I lunged at him. "Wait! Don't shoot him!"

"Island, he's my client."

"So am I, and you didn't kill me!"

God, I didn't like his voice. I would have preferred anger to this calm determination, not to mention that the guy in the trunk wasn't helping.

"Antonio is afraid of no one! I shit on your grave, *pinche cabrón*!"

I grazed March's arm with a trembling hand. "I'm sure he didn't mean it! Let's try to solve this in a civil manner."

"I *am* being civil. Please step aside."

He had waved my hand away and avoided my eyes, so I switched to plan B and jumped in front of the open trunk, shielding Antonio with my body. I had seen this in a ton of movies; it always worked. "You'll have to kill me first!"

March's bluffing skills far outweighed mine: I hadn't expected him to merely shrug and point the gun at me instead. "As you wish."

My breathing faltered. My eyes traveled up the gun's suppressor, the long black barrel, and to the wooden grip partially concealed by a leather glove: the shortcomings of my plan were becoming obvious.

The fat guy, who had been watching the entire scene with wide eyes, stepped in and tried to reason with March in his turn. "Whoa, whoa . . . Let's all cool down! March, man . . . seriously?"

I backed my new supporter with urgency. "Please, March!"

He took one step closer, and the suppressor pressed against my chest. Part of me was still terrified, but my body and mind reacted as if this were some strange intimacy. It's hard to explain, but I was now certain he wouldn't kill me. I didn't even think he would hurt me. I locked my eyes with his, and I saw the conflict in them. He didn't want to shoot me, and he probably didn't want to kill Antonio in front of me either. I guess he didn't like seeing himself in my eyes, and rightly so.

"Island, you have no idea who this man is."

"No, it's true, but I know who you are . . . Oh screw that, I'm not gonna bullshit you and say you're better than this. Just don't kill him, please. He's defenseless! Everybody deserves"—My gaze fell on the tattoos covering Antonio's cheeks. Wasn't it one teardrop for each person killed or something? 'Cause he had a shitload of these all the way down to his jawline!—"yet another chance. Antonio will *change!*"

The culprit seemed to have finally figured that calling March's mom a slut would get him nowhere, whereas helping me weigh in on this unexpected moral dilemma might prolong his life to some extent. He shouted from behind me, "She's right! That thing with Somoza's sister, it's in the past already!"

March took a deep breath, perhaps battling his inner douche, and slowly lowered the gun. Once the weapon was safely back in its holster, he took out a phone from one of his jacket's pockets, and all three of us held our breath as he made a call.

"Good evening, Phyllis. Can I ask you to call Mr. Somoza and tell him that . . . personal circumstances are forcing me to cancel our agreement. Yes . . . Exactly . . . Wire everything back and send his mother a box of chocolates with my regards . . . No . . . It's going fine. I simply prefer to concentrate on one thing at a time. Have a pleasant weekend. I'll be back in a few days."

The fat guy scratched his head. "So, do we just let him go?"

"Yes." As he said this, March bent down to untie the straps restraining Antonio, and I could almost have hugged him. Almost. Once he was done, the newly freed Antonio exited the car and stretched lengthily before smoothing out the wrinkles from what looked like a tux. Our ex-hostage flashed me a bright smile, and his right hand moved to reach inside his jacket, causing March and his host to do the same with hostile expressions.

No one got hurt. All Antonio took out was a red business card. He handed it to me. It bore a single phone number, embossed in the paper.

"*Querida*, if you need anything, you call . . . Antonio."

I liked the way he struck a little pose with his index finger and thumb, forming a gun as he said his name: maybe March should have considered coming up with a pose of his own. We watched him walk away on the tarmac with calm, confident strides, headed for God knew where, and after he was out of sight, March spoke. "Island."

"What?"

"Please don't interfere with my work again." Ouch, the cold killer voice.

Undeterred, I pointed at the car accusingly. "Why was he even in that trunk? Aren't you supposed to be dealing with me?"

"I have occasional schedule conflicts just like anyone else."

"No, you don't." The fat man seemed to know a lot about March's working habits.

Ignoring his colleague's accusing tone, March fished for a tube of mints in his pocket and munched on a couple of them without even bothering to let the sugar melt in his mouth like you're supposed to. His teeth ground the sweets with sinister cracking sounds, and I thought it was a super hardcore way to do mints, kinda like he was an addict. Once he had his fix, he cast me a brief glare and closed the incident with a gruff warning. "All right, there's room in the trunk now, if you're interested."

SEVEN

The Veneers

"Malcolm flashed her a seductive smile, revealing a row of teeth so white that she felt engulfed by their light, as if she had been hit by a supernova."

—Livia Torrente, *The Billionaire's Beautiful Waitress*

The fat man and I appraised each other silently under March's gaze.

He spoke first. "Still cute as a button . . . March, you dog!"

I was about to open my mouth to ask why that guy acted like he knew me already, but March placed his finger on my nose again, and the words died in my throat. I wondered if there was some valid scientific explanation behind this technique, like a neurological reflex that would short-circuit the speech center of the brain when someone touched your nose. That or he kept doing it because he thought it worked, and I kept shutting up because it's plain weird when someone does that to you.

Placing a friendly but somewhat invasive hand on my back, the fat man walked me to the aerodrome's hangar. March tagged along, his posture relaxed, a sign that our host could be trusted, I assumed. He led us to a small office located in a corner of the building and made some coffee. I was grateful for this, even if I wasn't a fan of the beverage. My stomach had been singing the sad complaint of a burgerless gut for the past hour, and I feared I might start hallucinating soon if I didn't get something to cheat my hunger.

Settling into an office chair, I offered our host my nicest smile as I warmed my fingers against a mug stating that everybody loved a Jersey girl. "Are we flying to Paris from here?"

"Nope, you're going to Le Havre," he said, opening a thin laptop.

I grimaced, thinking of the large port city about a hundred miles northwest of Paris. It had essentially been wiped out during World War II, only to be rebuilt in a style reminiscent of the Soviet era's best architectural efforts. He ignored my blatant disappointment and resumed his typing. "Now, make yourself at home . . . Need to make some arrangements to get you guys a passport for the countess and pre-clearances. Paulie Airlines got it all under control!"

So it was Paulie. Well, I did find Paulie pretty reassuring, much nicer than March, despite the fact that his excessive veneers made his mouth look a little strange. He noticed I was staring and, fortunately, took it as a silent compliment.

Pointing to his blindingly white teeth, he turned to March. "Wad-dya think o' these, man? Care to get the same? Can give ya my dentist's name. That man . . . he's an artist. Know what Jackie says?"

March shook his head, allowing him to go on, and Paulie proceeded to ask me the same. "Know what my girl says?"

I shook my head in the same fashion.

"She says, 'Paulie, you still got your goddamn salami breath, but these look so hot I could kiss you!' "

He nodded for good measure. I thought he must definitely be a nice mobster if his girlfriend could get away with saying he had "salami breath" without getting shot. I was starting to really like him.

"So she kisses you a lot?" I asked.

Spotless

"Nah . . . You know women, all talk, no balls," he said, raising his head from the computer with a long-suffering sigh. "Stand up and get to that wall, will ya?"

I complied, and he grabbed a reflex camera from a shelf. Getting the idea, I tamed my short hair into something that looked less like an alpaca's haircut and more like a decent bob, plastered a neutral expression on my face, and let him take a few pictures.

I watched in awe as he transferred them to his laptop. In the evenly lit office, the white wall produced a great effect, quite similar to a photo booth. I thought third-degree forgery was pretty cool . . . for a felony, that is. He took my hand and helped me press my fingertips on the surface of a small scanner.

Once he was done, Paulie clasped his hands together. "There you go! By the time you guys land, our good pal Ilan will have everything ready for you!"

I forced a smile on my lips. I was going on an adventure, and in an itsy-bitsy tiny private jet no less! I get that this distorted take on reality was merely a way to distance myself from what was truly going on here: I was being smuggled outside the US by a professional killer and a mobster with bad veneers.

———

"Which one of you is going to pilot?"

My question was probably nearly incomprehensible, since I had stumbled on a vending machine in the hangar a few minutes earlier and had been busy stuffing myself with candy bars since. Dinner was on March, so I had made sure to spend his change down to the last cent.

"None of us, honey. Your pilot will be here real soon," Paulie said, sorting papers on his desk.

March had been silent for the past twenty minutes. Was he maybe

59

nervous about the whole plan? Cutting deals, putting clients in the passenger seat, juggling two jobs. It was becoming clear that none of this fit his usual modus operandi, and I couldn't help but worry that we might both be making a huge mistake. Gobbling down my third Mounds, I turned to our host.

"What sort of pilot shows up in the middle of the night to fly random people to Europe anyway?" I asked Paulie while folding a piece of candy wrapper carefully—God, I hoped March wasn't getting to me with his OCD thing!

He shrugged as if it was obvious. "The sort who needs the money."

"Why?"

"He . . . he—" Paulie scratched his head. He seemed suddenly very embarrassed.

March came to the rescue. "He's doing meth. Terribly expensive."

I stared at him, aghast. "Our pilot does *drugs*?"

"Don't worry, it has no impact on his skills whatsoever."

He looked relaxed enough, so I decided to trust him on this. I wasn't truly scared of flying, anyway; I just thought about plane crashes a lot. And by a lot, I mean that I usually listened to black box recordings on YouTube the night before taking a flight. Nothing like a French pilot shrieking "Shit! We're going down!" in horror before crashing an entire Airbus in the Atlantic Ocean, children.

The sound of an engine echoed outside of the hangar, and when the guy slid open the large metal door, I scanned every inch of him, searching for any sign that he might be unfit for the job. He was a relatively short, friendly-looking man in his forties: messy black hair, brown eyes, wearing a blue flight jacket and carrying a small suitcase.

March had been right: so far, I could find no evidence of his addiction affecting his behavior in any significant way. He didn't even look tired.

"Nick, man! How's life?" Paulie was already on his way to greet our pilot, and I decided to do the same.

Walking to him, I extended my hand. "My name is Island. Thank you for coming so late."

His handshake was firm and warm; I relaxed a little and allowed a tentative smile to stir my lips. Within seconds, though, I felt March behind my back, pulling me away gently.

"We'll let you get ready, Nick. Right, Island?" His voice was smooth as always, but it was an order rather than an invitation, really.

Nick winced. "Okay. Always a pleasure, March."

Watching him stroll toward our plane, I felt something swell in my heart, like an urge to do things right because my time was probably running short and I no longer wanted to miss a single opportunity in what was left of my life. Freeing myself from March's grasp, I took a few steps outside the hangar in the cold night and called him back. "Nick! I just wanted to tell you . . . Please don't buy drugs with the money from this flight. Do it for me. I'm sure you're better than that!"

I was on the verge of tears, Paulie looked petrified, March had been performing a slow face-palm as I spoke, and Nick looked . . . mad?

Walking back toward us, he pointed an angry finger in our host's direction. "Paul, you really need to stop doing that!"

"Nick, man . . . I'm just trying to help! And this one was March's idea anyway!" Paulie whined.

The culprit stepped back and raised his hands, indicating that he wanted nothing to do with their dispute.

I was completely lost. "You're not a meth addict?"

"Jesus . . . Of course not!" Nick replied, rolling his eyes. "And I don't have gambling debts; I don't owe three hundred grand to the mob; I don't need to fund my teen porn start-up—" he went on, shaking his head, "I just have a family to feed!"

I turned to Paulie and March, Nick's indignation rapidly fueling my own. "What is this about? Why did you tell me he was a junkie?"

"It's . . . I'm just trying to protect his reputation. Guy married a

Mormon gal who popped him eight kids. You know . . . Don't sound good in our line of business!"

March silently nodded his agreement.

I was outraged. "How can you two keep lying to me like this? This one is even *worse* than the meth one! It's not even funny!"

"But it's true."

I looked back to Nick. "What . . . You really have *eight* kids?"

"Yeah, why else would I fly on my days off?" He shrugged.

No wonder Nick had looked so normal in the first place: he almost was. I was especially disappointed in Paulie. I expected nothing from March—obviously—but he, on the opposite, had sounded like someone one could trust. Well, one couldn't.

Sighing, I went back into the hangar, closely followed by my chaperone. As Bonnie Tyler used to say, "Where have all the good men gone?"

EIGHT

The Chest Hair

"He was absolute perfection: a smoldering batter of pure maleness, baked by the sun into a golden, smoking-hot beefcake."

—Terry Robs, *Glazed by the Cook*

Our plane's cabin wasn't the tiny space I had first imagined it would be; far from it, in fact. It was pretty spacious and even impressive with its large and comfy beige leather passenger seats, two long sofas facing each other, and wooden inserts that gave the interior a lavish touch.

The first two hours of the flight were spent in tense silence, March and I facing each other like cowboys before a duel. Although I was dying to explore the aircraft and open every single cabinet around me, I kept my hands locked on my lap. My earlier experiment in his car had taught me all I needed to know about disrupting his immediate environment.

Truth is, there was a question hanging in the air—well, at least in my air. I leaned forward a little, forcing myself to look at him in the eyes. "March . . . did you ever meet my mother . . . when working for that Board thing?"

His brow jerked up before he composed himself and gave me his usual poker smile. "I never worked with her. But she did possess a solid reputation before her death. No killer, but rather the type of professional you'd hire to secure valuables or intel with minimal disturbance."

"I guess I'm relieved to hear she wasn't . . . like you, but I still can't believe she was a thief. She was honest, you know," I countered.

"Personal moral standards have nothing to do with jobs like ours. I pay my taxes down to the last cent, and I'm sure your mother did as well. Yet she was breaking into embassies, and I play Krampus for naughty drug lords," March replied dryly.

"Oh, I'm sorry. I almost forgot you're a good citizen who doesn't speed on the highway. The kneecapping is just a *hobby*, right?" I knew I was playing with fire, but I couldn't help it. I needed to snap at someone to ease my stress, and he was the only one around.

His eyes narrowed. "Enough."

"Or what? You want to talk about something else? How about this? What's my price tag, March? The pay must be good, right? How much for all this? To spy on me, to search my apartment, and even pay for a trip to France in a private jet?"

"How much I get paid is none of your business."

He almost sounded angry. Was the money not good enough? Or was it because he had been forced to let Antonio go and give that Somoza guy a refund?

I remained silent for a while, struggling to cool down before probing again. "Will you let me go? If I help you find that diamond, will you send me back home?"

"Yes."

For the first time in twenty-four hours, I saw a light at the end of the tunnel. Was he a man of his word, though? Hard to tell, especially since I had already heard and seen a lot more than I should have, and taking me out of the country seemed like yet another serious breach of his "partnership" with Creepy-hat. I wondered if things were so easy for him. "Say . . . hypothetically, don't you risk getting in trouble if you let me go? Like you're betraying the family?"

He ducked his head, as if to conceal his eyes. Was I onto something? "Island, I'm not tied to any family. I sometimes work for the Board, and when I do, I only answer to its head, the Queen. As long as the Queen is satisfied with my services, anyone else's opinion is irrelevant."

I thought it sounded great on paper, but I wondered if his employer saw it that way too. "If you say so. But don't come complaining if you end up inside an industrial meat grinder."

He let out a warm, throaty laugh. Damn, I really liked his laugh. Too bad he was nothing more than a callous hit man with some manners. "Don't worry. I enjoy a reputation that allows me some leeway."

I wasn't sure why, but his carelessness made me a little sad. "You're an arrogant asshat, and it's going to get you killed someday."

His gaze turned pensive. "Your concern is very touching. It's rather unusual coming from a client."

I felt my ears heat up again at this oddly turned compliment. My own fate should have been my priority right now, not the way he did his job. My reply was halfway between an embarrassed mumble and a yawn. "I don't care about you, March. All I want is to survive this mess."

"Understood."

His calm words are the last thing I remember. I was struggling more and more to keep my eyes open and eventually lost the fight.

I woke up in France. Well, in the French sky anyway. As I opened my eyes, bleak weather could be seen through the plane's windows, and Nick made a captain's announcement that it was past ten a.m. local time and we would be landing in half an hour or so. My seat was in sleep position. I was wrapped in some blue cover . . . and March was gone.

My eyes searched the cabin, and I noticed that the lavatory door was wide open. Alerted by the sound of water running, I decided to get up and make sure he wasn't getting ready to waterboard me like they do in Guantanamo. I was stopped by a sharp pain in my right wrist and the impossibility of moving my arm any further. *Someone* had hand-cuffed me again—perhaps worried that I might try to strangle him in his sleep. I sighed in frustration as my eyes scanned the long black chain. The other end of the cuff had been locked under the seat, leaving no means of escape.

Undeterred, I bent to my right side as far as I could in a poorly designed maneuver meant to get a glimpse of what was going on inside that damn lavatory. It was a complete disaster. I ended up falling from the seat and hitting my head on the floor in the process. My arm still tied to the seat but now painfully twisted, I groaned in mild annoyance as I raised my eyes to the lavatory's entrance. March was indeed there, shirtless and getting ready to shave. His jaw and chin covered in shaving foam, an old-fashioned safety razor still in hand, he took in my undignified position and arched a questioning eyebrow.

I swallowed whatever was left of my pride. "Could you do something about the cuff?"

He looked down on me—literally—and merely resumed his activities. "No, Island. I won't help you, because, if I do, you won't learn anything."

It was almost surreal, the way he was able to perform his morning routine undistracted as I lay sprawled on the aisle's gray carpet with pleading eyes, only a few feet away from him. I gave up with a dejected sigh, resigning myself to wait until he was done. Surely he wouldn't step over me to get his coffee, right? Glancing up at him again, I inhaled sharply and felt my cheeks heat up a little. He had shifted his position to get a better view of himself in the small mirror as he shaved and, in turn, was giving me a much better view of his bare torso.

I wasn't sure I liked what I saw at first. March had a body that fit his choice of career, and there was nothing wrong with that. It's just that I wasn't used to seeing that sort of thing. To the best of my knowledge, muscular, ripped males belonged exclusively on TV and in sports magazines. I had sometimes met guys who looked like they worked out a lot; however, overly conservative social boundaries had restrained me from tearing their shirts open in public to check the goods. So, shapewise, this was actually my first close encounter with a male body that looked . . . well, that fit.

The second detail that left me a little uncertain was the hair. Since Joy's conquests always seem to be unrepentant chest-shavers, and 98 percent of all males I saw on TV flaunted these baby-smooth chests as well, I had come to perceive this as the norm—something especially true since the remaining 2 percent formed a heterogeneous group that included Alec Baldwin and the Ewoks. In this particular case, March's chest didn't really disgust me. I just found it . . . weird. As crazy as that may sound, the soft-looking chestnut hair covering his pecs and running in a diffuse line down his stomach seemed unnatural to me. Real men didn't have hair, in my opinion.

Taking in every detail, from the scary washboard abs to the way his biceps rippled under his skin when he moved to finish a spot on his chin, I discovered that he sported more than a few scars on his body. While some were little more than a thin line made somewhat paler by sun exposure, others looked like deeper dents in his flesh. One of them particularly stood out, because it wasn't a scar . . . but rather a scarification. I hadn't noticed it at first because it was on the back of his left shoulder. However, as he moved to finish his left cheek, I caught a glimpse of a frightening series of marks that formed an emblem forever engraved in his flesh.

It looked like a large disc with an intricate ethnic pattern—African, maybe?—and a fierce lion head in its center, taking most of the surface. Apart from the fact that merely looking at these ridged white lines hurt, I found it at odds with the rest of his persona. With his impeccable shirts and grandpa quirks, he hardly seemed like the type to go for tattoos or body modifications.

At any rate, March was a bit battered but overall a fine male specimen, and, as much I hated to admit it, his half-naked figure wasn't entirely without effect on me. I averted my eyes, feeling a full blush bloom on my cheeks when I realized that my fingertips were itching to cop a feel of that damn chest hair.

Now, that was . . . *Wrong*. Yes, with a capital W. True enough, since the age of sixteen or so, I had failed each stage of my sexual development, but this . . . This was a new and spectacular low.

—Braces and zits until the age of nineteen? Check.

—Silently stalking a gorgeous law student until you catch him kissing his girlfriend? Check.

—Spend an entire night crying and eating ice cream? Check.

—Trying online dating? Check.

—Giving up altogether and reading romance books instead? . . . Check.

—Daydreaming of fondling the chest of a sociopath who kidnapped you? God . . . *Check.*

Ladies and gentlemen, I give you . . . Rock Bottom!
Now that I'm thinking about it, I realize that those ten years searching for love—please stop laughing—hadn't been entirely lost. My Yaycupid dates did provide me with fascinating behavioral data, which I later compiled into a chart *(as follows)*.

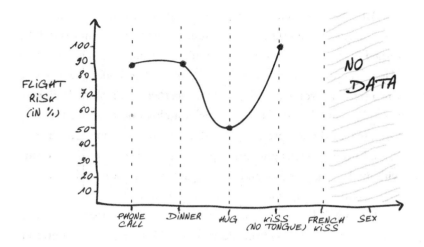

We can observe that, up to a certain point, the more you wait to confess you're still a virgin, the higher the chance that the candidate will agree to pursue the courtship process anyway (as evidenced by the fact that 90 percent of the men who were informed I was a virgin upon calling me to schedule a date chose to interrupt said process immediately). Results, however, show that while only 50 percent of the participants who received this critical bit of information after a hug decided to call it quits, 100 percent of those who got told after a first kiss with no tongue ran to the hills. Data could be inconclusive because it was only this one guy, and I jerked back in surprise when he tried to lick my lips, so maybe that's the reason he left, rather than the virginity thing.

Please don't thank me. I serve science.

————

Back to March and that sexy chest hair, because, yes, it *was* a little sexy, and it's not a crime to admit it, dammit. He was rinsing his face, a clear indication that he would free my arm soon—or so I hoped.

After he was done massaging some aftershave into his skin and methodically wiping the sink and counter dry like my grandma did, he turned his back on me to tuck away his razor and picked a flat, white plastic bag printed with a blaring ad claiming that Madam Wragg gave you a refund if you could find a single crease on your shirt. I cringed: I could see him being Madam Wragg's number one source of financial loss. He pulled out a pressed white shirt that looked similar to the one he had been previously wearing, put it on, tucked it in his waistline with meticulous gestures, and, at last, gave me his undivided attention.

"Good morning. How are you today, Island?"

I groaned. I was in as deep a shit as could be, my arm was sore, I was still a little numb from sleep, and, minutes ago, he had given a whole new meaning to the term "disdain." I was great, splendid even. "Get this thing off of my wrist!"

Kneeling down he took out the key from his pocket, unlocked the cuff, and I was free to move again. He did help me back to my feet. I have to concede this.

"Can I use the bathroom?" He had made me envious of his clean state, and I wanted to refresh myself too. A little soap and some warm water sounded like the best way to fully wake up and face the upcoming day.

"I'm afraid the answer is no. We'll be landing in less than five minutes," he said, checking the nice black chronograph on his left wrist.

I jumped back, beyond shocked. "What? How could you do this to me?"

"I'm sorry, do what?"

"Take all the bathroom time!" I choked out.

"Well, it seems to me you're the one who overslept. And you could have asked much earlier—"

I cut him short, in part because I was getting tired of being treated like a package with no rights, not even a right to wash, and mostly because I was starting to feel a familiar throbbing in my forehead.

"Look, drop it. Do you have any aspirin?"

I caught a fleeting look of concern in his eyes, but it was quickly traded for his usual efficiency. He left me for a few seconds to look for something in a black suitcase and returned with a box of Tramadol. "Will that do?"

"I guess."

At least I still had the right to minimum medical care. I didn't understand, though: Cuffing me, pretending he was going to break my arms, it all seemed okay in March's book of how you treat the ladies. The migraines, however, clearly bothered him, as if everything was acceptable short of nasty pain.

After a few minutes, Nick's voice resounded in the cabin. "I need you guys to fasten your belts. We're landing."

We both sat back, buckled up, and I thought I saw March close his eyes for a brief second when the plane's wheels screeched against the ground. Had the recent events somehow taken their toll on him as well?

NINE

The Facilitator

"Money plays a significant part in landing a willing sexual partner. If you happen to be extremely rich, skip directly to page 93. None of the chapters regarding how to attract a man apply to you since you can just buy one."

—Aurelia Nichols & Jillie Bean, *101 Tips to Lose Your Virginity after 25*

To say that my walk was stiff when we reached the small customs office would be a significant understatement. I had turned into a fricking Lego. Ten minutes earlier, a young ground attendant had come to meet us on the tarmac, discreetly handing me a brand-new passport, as fake as the smile plastered on my face to greet the customs officers. The offending document was scorching my fingertips, and every step that got us closer to the desk seemed to make it worse. I'll be honest: Paulie's special skills and connections didn't seem so awesome anymore, and I was starting to regret having ever thought that forgery was cool. I'm almost positive my cheeks burst into flames when one of the officers, a black-haired woman, extended her hand to me. "Votre passeport, s'il vous plaît."

Attempting to mimic March's confident gesture, I handed her the document and noticed that she looked as flushed as I did, if not more. What I didn't notice, however, was March's arm wrapping around me, and my breath caught in my throat when he pulled me in a tight embrace. What the hell was he doing? Why was it so hot in this little room?

The woman eyed us warily before clearing us for exit and handing our passports back. Beads of sweats had pearled on her temples, and her voice seemed a little hesitant. "Welcome to France, Monsieur and Madame May."

I jerked at her words. I hadn't read my name on the passport. March and I were a married couple now. A married couple with a shitty last name and an immediate need for domestic abuse intervention.

He took a step forward and dragged me along, still holding me close. "Don't look back. She's here to let you in."

I did look back, and in her black eyes I saw fear and shame that probably mirrored mine. Was she being paid by Paulie? Or by the friend he had mentioned maybe? Was she even being paid at all? An image of a fierce-looking mobster holding her cat hostage in a dark basement flashed before my eyes, and I prayed that I hadn't made myself an accomplice to some horrendous pet blackmail scheme.

As we made our way through a long hallway and into the airport lobby, our surroundings came to life. Le Havre-Octeville was a small airport, but it did attract quite a few French travelers, even Parisians willing to drive more than a hundred miles to get a better bargain on charter flights to Spain or Italy—anything for a little sunlight.

March led us toward the parking elevator, and my heart was still beating fast, since he remained way too close for comfort. Maybe he worried that I would try to bolt through the crowd and to the airport police office at the other end of the hall. I tried to push him away, but his grip tightened almost painfully.

"Please don't let people around us assume that you are unhappy to be Mrs. May. As a devoted husband, it would hurt my feelings," he whispered in a warning tone.

My temper flared at his remark, and I tried to free myself again. "Let me go!"

Our exchange caught some unwanted attention from a group of teens who were waiting nearby with large sports bags. Among them, a sinewy black boy with braces decided now was the best time to become a hero; he approached us. "Hé . . . Ça va, madame? Il te prend la tête?" *Hey . . . Are you okay, lady? Is he messing with you?*

March closed his eyes, inhaling sharply, and his hand squeezed my arm even harder.

Glaring at him, I issued a warning of my own. "I could scream for help and make your day a nightmare. Let me walk on my own. I will *not* try to escape."

I felt his grip loosen and cheered inside. Not wanting to push my luck any further, I offered the brave teen a cheeky grin and reassured him that women were perfectly safe and comfortable in the loving arms of the dear Mr. May. "Ça va . . . merci." *I'm okay . . . thank you.*

I took a few confident steps with March walking silently behind me, and the moment the boy and his friends resumed their discussion, I felt March's hand on my neck. My scalp prickled, a shiver ran down my back, and I believe I learned the true meaning of the word "goose bump" that day.

I stopped dead in my tracks as his body pressed against my back and warm lips brushed the shell of my ear, his breath tickling me. He smelled of aftershave, coffee, and mints—a delicacy I was starting to suspect he consumed abundantly. When he spoke in a husky whisper, my toes curled inside my ballet flats of their own volition. "I won't say this again, Island: behave, or *I'll* make you behave."

I swallowed as he went on in the same petrifying voice. "This is not a game. I'm not here to indulge the tantrums of some woman-child . . ."

Tears of shame formed in my eyes that I tried my best to hold back. "I'm not a child, and I'm not a package. Don't you *ever* fucking touch me again, March," I said through gritted teeth.

I felt him pull away, and I sniffed angrily. One tear had made it past the corner of my eye and was now rolling slowly down my cheek. When he reverted back to his usual Mr. Nice Guy act and tried to help me wipe it, I slapped his hand away.

I heard him sigh, and we resumed our walk, careful not to look at each other.

I had never been like this, never fought with anyone. You know how the Hulk says to Captain America, "That's my secret, Captain. I'm always angry"? Well, until then, that was my superpower: I was never really angry. This wasn't me. I didn't snap back, and I never cried. For God's sake, I hadn't even been like that as a kid!

March might have been right when he called me a child. I was regressing by the minute, and if things went on like this, I'd be two feet tall and soiling myself by the end of the day.

———————

Underground garages are bad.

Underground garages are where gang rapes and hubcap thefts happen. They're also the place where creepy gypsy ladies jump at you to curse you into the flames of hell. Those were the thoughts I entertained as we waited for . . . whatever or whomever March waited for.

My ears perked up at the increasing rumble of an engine in the distance. A large black Audi appeared on the parking garage's entrance ramp and stopped right in front of us. The driver's door opened, and a Mediterranean-looking man in his late forties wearing a black leather jacket and cargo pants stepped out.

If this guy was Ilan, well, then Ilan was impressive, to say the least. I had never seen such large shoulders before. I even wondered if they were fake and there was some sort of padding involved in this business. His face was intriguing; a complex maze of deep wrinkles ran across his olive skin and circled his green eyes, as if telling the story of a harrowing life, and the thick stubble on his jaw was studded with white hair, giving it a silvery appearance that I really liked. But then again, I've always had a secret little thing for older men.

He walked to us, his tired gaze locking itself straight into March's; his brow furrowed into a hostile expression. "March . . . still alive." The words had been spoken in a low baritone voice, with a strong French accent.

I winced a little. *Ouch. Apply cold water to burn area.* Okay, March had crossed him somehow.

He gave Ilan a predatory smile. "It's always a pleasure, Ilan. How are you these days? Still worried I might ring twice?"

I caught a flash of anger in Ilan's eyes, and I would have sold a kidney to know what the subtext in this comment was. It looked like these two were standing in a ring. Well, if they had been, no doubt March would have lost against that giant.

"Vous êtes le pote à Paulie?" *You're Paulie's pal?* I asked.

He nodded, his lips pressed in a stern line. "I am. And I take it you're Island, the crazy French girl . . ."

Toasty! Ilan wins. Fatality.

Dammit, I didn't even know that guy; how could he blast me too, already? I also noted that whereas I had asked my question in French, he had replied in English, perhaps not to exclude March from such a friendly conversation. At any rate, I felt butt-hurt by his comment. "Did Paulie say that, that I was crazy and all?"

Ilan shrugged. "No, he said you were Franco-American. The crazy part I figured myself when he said you were March's girl. Goes with the territory."

My legs almost gave way. "He said . . . what?"

Through my anger, I noticed that a crease of displeasure had formed on March's brow, and his lips were pressed in an expression of annoyance. I assumed that it would be bad for his reputation as a ruthless pro if word got out that he randomly banged his targets.

"Island is my client. Nothing more, nothing less. I'll have a word with Paulie regarding the issue," March clarified for Ilan, who nodded in understanding.

I couldn't have agreed more.

"Let's go," March concluded.

Ilan opened the car, and we stepped inside. Once I was seated, I scrunched my nose at the strong tobacco smell and the telltale little pine tree hanging from the mirror and grinning at me. Ilan smoked a lot. Maybe that was the reason his voice was so deep. Looking at March, I noticed he had kept his black suitcase with him instead of putting it in the trunk. I wondered if there were weapons inside it, and whether he kept it because he didn't trust Ilan.

The engine roared to life, and soon enough we were speeding on the A13 highway in the direction of Paris. Ilan had no regard for speed limits and a good radar detector; I found his driving immensely relaxing, much more so than March's.

As we passed yet another herd of bored cows, Ilan shifted the mirror to look at me. "Say . . . it's one strange notary you got," he remarked, his tone knowing, almost playful.

I fidgeted uncomfortably by March's side, noticing he was now staring at me as well, his eyes unreadable. "What do you mean?"

"Well, he's not exactly the kind of notary that went to law school, and to be honest, I'm still trying to locate him." He seemed to check for my reactions before continuing. "Paid a visit to his assistant early this morning. Obviously, I wasn't the first one: she had some nasty bruises and a couple of teeth missing." He shook his head with a sigh. "She told me her boss had gotten a tip around one a.m. that a bunch of gorillas were looking for him. Étienne managed to run away, and she's the one who got wrecked instead."

I grimaced at those macabre details and turned to March. "Do you think those guys were looking for the stone?"

He frowned. "Likely so. Did you tell anyone about your mother's notary?"

"No! I think my dad is the only person I ever discussed this with." Blood drained from my face. I turned to March, grabbing his arm urgently. "Oh my God, March! What if someone kidnapped him too! You have to let me check that he's okay!"

The muscles in his jaw contracted. "Even so, there's nothing we can do now."

"Let me call him!"

His nostrils flared. "Island—"

"March, fais pas ton connard." *March, don't be a dick.*

I looked at Ilan in surprise. Could March understand that sort of . . . exhortation? Apparently yes. My eyes widened when he pulled out his phone and handed it to me with a warning glare. "You're only calling to check on him. No games, Island."

I nodded, although I did briefly envision myself calling my dad for help. I decided against it: There was no telling how March would react if I betrayed him again. I dialed my dad's number. The phone rang twice, and when I heard someone pick up, I realized it was five a.m. in New York. My shoulders slumped in relief as his tired, grumpy voice resounded. "Simon Halder speaking, who the hell is this?"

"Hi, Dad, it's me."

"Island?" A typical grunt at the other end of the line. Thank God, my father seemed to be in perfect health.

"Sorry, I think it was a pocket call," I stammered, looking up at March.

Another grunt, louder. "A pocket call—honey, how many times did I tell you that Apple was rubbish and we needed to buy you a new phone? Why do you call from a private number anyway? Are the settings on that damn phone broken too? We'll go to the shop together, I'll ask for the manager—"

"It's okay. I'll check the settings, it's probably nothing." He sounded his usual bearish self so far, but I needed to make sure. "Dad, I'm sorry I woke you. You seem tense, is everything all right? Did anything happen?" It was a stupid question, since my dad was basically born tense, but I figured it'd get me somewhere.

Two grunts. Bad omen. "Did Janice tell you?"

My fingers tightened around March's phone. "Tell me what?"

"About the tapioca!"

I blinked, while in the receiver, the gates of hell opened.

"She's having us go gluten-free! She force-fed me some goddamn rubbish tapioca pearls cake! Blocked me entirely! Haven't been able to go to the john for two goddamn days!"

March cocked a suspicious eyebrow at the inflamed rant rising from his phone.

I winced. At least my father was okay. Well, badly constipated, but okay. "Dad, I have to go. I'll call you soon!"

"Island, wait—"

I handed the phone back to March with a sigh. "I think it's okay. He didn't sound preoccupied or anything."

Ilan laughed. "He sounded pretty preoccupied to me!"

"No . . . It's just that his digestive tract got blocked by a tapioca pearls cake."

I looked up to see March's eyes, wider than I had ever seen them since our first encounter. "Tapioca is excellent. There's something wrong with your father."

I heard Ilan snicker some more, until he seemed to calm down. "So, back to business. Anything you can tell us about your mother's notary?"

Much like March, he never lost track of his targets . . . "I already told March everything I know, which amounts to basically nothing. But you said he never went to law school; is he some kind of fraud?"

Ilan shook his head as he casually passed a semitrailer on the right, earning himself a disapproving snort from March. "Not entirely. He does oversee his clients' assets and turns dirty money into clean wills."

"A notary for gangsters?"

"Let's not use big words!" Ilan laughed.

Past the initial shock, a terrible sadness washed over me. Once again, I felt like I was discovering my mom. "March said my mother was some sort of spy, a thief, but it's . . . I still can't believe it."

"Didn't your father tell you anything after she died?" Ilan asked, his voice tinged with surprise.

I blanched. "What do you mean? He said the notary had never sent him the papers, that there was probably nothing!" The idea that my dad might have lied to me knotted my stomach.

"To the best of my knowledge, he's the one behind this. That woman I questioned told me she had been in charge of the rest of Léa's assets. She said that when she contacted your father after Léa's death, he refused to listen. He wanted nothing to do with them, even if they were technically your inheritance," Ilan recounted. "She insisted, and he told her to let the money sleep. He never contacted her again after that."

My fingers were itching to grab March's phone again and call my dad back to treat him to some rage-fueled ranting of my own. I gritted my teeth and put a lid on my rising anger. "I'm not sure I follow you . . . HSBC sent me a check. I received the remaining balance on her account plus interest."

March stroked his chin. "The six thousand dollars you told me about? I did find the amount a little surprising."

"Yes, why would that be surprising?"

In the driver's seat, Ilan broke into a gravelly laugh.

"What's so funny?" I snapped.

"Island, your mother spent fifteen years serving the Board. Do you seriously think all she had was a little cash?"

I looked back and forth between him and March. "I don't understand."

Ilan shrugged. "I'm not gonna list everything, but I'd say you're sitting on roughly twenty million euros. By the way, would you take an offer on that apartment in Monaco? My wife loves—"

I cut him off abruptly. "It's a joke, right?"

"I don't think so, Island," March replied.

My eyes squeezed shut.

I often dreamed that I was taking an elevator, and it suddenly stalled for a few seconds before falling into a bottomless pit. That feeling of losing ground, that millisecond of dread and weightlessness, my stomach heaving before the fall . . . were precisely what I was experiencing at the moment. I wanted to laugh at the irony of the situation: minutes ago I had been talking to my dad—perhaps for the last time—and he had bullshitted me about tapioca cake. No mention of the fact that he had stripped me of every last bit of my mother's legacy.

An "oversight," no doubt.

Who was I kidding? This was exactly the sort of thing he would have done. Simon Halder was a kindhearted and generous man, a loving father, but also a damn controlling and anxious one, and I could guess that he had firmly intended to keep that secret from me until the day he died.

It wasn't the money that made me angry. I had more than enough to live on my own. I didn't need any of it. It was the idea that he had robbed me of a part of my mom's identity, of something that might have helped me know her, understand her. To be honest, I already secretly blamed him for the way he had cleared our apartment in Tokyo and kept none of my mother's personal belongings after her death. But this was worse. My dad had *known* about my mother's activities, about her will, and he'd chosen to conceal the truth from me. And, in a way, I had allowed this. I could have told him I was hurt by the way he had meticulously wiped away all traces of her, told him that I hated the way he'd sometimes lock himself in his office to take certain phone calls after her death. I hadn't. I had retreated into a shell of my own and chosen to forget about that open gash between us, for fear of having to confront him.

"If you try to talk to him about Étienne now, he'll suspect something, and it might endanger him. What is done is done; he's better not knowing that you learned about your inheritance for the time being," Ilan commented, apparently reading my mind.

My eyes slanted at March. "Don't worry, Ilan, it's not like I have a phone anyway."

I hoped I wouldn't get killed, because I planned on having a long conversation with my dad when I got back to New York. I stole another glance at March, who seemed to be plunged in deep thought as well, his brow furrowed. March . . . who embodied every sort of trouble my dad had tried to protect me from by hiding that will from me. What was it that Paolo Coelho said in *The Alchemist*? "What good is money to you if you're going to die? It's not often that money can save someone's life."

Well, Paolo was damn right, and so was my dad, to some extent. Taking a deep breath, I made up my mind and looked at March. "I'll help you find the Ghost Cullinan if I can, but I don't want to know anything about the rest. I won't take stolen money. I'm in enough trouble as it is."

"No, it's money paid in exchange for stolen goods," Ilan corrected.

"Totally different," March concurred with a little nod.

Aggravated by the fact that I was being given life advice by guys with failing moral compasses, I slammed back into my seat and crossed my arms. "I'll pretend I didn't hear this. This conversation is over."

Ilan was, however, one of those "macho macho men" who decide when conversations are over and when they aren't. "You know, if money makes you feel bad, you can always be like March. Save it all and live like a Jesuit in a cubicle," he said with a cunning smile.

A mixture of embarrassment and annoyance flashed in March's eyes. "My house is big enough, thank you."

"I think you're exaggerating, Ilan. A real tightwad wouldn't fly private," I offered in defense of my captor.

Ilan guffawed. "He negotiates Paulie's prices!"

"I'm merely enjoying the benefits of his frequent flyer program," March replied indignantly.

"Paulie *doesn't have* a frequent flyer program." Ilan snickered.

"Well, thanks to me, now he does."

I couldn't help it: witnessing the outrage in March's expression, I dissolved into laughter.

Between two hiccups, I heard Ilan's amused voice, addressing March. "Putain, c'est bien la première fois que je te vois faire marrer un client." *Damn, it has to be the first time I see you make a client laugh.*

I was surprised, to say the least; Ilan had talked in a rather colloquial French for the second time, and I hadn't realized March could understand the language so well. It was becoming obvious he had been here before.

I spent the rest of the ride in silence, counting the cows and trying to figure what to make of all this. How many facets were there to the man people just called March?

TEN

The Goddess

"She was a mysterious, sensual goddess, gliding across
the ballroom with effortless grace. Upon seeing her, Ryker
immediately felt his pants tent: he had been hopelessly bitten by
the potent arrow of love."

—Gilda Sapphire, *Scorching Passion of the Billionaire Werewolf*

Ilan must have been a wedding planner before turning to a life of crime, because when we reached the outskirts of Paris, he took charge naturally, March letting him do so without questions. I doubted it was a display of submission, though, more like he didn't care and would do as he pleased in the end anyway.

A series of text messages made Ilan's phone vibrate in his front pocket, and after he was done checking them, he looked at March in the mirror. "Your guy was seen at the Rose Paradise two nights ago. He's a regular there. I'm sending someone. Shouldn't be long until we catch him. I booked you a safe room, and your car is ready, but we'll stop at my place first. She said she absolutely had to see you if you were in Paris."

As he introduced the program, I recorded each single word in that special area of my brain where I store all data that could lead to shocking revelations and drama. Who the hell was "she"?

Ilan drove us through Paris until we reached rue Saint-Dominique, a narrow, crowded shopping street resting in the shadow of the Eiffel Tower and mostly bordered by low nineteenth-century buildings. I marveled at the store displays: shoes, clothes, jewelry, perfume, pastries . . . The place was a Parisian girl's dream. We turned right on a smaller street and stopped in front of a more modern white building. Fumbling in his pockets, Ilan pulled out a small remote and opened a garage's roll-up door.

Once out of the car, he led us to an elevator. As I stepped in cautiously, my brain sizzled with curiosity. Who was the mysterious lady who wanted to see March so badly? A friend? A . . . girlfriend? Ilan's mom? By the time we reached the seventh floor, I was busy weaving an elaborate scenario in which their rivalry stemmed from the fact that March was doing Ilan's mom.

We stepped out, and I noticed that there was only one set of black doors at the end of the hallway—someone seemed to own the entire floor. Ilan pushed them open to reveal a huge living room furnished with tasteful pearl-gray-and-white designer stuff—the sort that makes you wonder how much crime pays—and there, standing on the dark wooden floor, was an apparition.

A woman, perched on high pink platform heels, with skin as dark and silky as the coat of a Bombay cat and indecent curves hugged by a beige bandage dress. It might have been a bit rude, but I stared. Almond-shaped eyes, long wavy hair, full lips, and impeccable makeup. She was a fricking goddess, and judging by the way she smiled seductively and poised herself, she knew it all too well.

My eyes traveled down to focus on her generous breasts. How could girls like me be expected to feel good about themselves when such creatures roamed the earth? It was almost unfair. Finishing my inspection, I noted she wore a series of large golden bracelets on her right arm. They clinked softly as she approached March.

I watched, aghast, as the sublime creature draped her arms around him and caressed his hair, greeting him with a suave voice. "T'es toujours aussi beau." *You're as good-looking as ever.*

A thousand questions whirled inside my head. Who was she? Ilan looked super mad. Was he going to hit March immediately, or would he wait another minute? Could March escape her hug without an embarrassing boner?

I inhaled her powdery perfume as she moved away from him. March seemed okay, not stiff in any way, not even moved. He looked . . . content. He had welcomed her attention with a gentle smile, and his hand lingered on hers in what looked more like a friendly gesture than a genuine attempt to score.

Clear disapproval burning in his green eyes, Ilan broke the spell, looking at me as he introduced her. "Meet my wife, Kalahari."

I gaped. March's voice as he taunted Ilan about ringing twice resounded in my head. *Please don't tell me he's banged Ilan's wife. Please. I wanna live.*

She locked her hypnotic brown eyes on mine. "March, aren't you going to tell me more about your *friend*?"

There was a lovely accent in her French. She was probably an African native who had settled in France at some point in her life, something common, especially in Paris.

He placed a controlling hand on my back and complied. "Kalahari, this person is here to fulfill a small business agreement with me."

She gave March a strange look. "Oh? And *this person* doesn't have a name?"

"Clients don't have names."

Kalahari's warm expression morphed into an icy one. Her nostrils flared ever so slightly, and a fascinating chemical reaction occurred that turned the honey in her voice into the kind of hydrosulfuric acid that can melt spaceships, like in *Alien*.

"March, j'espère que tu te fous de ma gueule . . ." *March, you'd better be fucking kidding me . . .*

My mouth fell open for the second time in five minutes. Her refined manners had vanished, and she was now voicing her discontent in one of the harshest ways the French language permitted.

Both men furrowed their brows at the same time, apparently aware that Kalahari was to be handled with extreme caution from this point on.

March's features hardened. "Kalahari, stay out of this. Please."

"You're unbelievable . . . *fucking* hopeless! How can you do this to—"

"Kalahari!" March roared, cutting her off.

Against all odds, it was me who jumped, not her. March had never raised his voice since we had met. Not even once. It didn't work, though. *I* would have cowered in fear and begged not to be shot, but she seemed to be immune to his wide range of intimidation tricks. Fearing she would claw at his face soon, and aware that Ilan seemed unwilling to step into their quarrel, I chimed in to give March what little credit he deserved in an effort to appease her. "It's okay . . . I'm getting special treatment. I don't go in the trunk." My chest burst with pride as I said this. I was no ordinary client, and I thought the world ought to know so.

March nodded his appreciation of my short and positive input on the current situation, and I felt his hand push me forward. "Well, I'm happy I was able to see you, Kalahari. We'll be on our way now. Ilan, can you give me the car key and the additional equipment, please?"

Well, that had been one helluva short visit . . . except not.

Before Ilan had the time to comply with March's request, she pointed an accusing finger in my direction. "You stay here!"

I felt his hand steer me toward the door while the anger in her voice nailed my feet to the floor, and I thought of King Solomon's judgment. Were they going to split me in two to solve their dispute?

Kalahari glared at him. "For the love of God, look at her! She's dirty, her pants are torn, and I swear I've been listening to this annoying gurgle coming from her stomach ever since she passed that door!"

I bowed my head in shame. It was true. I was in used condition, and my belly had been growling nonstop for the past hour.

March seemed embarrassed by her accusations, but he resisted bravely, fighting for his constitutional right to treat me like crap. "Island will have plenty of time to eat and take a shower later, and she's doing fine. She told you so herself."

I managed a crisp smile meant to confirm his bullshit and soothe her, but she would have none of it.

"How can you look at yourself in the mirror? I'm *so* disappointed in you!"

March recoiled, at a loss for new excuses, and Ilan finally stepped in, attempting to calm his wife. "*Chérie*, it's the job. He can't . . . you need to understand—"

"Like hell it is! Would you do that, Ilan? Would you dare to treat me like this?" I noticed she was trying to ball her fists in anger, but she couldn't because of her long nails. Her fingers were trembling, though.

He caved. "It's different!"

"A true gentleman keeps his girl well-fed, well-dressed, and well-fucked. That's final!" she yelled, emphasizing each part of this primitive triptych with a resounding slam of her high heel against the apartment's wooden floor.

I tried to assess the situation. Ilan no longer controlled his dark Aphrodite, March was staring at me as if all of this was somehow my fault, and Kalahari was adamantly advising him to screw me. I was scared shitless, but I realized I could make something of the chaos unfolding before my eyes.

"I-I think we can cut March some slack regarding that last point. I'm sure he has other things on his mind right now, but I could do with a meal and a shower." I held out my hands to protect myself as I said this, fearing swift retribution from the so-called gentleman.

The sound of my pleading succeeded in appeasing her wrath, and she turned to March, planting her hands on her hips.

I gulped and looked up at him. "Would that be okay with you, March? I know your time is precious, but it's been a rough two days. Please—"

I made sure to make my tone weak and begging like the plaintive mewl of a fuzzy kitten that got hit by a Hummer, to ensure that he would have no choice but to indulge Kalahari. She obviously held some sort of superpower over him, and I intended to use it to my advantage.

His soft, calculating smile returned, and the hand that had been resting on my back for the past five minutes receded slowly. "Kalahari is right. Island, I'm terribly sorry for denying you the comfort you *so much* deserve."

Ouch. Here came the fake apology . . .

"Please sustain yourself and take the time to bathe. Then we can leave, and before we part, I'll make sure that I've *thoroughly* abided to all of Kalahari's prescriptions."

And there was the threat. Double ouch.

I won't lie, I was a little miffed. I had earned some momentary relief, but March was now implying that he would make sure to "thoroughly" rape me before he let me go, so the results of my little strategy were mixed at best.

ELEVEN

The Cake

"She licked her lips slowly as she swallowed the last bite of her banana cake. 'I love creamy desserts,' she whispered huskily, her eyes devouring him whole."

—Terry Robs, *Glazed by the Cook*

Ilan and Kalahari's kitchen was even nicer than their living room. (For the record, I liked their shiny chrome toilet-roll holder a lot too. And they had black toilet paper, something I had never seen in my entire life. I stole some and stuffed it in my back pocket.) Examining the furniture, my eyes lingered on the long dark lava stone countertops and the coordinated black lacquered appliances. They almost made me wish my place had looked like an issue of *Metropolitan Home* too.

The meal itself was simple—fried eggs and a yummy little fruit and vegetable salad—but I had to admit that Kalahari was a remarkable cook. The joyful blend of fresh mesclun, grapes, pomegranate, and tart balsamic vinegar was absolute bliss. Plus I had skipped breakfast and was literally starving. I wolfed down my plate faster than a raccoon raiding the trash at McDonald's, went for seconds, and when I looked up to see that the dish was now empty, turned my attention to March's plate. He seemed disturbed by my keen interest in his remaining egg, perhaps because I was practically drooling.

"Are you gonna eat that?" Let's be real, he wasn't going to. It was mine for the taking.

March didn't see it that way, though, and proceeded to drag his plate away from me and closer to himself, staring at me intently as he did so. "Yes."

Narrowing my eyes, I raised my fork in an offensive position. I knew what I needed to do in order to get that egg. Before he had the time to dig in, I gathered a pinch of breadcrumbs from the table, where Kalahari had cut some slices of baguette, and threw them onto his plate. They landed on his egg yolk like shrapnel, irremediably tainting it. I saw his throat constrict, and his fork stopped midair. I had won.

Kalahari burst out laughing at this, and even Ilan couldn't suppress a chortle. March gave me a look of pure contempt and pushed his plate in my direction. "There will be consequences," he stated coolly.

Ignoring his warning, I helped myself to the rest of his food while Kalahari went to fetch a well-garnished cheese platter. There were five different sorts of cheese, and a couple of them smelled like a pile of dirty diapers abandoned in a stable: I couldn't wait to dig in. I cut a large slice of runny Muenster and spread it on a piece of bread with a regal gesture. Next to me, March was very still, and he politely declined when Ilan handed him the knife. Needless to say, curdled milk that's been left to rot in a cave for years probably didn't rank very high on Mr. Clean's list of approved delicacies.

I, on the other hand, closed my eyes and moaned in delight. That Muenster tasted like it was older than me. "It's been years since I had cheese that good!"

Ilan served me a slice of Reblochon as well. "How long has it been since you last came to France?"

"Four years. But we stayed in a hotel back then, and they don't serve the same kind of cheese."

He swallowed a large bite of graying, moldy goat cheese and nodded. "Yeah, food safety freaks . . . They don't know what's good."

"My mother was like you, she always insisted that mold is good for your immune system and only pussies cut it out."

"Spartan parenting?" Kalahari smiled.

"Pretty much. She'd be gone for days at time, and she really took advantage of how independent I was. She'd just plop me in a new apartment, say, 'Computer's here; microwave's here. Be good,' and . . . *whoosh*," I explained, flinging my arms in the air.

Whoosh . . . My eyes met March's, who had been listening to the conversation silently in front of an empty plate, and something tightened in my chest. Would I have been able to learn the truth by myself if I had tried to? Had my mother been that good an actress, or had I turned a blind eye on all those times when she'd seemed a little too tired, a little too lost?

"Ah, tu sais dans la vie, on court, on court!" *You know, life is all about running, running all the time.* How many times had I heard her say this when she came home late at night and let herself fall on our couch, exhausted? I had always thought she was one of those overworked career women—a diplomat, a woman of the world, speaking a dozen different languages without the slightest hint of an accent, and sirening her way through glamorous parties. Except she hadn't been there to binge on petits fours; she had been risking her life, night after night.

For me? To make money to support us?

No. As much as my mother had loved me, the new portrait that was progressively sketching itself in my mind suggested that she had been addicted to this life. She could have made just as much money by marrying my dad—no doubt he would have agreed, if the spark in his eyes whenever he mentioned her was any indication.

Across the table, Kalahari seemed in deep thought. "But didn't you go to school?"

I stared down at the gooey cheese on my plate as I recalled those first fifteen years of my life. "No. We moved all the time, so my mom would sign me up for all kinds of distance-learning programs. Some relevant, some not so much. I ended up following a course on slaughterhouse management once, when I was ten."

March's eyes widened in an expression of scandal, Ilan's mouth twitched, and tears of laughter built up at the corners of Kalahari's cat-like eyes.

"Yeah . . ." I sighed. "I'm not sure she read those leaflets before signing the application papers."

"What about your father?" she prodded. "Didn't he live with you?"

I shook my head. "You know that old song from Jean-Jacques Goldman? Elle a fait un bébé toute seeeule . . ." *She made a baby on her ooown . . .*

She answered my singing attempt with a bright smile. "C'était dans ces années un peu folles ou les papas n'était plus à la mooode!" *It was in those crazy years, when daddies had gone out of style!* "I love that song!"

"Well, it was sort of like that. I think they had a two-week fling in London, nothing more. And then, nine months later, there I was. I suppose he was a little disoriented, but he tried his best. He'd give me toys for Christmas, my birthdays, and my mom sometimes sent me to spend a couple weeks with him in New York," I recounted.

"You went to live with him after her death?" Kalahari asked.

"Yes . . . I was fifteen at the time, and it was a pretty drastic change of environment."

"But it was better for you," March stated, breaking his self-imposed silence.

My head shot up and I frowned at him. "It's hardly your place to judge that."

I expected him to back out and dismiss the topic, but to my surprise he insisted. "Children need a stable home, parents who'll send them to school. Your mother—"

"You'll never guess what's for dessert!"

Kalahari had suddenly shot up from her chair, cutting through March's judgmental little tirade before he could give me enough reason to throw my plate in his face. From the corner of my eye, I caught Ilan shaking his head at March. Kalahari looked at him as well, but there was no blame in her eyes, rather tenderness and sadness laced together. I thought of what March had told me the day prior in his car, about how he had dropped out before even reaching high school. What kind of family had *he* grown up in?

I pondered this over while Kalahari took a plate from a large side-by-side fridge. When I got a good view of the treat, I quivered on my chair. She was carrying a sexy, yummy *fraisier* cake. She laid the pastry on the table, its pink icing glimmering under the ceiling's lighting.

"Your favorite!" She winked at March as she said so.

I peeked at him. He didn't seem the type to like *fraisier*. Those luscious layers of sponge cake, vanilla butter cream, and strawberries seemed way too indulgent for a guy like him. I would have sworn he was into more manly stuff, like oatcakes.

I was wrong. Kalahari served him nearly a quarter of that hottie, and it started disappearing from his plate at a surprising speed. He kept a deadpan face while he ate, though, as if he didn't want us to know he was enjoying it. I was so engrossed in watching him that I forgot about my own plate, and what a tactical error it was.

"Seconds?" Kalahari's hands were already moving to cut him another slice.

He shot me a dark look as he answered her. "Please don't bother. Island won't eat hers."

My eyes widening in alarm, I reached to grab some breadcrumbs again, but he had been ready for my trick and outsped me. By the time my fingertips started gathering ammo on the tablecloth, my plate was gone and March's spoon was covered in the blood of my strawberries.

Kalahari burst out laughing, and Ilan's lips pressed together in apparent consternation. Gesturing to the remaining cake, she offered to replace my serving, which now rested in the depths of March's stomach.

His lips quirked in a smug smile. "I don't think Island has time for more cake. She needs to get cleaned up, and we're on a tight schedule."

I glared at him before leaving the table to follow a still giggling Kalahari. She led me down a long hallway and into a large bedroom decorated with white furniture. In its center stood a massive four-poster bed covered with a swarm of colorful Indian cushions. There was a fruity fragrance in the air, which I soon associated with a couple of scented candles resting on one of the nightstands. I inhaled deeply and reveled in the warm, cozy atmosphere surrounding me.

Crossing the room to open the doors leading to a white-tiled bathroom, Kalahari pointed at my clothes and made an elegant circular gesture with her wrist. "Get rid of all this. You're in desperate need of a bath!"

It was true. I couldn't ignore the mud stains on my jeans or the faint smell of sweat floating around me, and I was a little ashamed of my state of disarray. She walked to a large polished concrete tub and turned the hot water tap on before squeezing some bubble bath in the rising water. Once she was satisfied with the water's temperature, she returned to the room where I was still standing.

I gave her a sheepish smile. "Thank you. Can I borrow a towel from you?"

"Of course you can! There're clean ones in the bathroom; just help yourself once you're done."

I nodded and was about to go jump headfirst in that tub, when Kalahari took a few steps until she stood in front of me. Her face had lost her joyful expression in favor of a soft, thoughtful one. "You're going to be okay. Just relax for a little while."

I wasn't so sure that I was going to be okay, but I was at least being offered some momentary relief. I gave a grateful smile and entered the bathroom. I had first intended to make this quick, but once I had sunk into the warm, flowery-scented water, I fell prey to its emollient effect and allowed myself to laze around. After an undetermined amount of time during which I stared at my toes, a soft tap echoed on the other side of the bathroom's door.

Kalahari's voice resounded. "Did you fall asleep?"

"No! Sorry, I'm coming out."

I extracted myself from the now tepid water with clumsy movements and wrapped myself in a large gray towel that looked like a long dress on me. Confident that I was decent, I stepped out of the bathroom.

March had nothing on Kalahari where efficiency was concerned: by the time I entered the room, I discovered that she had prepared some clean clothes and even found a spare toothbrush for me—something that seemed like a small luxury, in my predicament.

TWELVE

The Octopus

"Every time his eyes plunged into hers, Honestee felt desire's inescapable tentacles slowly wrap themselves around her body, their suction cups clinging to her skin."

—Georgia Stilton, *The Shifter's Mail-Order Bride*

Half an hour and a few fittings later, I was wearing a pair of beige jeans, a plain white T-shirt, and a navy-blue hoodie that wasn't unlike mine except its back boldly advertised me as having been a part of Abercrombie & Fitch's Physical Ed class since 1892. I could live with that. A little cleaning in the bathroom sink made my ballet flats as good as new, and I was ready to face the rest of the day.

I didn't make it far. I got ambushed.

"What's your sign?"

I blinked at the magazine Kalahari had just fished from her nightstand. Were we really going to take astrological tests in the middle of my kidnapping? I feigned disinterest. "I don't know, I'm not really into this—"

"When were you born?"

"September 20."

She waved the magazine in my face. "Then you're a Virgo!"

Yes. *Indeed*. I was.

Ignoring my frown, Kalahari checked the latest predictions for Virgos who got kidnapped by hit men. "It says you're in danger of losing your good reputation because you flirt too much and you need to stop sleeping around. It also says you have no boundaries and you can't resist the temptation of . . . your heated core."

"No it doesn't say that!" I snatched the magazine from her hands.

It did say just that. I reread the part about my "heated core." Kalahari had been kind enough to spare me some of the worst details: that magazine was basically calling me a slut. My mouth fell open in an expression that probably made it look like someone had just crushed my toes with a hammer.

She laughed. "Come on, maybe they're exaggerating a little, but it's not like you're a nun either!"

Maybe it's because my face became really, really red; maybe it's because you're not supposed to look aghast when someone suggests the possibility that you have occasional intercourse: whatever the cause, she *guessed*.

Kalahari's smile faded, giving way to something halfway between awe and horror. "Don't tell me you've never—"

Instead of a firm denial, a faint whistle escaped my throat.

It was her turn to gape like a trout. "Oh . . . my . . . God. But you're what, twenty-two, at least!"

I coughed. "I'm twenty-five."

Her hands flew to her mouth. "Stop shitting me!"

I handed her the magazine back. "See? I'm the living proof that those predictions are random and baseless."

She took the offending publication, placed it back on her nightstand, and kept staring at me, tilting her head as if examining a new species.

"What?"

"Nothing. I was just wondering why . . ."

I shrugged weakly and looked away. "I don't know . . . it just happened to be like this."

"Island. Abstinence doesn't 'happen like this,' sex does," Kalahari chided as she sat on the bed.

I joined her. "Like I said, I don't know why. I guess the conditions were never united, that's all."

"What conditions?"

"It's difficult to explain . . . for starters, I had zits and braces until college, so most boys steered clear because I really wasn't that hot."

She smiled knowingly. "That sounds more like an excuse . . ."

"Well, I did have some sprinkles, and used to be able to stick a pen between my front teeth." I opened my mouth to demonstrate. "But, really, I think I just . . . didn't want to get close to anybody. School, people, I didn't want any of that. I didn't fit in."

"Because this life was too different from the one you had known with your mother?"

"Maybe . . . I had gotten used to taking care of myself, to spending my time either alone or with adults. And there I was, going to school for the first time in my life, and all people around me cared about was sneaking out beer from their parents' fridge and, well, sex."

A bubbly laugh escaped her. "What did *you* care about?"

"Super Mario 64."

"But this was high school, right? What about after the braces and the zits were gone?"

"I went to college."

"Perfect place to experiment with sex, or so I've heard," she observed with an impish grin. "So?"

"So, nothing! I had read all those romance books, and I had high expectations. I thought I would be courted by some perfect guy, hold hands, wait for the right time, and make sweet love."

A chortle made her shoulders shake. "In *college*?"

"Yeah, I know . . . By the time I figured out it was never gonna happen I was twenty-three and had a master's degree. That's more or less when I realized I had missed the train," I concluded. Kalahari was the second person after Joy to hear this, and I wasn't sure it made me happy. Scratch that: it was mortifying.

"Twenty-three is a bit young to give up, don't you think?"

Resigning myself to the fact this conversation was happening whether I wanted it or not, I resumed my tale of woe. "I was afraid to talk to guys, afraid of their reaction when they'd discover I didn't have any experience . . . I didn't want to face rejection."

She rolled on the bed to rest closer to me. "Don't worry so much. Truth is, if you don't say anything, most men won't even realize!"

I let that sink in for a second. "So they just don't care? How can they not notice—"

"Well, if the shoe fits . . ." She shrugged.

I winced.

Kalahari seemed to realize I was thinking of battering rams and ice-breakers: She gave me a comforting smile and patted my hand. "Don't worry, March takes excellent care of his turf."

I chose to ignore the many possibilities outlined by this choice of words. "I'm not his—well, I am, but not in the way you suggest," I mumbled, trying—and failing—to block any wayward thought. Was he a good kisser? Would it taste like mints?

"Sorry! I guess I have to try to plead his case because that's the part he's not great at!"

Understatement of the year, although I highly doubted March was trying to lure me under the sheets. If he was, then it probably qualified as the second-worst attempt at seduction ever in the animal kingdom—the worst one being, in my opinion, the way some octopuses tear their own penis off and throw it in their girlfriend's general direction, only for it to swim toward the lady and latch onto her body. No. Just *no*.

A horrifying mental image of March doing the same flashed in my mind, and I knew I'd never get back those two seconds of my life, or manage to scrub my brain clean of that particular visual.

Kalahari's voice broke through my zoological considerations. "Island . . . how come you're not asking?"

"Asking what?"

"About March and me. Aren't you curious?"

I wasn't sure I wanted to venture into this particular territory, but I indulged her nevertheless. "Well, okay . . . Are you his ex?"

"Yes."

I didn't even bother with a surprised look. It had been completely obvious. "So, what happened?"

She sighed. "We were both too young! I was twenty-three, he was twenty-four, and we had no idea what we were doing."

"What do you mean?"

"He had helped me out of a pretty shitty situation, so he felt responsible for me, and I had gratitude and love all mixed up. In the end, it took us a while to figure out that friends didn't necessarily have to be lovers."

I hated to admit it, but she had piqued my curiosity. "How long did you two stay together?"

"A year or so. I had nowhere to go, so we basically lived together from the start."

"Oh my God . . . with the cleaning and all?"

To my horror, she nodded with a smile. "Yes, but that was okay. He was really sweet to me. It's just that the relationship was bad for both of us."

"Why?"

"Because he's the control fairy, and I needed someone to help me grow and become independent."

Figured. With his strange cleaning obsession and at times arrogant attitude, March hardly seemed like the best candidate for a long-term relationship—unless you were a French maid, that is.

"He was smothering you, right?"

"Exactly. And I don't blame him. I was all too happy to play along. He did all the thinking for two, folded my clothes, gave me money to go shopping, and I didn't have to face life at all."

I listened silently, fascinated by her tale. She went on. "You know, I think he would have married me. He started talking about it at some point—"

I cringed at the idea of a hit man juggling contract killings and a wholesome family life. "What happened?"

"He grew up a little, enough to realize that our relationship only made his controlling streak worse, and I'll never thank him enough for that."

My mouth hung open for a few seconds in shock. "So he . . . dumped you?"

"You could say that! He actually supported me until I was back on my feet. I came to France to work in my aunt's beauty salon, and later he helped me start my own business. I met Ilan after that. He was still working for the DGSE at the time, so we had a rough start when he learned that my ex was . . . well—"

Still struggling to control my slack jaw, I processed the information she had given me. "Ilan used to work for the Secret Service? March has shares in a beauty salon?"

She nodded enthusiastically. "Well, you can call Katmosphère a chain now. I opened a second salon on rue de Rivoli in June. We'll be launching a product line soon!"

I was impressed, to say the least. Not only was Kalahari drop-dead gorgeous, but she was also in fact a successful entrepreneur. That being said, I didn't like the way it made me feel to discover that March did possess a soul like anyone else and was capable of an act of kindness—or, worse, potentially capable of committing marriage. I found the idea unsettling. It made my imagination run wild with terrifying scenarios of him having his baby perform a three-hour shift in the living room with one of those mop onesies.

Lost in visions I suspected were far more pleasant than mine, Kalahari closed her eyes. "You know, I don't love him the way I love Ilan, but he's my best friend."

I had never felt at ease with big words like "love," so I didn't know what to say. I chose to play it safe and merely acknowledge the obvious. "I'm sure he likes you too. You had him wrapped around your little finger back there. It was amazing!"

"Hey, only Christmas call he ever makes! That's how powerful I am!"

I broke into a fit of giggles at this detail; she truly had him on his knees. My breath was still short when she resumed speaking with a wistful smile. "You know . . . you resist March in a way he likes."

"I don't think so. He seems pretty pissed to have to deal with me."

She propped herself up on her elbows. "That's because he's been alone for years. He's used to his little comforts. Give him some time."

I jackknifed up in my turn. "He kidnapped me, for God's sake! What exactly are we talking about?"

"You're so cute when you pretend to be angry! Don't you like anything about him?"

"I like that maybe, if I collaborate with him, I get to stay alive," I stated grimly.

Why was she implying things about March and me? Was this some sort of punishment for having fantasized about him, even for a second? Her suggestive wink did little to comfort me. "Don't worry about that. He'll take good care of you. I'll kick his ass some more if he doesn't spoil you!"

All right, now I knew without a trace of doubt that she was hiding something from me. Was there no end to Paulie's shitty gossiping? "Look, I don't like this. It's like when Paulie said I was March's girlfriend. It's wrong . . . and embarrassing!" I felt bad for snapping at her like that when she had been nothing but kind to me, but I hated to be toyed with.

She got up from the bed too, and her eyes turned way, too serious for my liking. "I'm sorry, Island. What I'm trying to say is that I think

I know who you are. I realized it was you when Ilan told me about the job yesterday. March wouldn't say much, but Ilan knew your face and your name, so it was easy to put the pieces together."

"Kalahari, what the hell are you talking about?"

Uncertainty suddenly flashed in her eyes, and her delicate eyebrows knit together in an expression of dilemma, as if she suddenly remembered that March might object to her sharing the details of his private life with a perfect stranger.

"I shouldn't tell you this . . . I think he took the job because it was you, but it must be hard for him."

Sweat started to form on my brow. She wasn't going to leave me hanging like this, right?

"You're his Barefoot Contessa."

"What the—" I remembered how Paulie had called me a countess, back at the airport, and I was about to pester her until she explained herself, but a faint knock on the other side of the door cut me off. "Shit! I think they're waiting."

"Oh, let them wait!"

My eyes traveled between her and the door. She was right, they could wait. I *couldn't*. "Why are you saying I'm a contessa?"

Her lips curled into a knowing smile. "You need to have this conversation with March. If he doesn't have the balls to tell you, I will. But I think it would be wrong. He's made it this far, found you again . . . he *has* to tell you."

Again? Oh God, what did she mean by that? My mouth had opened to question her some more when the same impatient knocking resumed.

She shook her head with a sad smile. "It's okay, go."

I headed to the door with a sigh; Kalahari's riddles had me on edge, and I still had a long and potentially bad day ahead of me. She followed me into the living room, where Ilan was busy showing March what looked like a big bullet, arguing about the unbelievable amount of damage it could do. She swayed through the room until she was sitting on her husband's lap and placed a gentle kiss on his forehead. "It's all fun and games until someone loses an eye."

"Are you ready to go, Island?" March's voice turned my spine to ice. Of course I wasn't. I wanted to know more about the Barefoot Contessa thing. I wanted to run away and return home. I was essentially ready for everything except spending the rest of the day alone with him.

Getting up, Ilan reached me before March could. "Look, it won't be long until my guy catches your notary, twelve hours max. As soon as we're done, if March doesn't need you anymore, I'll send you back home."

His voice was firm, reassuring, and I desperately wanted to believe him. Kalahari gave me a gesture of encouragement with her two thumbs up, and I nodded.

I was going to be okay.

Right?

THIRTEEN

The Choice

"Some people will tell you that even when looking solely for sex, you can occasionally draw the line and dump a guy on the premise that he really isn't good for you. _BULLSHIT! DON'T DO THAT!_ Being picky is the best way to remain a virgin."

—Aurelia Nichols & Jillie Bean, _101 Tips to Lose Your Virginity after 25_

The enchanted interlude ended roughly five seconds after we passed the building's entrance. March turned to me, creepy poker smile etched on his features, and once again, I felt like I had in that glade: ready to bolt. He led us to a gray Mercedes that had likely been provided by Ilan and opened the passenger door for me. As soon as I heard the powerful hum of the engine, I fastened my seat belt in a hurry: I knew March enforced road safety rules strictly, and his thinly veiled threats had made a lasting impression on me. Better not end up in the trunk over something as trivial as failure to buckle up.

He nodded his agreement as the seat belt alarm went off, and the car started moving. We passed the Esplanade des Invalides with its church's extravagant golden dome, slowing down for a bunch of female joggers to cross the rue de l'Université, and as we drove along the Seine, a wave of corny nostalgia washed over me.

Paris runs in the blood, I think, and my mom had never been able to stay away for long. We moved all the time, but every three months or so she would find a good reason to come back here, if only for a few days. The bond wasn't social in nature: her acquaintances were scattered all around the globe, and she had no family left in Paris that I knew of. It was, I believe, the same type of visceral attachment that I felt as soon as I stepped on Parisian soil too—the need to stroll down deserted avenues early in the morning or inhale the delicious smell of roasted coffee and crack a hard-boiled egg on the counter of a noisy *bistrot*. It had been nearly four years since my last trip to France. Though I tried my best not to think about all these little things, and fit into my "normal" life in the US, being back in Paris shattered that intimate balance all over again.

I missed her . . . I missed her so much.

We paused at a red light, side by side with an old white BX whose driver's window was open, and inside the car I could hear the radio blaring Mort Schuman's "Allô Papa Tango Charlie."

His slow, depressed voice fit my current mood perfectly. I closed my eyes, mouthing the lyrics. "J'ai perdu celle que j'aimais, je ne la retrouverai jamais. Je vais noyer ma solitude dans le triangle des Bermudes." *I've lost the one I loved. I'll never see her again. I'll go drown my loneliness in the Bermuda triangle.*

Whether because he noticed I was crumbling and wanted to depress me further, or simply out of boredom, March shattered my reverie with a seemingly innocuous remark that felt like a kick in the shin. "I trust you had a pleasant time with Kalahari?"

My dream plane came crashing down in flames, and I felt my ears heat up to an unbelievable temperature. Had he overheard the conversation about Kalahari's Barefoot Contessa thing? Never in my life had a question tortured my mind more. I could feel it on the tip of my tongue, forcing its way out. I chickened out, though, like every time something touched me intimately, and I chose to divert our conversation to safer grounds. "Yes . . . I guess it was kind of them to welcome us into their apartment. It's a nice place."

"Yes, very typical of the French postwar architecture: bright and spacious."

Wow. March was a master of making small talk. I bet he had a complete set of premade conversation starters encompassing a broad range of fascinating subjects such as the weather, the price of bullets these days, or how to clean your windows with newspaper to get a perfect finish . . .

Tangled in a web of confusion and frustration, I curled up in my seat and looked away, staring at the ballet of cars driving through the Place de la Concorde. "T'es vraiment un mec horrible." *You're really a horrible guy.*

He laughed. "Thank you. Why are you no longer talking to me in English?"

I went on, still in French. "Because you understand French, and I felt like it. How long did you live here anyway?"

"What makes you think I lived here?" March asked, a touch a suspicion in his voice. It was the first time I was hearing him speak French. His English accent was unmistakable, but, as I had suspected, his grasp of the language was excellent.

"Kalahari told me things . . . about you."

His driving became more aggressive. He actually sped up when he had room to do so. "I've been here often, but I've never lived in France."

The blocks clipped together in my brain, and the answer escaped my lips at the same time. "No, you lived in Africa."

I couldn't be 100 percent sure I was right, but I thought it made sense. The scarification on his back, Kalahari's claim that she had arrived in Paris after their breakup, the fact that he understood and spoke French but claimed to have never lived in France.

"Please mind your own business in the future," he snapped back.

Africa it was.

The car took a sharp turn along the Seine, on the Quai d'Orsay, and March deemed it necessary to complete his warning. "Listen, Island, I won't ask what Kalahari told you while you were alone with her. I will, however, tell you this: it doesn't change *anything*. I have a job to do, and I will do it."

Before I could ask what didn't change anything, a monstrous shock shook the car. March hadn't seen it coming—likely because he had allowed our conversation to distract him—and I obviously hadn't either. Needless to say I couldn't have imagined that the second car accident of my life would happen with him. Statistically, it should have occurred in my father's car, doing ninety miles per hour on I-84, not in March's Mercedes, waiting at a red light like decent road users.

The vehicle came from a small one-way street on the right, crashing into our side and blocking the car. I have this memory of a huge noise and my entire body being projected to the right, with my head slamming violently against the side air bag I hadn't even seen burst out. There was talcum powder everywhere, in my eyes and on my burning cheek, but also a dull pain in my abdomen. The seat belt had locked itself during the impact and was squeezing me tight. March's hand pushed my head down so hard I thought he was going to break my neck. I was in a complete daze: my ears were buzzing, and when my nose crashed into my own lap I was still wondering what had just happened.

Well, what had happened is what I believe to be called an ambush—though it didn't fully dawn on me until I heard the first gunshots. I kept my head down and shrank to the size of a lawn gnome while March tried to maneuver us out of this mess. A choir of panicked screams and wails rose in the street: around us, drivers and passengers had started scrambling out of their cars. Soon the Mercedes was surrounded by empty vehicles encasing ours in a trap.

Still dizzy, I felt March undo my seat belt and pull me toward him while he unlocked the driver's door. A projectile slammed into the windshield with a loud noise; it would have ended its course in March's head had it not been blocked by bulletproof glass. I glanced up at the crystal-like star now decorating the glass. God. He wasn't seriously thinking of getting out while people were shooting at us, right?

I felt him shift next to me and peeked up again. He was removing his jacket, under which a black holster circled his shoulders. Was it the best time for stripping? I felt the navy-blue garment fall on me, strangely heavy and smelling of his clean scent and Kalahari's perfume. Frightened, confused, I stared as he pulled out that black gun with the long suppressor and unlocked his door.

Then I heard it.

A voice, a yell in the midst of chaos, echoing between gunfire, terrified shrieks, and the distant sounds of French police sirens approaching.

"Mademoiselle Chaptal! DCRI, on vient vous aider!" *Miss Chaptal! Homeland Intelligence, we're here to rescue you!*

My heart exploded in my chest as if I had scratched a goddamn winning lottery ticket. I jackknifed up, shrugging off the oversized jacket, and looked through my window to see a blue minivan and a guy standing in front of it, wearing the bright orange armband identifying a French police officer. March's determined blue eyes met mine, and he certainly read my distrust, a reminder that he wasn't the good guy here. He was the bad guy, and I was being given one single chance to escape him and that Board organization.

"Island, don't! Stay here!"

A large hand clasped around my wrist, cutting the blood flow there, and I struggled against his grip, kicking him, pulling desperately at my arm. I cried out in pain as his fingers tightened, bruising the translucent skin protecting my veins, and he let go. My free hand flew to my door handle and tugged frantically. Damn thing wouldn't open! I remembered that there was a button near the wheel commanding the door locks. Panting, I batted his hands away with all I had. At some point I dug my nails into his skin until he bled and managed to hit that damn button.

When a dull sound indicated that my door was unlocked, I tried the handle again. The door opened, and I tumbled into the street, my legs reflexively kicking in response to March's forceful attempt to grab them.

The gunfire had ceased, perhaps because the cops were waiting for their announcement to produce some sort of effect. The sirens seemed to grow closer, and I was progressively being filled by a sense of incredible hope. Later, it took me several sleepless nights of replaying the scene in my mind to understand how and why I was able to exit that car: March had hesitated. He could have stopped me in a hundred different and equally painful ways, grabbed one of my ankles again and simply broken it to incapacitate me, but the couple of seconds he spent trying to make that decision proved to be too long.

I finally managed to crawl away from the wrecked Mercedes, and I registered a flash of panic in his eyes. I didn't give a shit; I couldn't hear anything but the sirens calling, and at the time I assumed he was mad because of losing his paycheck and ending up caught by the police.

I saw the cops shooting at our windshield again to stop March from going after me. I think he managed to get out anyway. I heard more gunshots and a scream behind me. My eyes darted to the left; the driver of the car that had rammed into ours had since come out and tried to fire at March as well. I barely had the time to see the shooter collapse, a stain of deep red blood rapidly spreading on his chest.

"Couvrez la!" *Cover her!*

It was that bald guy near the Citroën minivan who had shouted, shielding himself behind the vehicle to avoid ending up like his unfortunate colleague. A second black-haired cop wearing the same orange armband stepped out of the minivan and fired at March with what looked like a powerful automatic rifle, successfully stopping his progress toward me. I looked back to see March plunge to the ground and shield himself behind an open car door.

The strangest thing happened then. All the adrenaline pumping in my blood was still propelling my feet forward, and I didn't stop running toward the cops, but part of me wanted to look back again to see if March was okay. Thank God I was a rational person, the type who steals toilet paper but doesn't let inappropriate feelings for her kidnapper stand in the way of her freedom.

I blocked that thought and ran toward the voice, my arms flailing, snot running all over my nose and mouth. This had been no dream. There, standing behind the minivan and already opening the sliding door while his colleague fired again and again into the car shielding March, was the man who had called my name. A tall young man with a neatly shaven skull, a black parka, and that flashy, goddamn-beautiful orange armband.

The time it took me to cover the distance between us felt way too long, but really, the whole thing—car crash included—had probably taken less than a few minutes. Soon I was collapsing in his arms and sobbing with relief. He helped me inside the vehicle, and within seconds it was all over. We were driving fast along the Seine's right bank, and my bizarre adventure was reaching its conclusion. No one would ever search my things again, or even threaten to tenderize me.

"Complètement conne, ma parole . . ." *I swear, she's completely retarded . . .*

My head shot up.

I looked at my savior in surprise. He was sneering at his colleague's statement, and a surge of panic washed over me, making my skin prickle.

Turned out I had been right: it was over, and quickly so. The bald man grabbed my neck, pressed my carotid, and I blacked out.

I know it was a little late for that, and maybe I deserved what I got anyway, but my last conscious thought was of March.

FOURTEEN

The Table

"Ramirez tore Rica's red blouse open, revealing the sumptuous globes of her breasts. 'You are mine, Rica! Love is the sentence, and my shaft is the needle!"

—Kerry-Lee Storm, *The Cost of Rica*

Have you seen that movie—*Being John Malkovich*? The one where everyone had John Malkovich's face? My dream was kind of like that, except everybody had March's face, and it was terribly creepy. I had sometimes dreamed of the months my mom and I had spent in Tokyo or of my stay in the hospital, but never of the accident itself. Those few minutes and the two weeks that had ensued remained a complete black hole.

At the moment, however, and for the first time in ten years, I was back in the car, driving down the Keiyo Dori with her. She was talking about where we would go next—Australia, maybe? I could see the flicker of sadness in her green eyes, concealed by a bright smile. Did she miss the man in Pretoria? Had she perhaps loved him a little?

I was trying to focus on her lips, on what she was saying, but the passersby all had March's face, even that little dog, so it wasn't easy.

Suddenly, my mom's head jerked a little, and she went limp. I watched in incomprehension as her hands slid off the wheel. Had she passed out? Was the blood on her shirt coming from her head? Everything went quiet save for that soft buzzing in my ears. My own voice. I was screaming so loud my throat hurt, but it was muted. I couldn't hear myself.

The car was still moving. I had no idea how to stop it, and we were almost at the gas station. I already knew what happened next: we were going to crash into that white car, the one with an old man filling the tank. He ran away, dropping the nozzle, and everything felt fast, and slow, and inevitable. When we hit the white car, I was able to hear again—metal crashing and panicked shrieks. The heady scent of gas permeated my nostrils, and I saw the first flames rising from the rear of the white car and licking the blue hood of ours.

Everybody still had March's face, and they were all looking in our direction, but no one was doing anything. They were certainly afraid to go near the cars, afraid that they would explode. I couldn't move. My entire body seemed numb, and my head hurt where it had slammed against the headrest. I didn't open my door because my hands were trembling too much, but someone else did. Another March? No . . . he was the only one who didn't have March's face. Well, not exactly. My savior did look a lot like all the other Marches, but he had longer hair, and he was much younger. He cut my seat belt with a small incurved knife, and I thought it was nice for a man to carry a knife around like that. How handy. He cradled me while pulling me out of the car. It almost felt like a hug, but I couldn't hug him back. My body was sort of paralyzed, and the street, the faces around me were starting to blur into a white haze. I wondered if that man smelled like mint because it was a dream where everyone was March, or if he liked eating mints as well.

I wanted to tell him to save my mom too, that maybe she was okay, but an insistent touch on my face made my eyes flutter open, and I floated back into reality. Someone was tapping against my left cheek, and there was a soft masculine voice.

"Wakey-wakey, sweetheart."

I squinted. Surrounding me was a blinding light that made my eyes hurt. There was a pungent smell—Listerine, maybe? I felt a little cranky; I wished I had slept some more. I didn't freak out until I noticed I couldn't move my arms and legs. Then I felt the particular tightening in your chest that starts when things go wrong. And, sweet Raptor Jesus, they were going extremely wrong. With a quick, frantic motion, I shifted my head right and left, trying to make out the rest of the room through the white light engulfing me. I came to realize that I was in what looked like an old white-tiled hospital room, entirely naked and secured to some sort of black leather operating table.

This mildly romantic setting wasn't my biggest issue, though. Indeed, possibly worse was the fact that I was now staring into the rainy gray eyes of none other than *holy fucking Creepy-hat.*

You know how sometimes you've done something silly and you hear yourself squeak "oops" in your mind? I heard that then; I heard it loud and clear. As I took the time to reacquaint myself with Creepy-hat's pale and surprisingly smooth skin, one specific moment kept playing over and over, furthering my considerable dismay. Resounding in my ears was the word March had said back in the car, the one I had refused to listen to: *"Don't."*

So, at this precise moment, the only two bricks my neurons were able to assemble were "Don't" and "Oops."

And I wanted to cry very much.

"Oh no, please don't cry."

His voice was a syrupy whisper as he took a square of gauze on a nearby metallic tray to wipe tears I hadn't even felt roll on my temples.

I watched him through blurry eyes. He was wearing some sort of lab coat over his dark suit and white surgical gloves. My gaze lingered on his features, noticing for the first time how strange they seemed: Creepy-hat didn't look young, yet he didn't sport obvious wrinkles either. His face was delicate and chiseled, like there was almost no fat underneath his skin. I hated his eyes. They looked too intense, too . . . eager. I was no longer so sure how old he could be, now that I was seeing him up close. Maybe he was ageless after all, like Dorian Gray. The scar on his cheek looked less impressive than it had when I had first seen it in the glade in Pennsylvania, more shallow perhaps, and it didn't have a different color than the rest of his pale skin.

The whole situation didn't feel real. It couldn't be real. My deal with March, the flight to France, Paulie, Nick, Ilan, Kalahari. All this to end up back to square one, on the infamous table I had been spared from the day prior. Creepy-hat's hands approached my body, and a wave of nausea contracted the muscles of my stomach as his fingers touched it feverishly. When they reached higher and traced my breasts, I convulsed, letting out a desperate wail.

He didn't seem to care. "I want to make you feel better about all this. I'm not like March. I don't enjoy inflicting pain."

Hearing March's name gave me the strength to focus. He had suggested he knew Creepy-hat, and the guy seemed to know him well enough too. "You'd better not touch me! March won't let go of his contract that easily. If you steal his job from him, he'll kill you!"

I had no idea if this was true, and to be honest, rational logic would have demanded March drop the issue altogether at this point, because I was probably becoming more trouble than I was worth. It's just that making up that sort of bullshit made me feel better. I half-expected Creepy-hat to brush off my threats as nonsense, but he did worse: he laughed.

His high-pitched cackle echoed throughout the room, sending a painful shiver through my chest. I had never known I could be that funny. Once he had calmed down, he let out a contented sigh. "You're one of the sweetest patients I've ever had. I'll save a part of your liver for March, if you don't mind. That will teach him some manners."

The index finger of his right hand scratched his long scar nervously as he said this, and, apart from being on the verge of passing out at the prospect that my liver might somehow leave the safe haven of my abdominal cavity, I wondered if March had anything to do with this wound. Was he somehow responsible for Creepy-hat's scar?

"I hope he kills you!" My voice cracked, and it was becoming hard not to let go and beg for mercy.

"Oh, I love that! He played good cop with you, huh?" His intonation turned seductive, his hand reaching between my legs as he suggested this.

My breath hitched in revulsion.

"Did he play down there, Island?"

I squeezed my eyes and gritted my teeth in an effort not to scream as his fingers probed me. I clenched my fists until they hurt, praying he would stop. He eventually did, and a look of surprise appeared on his features. "Now, that's . . . unexpected. We'll have to examine it again."

I thought I was in hell already with that creep assaulting me and planning to further examine my hymen, but I soon found out that we were only getting started. A cold hand traced my collarbones. "You know . . . March would have brought you back to me anyway."

"You're lying. He hates your guts," I hissed.

"Yes, as he has aptly demonstrated in the past." He sighed, scratching his scar again. "But it doesn't matter. Once in the pack, always in the pack. If he had any idea who I'm working for, March would be here right now, crawling at our feet, waiting for a chance to lick his master's hand." I tried to make sense of his rambling, in hopes that it would delay the rest of our program.

"March already knows. You guys work for the Board. He told me that," I said.

"Oh, sweetie, I'm a fickle man. I may take a job from the Queen, but it doesn't mean I won't keep an eye open for other opportunities," he said, still caressing my neck.

I squirmed to escape his touch. "What are you talking about? Did you—"

He pinched my lips shut before I could finish, chuckling softly. "*Chérie*, we're getting carried away! Take a deep breath and relax. This is for you and me. It's the most intimate thing you'll ever share with anyone."

My eyes widened in panic, and I thrashed desperately against the thick black straps holding me down. "I already told March I know nothing about the diamond!"

He shook his head as he prepared a long needle and several bottles. "All right, all right. I knew you'd say something like that. So, let me introduce you to what we're doing here. The way I see it, it's like a reasonable exchange. I'm removing some parts, but if you tell me what I need to know, I put them back. There's no pain involved. You don't need to worry about that. I have excellent medical skills."

I won't lie. I *was* getting worried. And not just about whether he had an accredited medical degree. "W . . . what are you talking about? Please . . . don't do this!"

"Calm down, Island. As I mentioned, ultimately you decide if I put them back. I'm your slave here. All you have to do is talk."

I was crying again, and losing it for good. Of course, as a beginner, I immediately fell straight into torture's most common psychological pitfall: hoping to escape the treatment by offering to confess everything and anything upfront. I was shaking and sobbing so much I'm not even sure if I made any sense. "I-I get it! I stole the diamond! I'll tell you where it is if you let me go, please!"

He laughed again, and this time there was an edge to it. He was excited. "Island . . . I know you mean well, but years of experience have taught me that the amount and quality of the information you'll provide simply *isn't* the same once you're staring at your own kneecaps on a steel plate."

I'll never know where I found the strength to control my aching bladder during this conversation. By the time he was done talking, he had a syringe ready, and my lungs were giving up on me. When he stabbed my right thigh and injected its contents, I produced a sound I didn't know I was capable of, which probably qualified as a scream. A distant part of me thought I sounded like a million shards of glass were exploding in my throat, ripping it from the inside.

"Please, please don't cry. You're beautiful, you're sexy, you're confident—" His voice was trembling with excitement, and his gaze was fierce. He was kneading my thigh, and soon I couldn't feel his hand so well. My leg had grown numb.

After having massaged my flesh for a while, he gave my skin a strong pinch that elicited no pain. "See? Like I promised."

He moved to kiss my forehead, and I cried even harder, no longer able to process anything. I shut down as he prepared his instruments. My eyelids slid closed, I stopped feeling the cold drops of sweat running all over my body, and I was no longer listening to him, retreating into a world of my own, filled with math and mints.

Creepy-hat didn't like it, not one bit. He slapped me twice, and when I opened my eyes, he looked frustrated. "Island, don't drift off on me like this. I need you focused, honey!" He was starting to sound a little hysterical. Was he angry?

Satisfied that he had some of my attention back, he allowed the grin to return to his lips. "Now, give me a smile!"

It's funny. It was only when I heard him ask me to smile for him that it hit me. This guy wasn't bad or cold or whatever . . . he was clinically insane.

I complied, although I didn't know why. It was more of a rictus, anyway, that grew wider, which Creepy-hat seemed particularly pleased with. Once he was ready, he started to work, shaking his hips as he mouthed some little song in his head. Within seconds, he was done drawing marks around my thigh to guide his hand, and a small scalpel was tucked between his thumb and forefinger. I lay motionless and broken. Tears were still running down my temples, but it didn't feel like I was crying. All I could do was stare at the massive lamp above me.

The human sense of self-preservation is a wonderful thing. I didn't have much experience on how to proceed when you're about to fight a battle for your survival, but the right words came anyway. Creepy-hat's blade had already started biting into my skin, an inch above my knee, but I couldn't feel it; I think that's what allowed me to collect myself. "Did March do that? That scar on your cheek?"

His hand stopped, and his gaze shifted from my leg to my face. "Yes. Why do you ask, sweetie?"

I struggled with the lump inside my throat and went on. "It looks like it must have been painful. Why did he hurt you like this? What happened?"

The blade in his hand hovered above my skin, grazing my belly, breasts, and neck until it settled on my cheek, in the same area that March had wounded Creepy-hat. At that point, I did start to question my strategy.

"We were hired together for a mission in Colombia two years ago. He was expected to recover the client, who was hiding in the jungle. Las Cotudos . . . charming place, have you ever been there?" he asked.

I shook my head.

"He did his job, and I did mine, which was to interrogate the client. Now that we're together, you can see it isn't so bad, right?"

"Yes." Now, that's a yes that cost me *a lot*, mind you.

"Well, March wouldn't agree with you. He interrupted me when I was almost done with our client, and—wait for it—demanded explanations. As if . . . as if he himself had never questioned anyone before!" His voice had become a little hysterical again, and I gritted my teeth as he went on. "You know me, I don't pick fights, so I merely told March that most clients prefer my methods to the kind of brutal approach men like him profess. You agree, don't you? Would you rather I break your fingers?"

"No . . ." I breathed.

This conversation was getting completely surreal . . .

"He gave me that nasty look and said that when I was done stitching the client, I should stitch myself," Creepy-hat recalled in a brittle voice as he scratched his scar again. "And after that, he pulled out a knife and slashed my face. He sectioned two facial nerves . . . Can you believe I've lost taste on that side of my mouth? I would *never* do that to a client!"

Creepy-hat and March's collaborations were bound to fail miserably one after another, I guess, because, as Creepy-hat said this, we both heard screams and gunshots coming from behind the tiled room's black door. I saw his expression harden in a split second, but he didn't move to escape. He certainly knew we were trapped, anyway.

"Don't worry, honey," he said in a firm voice, one I assumed he intended to be reassuring.

Moments later, the black door was smashed open with a loud cracking sound. Creepy-hat might have been insane, but he was still well-trained. He efficiently dodged the bullet that was fired at him as a greeting, and I heard it shatter the tile somewhere behind me.

Was I happy to see March standing in front of us? Hard to tell. I was so terrified, so exhausted that I'm not even sure I felt anything anymore. Of course, not getting your kneecaps removed, your liver fiddled with, or whatever Creepy-hat had been planning on doing to me, all these things spoke of a positive outcome, but I couldn't focus on that. My eyes were locked on the sight behind March's shoulder, and it was difficult to focus on anything else. The fake police officer with the shaven skull was hanging a few feet away from the door. I say "hanging" because a knife had been used to pin his throat into the hallway's grayish plaster wall, and his feet were no longer touching the ground. His eyes wide open, he was producing eerie gurgling sounds as blood poured from his neck in a steady flow and dripped on the tiled floor.

I was mesmerized.

I raised my head to look at March. He was holding that same rather scary-looking gun I had seen before. I know it's a little unfair, since he looked extremely pissed, and a little out of breath, but I thought of what he had told me in the woods about wanting to tenderize me, and it made me wonder if he had done this on purpose. Had he been waiting behind the door for the right moment to intervene, as a punishment for escaping?

"You don't need to pretend to be saving me again. I really don't know anything . . ." I was so tired; I didn't see the point in trying to believe in this play anymore, and my voice was down to a whisper.

Incomprehension flashed on March's features before his ever-reliable poker smile came back to mask his thoughts. "Good evening, Mr. Rislow. I'm sure you won't mind if I recover my client."

My eyes shifted to Creepy-hat. He looked tense but collected, scalpel still in hand, like he was weighing his options. "I seem to have no choice. Will you go easy on my assets, though? You have no idea how hard it is to find and keep decent employees these days."

Creepy-hat hardly looked worried, and since he was implying that March's killing his men was little more than a running gag between them, I assumed both assholes were on the same page, and he had never intended to let me live in the first place. I stopped caring. I thought it was a little cruel for March to keep acting like he was going to save me, though.

"Go away."

March took a step toward the table and placed his hand on my forehead. "It's okay. We're leaving."

Tears welled in my eyes again, and this time I spoke louder. "I said, go away! All you people do is lie to me! He said he doesn't work for the Board. He works for your *master*!"

I registered a certain confusion on March's face before he raised his gun to his colleague. "Island, what are you talking about?"

I went on, still sobbing. "He said you'd bring me back to him anyway because you'll never leave the pack!"

His eyes widened at this last word, and Creepy-hat paled, his own eyes darting around for a possible way out. To my surprise, March parted his jacket to place his gun back in its holster. He no longer seemed mad: all I could perceive was cold determination as he spoke to Creepy-hat. "We're done here. I'll take care of any new developments and inform the Queen that your mission is over."

Upon hearing this, Creepy-hat smiled at me tenderly. "Don't worry, sweetie, he's bluffing. He's not going to kill me. He's smarter than that."

Something dark filled March's gaze as he glanced at my naked form, the blood running on my leg, and the equipment surrounding me, and his jaw clenched imperceptibly as he confirmed Creepy-hat's statement. "You're right. I'm not going to kill you."

If you ask me, I'd say he did, but March seemed to be an expert at playing on technicalities. I caught the look of surprise in Creepy-hat's eyes when his former colleague lunged at him and easily wrenched the scalpel from his slim hand. A black-gloved fist brought him crashing face-first against the instrument tray, and I barely saw the small blade shimmering under the surgical light before it plunged in his nape, above his shoulders. My eyes squeezed shut at the sick noise of bone cracking. Creepy-hat slumped on the floor with a quiet whimper, much like a wounded puppy. I was so out of it that I didn't even feel vindicated that the man who had been planning on disassembling me minutes ago was now a disarticulated lump sprawled on the floor.

March undid the straps holding me to the table, and I was free. Yet I didn't get up. I still couldn't feel my right leg, and my body wouldn't move. Rolling to my side, I managed to curl up a little. I stared at the tiled wall, physically and emotionally drained. All I wanted to do was wait—not wait for something specific, just wait. March had other priorities. His dark jacket landed on me to cover my naked body, and I registered its unusual weight again; I figured it was bulletproof. He bent over me and reached to clean the cut Rislow had made earlier and place a few transparent strips across the wound.

"Butterfly bandages. You'll hardly see the scar." His voice was soft and soothing. That's what he did, I realized. He got me hurt, and then he smoothed me back into shape, only to do it all over again. Until when? Or what?

Dismissing that depressing thought, I snuggled into the warmth of his jacket, breathing his scent and slowly recovering from my state of shock. "How did you find me?"

"I didn't. Ilan did." The muscles in his jaw tightened. "He pulled every string in Paris's underworld to find this place." I could tell he was grateful for that, and a weak, cheesy part of me wondered if maybe March had been scared that I would die, if maybe . . . he cared a little.

A low sound broke our exchange. Below us, what was left of Creepy-hat was trying to speak. It was almost inaudible, a wet, raspy murmur, but we both heard the words before he passed out. "You picked the wrong side."

March didn't even blink, but somehow, I got the feeling that Rislow's point had landed close to home. Perhaps in that secret place within himself where he locked away his doubts about this odd job and the pact he had made with me. Ignoring his victim's insinuations with disconcerting ease, he helped me put on his jacket, cradled me in his arms, and carried me through a maze of decaying and deserted hallways. I tried to avert my eyes every time we passed the still form of one of Rislow's men. I counted seven bodies, including the bald guy now decorating the wall, and as we reached what seemed to be the entrance door, I wondered if there were more.

Once we were outside, he walked us through a sinister park. Granted, it didn't help that the sun was setting and we were in fall, so half of the trees were leafless already. There, despite the declining light, I got a better view of the building, an abandoned mansion with several broken windows and brick walls that threatened to be swallowed by brown ivy. A dilapidated signboard dating from the nineties helped me connect the dots. We were less than an hour away from Paris, in a small suburban town called Maincy. The place had been a private clinic at some point until it had been shut down. On the estate's rusty gates, several other public signs regarding a series of city-approved building permits suggested that the project to rehabilitate the clinic had fallen prey to France's inextricable administrative maze for the past twenty years, allowing the place to turn into some sort of improvised haunted house for Rislow's sick enjoyment.

When he stopped in front of a brand-new black BMW, I assumed Ilan had played fairy godmother again and replaced the unfortunate Mercedes. March helped me into the passenger seat and worked on fastening my seat belt—safety first, right? As he adjusted the belt, I noticed a few dark stains on his jacket, some on the shoulder, another on the front, near my breast. Without thinking, I brought my hand up to touch them.

A cool wetness coated my fingertips. Red transferred from the fabric, staining my skin. I stared in horrified fascination. This wasn't March's blood. More likely that bald guy's, and perhaps the blood of a few others. Against the pasty, almost bluish white of my skin, it looked surprisingly dark. I inhaled the earthy, metallic scent permeating me, a combination of fresh blood, dried leaves, and musty walls. I probably zoned out for a few seconds, since the vision of his hands cleaning mine with a small wet wipe surprised me. I couldn't remember having seen him move to fetch it.

He was thorough, gentle, wordlessly wiping my fingers several times, insisting on getting under each nail—out of habit, no doubt. His hands were warm. He was a different man from the March I had seen maim Creepy-hat minutes ago, the March whose jacket was drenched in the blood of the men he had killed, and I found myself unable to reconcile those two faces of a same coin. Once he was satisfied with my hands' state of cleanliness, he folded the wet wipe over and over, until all that was left was a tiny reddish square that he carefully slid into a plastic bag. He then moved to work on removing most of the bloodstains on his jacket with a second wet wipe.

His eyes were focused, his gaze empty.

"Are you sad?"

He paused upon hearing me murmur the question, but didn't look up at me.

"No."

I felt my eyes tear up, but I had no idea why. "Don't you regret it . . . when—"

I heard him swallow. "No. After a while, you no longer think about it. You don't think about anyone specifically."

When his hand resumed wiping the front of the jacket mechanically, I wrapped my fingers around his wrist to stop him. "But you're sad . . . right now."

His eyes still wouldn't meet mine, but I saw the corner of his lips twitch in a derisive smile, not even enough to reveal a dimple. "Let's call it a general sadness. I'm not sorry for any of them, Island."

I let go of his wrist. "No. You're sorry for yourself, for what you are."

Whether my assumption was true or not, March didn't bother with a reply. He disposed of the second wipe and took the wheel.

FIFTEEN

The Contessa

"I returned for you, Cathy, for your love! Even after the aliens reinitialized my brain, you were the only thing I never forgot!"

—Breyannah Steel, *Galactic Passions*

I think I slept a little on the way back. It was now dark, and the colorful lights of Paris's Boulevard Périphérique danced before my eyes. The large dual ring road marked the administrative and social boundary between Paris and its suburbs. You either lived on the good side or the bad one, and crossing it was in many ways the incarnation of the Parisian dream—a long climb up the proverbial social ladder until you were rich enough to afford a tiny chunk of the capital's outrageously overvalued housing market.

I rolled my head lazily to watch March as he drove us. Something bothered me, had been gnawing at me since we had left Maincy, and I needed it out of my system. "Why didn't you ask Rislow who he was really working for?"

"Because he wouldn't have talked," he said, his eyes never leaving the road.

"Wrong. You didn't ask because you already knew. You looked shocked when I mentioned the pack thing. So who's the guy?"

"Don't worry about it."

I let out a little grunt. "March, your *colleague* tried to extract my kneecaps and my liver. I worry."

"I told you not to leave."

"It won't happen again."

"Good." He nodded. There was a long pause before he resumed speaking, in a low, almost resigned tone. "His name is Dries. I have no allegiance to him. I only serve myself and my employers."

I stared at him for a couple of seconds, winded. Had March just been honest with me? "So . . . you think he heard I had the diamond and cut a deal with Rislow?"

"No. Rislow was certainly lying."

I was tempted to tell him that there would have been no reason for Creepy-hat to lie, even less so when he was alone with me and trusted I wouldn't be able to repeat anything, but as I reflected on this, a detail caught my attention. "Where is he from? Dries sounds Dutch or something."

Or maybe South African . . . but I couldn't bring myself to say it because the idea that he might in fact be the tall man from Pretoria made me sick to my stomach. I remembered my nightmare that Creepy-hat had interrupted: my mother's body going limp after a gunshot wound. She had been murdered. By that man?

"He's from South Africa."

My eyes fluttered closed. "Do you think he's the man my mom was seeing? Wouldn't it explain every—"

We almost ran a red light, and the car halted abruptly. March grabbed my shoulder to turn me toward him, a whirlpool of scary emotions forming in his eyes. "Dries would have never done this. This is not . . . This is *not* the way we do things."

I swallowed painfully. God, I didn't like when he raised his voice. It was out of character and downright terrifying. "What do you mean *we*? How can you be so sure of that? Maybe he helped my mother steal the diamond for him. Maybe he killed her because he wanted it only for himself!"

For a couple of seconds, he stared at me as if he were seeing me for the very first time. The light turned green again, and he averted his eyes to look at the road, tapping his index finger against the wheel. "Dries did *not* kill your mother."

"Then who did?"

"I don't know," he replied through clenched teeth, his nostrils flaring.

Creepy-hat's words rang inside my head, and I finally understood them. He had been right. If that Dries guy was my mother's lover, her accomplice, and the man competing with the Board in the search for the Cullinan, we had a serious problem because it was obvious March couldn't—wouldn't—accept the notion. Clearly, that "we" meant something along the lines of "Dries's and my little killer club that you're *not* admitted to."

"If it can ease your mind, I'll try to contact Dries. Maybe once we get to your notary, we'll learn more about that third accomplice," March reasoned, regaining his composure.

Letting out a deep exhale to control my temper and avoid yelling that he needed a fricking reality check, I touched his forearm tentatively. "Is he your friend?"

March seemed to hesitate before answering, as if he himself wasn't sure of that. "No. Dries is not my friend."

"What did Creepy-hat mean when he said Dries was your master? Did he . . . teach you—"

I had gone too far; he shut down. "I already told you I don't serve him, and he has nothing to do with this."

We both sulked for a while, March driving with a grim look on his face, me staring absently at the traffic. I didn't even try to play with the radio, and he gobbled down half a dozen mints. That's how bad it was. He was much better at sulking than I was, though. After fifteen minutes of the silent treatment, I started to get bored, and soon the tip of my tongue itched with yet another touchy question, one that had to do with Kalahari's unfinished tale. "March, how long have you known me?"

He glanced briefly at the round black clock on the dashboard. "Fifty hours."

I groaned in frustration. "And you're lying again! Kalahari knew about me before you took the job!"

The Paris mayor's office dedicates a considerable amount of time and effort to ensure that the Périphérique remains at least partially jammed at all times of the day. It was seven thirty, and this Sunday evening was no exception. Soon, March couldn't even pretend to be driving in order to avoid answering my question, as the car had all but stopped. I looked at his profile, outlined by the lights around us, and waited.

He eventually answered. "I did know you before we officially met. I'd seen you a few months ago."

I almost jumped in surprise. "What? Were you stalking me before that Queen person asked you to recover the diamond?"

"No. I was interested in one of your father's clients, well, his right-hand man, to be precise. I was at Halder Equities' Christmas party with Paulie last year."

He sounded like he wanted to leave it at that. I didn't. "Seriously? You were there? I don't remember either of you."

"I know. I don't think you ever looked at us. You were . . . busy."

Busy, indeed.

I had always found my dad's corporate Christmas party to be a well of unfathomable boredom, a tiresome scripted parade for the wealthy, where the hedge fund's board members would give the troops and clients a small pep talk while everybody drank champagne to celebrate the miracle of being rich. I know I'm sounding like a spoiled brat, the wealthy Simon Halder's pampered daughter, and I guess I am to some extent. The Christmas tree was, after all, always nice, and there are worse places to dine at than the Waldorf. Still, is good food worth an entire evening spent smiling until your face hurts? Not sure.

Which brings me back to how busy I had been that specific night. Feeling lost among all these people I hardly belonged with, I had retreated into the farthest corner of the room. There, I started playing with two equally bored Russian kids, showing them how to curdle Bailey's with Coke and introducing them to the fascinating world of acidic reactions.

There was still a long line of cars in front of us when March turned to look at me, his eyes filling with such warmth that I felt defenseless. "You were conducting science experiments with Mr. Agdanov's sons. Your dress was pretty."

I was having a hard time figuring where he was going with this. My black flapper dress had been too big, and overall a monument of ridicule compared to the swarm of elegant designer gowns surrounding me. I scratched my head in mild confusion. "So you were interested in Agdanov's secretary, the guy with the missing pinkie?"

He nodded, and I winced at the memory of the tall blond guy with deep bags under his severe eyes. "He creeped me a little. Was he dangerous?"

He seemed to search for his words before answering. "He had a crowded résumé."

"Had?"

March apparently thought it best not to elaborate on the whereabouts of Mr. Nine-fingers. He went on, deflecting this sensitive topic. "You also removed your shoes at some point. I think you believed no one would notice if you stayed away from the other guests."

His dimples creased into a faint smile as he recounted this, causing me to blush a little. Thank God we were in the dark. "My toes hurt. Look . . . I know I made an embarrassment of myself—"

The car in front of us sped up, and he looked away, making a little show of concentrating on driving at eight miles per hour. "It's not what I meant. I actually thought you were the most interesting feature of the party. I can even say I toyed with the idea of chatting you up while you stood barefoot in that little black dress."

He was maintaining a remarkably deadpan face as he recounted how he had met me ten months ago and considered flirting with me at my dad's Christmas party. Worse was the fact that he had somehow discussed this with Kalahari, which suggested our non-encounter had been kind of a big deal to him. I *needed* to get to the bottom of this. "What stopped you?"

"I wasn't there for that. Anyway, Mr. Halder arrived, and you lost all your appeal."

I didn't miss the way his fingers tightened briefly on the wheel at that specific memory.

"Scared to make a move in front of my dad?"

"It had nothing to do with that. I couldn't have cared less."

I rolled my eyes at this surge of typical male arrogance. "Yeah, right . . . what made you back off then?"

"You. As soon as he was done lecturing you about your appearance, you quite literally disappeared. One minute you were the Barefoot Contessa, and the next, nothing, a mediocre girl with her eyes downcast and no meaningful input on Jackson Pollock's work."

Hearing Kalahari's mysterious words cross March's lips made my chest heave with a flurry of emotions—pleasure, confusion, fear . . . and anger, since I had apparently been the Barefoot Contessa for less than half an hour before, of his own admittance, retrograding to utter mediocrity. I snorted in derision. "Thanks for the compliment . . . I guess."

A ray of light danced on his cheeks, painting the most infuriating smile. "You miss my point, but you're welcome."

There was no longer any doubt that March had somehow turned my once endless fuse into a one-inch firecracker. Flustered by the idea that he had in fact witnessed one of my many social shortcomings, I exploded. "What did I miss? The part where you said I'm mediocre? I'm not stupid, you know. I don't compare myself with girls like Kala—"

"Will you stop that? It's terribly annoying!"

Holy shit. He had raised his voice again. I clammed up, wrenching my fingers as the black sedan glided along the Seine's right bank. All around us, old baroque buildings bathed in the gold of public lighting glimmered against a dark indigo sky, enveloping the car in that copper hue so typical of Paris at night. March ignored me for a few minutes and pulled out to take the nearest exit. When we reached the Pont au Change, I raised my head to gaze at the four stone sphinxes guarding Place du Châtelet's fountain, each continuously spitting a long stream of water in a large circular pool. He parked in a nearby alley, causing me to snap back to attention.

"I thought Ilan had arranged a hotel room."

I registered an exasperated sigh. "He has. I simply didn't want to finish this conversation while driving."

I wrapped his jacket tighter around my body and curled into the seat, remembering my state of undress. Somehow, it hadn't mattered to me before, but he hadn't been looking at me the way he was now that he was no longer concerned with the traffic around us.

March took a deep breath. "I never meant to say that you were intrinsically mediocre . . . and you should stop comparing yourself to other women."

"Why?"

"Because you don't need to. You're in a league of your own."

The words had escaped his lips in a hurried mumble, as if it were difficult for him to say them out loud. My brain wasted no time in reviewing every single interaction with the opposite sex it had ever recorded, and its verdict was final: no man had ever suggested that I was a countess who didn't compare to other women because she boxed in her own league.

I wanted to dismiss his compliment and say something lame like "Wow, thank you. Nice weather, by the way," but instead, I kept digging us both into a hole. "Is it the reason you're helping me? Because you—" My throat was dry. I couldn't go on. Say what, anyway? Ask him if he still felt the way he had at the Christmas party? What was the point now that I was his client?

He answered in a tight voice. "It's a possibility."

I wondered how much it cost for a control freak like March to admit such a thing, certainly as much as it did for me to do the same. "I know it's a little easy to say this now, but . . . I wish you would have talked to me that night. I wish we had met."

I looked away, as if I could pretend someone else had spoken. After a few seconds of embarrassing silence, I took a timid peek at him to assess the damage. I didn't understand the expression on his face. Surprise, sadness? Without a word, he peeled off his black leather gloves, his eyes never leaving mine, and a foreign tingle spread in my body when he extended a now bare hand to cup my cheek, his thumb stroking my skin. I laid my right hand on his, and I closed my eyes at the feeling of the warm skin under the pads of my fingers.

I opened them again. Suffice to say I shouldn't have: it was like standing on the edge of a cliff. I looked down and felt myself spiraling in those dangerous blue pools. I think I let go of his hand on my cheek and leaned forward to rest my palms against his chest while he pulled me toward him. I have the memory of his face inching closer and closer, his fingers threading into my hair, the smell of the mints, and that little voice inside my head that kept shrieking, "First base! *First base!*"

Fun fact: there are approximately 2,249,975 inhabitants in Paris, 47 percent of whom are male, and 25,056 of whom are not only male, but also homeless. So, in the event that a weird guy squishes his face against your car's windshield and groans that he needs change and will definitely *not* use it to purchase booze, there is therefore a 2.38 percent chance that he is in fact a bum. Or maybe a 100 percent chance.

Whatever. What I mean to say is that March pulled away abruptly, drew out his gun, and my near mint-flavored-kiss got ruined.

He immediately relaxed when he saw that there was no imminent threat, save for that of greasy fingerprints on his windshield. Meanwhile, in front of the car, our visitor wasn't yet drunk enough to ignore that someone was aiming at him with a suppressed gun: he backed away slowly, hands up in the air, fear and disbelief painted on the leathery contours of his face.

"Il est pas bien celui-là, il est pas bien . . ." *That dude's crazy, he's crazy . . .*

We watched as the guy eventually ran away with a slew of curses. "Va voir un psy, sale enculé!" *Go see a shrink, fucker!*

Once he was gone for good, the blush that had been heating my cheeks for several minutes turned fierce. The spell was broken, and I had no idea what to do with myself. March seemed just as confused by our mutual lapse in judgment. In his eyes, I could now read guilt. He cleared his throat, eyes darting away from my body, only half-covered by his jacket despite my best efforts to keep it wrapped tight around me. "I think you've been under a lot of stress, Island, and I'm perhaps a bit tired as well."

His polite rejection did sting, but he was right. Sweet compliments or not, I wasn't cut out for this: the whole Parisian romance cliché belonged in my books, not in real life, and kisses weren't supposed to be interrupted by your partner pointing a gun at some inebriated onlooker. I shook my head, coming back to my senses. This entire conversation, along with the non-kiss that had ensued, were nothing more than regrettable accidents, and March was just another dot on my dating chart, one to file under the "gave up after bum attack" category.

That little voice in my head commented that, had our interactions not been subjected to Murphy's law, I would have gladly let March ravish me. I told the little voice to shut the hell up and cut me some slack: I had narrowly escaped being dismembered alive on an operating table a few hours ago, for God's sake!

Straightening in the seat, arms still crossed around my body to better hold his large jacket, I managed a nervous laugh. "Wow. I think I was a little tired too. Er . . . how about we never mention that again?"

March's casual smile came back. "Agreed. Let's get some rest before hunting down that notary of yours."

He started the car then, his gaze leaving mine to look at a couple of teens crossing the street against the red light.

SIXTEEN
The Sheikh

"Tell me, Swanella, now when did you last let your heart decide?"

—Lory Deesire, *Accidentally Married to the Billionaire Sheikh*
(Possibly borrowed from Disney's *Aladdin*)

March and I were driving up the Champs-Élysées, minutes away from
our hotel, when an insignificant detail hit me like a pie in the face.

"I'm still naked . . . under your jacket."

His mouth twitched. "Yes, I did notice."

God, I was starting to deeply regret this brief bout of flirting with
him. Regular March was back, and with him, most—if not all—of my
problems.

I glared at him. "I will *not* enter a hotel naked. I need clothes."

"I'm afraid it's a little late for that," he said, gesturing at the clock on
the dashboard. Past nine. Damn, most shops closed at seven in France.
There was still a glimmer of hope, though.

"Take me to a Monoprix. They close at ten, and they sell clothing."

Watching for an opportunity as he drove down the avenue, I pointed
a dramatic finger at a bright red storefront on his left, and he complied,

stopping the car. I heard my door unlock before he turned to me with a cruel smile. "After you."

Technicalities. It's always those damn technicalities, like wanting clothes but not wanting to wander through the aisles of a crowded supermarket wearing only an oversized men's jacket and no underwear.

I huffed, puffing my cheeks for good measure. "Can I give you a list? Please?"

"I'm not leaving you alone in the car for that long." The mirth was suddenly gone from his voice. I knew we had reached an impasse.

Taking a long breath, I summoned the badass within me. I was getting used to perpetual shaming anyway. "March, can you swear on your dead body that your jacket is long enough?"

He nodded. Balling my fists, I opened the door, and he followed me. I thought my first steps in the street would be awkward because I was barefoot and butt-naked, but the most annoying part was actually my leg. The muscles were still numb, and each step felt weird, like walking on cotton. I think he noticed. He made no direct attempt to help me walk, but his left hand hovered behind my back the whole time, ready to catch me if I fell.

As expected, everyone was staring at me. Burying my head low in my shoulders like a pissed chicken, I tried to ignore the quizzical stares of the shoppers passing by. So I had no pants and no shoes, so what? Fuck you, France!

I guess March was rubbing off on me, because this shopping was nothing but efficient. Clothes, shoes, and basic hygiene products piled into the plastic basket he carried for me at a surprising speed. I didn't even bother with fittings: I wanted this over quick, especially since that old guy in the underwear aisle had been gawking at me for several minutes already.

It wasn't him, however, who spoke behind me as I shoved several pairs of panties in the basket with reddened ears. "The cream lace ones looked much better."

I tried to conceal the offending items under a pair of jeans in the basket with nervous hands. "This brand is too expensive." I *didn't want* to have this conversation. Not with March, not after what had happened in the car, and certainly not in public while I wasn't wearing any underwear.

"You're not paying, and I saw your hand linger on them before you picked the discount cotton ones." He was straightforward and matter-of-fact, as usual. Except he was discussing lingerie. My lingerie.

Fearing he might keep badgering me for lack of a better thing to do, I swallowed my pride and replaced the cheap cotton knickers resting in the basket with the delicate silk and lace panties. Flustered, I pointed a decided finger at the registers. "We're done here."

He didn't budge. "You didn't switch the bras. Your underwear won't be coordinated."

Sweet Jesus, it was OCD time.

I made it back to the rack with a growl and, this time, traded the discount bras for their elegant counterparts. Dropping them in the basket, I gave him a challenging glare. He nodded his approval and consented to resume walking.

"Seriously . . . I wish I could see you when you run away from bed because you got a panic attack over your partner's mismatched underwear," I mumbled as we waited for our turn.

He shrugged. "I don't. It's just a matter of personal taste." He gave me a sideways glance as he said so, and I rolled my eyes to the ceiling.

Never in my life had I wished so hard for a thousand-foot-wide asteroid to change its course to hit someone directly in the face. Granted, it would have wiped out the entire country and possibly caused an impact winter on Earth in the process, but the greater good of mankind was worth some modicum of sacrifice. At any rate, there was at least one good thing coming out of this: I was now officially over March. Whatever I had experienced in that car had clearly been a mirage. Case closed.

Now, I realize I'm presenting things in a rather negative light. To be truthful, I'll concede that there weren't exclusively lemons on my plate, but also a few treats. Kalahari's overwhelming kindness had been one of them, and our hotel turned out to be another.

I can't say I had ever dreamed of staying at Paris's super glamorous Bristol Hotel, because I'm not the type to fantasize about wearing Louboutin heels or bathing in champagne. Still, I was a little lightheaded when I entered the huge white lobby. As March took care of check-in, I marveled at the long red carpets, lavish furniture, and impressive crystal chandeliers hanging from the ceiling. At some point, I nearly started counting the roses in a massive round bouquet that stood on a mahogany table in the reception.

I was about to follow him to the elevator when I caught movement in my peripheral vision; something fluffy was wiggling under a large burgundy armchair. Wasting no time, I squatted and tried to reach under said armchair. Two gorgeous aquamarine eyes glared at me, and a small creamy paw met my fingers, encouraging me to leave its owner alone.

"His name is Fa-raon. He's the hotel's mascot."

I looked up at the owner of the gentle voice that had introduced me to the cat—a woman in her late forties, of Middle Eastern descent maybe. Her tall silhouette was hugged by an impeccable gray dress, and around her neck a single white pearl tied to a silvery chain shone softly between long raven tresses. She gave me a polite smile, which I returned. "You know him well?"

"I love cats, so I pet him every time I stay here. I am Guita, by the way." She extended a smooth hand ending with long burgundy nails as she said so.

Shaking it with a timid gesture, I peered over her shoulder and noticed March was watching the exchange, staring at Guita's back intently. Was he maybe into older women?

"I'm Island. Thank you for introducing me to him. I have to go, but maybe we'll see each other around."

"We *will*. I'm certain we will, Island."

She exuded a blend of kindness and self-confidence that reminded me of my mother: would she have been like Guita if she had still been alive? Would a dozen more years have lowered her voice to the same kind of soft alto as this woman's? I didn't really believe I'd ever see Guita again, but as she watched us step in the elevator, I felt a small pang of regret. She had seemed nice.

After the bellhop finished showing us into a suite decorated with eighteenth-century French furniture and some intricate white-and-teal vegetal pattern on the curtains, seats, and bed linen, March ushered him out and started making himself at home. I watched in silence as he retrieved a few things from the mysterious black case that never left him, before inspecting the suite.

I tried to peer at the contents of his suitcase when he opened it. I assumed there were more than shirts and socks in there, and I was curious about what it could be. Guns? Obviously. Grenades? Maybe . . . A flame-throwing pen? Okay, maybe not. Admitting defeat, I opened the bedroom's wardrobe, claiming a shelf for my Monoprix bag.

Once we were done, he turned to me with a full-blown poker smile. "I need to run some errands. Can I trust you to make yourself comfortable and not do anything stupid?"

My eyes widened. "You would trust me alone in here? Even if—"

"Not a single second. The doors and windows are locked and bulletproof, and someone will warn me if you try to escape."

I shook my head in disbelief. I had known that it was possible for hotels to buff up the security of some suites—like the presidential ones—but I had no idea gangsters could have their own bunker suites as well. My eyes darted to the windows. Indeed. Top floor, no balcony, no vis-à-vis. If on top of that the windows were bulletproof, I wasn't going anywhere anytime soon.

"All right . . ." I sighed. "Can I at least get something to eat?"

He tilted his head, charming the living daylights out of me as he defined the terms of my incarceration. "I'm afraid it will have to wait for my return. No one comes in."

And with that he was gone, leaving me to stand in the middle of the suite, flabbergasted. Scratching my head, I decided to take a bath while he was out doing whatever it is that professional killers do when they roam the streets at night. My gaze traveled over the white furniture and light gray marble of the suite's bathroom while I undressed tiredly. I examined the long porcelain tub; it was pretty nice, but nothing mind-blowing, at least compared to the one I had seen during a girls' weekend in Las Vegas for Joy's birthday. You don't know how much you need a futuristic hot tub with light effects until you're sitting in one. It's all I can say.

––––––––

I was almost done showering when I heard the room's entrance door click. I turned the tap off, dried myself, and slipped into one of those cool free terry robes that they bill you for if you smuggle them in your suitcase. The white cotton was top-quality, and I felt pretty good, considering how bad my day had been. I opened the bathroom's door. March was back.

"Glad to see you took some time to refresh. Feel better?" He was standing in the middle of the room, and his intimidating gaze appraised me for a few seconds, eyes gleaming with interest.

I fidgeted uncomfortably. "Is something wrong?"

"No. You might want to either tighten that belt or get dressed, though," he said, looking away.

It took me a couple of seconds to figure out the meaning behind his remark, until I looked down.

Oh. My. God.

Oversized terry robe is oversized.

It wasn't a complete disaster yet—and March had seen me entirely naked on Rislow's table already anyway—but I had been rather careless, and the top of the robe was gaping in a way that left little to the imagination. Sweet Jesus. A nipple slip in front of a guy I had nearly canoodled with less than half an hour prior. How much worse could it get?

"Sorry!" I tucked the terry robe's gaping décolletage against my chest and retreated into the bedroom to get dressed. When I came back, March was no longer in the living room, and I could hear the water running. Blocking any inappropriate thoughts of him under the shower—something made easy by replacing these with visions of him manically wiping the walls afterward—I sat down cross-legged in a large teal armchair, my gaze turned to the room's bay windows, through which I could see the Eiffel Tower shimmering in the night.

I'll be honest: there was this little perverted part of me that hoped he would exit the bathroom clad only in a towel, wet chest hair glistening and all, like in those Diet Coke ads. He didn't. He came out dressed in his shirt and jeans, and he had traded his brown oxfords for the hotel's complimentary slippers. *Meh.*

I eventually turned the TV on, and he called room service while I watched that old show where the guy's voice dubs baboons. I returned to the living room to discover that several tempting plates now stood on a small ornate mahogany table flanked by two Louis XV armchairs. Settling in one of the seats, he motioned for me to sit down. I plopped myself in front of him. "Thank you."

"You're welcome."

Blame France all you want, call the French cheese-eating surrendering monkeys who wash only once a year, but there's nothing like French haute cuisine! Closing my eyes in delight, I porked my way through a bunch of sexy little crayfish makis swimming in a creamy lobster sauce. As I considered the idea of drinking that wonderful sauce straight from my plate, my brain chose to remind me of a few practicalities.

"March, I've been thinking . . . tomorrow's Monday. People are going to notice I'm gone. What are you going to do about that?"

He looked up from his Caesar salad, his eyes reflecting no traces of worry. "Work shouldn't be an issue. You e-mailed EM Tech's HR an hour ago to inform them that you would be taking a few days off for personal reasons."

I choked on a crayfish and coughed loudly upon hearing this. "I . . . what? I never . . . did you hack my e-mail account?"

His eyes lit up, and he flashed me his trademark all-knowing poker smile. "Yes, I had someone take care of it. I realize it's a little unpleasant, but it was a necessity."

I need to run some errands . . . Asshole.

Once I had reined in my anger at his utter lack of regard for my privacy, I fought back a burp and dragged one of the two dessert plates toward me. My mouth watered at the sight of the gorgeous lacquered chocolate dome. "What about Joy?"

"Well, I was hoping you could do something about her."

I licked chocolate mousse from my lips. "You mean call her and pretend I went on some improvised romantic getaway with you?"

He laughed. "It's close enough to the truth."

"To help you in your job, which was, if I recall properly, to abduct me, torture me until I gave you the diamond, and kill me afterward? The job for which you're likely being paid more than what I make in an entire year?" My eyes narrowed with each detail, the chocolate in my mouth turning bitter. "It's gonna cost you."

He leaned forward, resting his chin on intertwined fingers. "Name your price."

I eyed him pensively for a while, and when his gaze met mine, with that warm expression that belied everything he was, my skin tingled at the memory of what had nearly happened in the car. An idea crept into my mind.

A bad one.

And therefore a tempting one.

Could I ask him such a thing? Would he laugh and say no? As I tried to sort my feelings about the whole plan, it struck me that I had to ask him because it was the best I could hope for. No one would ever love me "just the way I was" and kiss me in the snow like Mark Darcy did to Bridget in *Bridget Jones's Diary*, but at least I would have this.

"I want a date."

His eyebrows jerked, and a deep laugh echoed in the room that lasted for a good ten seconds. When he ended it, shaking his head with a smile, I tried hard not to blush. "A date? With *me*? What for?"

I swallowed my pride upon hearing him laugh his ass off at the idea of dating me and straightened in my chair, ready to demonstrate my point. "Have you read *Accidentally Married to the Billionaire Sheikh*?"

March cringed. "No, I haven't read . . . *that*."

"You should. It's a compelling read and an insightful look into the dynamics of relationships that start with abduction and forced marriage." I narrowed my eyes at him as I said so, in hopes that *Mr. May* would get my point. "In the beginning, Swanella—"

"Wait, the heroine's name is *Swanella*?"

"I think it's an homage to *Twilight*; let me finish. So Swanella is super mad that Sheikh Hedwardh kidnapped her, told her family she was dead, and staged her burial to force her to marry him."

His brow furrowed. "Why did he do such a thing?"

"Because she's the only girl beautiful enough for him, so he flew to America to ravish her."

He seemed lost. "But how did he know her? How did he know she was beautiful?"

"She's this world-famous supermodel, and she also founded her own non-profit that saves abused children."

The corners of his lips turned down in an expression of profound respect. "That's remarkable. How old is she?"

"Eighteen."

He gazed at a spoonful of chocolate cake thoughtfully. "So Swanella is young, successful, kind, and beautiful, and she's looking at a few years of marital rape. Where does you and I going on a date fit into all of this?"

"Like I said, she's mad, so Hedwardh offers her a beautiful dress and takes her on this glamorous date so she'll fall in love with him."

"Does it work?"

"And how! He pops her cherry right afterward," I said, accompanying this conclusion with a heartfelt thumbs-up gesture.

He tilted his head, the corners of his eyes crinkling with mischief. "Are you suggesting you want me to deflower you?"

"Of course not!" I blushed profusely before regaining my composure. "All I'm saying is that you're a villain who kidnapped me, and you want me to call my best friend and pretend I'm okay, so you *owe* me. And what I want is this; I want the kind of date girls like me never get."

"Define 'the kind of date girls like you never get,'" he answered with a quizzical look.

I raised my arms in the air in an enthusiastic gesture, and years of ninety-nine-cent romance books and direct-to-DVD rom-coms poured out from my lips. "The whole dreamy boyfriend experience! Dinner, champagne, candlelight . . . Also you'll pretend you care, like you did in the car. I want stars; stars and fricking satellites!"

He swallowed a bite of cake and nodded slowly. "I see. What makes you think I'm qualified for this?"

I shrugged. "You're a good liar."

"All right then. It's a deal. Call Joy for me, and I promise to give you my best impression of a glamorous date." He laughed, extending his hand.

I shook it firmly, reveling in the contact of his skin against mine. "Deal. I expect you to spare me no compliment. I'll make you a list, if you want."

"A list?"

"Yes, things like 'Baby, God stole all the stars in the sky and stuffed them in your eyes.'"

March winced. "I will *not* say something like that, Island. Where is it from anyway?"

"*Slave to the Rich and Sexy Vampire.*"

"Oh. This one is not a billionaire."

"No, he keeps it low-key."

Visibly pondering over this, he rose from his armchair and pulled a smartphone from his pocket. Then, unlocking the device, he handed it to me with an expectant wink. "I believe you owe me one phone call."

"All right, give me that."

It went better than expected, mostly because, thanks to the time difference, it was four in the afternoon on the East Coast, and Joy was still in Southampton. I felt bad for lying to her, though, and even worse for making up that ludicrous story about embarking on a last-minute romantic getaway with March in Paris for the weekend. He listened attentively, watching for any sign that I might be trying to convey a hidden message, I assumed. While Joy did ask me several times if I was high, she eventually bought into my story—certainly because she would have done that sort of thing in a heartbeat, had the opportunity presented itself. I lied about our hotel's name under the silent pressure of his gaze, and once we were done exchanging banalities about the local weather, Joy inquired on the only thing that truly mattered in life.

"Is it big?"

I cringed at her direct question, and I'm not sure what came over me, but I stared insolently into March's eyes as I answered Joy. "No, super small . . . yeah, like a mini hot dog. Also he's like forty, so you know . . . it's all soft."

The slight twitch of his lips promised a world of hurt later on, but I figured life was too short for regrets anyway—especially mine. Joy groaned in despair on the other end of the line, encouraging me to dump him right away because small, limp dicks were a total deal breaker. I don't know if it was guilt over my claim that he was poorly endowed, or because I knew he could hear Joy making terrible jokes about overcooked mac'n'cheese through the speaker, but I felt the need to rectify my account, even a little.

"He-he's a decent kisser, though," I stammered, feeling my face heat up at this particular lie—was it even a lie?

In any case, it was no use. Joy believed nothing in this world could redeem a mini-hot-dog dick, and we decided to leave it at that. I felt a diffuse weariness when we said good-bye before hanging up, perhaps born from the fear that my adventure wouldn't end well and I'd never go home, in spite of March's best efforts.

I handed him his phone back without meeting his eyes. As expected, there was a price tag on that mini hot dog. I didn't think it would be so high, though.

His lips quirked. "I'm actually thirty-two, and I never thought I'd hear a socially crippled virgin who binges on romance books speculate on my size. You made my day."

I had earned that one, and it hurt in all the right places. I got up from the sofa with gritted teeth and gave my best shot at a haughty glare. "I'm going to sleep. I'm taking the room. You get the couch."

I saw the smugness vanish from his face and his hand rise in an attempt to stop me, but I ran into the bedroom before he could open his mouth, slamming the door behind me. Once I was inside, I allowed myself to fall to the floor, my back sliding down against the door.

SEVENTEEN

The Ostrich

"He was a billionaire with a fortune of cosmic proportions, but he yearned for one thing only: the beautiful waitress who worked in his massively big skyscraper's cafeteria."

—Livia Torrente, *The Billionaire's Beautiful Waitress*

"I never thought I'd hear a socially crippled virgin who reads romance speculate on my tiny Jell-O junk, mmmhh'kay!"

Some people blow off steam through exercising, others do drugs, a few eat mints and kill people. *My* way had been the same for years: imitating people I hated with the voice of *South Park*'s Mr. Mackey.

I was lying in bed, clutching the teal comforter in aggravation, my recent interactions with March replaying over and over in my mind. Who the hell did he think he was to call me socially crippled and mock my reading choices? So he had nearly kissed me. So what? Did that give him the right to play with me like that? To monopolize my thoughts? Of course not. He was nothing special. Other guys had kissed me— really kissed me! Those had been great, memorable kisses.

Super hot, actually.

Yeah.

No, March was just some OCD-ridden freak with too much attitude, and his chest hair was lame. I slammed my fists on the bed with determination; I wasn't going to let him walk all over me.

I was still seething, and repeating to myself that I too, was a warrior with balls of stainless steel, when I realized that some parts of my body were, in fact, *not* made of steel.

There was a dull ache in my bladder. I needed to pee.

Since my scalp was prickling at the idea of having to face him to access the toilets, I decided that nature could wait. According to the TV's clock, I struggled for fifty-four minutes before the urge became intolerable and I had to get up. Mortified, I slid into my jeans and tried to crawl out of the bedroom unnoticed, to no avail: March wasn't asleep. He was resting on the room's long sofa, reading something on his phone.

Detaching his gaze from the screen, he gave me a lazy smile. "Shouldn't you be sleeping?"

"I need to . . ." I gestured to the toilet's door, scratching my tangled hair, eyes still half-closed.

He nodded his understanding, and I scurried across the room to lock myself in. Hell-bent on making sure March didn't discover that I possessed a bladder like the rest of mankind, I stuffed the bowl with toilet paper to muffle any undignified sound—and yes, I'm aware that this is stupid and I could have clogged the toilet. Having a crush is complicated. Flushing proved even more of a torturous process, especially with all that paper. I shuddered at the loud gurgle that sounded like a thousand voices yelling, "Hey! Island went to the TOILET!"

I washed my hands and headed back to the bedroom, only to be stopped by his voice. "You seem tense. Are you still angry?"

"No," I mumbled.

"I see. Still angry, obviously."

Ignoring his snide comment, I leaned against the bedroom door, focusing my gaze on his phone to avoid his mocking eyes. "What are you doing, playing?"

"No, I'm checking the messages coming from my website."

I gawked and scuttled across the room until I was standing near the sofa. "You have a *website*?"

"Yes. I suppose it's important to keep up to date with today's latest technologies. It's responsive too," he explained, turning the screen of his phone so I could get a better view of it. I struggled to adjust my sight to the blinding bluish light and examined the page. March's website included three elements: a single line of text that said "Please fill in the following form to contact me," a contact form—indeed—and . . . a close-up picture of an ostrich.

"Whoa. It's . . . nice," I lied. "Why the ostrich, though?"

"Well, the engineer said I should put a personal touch. I like ostriches. There's a certain depth to their gaze," he mused quietly.

I knew there was no reasoning with personal tastes; I didn't press the issue. "So you get the messages, and what? How does it work?"

"My assistant sorts them first and forwards me those worthy of a second read."

"Phyllis?" I asked, remembering the phone call he had made before freeing Antonio from his trunk.

"Yes. She runs my place, takes care of the paperwork, and updates the website."

I twitched. "March, there's nothing to update here."

He gave me a surprised look, as if I was missing the obvious. "She changes the picture, of course! I have this folder where I collect my ostrich pictures. She changes it every Monday."

I stared at him, baffled. Who the hell was March? Was he the ruthless professional killer who had killed at least eight people since Friday night? Or the gentle and slightly lunar guy telling me about his collection of ostrich pictures? I figured that since he seemed to be in the mood to chat, I'd seize this opportunity to further my study of the market dynamics of the criminal underworld. "Speaking of your job, you never answered me, back in the plane. Say that you get a serious message, how much for a day of March?" I asked, kneeling on the carpet by his side.

His expression turned challenging. "Why do you want to know?"

"Just curious."

"Two hundred, plus expenses."

It took me a couple of seconds to figure out what he meant. "Like . . . two hundred . . . grand?"

He nodded.

I did the math in my head. "That's . . . more than six thousand bucks for a backrub!"

A mischievous smile curved his lips. "Would you like one?"

I recoiled in horror. "God no! I don't spend that kind of money!"

He laughed, and I think that little game might have gone on if his phone hadn't started buzzing. March picked up, and I listened anxiously in the dark. I couldn't make out the entire conversation, but the deep voice on the other end of the line sounded like Ilan's, and March's body language was getting less and less relaxed as the conversation progressed: he didn't like what he was hearing. Once the exchange was over, he remained silent for few seconds and then got up from the sofa, suggesting we were done for the time being.

"March, what's going on?"

"Ilan had a cleaning team take care of Rislow's hideout. They found him dead," he explained.

"He didn't survive the wound . . ." I looked away as I said this, almost angered by the realization that I cared, even when Creepy-hat had been the most worthless piece of shit to ever roam the face of the earth.

"He was shot in the head."

My head snapped up. "What? Someone came afterward?"

"Yes."

March's eyes turned dark, concern lurking in their depths, and Creepy-hat's words rang in my ears. "Does it have anything to do with what Rislow said? He said you picked the wrong side, and Dri—"

He knelt down to be at eye-level with me, and before I could ask if he thought Dries was the one who had killed Rislow, that damn finger landed on the tip of my nose again. "Island, I can't discuss this with you. All you need to know is that you are *my* client, and I won't let anyone near you."

I closed my eyes in frustration. There was such a thing as too many secrets, and March embodied the concept perfectly. He had me feeling like I was standing in front of a two-hundred-foot-tall onion with nothing but a table knife to work my way through all those layers, and I feared there might be tears. Lots of them.

"Are you gonna brush me off like that? I'm not stupid, you know. I can tell there's been something wrong from the start. You weren't supposed to take care of me; Rislow was. Did that Queen person hire you because she suspected he might be working for Dries? What's really going on, March?"

His lips pressed in a grim line as he picked a shirt from the mystery case. "I'm not entirely certain."

"Have you talked to Dries?"

"Phyllis is looking for him."

Getting up from the sofa, I watched him strap on his holster. "Where are you going anyway?"

"To have a word with your mother's notary."

"In the middle of the night?" I asked incredulously.

He checked his watch. "Yes. One of Ilan's informants called to warn him that Mr. Étienne had shown up in a club where he's a regular. Given the circumstances, I'd rather not wait any longer to question him."

"The"—I scraped my brain for a memory of the club Ilan had mentioned during our trip from the airport to his place—"Rose Paradise. What sort of club is that?"

"A strip club."

I stretched my neck and arms before walking to the wardrobe. "Okay, just let me grab a T-shirt!"

A stern expression appeared on his features. "You're staying here."

Two could play that game.

"I *am* coming, and instead of bossing me around, you should thank me for not asking what else you're lying about. Should I ask what makes you so sure Dries didn't kill my mother? Maybe it's because *you* did," I said, glaring at him.

I feared I had gone too far with such a ludicrous accusation when his jaw ticked in rising anger, but his gaze eventually softened, and he gave in. "Get ready. Ilan will be here in a few minutes."

EIGHTEEN
Them Bitches

"Rick loathed the idea of cheating on Belinda with a stripper spy, but he had made a commitment to serve his country, and the CIA demanded that he draw his weapon."

—Sabrina Boys, *Slip of the Thong*

When Ilan entered the suite at midnight sharp, March was ready, and so was I. Well, almost: clothes flew out of my Monoprix bag and all around me as I searched for a suitable pair of socks under their amused gaze. I finally found the perfect pair for a strip club night—pink ones, of course—and announced I was good to go as well.

March's horrified stare stopped me dead in my tracks. "What are you doing?"

"I-I'm going. I'm still allowed to come, right?"

"Yes. But not before you've done something about . . . this—" He gestured to the clothes on the ground.

My nose scrunched up in an expression of despair, but that didn't move him in the slightest. He watched me with unforgiving eyes as I

picked up every single item of clothing and folded each one meticulously before placing them back in the bag.

I feigned hurt. "Are you happy?"

"Yes, but I shouldn't have to ask. This should come as a reflex," he
said in a patronizing tone.

"You'll never change me, I'm a free spirit!"

His eyes narrowed. "We'll see about that. How much do you want to
bet that I'll break that free spirit into a spirit who picks up her clothes?"

I heard Ilan snicker behind us at this last remark, and I let March
steer me out of the room. It was only when we crossed the lobby that
my mind registered the obvious. When had the two of us started making plans for the future?

———

Oddly enough, I seemed to enjoy the Rose Paradise more than March
and Ilan did. Both appeared to be nervous, almost shy, when we were in
men's heaven—a divine garden of pleasure filled with enchanting rivers
of booze and where titties grew on trees. Go figure.

I, on the other hand, tried to make the most of this new experience,
since I knew I was lucky to have even been allowed inside. The two of
them had been admitted fairly easily, despite the fact that they weren't
wearing suits. When the bouncer had stared down at me, his cold glare
had said it all. Boobless little people who wore jeans weren't allowed in.
Thank God for guns, solid ties with the French police, and Ilan's threats
of summoning a raid on the place; all of these had helped us smooth
out our differences. Soon, I was frolicking among drunken executives
and gorgeous bikini babes on a pink leopard-print carpet, wiggling my
hips to the sound of electronic music.

Carried by the recent increase in my self-confidence levels, I quickly
mastered the complex administrative rules of this den of iniquity and

turned to March for some financial support while Ilan questioned a barmaid. "I need money for Rose tickets. Sasha here will agree to dance for us in exchange for one Rose ticket," I announced, beckoning over a blonde stripper in a black see-through nightie with a body that rivaled Kalahari's.

March looked at me and Sasha, aghast. "Island, I'm not entirely certain—"

"You don't like strippers?"

Ilan came back toward us, and Sasha gave him her brightest smile, perhaps in hopes he had some tickets to spend. He frowned in response. "Island, no man will ever admit to enjoying strip clubs in front of his girl. It's an unspoken rule, like the bro code."

I looked up at his tired green eyes, searching them for a sign that he was joking. "But I'm not March's girl, and I've never been to a strip club. If you don't want your tickets, I'll take them!"

Ilan shook his head in disbelief, and both men put a hand on my back, steering me away from the statuesque Sasha and toward a long, dark hallway decorated with a slew of erotic statues poorly imitating ancient Greek sculpture—I'm pretty sure Praxiteles's young athletes did not sport ten-inch boners. As we passed private booths where gorgeous girls performed lap dances on stoned businessmen bathed in a reddish hue, I heard Ilan whispering to March in French.

"Au moins, elle est pas jalouse. C'est déjà ça." *At least, she's not the jealous type. It's something already.*

I have no idea how it feels when you're sitting there with a stripper on your lap, struggling to control the business in your pants, and suddenly two big guys plop themselves on either side of you, kick your stripper out, and clasp a hand on your mouth so you won't scream. I guess watching the stripper go must be the worst part. We were worried she might tell security her client was in trouble, so we gave her lots of Rose tickets, and she blew us a kiss before strutting away happily.

The guy we were now holding hostage looked more like an adman than a notary: short and lean with an elegant dark suit, a red tie that I found too flashy, and red shoelaces that matched the tie—a sure sign that style was an important part of his life. I think it was the tie-coordinated-with-shoelaces thing and the gel in his graying black hair that made me dislike him almost instantly. I noticed a small bowl of peanuts sitting near a half-empty bottle of champagne on the low black table his stripper had been dancing on. I was tempted to dig in, but I remembered all those stories about bar peanuts being your number one source of germs and how eating them meant you'll get to sample several people's urine.

Since March was so good at pleasantries, he made the introductions while Ilan pressed his huge hand over the guy's mouth.

"Good evening, Mr. Étienne, I'm terribly sorry we had to interrupt your date. I'm Mr. May; I kill people for a living."

When he heard that, Monsieur Étienne showed a spectacular lack of balls. He started squirming and screaming against Ilan's hand, his face turning redder than his ugly tie.

Unimpressed, March went on. "My associates and I would like a word with you. Can I trust you not to scream again?"

He opened his jacket enough for Étienne to see the gun and nodded to Ilan to release his grip on the guy's mouth. Étienne remained perfectly still, his eyes darting around the booth in alarm, his voice a panicked hiss. "Je suis au courant de rien! Dites à votre boss que je sais rien!" *I haven't heard anything! Tell your boss I know nothing!*

God, he sounded like Pepé Le Pew. March went on in excellent French, with an ominous smile. "I'm here with Miss Chaptal, whose mother's estate I understand you are in charge of. She would like a word with you. Can I ask you to spare us a few minutes?"

Something shifted in Étienne's expression. His muscles seem to relax. "Chaptal? Léa? What . . . You weren't sent by Pizza Tino?"

March and I shook our heads slowly, looking at each other in puzzlement. Ilan, on the other hand, seemed to understand what was going on. "Tino? Is he still dealing car parts? I thought he was retiring. I heard the Corsicans tried to blow up his villa in Calvi—"

The notary's eyes widened again. "I know nothing about that; all I do is take care of the paperwork! I told his men I knew nothing!"

March stroked his chin slowly. "Am I to understand that the men who ruffled your assistant were there on behalf of Mr. . . . . Tino?"

The guy nodded fearfully.

Well, that shed a whole new light on our own plans. From the looks of it, Dries—or the Board for that matter—didn't suspect Mr. Étienne of any kind of foul play. They might not even know about his existence: if his current troubles with some small-time thug named Pizza Tino were any indication, he was a local player, small fry for the Board and their billion dollars' worth of machinations. The more I learned about my mother, the more I understood her, and this was one smart move: entrusting her little secrets to a guy who appeared too insignificant to show up on the Board's radar.

I cracked my knuckles. Time to make the scum talk. I lunged at Étienne, nearly sprawling myself on March's lap to grab the guy's collar. "What do you know about my mother's will? Talk, or we—" I exhaled and tried to make my voice sound deep and cool like March's. "We'll break every single bone in your body."

He let out a pitiful moan. "I know nothing!"

That was apparently his favorite line. "Wrong answer!" I roared under Ilan and March's amused gazes, before extending my arm to grab a few peanuts. To hell with hygiene. "Talk now or I'm shoving these up your nose!"

Mr. Étienne squirmed in Ilan's iron grip while I inserted the first peanut in his nostril with a wince—his nose was running, and it was disgusting overall. I couldn't see how guys like Creepy-hat got off on that sort of thing. My victim sneezed out the peanut with a sob. "If it's the money you want, I'll give you access to all the accounts, everything! I'll give you the paperwork. What the hell do you want?"

I paused and looked at March. That guy was right. In my eagerness to be the one tormenting people for once, I had failed to consider the possibility that he might have nothing else to reveal than what Ilan had already learned from his assistant in the morning. I let go of him and noticed that Ilan's hold had relaxed as well.

"I don't want the money—"

Mr. Étienne sighed. "Your father said the same back then."

"I know."

"He's an idiot. You should take it."

"You're being hunted by a guy who calls himself *Pizza Tino*; you don't get to call my dad an idiot." I grunted. "I just . . . I just want to know if she left anything else for me, anything personal."

I'll admit that in this instant I didn't care much about the Ghost Cullinan. I hoped for a little piece of her, a meaningful souvenir.

Étienne's eyes softened, and I wondered if maybe he understood. "There was also a book and a letter. They're still in my office. I can't go back there until . . . some things have been resolved. But I'll send them to you if you want me to. Does your family still live in New York?"

"A book?"

"A samurai story, I believe."

I raised an expectant eyebrow while he seemed to search his memory.

"*Across the Night* something," Étienne concluded proudly.

"*Across the Nightingale Flooring*," I corrected.

He nodded.

For all his social varnish, March showed limited interest in literature and shifted the topic to more pressing issues. "What was in that letter? Did you read it?"

Étienne looked embarrassed—of course he had, regardless of how personal it might have been. "It was a little long, I don't remember everything. She said things about your father and what she had decided about him . . . She also wrote that she had made a terrible mistake, and she was trying to make things right. She said that if someone ever came asking for something she had borrowed, you had to go see the man you loved in Tokyo, and that he would give you what you needed."

Ilan and March shot me a strange look, and I had the good grace to blush. I knew exactly who she meant, but I had no idea how and why Masaharu had agreed to become her messenger.

For the hundredth time since March and I had met, I found myself thinking that I had never truly known her, and it hurt. I gathered that all these lies had been a necessity, a way to protect me, and many things now made perfect sense, like why she had never allowed me to attend school and socialize too much with other kids, for example. These fragments of her truth, however, left me with more questions than answers, and the lingering feeling that she hadn't trusted me enough to tell me everything, to be herself.

I took a deep breath and squeezed March's jacket for comfort. "I think I know who she was talking about. I have no idea what became of him, though."

Mr. Étienne watched us silently for a few seconds, and he finally gave me a suspicious look. "Do you . . . work in the same field Léa did?"

I shook my head. It was obvious enough that I didn't belong in this world. Then, all of a sudden, he grabbed my hand and pulled me close to him, our cheeks brushing each other briefly, his lips pressing against my ear. March shoved Étienne away almost at once, rewarding him with the cold killer glare I knew so well. He turned to look at me, concern warming his gaze.

"I'm okay, don't worry."

He gave me a little smile before turning to the notary. "Can you explain—"

I bet when March stopped in mid-sentence to pull out his gun, Mr. Étienne thought it was for him, because he raised his hands to shield himself. It wasn't, though. The lucky winner was an Asian stripper who had slowed down while she walked past our booth.

Things moved fast—two seconds or so during which I thought March had lost his mind and succumbed to acute paranoia; one second for her to slide her hand inside her black panties and produce a tiny gun from them; two shots, and it was over. The girl was dead . . . and so was Étienne. She had shot him straight through the heart, milliseconds before March could lodge his own bullet between her eyes.

The notary's lifeless body slumped between March and Ilan, his face ashen. I realized that one of his hands was touching my arm, still warm. I jerked away, fighting a wave of nausea. My eyes fell on the stripper and the small dark wound on her forehead, from which blood trickled slowly. How much had she heard before killing Étienne? Did she work for that Dries guy? I felt March's hand clasp around my wrist; our eyes met. For a brief moment, I caught that same diffuse sadness I had seen in them back at Rislow's hideout. And despite his earlier claims, I thought that perhaps a tiny part of March, buried in a well-ordered bunker deep inside him, did regret when he had to kill.

There was no time to mourn, though: while March's gun was well suppressed—all I had heard was a snap, sort of like a door closing—that woman's wasn't. The sound of a weapon being fired had created an immediate commotion, which was amplified by the grim spectacle of her lifeless body outside the booth. Clients and girls started leaving their own booths and running down the dark hallway in panic, some shrieking, others calling security. As we tried to blend into that hysterical crowd to escape, I noticed Ilan had pulled out a gun as well—some big and unsuppressed semiautomatic; plus he kept making weird little hand gestures to March. Some sort of L with his thumb and index finger, then three fingers, as if he had been counting.

I had no idea what they were doing, but March seemed to understand, responding with an equally strange little pantomime. He mimicked what I assumed to be a hat over his head, and before I could ask what kind of game they were playing, Ilan pulled me with him into an empty booth. I barely had the time to see March shoot a guy in a black parka standing at the end of the hallway, whom I had previously assumed to be part of the club's security team.

Things went downhill from there, because Ilan's hand signals could have translated to "three dudes with automatic rifles and a limited sense of humor at twelve o'clock." I heard the last handful of people trying to escape scream for help, likely hiding in a booth, and the most terrifying din I had ever heard in my life broke out. I huddled against Ilan's broad frame as hundreds of bullets were fired into the line of private booths. Silk, glass, and plaster exploded all around us, and Ilan pushed me under a red sofa, where I curled into a ball, praying that the walls would be able to stop at least part of this deluge.

After a while, the shooting stopped, and I watched in horror as Ilan crawled on the floor to leave the booth, perhaps while the men reloaded. I hadn't seen March enter any of the remaining booths before all that shooting. Was he dead? Maybe not. That same muted clap I had heard when March had shot the stripper resounded again, and a second shooter fell to the ground. I could see the man's body in front of the booth's entrance, near the Asian stripper's, and he had dropped his rifle, which now rested a couple of feet away from me.

I expected the shooting to resume, but the hallway fell silent. I didn't dare call for either March or Ilan, and I couldn't see what was going on outside. I waited, every single muscle in my body contracted in fear. After a few seconds or so, I heard the sound of a small object bouncing softly on the hallway's carpet, and a voice that seemed to be Ilan's.

"Ah le con . . ." *Dumbass . . .*

A huge detonation suddenly made the booth's wall tremble. Call it balls of steel, complete stupidity, or a visceral need to win at any cost: the last man standing had unpinned a fricking grenade in the hallway. Certain that March and Ilan were dead, I lost it. Rolling from under the sofa, I grabbed the big black rifle that had landed near me earlier and stepped out of the booth, holding the weapon with shaking hands.

Curls of acrid smoke and plaster danced in the air, and half of the red spotlights were dead. March and Ilan lay motionless behind a large sculpture of a centaur taking a nymph from behind, and through the dust whirling around me, I could make out the third shooter's silhouette. He was still standing. I pointed the rifle at him and started to sob loudly.

"It's all right, biscuit. He's out of ammo. You can put the Famas down."

A wave of relief washed over me upon hearing these words, so intense, so sweet it was almost painful. Behind me, March's calm voice was calling me. I was in a state of shock, however, and my brain refused to acknowledge that the guy standing in front of me no longer posed a threat. Both men got up from the floor, pointing their guns as well at the guy in black military attire, who was still holding a rifle similar to mine and seemed to be under an equal amount of stress.

March kept cooing. "Island . . . I need you to push that little button under your finger all the way to the right and put the gun down."

"No! He's gonna shoot us!"

Ilan joined his plea. "His magazine is empty. Calm down and push the little button. *Don't* touch the trigger, Island."

I did try to do as I was told and let go of the trigger, but my adversary figured that a chimp would have better chances of handling a Famas properly. I can only assume he decided to die a hero, letting go of his now useless rifle to reach inside his jacket for a gun. Panicked, I pressed the trigger at the same time March fired his own weapon.

They never tell you about the recoil in the movies, you know, that backward momentum that your body is supposed to sustain when a weapon is fired. The one I didn't sustain and that sent me hurling to the ground while firing an automatic rifle. The guy missed me and collapsed with a horrifying scream while a slew of bullets flew in all directions, including the ceiling. I eventually let go of the rifle, which landed a few feet away from me . . . and I was fricking petrified.

March ran to check on me, his hands roaming all over my body to feel for potential wounds. Satisfied that I would live to see another day, he helped me up. "I told you to put the safety on."

I wailed in his arms as he patted my head. "Oh my God, I killed him . . . I killed him!"

"No. He's good, biscuit."

Walking to the guy, Ilan knelt beside him, pointing a gun at his head. "You scared the little lady. Tell her you're fine."

At first the guy just kept moaning, but Ilan poked him with his gun, and he croaked, "I'm . . . fine."

This proof of life brought me tremendous relief, but I was still worried I had hurt him badly. "How is he?"

"Mmm, let's see . . . Two in the thigh, one in the hip, and one . . . oh, excellent job, *chérie*," Ilan sneered as he examined our assailant.

"What . . . where's the fourth one?" I asked.

An ear-piercing shriek escaped my victim. "You shot me in the dick, bitch!"

My hands flew to cover my mouth. "I'm *so, so* sorry! Is it . . . did it fall off?"

"No." Ilan chuckled.

"But I'm going to rectify that if you don't tell me who sent you!" I looked up at March as he said this. His right arm was still wrapped around me, but his eyes were a frighteningly cold blue.

He pushed me aside gently to join Ilan at the man's side. Crouching on one knee, he reached under his jeans to reveal a black sheath tied to his leg. I watched with increasing worry as he produced a short, incurved knife that looked somehow familiar—maybe because its shape reminded me of the raptors' claws in *Jurassic Park*? The guy started writhing in fear, and Ilan pinned him to the ground while March undid his pants and exposed his bloody junk.

"In my country, people still sometimes do this as a means to punish an enemy, or to avenge rape. First, you cut the blood flow—"

He wasn't seriously going to do this, right? March tugged sharply on a drawstring cord that served to fasten the hood of the guy's jacket. It snapped, and he tied it around his victim's balls. I don't know what happened next, because I squeezed my eyes shut. I suppose the blade made contact with the guy's nuts, because he started screaming desperately, and I could hear his uninjured leg slam against the floor as he tried to free himself.

"I don't know anything! I don't know!"

"Stop lying to me, or I'll geld you!" March's roar sent a chill through my body, and I covered my ears. Some logical part of me knew that March wasn't really mad, and that he was merely raising his voice to increase the guy's stress and make the interrogation more efficient, but I couldn't help it. Hearing that booming, intimidating voice affected me almost as much as the man lying on the floor and about to be castrated.

There was some more atrocious howling, and—thank God—that poor goon broke. "Stop! We were supposed to kill you guys and bring him the girl! I swear it's all I know!"

"Why did that woman kill the notary?" Ilan asked.

"She worked for *him*. She decided to move first. She said she had the intel she needed for her boss, that she'd clean up and leave the rest to us!"

A loud scream suggested that March's blade had made some dreadful progress. "Him? The man who hired you? Who is he?"

"I swear I don't know his name! I only heard his voice!"

"All right."

I didn't like how calm March suddenly sounded. That didn't bode well for this man's already bloody crotch. I cracked an eye open, only to see March's arm move and Ilan hold the guy tighter.

The guy let out a broken sob. "He was Scottish! Please! Please! It's all I know!"

March spoke again, and this time his voice sounded normal again, if not a little puzzled. "Did this man tell you this, that he was Scottish?"

A series of short pants preceded the answer. "No! I guessed because he spoke English, but sometimes he rolled the Rs! Please let me go!"

I opened my eyes fully, and there was a long pause, during which all four of us looked at each other like poker players around a table. The mercenary was no doubt trying to figure out whether he would get killed or not, and Ilan and I were staring at March, daring him to bullshit us and pretend that the so-called Scottish villain who had sent men to capture me and rolled his Rs wasn't actually Dries, the South African. March himself looked like he was struggling with the notion that his former boss was one greedy and unscrupulous son of a bitch.

I thought of the stripper again. She had claimed to have enough intel . . . but those guys had intended to capture me anyway, rather than kill me. That probably meant that Dries couldn't solve my mother's riddles without my help. *Good.*

I know for sure that March didn't cut that guy's nuts . . . entirely. I think he had started to, and the guy talked before losing them for good. Ilan later swore to me that it was only a cut through the skin, and that no permanent damage had been done. It could be a lie crafted to make me feel better. Maybe that guy is alive somewhere, with only one ball left. I read on the Internet that it's enough to live a normal life.

A few seconds later, a freaked-out bouncer led us out of the club through the rear exit, and I was relieved to see that the couple who had sought shelter in the last booth was shell-shocked but still alive. This was my first brush with actual criminal activities—on the giving end anyway—and I have to confess I did feel a little thrill of impunity as we walked away in a darkened street and I saw the first police cars arrive at the scene, their sirens blaring on the Champs-Élysées.

———

We looked like bums. Bums gathered around a Mercedes, but bums nonetheless. Our clothes were wrinkled, covered in dust and some blood, for March and Ilan. While neither had sustained any major injury, there were a good deal of cuts and bruises. Ilan's left cheek looked like he had been punched by the Undertaker, because he had been blown face-first into a wall when the grenade had exploded. Face-wise, March had only a few cuts, but Ilan kept joking that he would be in for a rough awakening in the morning, since his bulletproof jacket had stopped a couple of bullets—pretty close call—and there were already large, nasty bruises forming on his back and side. Comparatively, I was more or less okay, leaning against the car and sucking on one of March's extra-strong mints while he stood by my side and munched on a handful of them like a junkie.

When he was done, he gave me a wry smile as Ilan opened the door for me. "Island, Ilan and I need to discuss a few things. Get in the car, please."

"No. If it has to do with Dries, I want to hear it. That stripper gave him intel, and I bet that letter and the book are already gone by now. We still have the upper hand, though, because he doesn't know where to look. So that's settled, I'm going to Japan with you."

I registered surprise on his face before his eyes hardened. "We're not repeating what happened in the club. You'll tell me what I need to know, and wait for me in Paris with Ilan. Then, once we're done, I'll send you back home."

Kalahari's words echoed in my head. This was the catch. It wasn't the fact that he had a cleaning disorder; it wasn't his job; it wasn't even the way he did mints to keep his stress-levels in check. It was the damn control issue. March wanted—needed—to control everything and everyone, and this aspect of his personality was pretty much a take-it-or-leave-it.

"I said *no*. It's not like you have a choice. I'm the only one who knows who my mom was talking about in her letter, and I'm in *no mood* to tell you right now," I snapped.

Ilan shot him a questioning glance, and when March took a menacing step toward me I thought he was going to try to scare me, but that in the end he would bend like he had until now whenever I challenged him. I was no longer afraid of his icy-stare-of-death anyway.

Turned out I needed to learn his body language better.

NINETEEN
The Lion

"Holly didn't want a good, decent man. She wanted a dangerous man, a mysterious lion who would ravish her and feast on her body in the savannah."

—Stephanee Dusk, *Hunting Holly*

I spent the entire ride cursing them both: March, for having dared to put me kicking and screaming in the trunk, and Ilan, for not bothering to slow on speed bumps. The car eventually stopped, and I squinted my eyes when the trunk door opened to reveal Ilan's face.

"Calmée?" *Cooled down?*

I shrugged off the wool quilt March had wrapped me in prior to locking me in the cramped space, and held up my handcuffed hands, glaring silently at Ilan. He undid the cuffs and helped me up. I was about to pounce on March for his distinct lack of chivalry, but I realized he was gone.

"Where is he?" I barked, as we made our way out of the garage.

"He had some shopping to do." Ilan shrugged.

I leaned against the elevator's wall. "When is he coming back?"

"Soon."

I shook my head and entered the living room with gritted teeth. There, two men stood in front of Ilan's apartment's door, both wearing orange armbands. Great, more fake cops. Ilan gave them a slight nod, and we all entered his living room. To my disappointment Kalahari wasn't there, and though I wanted to ask when or if she would be back, I was too pissed and exhausted, so I kept quiet. Ilan's guests looked me up and down, perhaps assessing how much trouble I could cause, and waited for him to speak.

"Island, meet Lieutenants Gomez and Tavares. They'll keep you company while I'm gone."

I performed a slow face-palm upon hearing names that had obviously been borrowed from a popular French cop comedy. "Sérieusement . . ." *Seriously . . .*

One of them, a young Arab man with alert brown eyes and a black leather jacket, winked at me. "On est des vrais flics hein. C'est juste que là c'est un petit extra!" *We're actually real cops. This is just a little extra to our job!*

Incredulous, and still pretty depressed over the evening's bitter conclusion, I let myself fall on Ilan's long gray couch while he gave them additional instructions in a low voice. I didn't hear everything, but from what I gathered, I wasn't going anywhere anytime soon. Ilan locked eyes with me one last time, his piercing green gaze sending me a gentle warning, and he was gone.

Sleep eluded me, so I spent two hours watching brain-melting crap on TV, hovering in a limbo of boredom, regret, and uncertainty regarding the future. Gomez and Tavares seemed pretty bored too, but I have to admit they were very professional about it. The only time I was allowed to remain alone was during a quick shower and a trip to the toilets. Also, one of them always stood by the living room's bay windows to watch for a while whenever a car could be heard passing down the street. I learned that the happy Arab guy was Tavares, and that he wasn't Arab at all. His father was Turkish and his mother Italian.

A tall man with dark skin and twisted hair, Gomez was less talkative. He kept stealing glances at me as if he was about to speak and would look away as soon as I caught him doing so. His little game lasted until two in the morning or so, when a fried Camembert sandwich got the better of him. Munching on a bite of the heart-attack snack, he stared at me for the hundredth time, his eyes shining with curiosity.

"My uncle . . . he says he knows that guy—the *Lion*, Ilan's friend."

My eyes lit up. "Are you talking about March? Why are you calling him a lion?"

He nodded, a crease forming on his brow. "Lions of Nergal—they're mercenaries, like an old, secret clan . . . mostly South Africans."

"Are they bad guys?" I asked candidly.

His eyes widened at my question, as if the answer was obvious to whoever had heard about them. "Killing machines. Few people can afford them, and you don't want to be around when they show up."

Part of me refused to believe that March had anything to do with a pack of bloodthirsty South African mercenaries, but given his ties to Dries, his questionable professional choices, and, of course, the lion carved on his back, maybe Rislow had been right after all. I had never killed anyone, never been on a battlefield. How could I pretend to understand the depth of the bond between March and Dries?

I tried to back away from that sensitive topic. "Look, I don't know anything about this—"

Gomez didn't care about my reluctance to hear the rest of his story, though. Motioning for Tavares to listen as well, he went on. "Before he fled to France, my uncle used to be a general in the army, back in Ivory Coast. He told me that three years ago, after the presidential elections, when the civil war started, two American spies—a man and a woman—got caught by Liberian mercenaries working for President Gbagbo."

He winced before resuming his story. "They got tortured . . . nasty stuff. They were burned, and they knew too much, so . . . the CIA sent that guy to clean up."

My throat tightened as he dragged his thumb across his neck in an explicit gesture.

"Hear this: he didn't just kill the spies. He wiped the entire unit that had captured them. They picked up twenty-five bodies! He vanished right after that, but when my uncle questioned his men, one of them swore on God's head that he had seen the mark."

I swallowed painfully. "The mark?"

"On his back, the lion's head."

There was a pregnant pause as both men observed my reaction, trying to gauge how much I knew about March. I suppose I wasn't good at masking my thoughts, because Gomez saw through me almost effortlessly. "You've seen it too, right?"

"That doesn't mean anything. I'm sure there are hundreds of men with a lion on their back." I didn't need to look into their inquisitive eyes to know how my voice sounded: hurried, worried . . . guilty.

"You honestly believe that?" Gomez asked mockingly.

The sound of a key turning in a lock diverted Gomez's attention to the apartment's entrance door before I found myself forced to answer his question. For the second time in forty-eight hours, Kalahari had saved me.

Both men watched as the door opened, right hands lingering on the guns at their side. Once she had announced herself and stood in the middle of the living room, perched atop precariously high heels, my wardens relaxed, greeting her with goofy smiles. True enough, those white leggings left little to the imagination.

There was a series of sharp noises as her boots hit the dark wenge in a way that had me thinking the expensive wood would never recover, and she flung her arms around me, hugging me tightly. "Oh, baby! Ilan told me what happened. I was so scared!"

Her warm embrace and sweet perfume momentarily quelled the whirl of doubts inside me, and I returned the gesture, burying my nose in the thick brown mane cascading over her shoulders. We stood like this for a moment or so before she pulled back enough to look at my weary eyes. "I'll lend you a pair of pj's, and you're going to tell me everything!" She then turned her gaze to Ilan's henchmen. "That won't be a problem, right?"

Both shook their heads, apparently under her spell, just like Ilan and March had been.

Once in the bedroom, I wasted no time in changing into the pair of oh-so-soft pink satin pj's she had picked for me. Kalahari changed as well, slipping into one of Ilan's sweatshirts, and we jumped on the bed, eager to hold an emergency meeting under the resident pigeon's disdainful gaze. She took some time to examine the various bruises visible on my arms and ankles after my recent misadventures. I winced when she trailed concerned fingers over a particular imprint I recognized as March's own handiwork, when he had tried to prevent me from leaving his car during the ambush.

"Let it all out," she murmured, shifting closer to me.

I lay down on the pillows and stared at the ceiling, allowing the past days' tension to ebb away. "He's an asshole."

She let me talk without interrupting me for at least half an hour. Grateful for her listening ear and her discreet encouragements to keep going, I provided a comprehensive account of the past thirty-six hours. The mini-hot-dog incident had her laughing to tears, and Kalahari insisted that my claim regarding the size of March's junk was completely defamatory. I had to cover my ears when she went ahead and provided precise measurements, along with unsolicited details regarding his use of said junk.

Once she was done tormenting me, she turned pensive. "Are you afraid of him?"

I pulled back the bed's comforter so I could slide underneath. "Not really. I'm not afraid he will hurt me . . . I'm afraid of what he might do to others."

Kalahari's tender gaze turned serious. "It's been ten years since he left the Lions, you know. He's a very different person now."

"Gomez says that he was in Ivory Coast three years ago and that he killed twenty-five people. There was even a woman!"

She sat up in the bed and brought her knees against her chest. "It's not what you think. She was . . . Who's Gomez anyway?"

"The guy with the twists, Tavares's friend," I said, gesturing to the living room on the other side of the wall.

Her lush lips formed a small O of indignation, and she yelled at them through the door. "Hocine, Abdoulaye, vous êtes vraiment deux gros cons!" *Hocine, Abdoulaye, you're a pair of fucking dumbasses!*

Okay, that settled it. They weren't the real Gomez and Tavares, but close enough, obviously. I heard snickers coming from the living room, which had me fearing she would go all Bane on them like she had with Ilan and March when they had dared question her orders. She dropped the issue, however, turning to me with saddened eyes. "Her name was Charlotte Covington. March did . . . He killed her . . . but it's not what you think. She wasn't a client. God knows he had negotiated hard enough to ensure that."

"I don't understand—"

She let out a deep breath. "Since he started his . . . business, March has often accepted jobs from the CIA. It's an easy way to stay on the US government's good side. He gets things done for them, and in exchange, they'll overlook the rest of his activities as long as he chooses his clients wisely. Of course, they never trusted him much, so a few years ago, this guy called Erwin came up with the idea to try to put one of his agents in March's bed. That sounded like the best way to keep a *close* eye on him."

A chill crept up my spine as I put the pieces together. "Charlotte?"

"Exactly. She had this cover as a humanitarian worker—way over the top, if you ask me. It didn't matter anyway because, right after they had met, March had one of his contacts screen her, so he knew she was CIA from the start."

"I don't get it, if he knew she was a spy, why did he care?"

A heavy sigh accompanied Kalahari's answer. "Because he's a moron, and he played with fire. He humored her for a little while until he realized he was completely hooked. That's when he came clean and told her that he knew about her mission, but that he loved her anyway."

"But . . . did she love him back?" I wasn't jealous, more like anxious to understand why March had killed this poor woman.

She shrugged. "Honestly, I don't know. I only saw her a couple of times. Judging by the way she looked at him, I'd say maybe a little, but not the way *he* loved *her*. March would have jumped off a cliff for her. You know the saying. 'First cut is the deepest.'"

I massaged the bridge of my nose, battling the first signs of a migraine. "He didn't get that she wasn't on the same page?"

"Correct. When he dropped the L bomb, she told him that she couldn't go on with her mission in these conditions and called it quits."

I cringed. "Ouch."

"Exactly. It takes a lot for him to take out a whiskey bottle, and it was one of those times. He nursed his wound for a while, and I thought we'd never hear about her again. Except eight months later, during the first weeks of the civil war, she got caught with another agent, spying on Gbagbo's Special Forces. Like I said, that NGO cover was complete garbage!"

"March went to her rescue?"

"He struck a deal with Erwin, and the CIA hired him for the cleanup job, with an underlying agreement that he would erase Charlotte from the grid instead of killing her, and no one would ask any questions."

"Gomez said that they had been tortured, that it was horrible . . ." I murmured.

She looked away, and her throat constricted. "March was too late. The Liberians were done with them. They were burned alive. By the time he reached the camp, there was . . . nothing left to do."

Bile rose in my throat. "You mean, he killed her . . . to end it?"

I couldn't imagine how it had felt for him, or how he had even been able to do it, for that matter. I could rationalize the fact that beyond a certain point, death was preferable to hopeless attempts at prolonging a life of agony. Yet the horror of the act was all I could think of. Had she asked? Had he made the decision for her? Had she been aware that he was killing her? The memory of my mother's body being left to burn inside our car filled my mind, and I felt a wave of nausea sweep through me.

I was in for another migraine.

TWENTY

The Prune

"The sexy doctor growled in barely contained desire as he examined Leigh's mouth. Soon, it would no longer be the depressor keeping her tongue down like this."

—Rayna Kissings, *Love Clinic #5: Doctoring Leigh*

Abdoulaye and Hocine might have been prone to picking ridiculous code names, but they were indeed real cops, which allowed them to obtain a box of anti-migraine meds from a drugstore down the block with badges in lieu of a prescription. Their superpowers weren't enough to escape being swindled, though: they came back with not only the precious drug, but also a bunch of useless vitamins and some moisturizing cream. Trust a French pharmacist to always bullshit you into buying additional "treatments."

After I had taken the pills, I slept for a couple of hours. Around six a.m., a muffled noise woke me up. Kalahari had fallen asleep too, at some point; she was sleeping soundly by my side. I crept out of the bed as silently as possible and tiptoed to the bedroom door to better listen to the voices coming from the living room.

"Tu veux du café?" *Do you want some coffee?*

Ilan was back, and there was no mistaking the deep voice that answered him with an English accent. March had returned from his little excursion as well. A third voice mumbled a few words in French, which seemed directed to him. I held my breath, straining my ears.

"How much have you slept in the past three days?" the elderly male voice asked—a doctor maybe?

"Eleven hours," March replied. My eyes widened at this. Come to think of it, I had never caught March sleeping since the beginning of our trip.

"Taking anything to help? Drugs, meds?" the voice asked with a hint of suspicion.

"Coffee, mints, amphetamines, sixty milligrams," he recited matter-of-factly.

The doctor and I seemed to have the same reaction upon hearing that March was taking speed to stay awake. "Humpf . . . do you often take stimulants?" I could almost picture the disapproving frown that came with that little grunt.

"Only on rare occasions, when my job doesn't allow for much sleep."

The man's voice softened a little. "All right . . . I'm probably wasting my time here, but I'd recommend that you go to bed and sleep for eight hours straight, rather than munch on speed and mints to stay sharp."

"Thank you, I'll keep it in mind." March's tone was as polite as ever, but having experienced myself his various flavors of civility, I gathered it basically meant, "Screw you; you're not my mom."

"As for this, you're still in excellent physical condition. It should heal well, but you'll feel it for a while." I figured he was talking about those large bruises Ilan had joked about earlier, and I wondered how bad they were. "Let me tell you something, though. Your body no longer heals like it did when you were twenty. You're reaching an age where you need to become more careful—"

March was no longer replying. Maybe he didn't like to hear that old French doctor call him washed-up.

"You still have a few good years left, but it's becoming tougher. You can feel it, right?" Damn, that guy lacked tact! "Family, kids?" he probed on.

"No," March said flatly.

"Then go make some. Only thing that gets guys like you to retire in time," the doctor concluded with a little laugh.

I felt bad for March, like when I had watched Sean Connery play an aging James Bond in *Never Say Never Again*. March wasn't that old, after all. Granted, he might have pushed his body further than most, but that preachy grandpa was practically telling him to go sit in a wheelchair and do crosswords! Feeling that someone needed to stand up for the truth and remind that mean old prune that *Sir* Sean Connery had still been performing his own stunts at the ripe age of fifty-three, I pushed the door with careful movements.

"Stop calling him old!" I whispered, worried that I might wake up Kalahari while serving justice.

In the dimly lit living room, March was sitting on the couch while a guy with a thick mop of curly gray hair and a little moustache put the finishing touch on a bandage around his torso. Near them, Ilan was checking his phone with a cup of steaming coffee in his hand. That doctor had taken care of him as well: large Band-Aids covered the side of his face.

Curly-prune turned to look at me. "Seems you have a fan club, Mr.—"

"April," March completed. Honestly, was a man who used such code names worth fighting for?

In the meantime, Ilan was staring me up and down with a look of slight astonishment. Intimidated by his insistent gaze, I looked away to close the bedroom's door behind me. "What is it? Is there something funny on my face?"

"No, but it feels strange to see those on someone else than Kalahari." He shrugged, gesturing to the pink satin pj's. I had always heard men paid no attention to what women wore unless it was slutty. Ilan must have been the exception to the rule, since he seemed to keep a close eye on Kalahari's wardrobe.

While Ilan paid Curly-prune and showed him out, I sat beside March and examined the doctor's handiwork. Okay, I'm lying. I couldn't focus on the bandages. I did try my best, but he was shirtless again, and my neurons short-circuited. The soft glow of a paper floor lamp near the sofa outlined his handsome features and the hills and valleys of his torso. He had showered recently. I could smell a fresh, soapy scent on him, like citrus. I knew it was wrong, but I pictured myself burying my face in his chest to rub my cheeks against that damn hair and inhale his scent, kinda like cocaine addicts do when they're at the end of the road and they just slam their face into the entire bag.

He looked at me questioningly when my eyes lingered on his navel—a most excellent one, I should say—and traveled down, following the narrow line of hair on his stomach that, combined with those strange V-shaped muscles, looked like a long arrow pointing down to his groin. I think I unconsciously licked my lips, and when I realized how such a gesture could be misinterpreted, I averted my eyes, reining in my basest instincts.

I plastered a neutral expression on my face. "You don't really deserve it, but I'm still gonna ask if you're okay."

"Splendid. How about you?" he inquired with a gentle smile. "Kalahari told me you had another migraine."

Dammit, why did he have to give me *that* smile? I looked at the dimples, those faint crow's-feet, the warm spark in his eyes . . . and I almost forgot about all the things that scared me. Dries, the secrets of his past, and the storm brewing above our heads. For a moment, none of this mattered.

Well, almost none of this. "You put me in the trunk."

"You were uncooperative," he reminded me.

I stared at him, scandalized. "Have you ever heard of *mediation*?"

"You didn't want mediation. You wanted to fight me."

Touché. I raised my hands in surrender. "I *may* have come on a little too strong, and I'm willing to admit that your shooting skills are marginally superior to mine."

"Apology accepted." March chuckled. His smile quickly faded in favor of a more thoughtful expression, though. "Ilan and I paid a visit to Étienne's office while you were sleeping. You were right: By the time we arrived, the office had been searched. There was nothing useful left."

I rubbed the bridge of my nose. Now Dries probably was in possession of whatever clues my mom had left . . . and I had just been robbed of the precious few souvenirs she had left for me.

"Still no idea why your mother would have left that book for you?" March asked, crossing his arms.

"No. But her letter hinted that the stone is in Tokyo, so maybe it was some kind of wink. I read that book when I was a kid, and I loved it," I explained.

March seized the opportunity to pick up where we had left off before my little trip in the trunk. "Speaking of which, what's the name of your mother's contact in Tokyo, 'the man you loved'?"

He *never* gave up. Too bad I didn't either.

I forced myself to look at him in the eye. "Look, I won't throw a tantrum again, but I need you to understand how important it is for me to go there with you. I may never have a second chance to learn the truth. We have a deal, March. I won't help you if you don't help me."

I thought I saw a flash of doubt in his eyes, but it was gone so quickly that I figured I had dreamt it. "When I say keep quiet, you keep quiet. When I say stay back, you stay back. When I tell you not to touch a weapon, you don't touch it. Are we clear?"

I nodded eagerly.

His smile turned a little smug. "Good. That name now?"

I was about to tell him when Ilan stepped in to give me the benefit from his twenty years of experience as a spy and shadow man. "Stop and think, girl! You have him by the balls. Make the best of that piece of intel. It would be a shame to waste it, just saying—"

March glared at him as he toasted us with his coffee cup, and I realized that Ilan had used me as payback for the worst affront a man can endure: having to be friends with a guy who you *know* banged your wife, and not only once. Heeding his advice, I closed my mouth and grinned at March. "He's right. I'll tell you as soon as we're *both* on a plane heading for Tokyo."

A bright smile lit Ilan's face, the smile of a man savoring the sweet tang of revenge. "See, Island, that's how mediation works. Now go get ready. He's got an order to pick up, and I'm taking you two to the airport afterward." With this, he grabbed my dear Monoprix bag, which they had retrieved from the Bristol's suite, and threw it across the room into my waiting hands.

March watched me silently as I retreated to the bedroom. Seemed like Mr. Clean wasn't used to getting owned.

TWENTY-ONE

The Burgers

"Yael sighed. Jake was perfect in every way, rich, kind, and sexy.
But he wasn't Jewish. They were never meant to be."

—Ruth Joseph, *Caged Heart in Brooklyn*

In the end, I wasn't able to get dressed without waking up Kalahari. An emotionally charged good-bye ensued, during which she called me her little cupcake and hugged me tenderly. When we finally left rue Saint-Dominique, it was still early, and while Ilan and March had treated themselves to some coffee before leaving, I hadn't eaten breakfast. My stomach was growling pitifully as we drove down Boulevard des Capucines. Looking at the Opéra Garnier's monumental facade on my left, I tugged on March's sleeve. "Have you ever tried that gourmet restaurant, the one that's inside the Opéra?"

He shook his head.

Ilan glanced at me in the mirror. "Don't worry, we're going to one of the best restaurants in Paris!"

Ignoring March's sneer, I grinned. "Really?"

"Yes!"

"No."

My gaze traveled back and forth between them. They had spoken at the same time, and I couldn't decide whom to trust. Ilan looked pretty relaxed, happy even. March, on the opposite, seemed a little queasy, as if they had served him a rat casserole the last time he had been there. Choosing to trust Ilan's confident smile, I rubbed my palms together in anticipation.

By the time we reached Boulevard Poissonière's legendary theater, the Grand Rex, it was past eight, and Paris had awoken. Cars struggled in the morning traffic, workers hurried down the stairs of Bonne Nouvelle's *métro* station to catch their train, and food trucks opened one after another on both sides of the boulevard. Ilan skillfully passed other cars until we were in a smaller, less crowded street and stopped on rue de Trévise, in front of a restaurant that boldly advertised itself as M.O.B. Heaven. I looked up at March.

"Minas's Organic Burgers Heaven," he clarified with a sour smile.

It was still closed at that hour of the day, but the bright red storefront was covered with large pictures of luscious, juicy burgers and menu information in various languages, certainly to attract tourists. As soon as we pushed the door, a loud, gravelly voice roared in our direction. "On sert pas les juifs ici!" *Ain't serving no Jews here!*

I recoiled, shaken to the core from being outed in public, and wondering just *how* he had guessed. "But I'm a non-practitioner! I eat bacon!"

March and Ilan cast me surprised looks, and the burly man cleaning glasses behind a long wooden counter dissolved into raucous laughter. "Ah vieux salaud! Ça te suffisait plus de venir, maintenant tu me ramène toute la tribu!" *Old bastard! It wasn't enough that you came here, had to bring the entire tribe with you!*

I looked up at Ilan, who was grinning from ear to ear, and realized that his name should have been a hint. "You're Jewish too?"

He patted me on the back. "Never one to turn down a ham sandwich, though."

"I never knew my grandparents, but my mom told me they took these things very seriously. I guess that makes us bad Jews." I smiled.

"The worst kind, my friend!" We all turned our attention back to the giant who had greeted us so fiercely. He was almost as tall as Ilan, a bit older, and his shaven skull shone bright under a series of colorful bohemian lamps decorating the small dining room's ceiling. With his thick gray beard he reminded me of an ogre straight from a children's book, and I stared at his forearms for a while, examining the various tattoos covering them: Jesus's face, Jesus with a gun, skulls, more guns, and a colorful little piece that seemed completely at odds with the other designs. "Why the Smurfette?"

He wiped his hands on his black T-shirt and laughed again. "Had it done for my granddaughter!"

I thought it was cute and that maybe he wasn't a bad person, just a guy who liked gun-toting Jesuses and sold burgers. I gave him my warmest smile as he leaned forward and planted his gaze on March's, black eyes burning with a disturbing intensity. "Your baby arrived an hour ago. I won't ask what you plan on doing with it, but I'll tell you this. You're one sick, sick man . . . and I like that."

Okay, maybe he wasn't a nice guy after all. March smiled, visibly flattered, and adjusted his black gloves. "Good. Has it been tested?"

"Yeah, saw to it myself. The Ukrainians updated the firmware a couple of weeks ago. Great new features, you're gonna love this. You sure you don't want DU ammo?" our host asked.

"Thank you, Minas, tungsten will be fine," March confirmed.

I had a feeling I wasn't supposed to interfere, but some questions have to be asked. "Exactly what kind of DU are we talking about?"

March's hand crept between my shoulder blades, a silent invitation to drop the issue, but Minas was perfectly at ease with this question and focused his bad-guy eyes on me instead, making my knees grow a little weak. "What kind do you think, little Jew?"

More anti-Semitic digs, really? Pricked, I treated him to a tough glare of my own and wiggled a finger at his broad chest. "I think you're selling depleted uranium ammo, and you're gonna get cancer!"

Minas's hand flew to his mouth in a gesture of consternation, but it was obvious he was trying hard not to laugh again. "Man, you need to talk to her about the birds and the bees."

"I'll think about it." March sighed. "Can someone serve Island breakfast while we finish this conversation downstairs?"

A female voice rose behind us. "Je m'en occupe. Va faire ton business avec Minas." *I'll take care of it. Go do your business with Minas.*

I hadn't noticed that curvy woman entering the dining room. She seemed about the same age as Minas, but her long tresses were dyed a bluish-black, perhaps to conceal gray hair. Her eyes were much softer than his, and inspecting her oval face, I gathered she had been a striking beauty in her youth. Her full red lips curved into a welcoming smile as she spoke again. "No one leaves Anouch's table hungry!"

I did see March wince, but I thought nothing of it and watched as Ilan, Minas, and he disappeared down a narrow staircase.

———

In the end, I didn't eat much in Minas's Organic Burger Heaven, but Anouch and I chatted pleasantly while we waited for the men to return. She showed me pictures of their baby granddaughter and confirmed to me that Minas shared his time between the restaurant and a second shop in the basement, where he sold weapons. I couldn't tell if the weapon shop was a good one—March seemed to be pleased with his purchase—but the restaurant made decent french fries, and their waffles were okay too.

I didn't try any of the burgers because Anouch explained to me that they had this awesome business model where they would purchase 50 percent lean horse and badger trimmings from Romania, only to grind them, relabel the final product as organic beef burger, and serve it to "retarded hippies." The profit margins were nothing short of amazing, and trendy young Parisians waited in line to try Anouch's cilantro and rosemary double goat cheese. It wasn't goat cheese either, but rather a mix of various fermented dairy specialties compacted together and subsequently cut into thin slices. Here again, great margins.

I was sipping a glass of water—I wasn't too sure about the "homemade" milk shakes—when all three men emerged from the tiny flight of stairs that led to the basement. I found myself hoping that Minas's business ethics were a little stronger when it came to weapons than burgers, because I didn't want March to get killed by his own weapon upon firing it or anything ridiculous like that. This particular concern was soon overshadowed by another more immediate one, though.

"What the . . . March, what the hell did you buy from him?"

I'm sure you've already heard the idiomatic "boys and their toys" before. Well, I was currently witnessing a typical case of acute boywithtoysitis. March was smiling smugly as he carried a long and large black metal case, which seemed heavy even for him, and Ilan had a look on his face that said, "Will you let me play with it?"

We were about to leave when Minas looked at the three of us before slamming a big fist against his palm. "Putain, j'ai failli oublier!" *Fuck, almost forgot!*

I won't lie. As I watched him rush down the little staircase again, my first thought was that Minas, indeed, sold weapons the same way he sold burgers, and he had forgotten the little screw that held the weapon's barrel in place—or it looked like a real screw, but it was only plastic. To my astonishment, I was wrong. When he came back, he was carrying a bunch of black T-shirts wrapped in transparent plastic and a few key chains. He gave one to each of us, and I stared for a few seconds at the T-shirt in my hands. I wasn't sure I would wear it since it was XXL and depicted a blood-covered skull in front of an AK-47 bearing Minas's burger shop logo. The key chain, however, was pretty nice. A small and heavy steel tube engraved with a Jesus. I was starting to understand that Minas liked Jesus very much.

Taking the object from my hands, he gave me a fatherly smile. "Check this out. Ain't no man gonna rape a Minas girl!"

My eyebrows rose in curiosity as he pressed the sides of the little tube, and a short, razor-sharp blade shot out. "This is so cool—"

Less impressed than I was, March gave our hosts a curt bow. "Thank you both. Minas, it's always a pleasure to do business with you."

Ilan helped March put the giant case in the car, but it was so big we had to fold a seat down for it to fit inside. Once everything was in place, I opened the passenger door, but before I could sit, I was stopped by March's extended hand. I stared at his upturned palm in confusion. "What?"

"I'm sorry, Island. Our arrangement specified that you are not to touch any weapons. I can't allow you to keep it."

I gave him the big, sad eyes. "But it was a gift . . . and it's not like I'm ever gonna use it on you."

Sad eyes didn't work—perhaps because he still had to digest Ilan's little stunt. His hand remained where it was, waiting expectantly. I dropped Minas's key chain with a sigh and climbed into the car, clutching the T-shirt against me. At least I had that.

TWENTY-TWO

The Bottle

"When it comes to kissing, less is more: if you have no idea what you're doing, _better not do anything at all_. Be a starfish. Starfish get laid. Except the asexual ones. But this section will be written under the assumption that you are a sexual starfish."

—Aurelia Nichols & Jillie Bean, *101 Tips to Lose Your Virginity after 25*

I wouldn't go so far as to say that I was getting jaded, but when we reached the tarmac of Coulommiers one hour later, I found it almost natural for us to fly private and depart from some obscure aerodrome in the middle of nowhere. Those were undeniably a safer choice for us, since I couldn't picture March passing airport security with the huge case he had acquired from Minas: whatever was in there seemed like the sort of paraphernalia even well-bribed customs officers would find difficult to ignore.

I was a little sad to say good-bye to Ilan: I had gotten used to his tranquil presence and the way I always felt so safe around him. I allowed myself to hug him, inhaling his delicious smell of spicy vetiver cologne and tobacco. To my surprise—and perhaps even more March's—he returned the embrace, squeezing me with his large hands. I never told March what Ilan whispered in my ear that day, but I've always wondered if he could read lips and knew anyway. At the time, I didn't realize the full meaning of Ilan's words; I thought he was just teasing me.

"C'est pas à moi qu'il faut que tu t'accroches, ma belle . . ." *It's not me you should be holding on to, sweetie . . .*

After he was gone, we strolled toward a white jet that was a bit longer than the one we had taken to come to France. My review of the paintwork will have to be a little harsher this time: I didn't like it at all. I mean, what paintwork? Do a couple of black lines drawn along the hull even count? Sorry, G650, you leave me no choice but to fail you.

March noticed my critical gaze. "You seem displeased."

"Legacy's paint looked better. This one is too plain," I observed, stroking my chin like some aeronautics expert.

He laughed. "Aren't we being a princess. Gulfstreams aren't good enough?"

"I guess not." I shrugged with a smile.

Inside the jet, a tall young woman wearing a pair of black leather pants and a nice black-and-white horizontal-striped T-shirt was waiting for us. She had the most incredible flaming red curls, and greeted us with a thick Eastern European accent. "Welcome on board. I am Ekaterina, I'll be your pilot today."

I extended a hand to her. "I'm Island, and I'm not really a criminal." Pointing to March, I went on. "This is March. He, uh—" I stopped as I caught a look in his eyes that suggested I didn't want to detail his rap sheet to Ekaterina.

She gave me a knowing look. "Don't worry, I fly and never ask."

As she said this, I remembered where I had seen those stripes on her T-shirt before. "Is that the Russian army's T-shirt?"

"Yes, *telnyashka!*" she confirmed, her green eyes lighting up as she proudly slammed her palm against her ample bosom.

"Awesome . . . So you were in the army?"

"No, my brother Vitaly. I stole it from him," she replied cheerfully. Then, looking at March, she gestured to the large camel seats behind us. "We'll be taking off in ten minutes."

He nodded and we settled for a pair of seats facing each other near the plane's galley. As Ekaterina disappeared into the cockpit, I looked at the small white door with envious eyes.

"Maybe we could ask Ekaterina for a brief visit of the cockpit after takeoff," March offered, reading my mind.

"Uhm, maybe," I said, not wanting to let him see how much his suggestion appealed to the child within me.

"Come to think of it, we could say I'm negotiating this for you, after you've given me the name of your mother's contact."

I huffed as the engines started. "I don't think your help will be needed, and I'll tell you when I feel like it."

His eyes narrowed. March was one tenacious bastard. "As you wish . . . try not to fall asleep during the flight, though. You never know what could happen."

Remembering the way he had cuffed me to my seat during our previous plane trip, I cracked my neck, deciding not to repeat the incident.

———

We had been flying for several hours, high above the clouds in a now darkening sky. The snowy and rocky landscape I could sometimes make out through the clouds suggested we were passing over Russia. March had spent a while reading something on his phone and was now busy doing crosswords, his features frozen in an expression of intense concentration. I fought a grin when I noticed the small label stuck to his magazine. He had a yearly subscription to *USA Crosswords Jumbo* under the name of Mr. December.

It wasn't much, but it made me happy. The fact that he trusted me enough to do what he liked instead of watching me silently like Kalahari's resident pigeon felt like a small victory. The pencil that had been hovering over the magazine's last page went down, and he scribbled a few letters, a self-satisfied smile curving his lips.

"Did you finish the last one?"

He closed the magazine before laying it on the small table between our seats. "Yes. Are you ready to tell me that man's name?"

I let out a heavy sigh, wondering if he had been thinking about that all along. Probably so.

Since I *was* in a plane headed for Tokyo, and therefore no longer had any excuse to deny him, I spoke. "His name is Masaharu Niyama. He should be around thirty now. He used to live in Kōtōbashi, but I have no idea if he's still there. I hope he's not dead."

March had pulled out his phone and typed something as I explained this. After a few seconds, his eyes skimmed through some data on the screen, and he answered me with a smug little smile. "Don't worry. Your man is still alive. Masaharu Niyama, thirty-three, unemployed. His personal address is the same as his father's: 4 Chome-14-4 Kōtōbashi."

I should have been busy celebrating the fact that I was going to rekindle my old flame and be able to follow Masaharu around again, but I have to admit I had other priorities. "Wait, you have an Internet connection in here?"

March nodded, and I lunged at him, reaching for his phone. "Can I?"

He moved the phone away from my eager hands. "Why?"

"I don't know . . . to check my e-mails, write to Joy, read the news . . ." I was also thinking of installing Triple Town on his phone and playing it for a while, but he didn't need to know that.

"Nothing crucial, obviously," he noted wryly. "Since you seem to enjoy bargaining so much, what would you like to offer in exchange for using my phone?"

Douche alert! There was no mistaking that sardonic smile. I was in for yet another bad time—if I wanted to check my e-mails, anyway. "You know I have nothing—" Well that wasn't entirely true. There was a little something that had been nagging since our brief encounter with Étienne at the club, but I didn't want to play that card yet, as it might come in handy if the situation became desperate.

"Too bad." He shrugged.

What can I say? I was a poor little geek who had spent almost three days without her laptop or an Internet connection, and notifications were piling up in my Facebook account. "How about this? You can ask any question you want until we land, and I'll answer! About Masaharu or what Kalahari told me about you . . . anything. In return, I can use the phone whenever I want, and you'll let me install any app I need!"

The way he looked at me when he handed me that phone . . . the cruel glint in those blue pools. I should have paid more attention instead of reading Joy's account of her weekend in Southampton and how she had met "Vince-the-cutest-photographer-in-the-world" at the Indian deli down the street. I spent a blissful hour replying to e-mails, building a castle in my Triple Town account, reading the weather forecast, and commenting on my stepmom's latest blog post. Janice has this vegan cooking blog that no one ever visits, so my dad and I are required to leave comments in order to make her feel better about her contribution to the World Wide Web.

When I placed the phone back in his hand with a grateful smile, his eyes softened, and he gave a gentle, playful tap on the tip of my nose . . . before nuking me. "What did Kalahari tell you about me? Take your time. I'd like to hear absolutely *everything*."

I felt my heart rate increase and my ears redden. *Oh shit. Everything?* "I . . . she . . . uh . . . Stuff, not much, I guess."

"What an ugly little lie. Let's try this again."

I took a deep, calming breath and told myself that, much like an ice-cold shower, this would be better done quickly and without thinking. "She said you're her ex, that you helped her buy her beauty salon, that you were nice, but you were the control fairy, and that your cleaning . . . *peculiarity* used to be worse. She said you talked about marrying her, but that you left her so she could fly on her own, and because you knew you were too controlling. She said you've been alone for a long time, that you're not great at selling yourself to women. She also said—" I swallowed. "That you're uncircumcised, that—" I buried my face in my hands to conceal my flushed cheeks at that point. "That you were a little too classic in bed, not very adventurous." I stopped, crimson with embarrassment. I knew there were two topics I had left out, though, and I prayed he wouldn't ask.

"What a *surprising* amount of details. Measurements, perhaps?" he asked with that unforgiving poker smile of his.

"Yes. I refuse to repeat those," I confirmed through gritted teeth.

"And I won't make you." He nodded. "Is that it? I sense a certain *tension*. As if you had omitted a couple of things you knew would displease me *immensely*."

He was no longer smiling.

I shifted uncomfortably in my seat. "I know about the scarification on your back . . . about the Lions."

"And?" he insisted, the dark blue depths of his eyes daring me to lie.

"And about what happened with Charlotte."

March seemed to be relieved for a brief moment, as if he had been expecting more, but soon his lips thinned. "And what are your thoughts on all this?"

My stomach twisted into knots. I wanted this little interrogation game to stop, *now*. "March, I'm sorry, I know this was none of my business, and I shouldn't have listened to these stories. I'm sure you had a good reason to leave those guys, and Charlotte—" My voice broke. "She . . . I can only imagine how you felt, how you still feel about what you had to do. It doesn't change anything for me. I don't think you're gonna kill me or anything like that."

I had no idea what Charlotte might have looked like when she had been alive. All I could picture when I thought of her was a charred body. The same charred body that I pictured when I thought of my mother in our burning car. I wanted to be stronger than this and bear with his questions until he grew tired of tormenting me, but I couldn't.

One tear, two tears.

Before I could stop myself, they were rolling freely down my cheeks, pooling at the tip of my nose like heavy pearls. There was a salty taste on my lips, and I wanted it all to be over. "I-I'm s-sorry!"

The cold mask that had been etched on his features for the past five minutes vanished, leaving an expression I had never seen on March's face before—a combination of sadness, guilt, and worry that made him look almost vulnerable.

He rose and moved to kneel by my side, resting one of his forearms on my seat's right armrest while his free hand touched my cheeks tentatively, wiping the tears there. He spoke in a soft voice. "Island, I'm a rather private person. I live alone, I don't have many friends, and there's nothing particularly glorious about my life, as you probably gathered from Kalahari's stories.

"I don't like being exposed, and I'll make sure she understands that. I shouldn't have taken my anger out on you; I apologize."

"But you'll stay friends with her, right?" I sniffed.

"Of course. Kalahari and I will have a frank discussion, and payback is on its way, but I know her. I know she meant well, and I suppose it won't be the end of the world." He smiled.

"Payback?"

"Do you know how long she's been waiting for that crocodile bag Ilan ordered for her from Hermès?"

I shook my head in response.

"Seven months. Do you know when it will be completed and delivered?"

I shook my head again.

"Never. Some 'asshat,' as you would put it, had his PA inform the boutique that the order was canceled." Now those eyes seemed positively *evil.*

I couldn't help but chuckle at their antics. March was pissed, but not *too* pissed, and I felt damn relieved. Reflecting on what had happened, I took his hand without thinking. "Again, I'm sorry. You're pretty strange, but you deserve to find someone who'll make you happy, March, and I'm sure that will happen. That being said, I stand by my words: you're an arrogant ass most of the time."

His thumb wiped one last tear that had been outlining my jaw, and I shivered at the feeling of his fingers trailing across my skin, lingering one, maybe two seconds longer than needed.

"I used to think about Charlotte all the time, used to wake up in the middle of the night thinking of her . . . but I realize I no longer do," March said wistfully.

I had no idea what to reply to such an intimate confession. In fact, I almost felt like I shouldn't have heard it. He had, after all, said that he was a private person and didn't like for people to pry into his life. Hoping to drop the issue, I got up from my seat with a weak smile. "I-I'll go get myself something to drink."

March moved, allowing me to reach the galley, and followed me, perhaps to get a glass for himself as well. Now, I think that at this point, I should mention that I don't believe in fate, predestination, or whatever: I have my own theory, which involves trollish subatomic particles ganging up to push you into awkward situations. In any case, those particles did their job—or maybe it was just air pockets. As I grabbed a bottle of mineral water in the mini fridge, the plane started to shake and undulate on the dark clouds, up and down like a fairground ride. I stumbled backward in a fit of panic, my shoulders hitting the galley's plywood wall, and March lunged to steady me.

There was that feeling of the plane swaying, the water bottle rolling on the gray carpet a few feet away from us, and I could no longer think. March's body was pressed against mine, flattening me against the wall, and he had bent a little, his face inches from mine. I could smell him, the mints, his faint laundry scent, and I didn't dare to look up because his chin was brushing against my forehead.

He remained silent.

I listened to his peaceful breathing and squeezed the sleeves of his shirt with trembling hands, as if he had been the only thing that kept me steady.

He shifted, and on my temple, the rough touch of the stubble on his chin was replaced by a much softer one, that of his lips.

That damn bottle was still rolling around, the water inside hitting the plastic walls with faint sloshing sounds, and my head was spinning in tune with its movements. When his fingers tilted my chin upward, I had no choice but to look him in the eyes; their dark, mesmerizing blue reminded me a lot of what had happened in the car. Gone was the calm confidence: all I could read was confusion, as if he himself wasn't certain what was happening.

Okay, this was definitely like in the car.

March's lips brushed mine for the first time since we had met, one of his hands pulling me closer while the other steadied me against the wall.

The kiss itself wasn't wild—I gathered from Kalahari's flowery confessions that he wasn't exactly the volcano type, regardless of how worked up he was—and he seemed a little hesitant at first. Once he had found his bearings, though, he proved to be a smooth criminal, patiently waiting for an opportunity to make it past the enemy lines.

I'm afraid my own performance was probably underwhelming, but I prefer to remember it as some super passionate and sensual demonstration. I mean, I didn't turn my head away when I felt his tongue dart at my lips, which made for considerable progress. I just closed my eyes, opened my mouth, and let March take the lead, allowing him to conduct a meticulous exploration of recesses usually reserved for toothbrushes and chocolate cake. I did try to kiss him back a little, but my timing never seemed to be quite right, so when our teeth collided for the second time, I gave up on that and simply held on to him for dear life.

I almost wished I had been in a state to formulate rational thinking, because there was so much to learn and file from that first proper French kiss: the strange, mineral taste of saliva, the flavor of the mints, and so many improbable nerve connections I had never heard about. Was it even normal to feel it all the way down to your breasts when someone tickled the roof of your mouth?

March eventually slowed down on the whole tonguing business—perhaps to breathe—but it took him a little while to fully let go of my lower lip. Not that it made much of a difference: I was in such a state of daze that I actually forgot to close my mouth. I stood there, still pressed against him, my fingers gripping his arms, lips parted in a silent O. His right hand cupped my cheek, and with a tender smile, March delicately brought my jaw up, manually closing my mouth after that complete system breakdown.

When the magnitude of the incident finally registered in my neurons, it took thirty more seconds of frantic blinking before I was able to form a complete sentence.

"You kissed me."

Nobel Prize–level scientific conclusions, people!

"I did."

"Isn't that kind of a big deal?" My voice broke, and I must have sounded a little distressed by this turn of events, but in truth, I was more unnerved by his apparent cool. I pushed him away weakly, my arms and legs little more than sticks of jelly. I could no longer meet his eyes, so I focused on a fascinating point on the carpet.

Above me, he sighed. "This is going too fast."

My gaze jerked back to March. That had been no question, rather an affirmation. He still had that same peaceful expression, and there was a knowing glint in his eyes, which almost made me want to contradict him for the sake of it. But he was right. It was too early for me to put words on whatever twisted bond was forming between us, and March was quickly filling my chart with things I wasn't entirely certain I was ready for.

Outside, the sky was almost dark on one side of the plane, while on the other side, a fiery sunset painted the clouds with vivid orange and pink hues. We were chasing daylight. The plane would land in Tokyo in late morning, and if I didn't sleep during the flight, I'd spend the day like a zombie.

"Maybe I'll try . . . to get some rest before we land."

"Excellent idea." He nodded, wrapping his arm around my shoulder as we returned to our seats. "We have a long day ahead of us, and if I recall, well, I still owe you a romance-book date." The corners of his eyes crinkled. "Perhaps this is where we should start."

I looked up at him as I sat back and reclined my seat until it was in sleep position, trying to figure the appropriate response. Was there even an official term for the stage of March's and my . . . proceedings?

Curling to my side, I watched him leave to retrieve a cover from one the galley's closets. He came back and draped it over me with a smile that made my chest tingle. As he moved to return to his own seat, I grabbed his hand, holding him back. "March . . . how does it work? Do we trust each other now?" I whispered.

There was the same blend of tenderness and confusion in his voice that I had witnessed in his eyes before. "I'm afraid so, Island."

TWENTY-THREE

The Ice Coffee

"Love is all-powerful, limitless, blind, Roger thought. Yes, his love was blind to the fact that Bernadette was, in fact, a man and his long-lost half brother, Bernard."

—Dany Butters, *Last Tango in Louisville*

If you don't mind, the official version will be that I landed the jet in Chōfu Airport, which is almost true. Ekaterina let me sit in the empty seat on her right and pull the landing gear lever—a decision March expressed considerable concern over. Don't worry, the gear worked fine, and my story doesn't end with a gruesome plane crash on the tarmac of a small regional airport in Japan.

Even though we didn't get arrested or anything, I doubted I'd ever get used to showing people a fake passport, and I wondered how March could be so relaxed about the whole thing. The huge black case drew some attention to us as we crossed the lobby, and I was extremely relieved when he retrieved the keys for a brown Honda SUV from some high-end car rental counter. After a brief struggle with yet another scumbag foldable backseat—I thought it was me, but that day,

I discovered that foldable backseats truly fear no one, not even guys like March—both black mystery cases had been stored in the back. In no time we were driving down the Chūō Expressway in the direction of Tokyo, under a heavy rain.

I hadn't traveled to Japan since my last year in Columbia. Back then I had spent six months interning for a big French bank's local branch to develop an intranet application for HR as my end degree project. So, first post-Fukushima visit, you could say. Not much had changed—in Tokyo anyway—and as I looked at the dense traffic and ad-covered buildings through my window, I was filled with a pleasant sense of familiarity.

We were entering Minami-Shinjuku, in the west of Tokyo, when March's phone started buzzing in his pocket. The slight twitch in his jaw was self-explanatory. He had forgotten to install the hands-free kit—proof he was terribly distracted—and had qualms about taking a phone call while driving.

"Do you want me to pick up and plug in your headphone?" I offered, though I didn't expect him to accept.

"Yes, thank you."

I was pretty surprised, to say the least, but I collected myself and pulled the phone and a pair of tiny earplugs out of his inner pocket, careful not to touch his arms, or the wheel. "It's . . . '0'," I informed him, looking at the single number displayed on the screen in guise of a contact name.

He nodded for me to pick it up.

"Mr. May's office, how may I help you?" I announced.

A sultry female voice answered me with a laugh. "Oh my, have I been replaced? I liked this job!"

"Oh my God! You're Phyllis!" I chirped.

Next to me, I heard him cough. "Oh, yeah, sorry! Seems like I don't have the right to talk to you. I'll just pass you to March."

"Thank you, Miss Chaptal. I look forward to hearing more of you when the circumstances will allow it."

I was tempted to tell her that it was unlikely, but I didn't want to hijack March's call, so I plugged in the headphones and placed one in his ear. I know it's silly, but the brief proximity we experienced as I touched his ear and the soft chestnut hair surrounding it gave me a pleasant little chill.

He made sure nearly nothing transpired of their exchange. All I learned was that she was the one who had arranged the car rental, as well as a hotel in Roppongi Hills. I could tell she had said something else, though, because at some point during the conversation he listened to her in complete silence for almost a whole minute, his brow knitted in an expression of displeasure before answering her. "I thought so. I've already taken additional measures."

What kind of measures was he talking about? The big suitcase he had purchased from Minas? Crossing my fingers, I prayed we weren't driving with a portable nuke in the trunk or anything like that.

When he hung up, I indulged one last time, even though he hadn't requested any help to remove the earplug, hoping he wouldn't notice my fingers lingering a second too long on the shell of his ear. God, I liked the soft fuzz there . . .

"I need your help. Where do I go, Island?"

His calm voice snapped me out of my daze. March seemed to be struggling with a notion I had discovered long ago. In Japan, you don't find addresses, addresses find you—if you're lucky. Indeed, with no street names and a complex addressing system relying on nonlinear building numbers, you could find yourself stuck in front of the wrong building with no idea where to find your apartment—which is exactly what had happened to my mom on the day of our arrival in Tokyo. We had eventually spent our first night in a nearby hotel, because she was exhausted and didn't want to hunt for the right number at one in the morning.

"First on the right, after the drugstore," I instructed. I could see myself again, at the age of fifteen, stalking Masaharu after his baseball game and watching as he entered the tiny gray house with straw blinds protecting his mother's bedroom window from the prying eyes of an old dude who lived in the opposite building.

March reluctantly parked the SUV on the sidewalk lane, for lack of a better option. It was still raining, and warm drops ran down my neck and under my beige T-shirt as we made our way toward the house's entrance. Halfway there, I felt him move closer to me, and it took me a couple of seconds to understand that he was shielding me from the rain, draping his right arm around my shoulder and keeping close to me so most raindrops would fall on his jacket rather than on my back. I didn't look up because the way his body brushed against mine had me turning pink. If things kept going like this, he was probably going to ruin me for any other man.

A strange impatience filled me while we waited for someone to answer the door. Would Masaharu recognize me? Would he even remember me? I took a deep breath when the small wooden door slowly opened to reveal . . . Masaharu's mom. There was no denying that all the weird beauty products Haru had been putting on her face back then had worked. She still looked amazing, even in her mid-fifties. I felt March stiffen behind me as he observed Haru's long black hair, broad shoulders, elaborate makeup, and lilac cotton dress, but he said nothing otherwise, allowing me to introduce us.

I cleared my throat, worried that my Japanese might have become rusty since my last trip. "Konnichiwa, Niyama-san. Watashi o oboete iru ka dō ka wa shirimasen . . . Namae wa Island Chaptal desu. Jyuuni nen mae, Sumiyoshi ni Haha to sunde ita. Masaharu-kun no yūjindatta." *Hello, Mrs. Niyama. I don't know if you remember me . . . My name is Island Chaptal. Ten years ago, I lived in Sumiyoshi with my mom. I was a friend of Masaharu's.*

She blinked a couple of times, and March and I waited as an expression of shock formed on her smooth face. Her pink lips puckered in a small O before stretching into a large grin.

An ear-piercing shriek soon welcomed my introduction. "Shinjirarenaiyo! Hontou ni shinjirarenaiyo!" *I can't believe it! I really can't believe it!*

I could tell March didn't like witnessing a conversation he couldn't understand, but I figured translating the exchange would take too much time, so I kept on chatting with her in Japanese under his confused gaze.

She cradled my cheeks in her hands, speaking in a cheerful, excited voice. "You've grown sooooo much! How's your mama? Is she here in Tokyo too? You two left so suddenly I never thought I'd see you again!"

I swallowed a lump in my throat. "She's dead, Haru-san. She died here, in Tokyo. I came back to see Masaharu."

Her hands left my face to squeeze my shoulders. "I'm sorry to hear that, Island-chan. Masaharu-kun isn't home, but would you like to come in for a second?"

I turned to March. "He's not home, but she's inviting us in. Is it okay?"

He nodded and followed Haru inside the living room, but not before having removed our shoes, as was customary. I didn't miss the glint in her eyes as she watched March do so. Unbeknownst to him, March had scored big-time with Masaharu's mom.

Masaharu's house was the same as I remembered, with its small, dimly lit rooms, cream wooden floor, old ink paintings, and celebrity posters on the walls. I gathered Haru still had that big rice cooker in the kitchen, as a pleasant smell of hot rice floated in the air. Once we were all seated around a wooden table with ice coffees, she shot March a smoldering look. "Who's that hot gentleman with you? Is he *American*?"

Presumably identifying the word "American" in her sentence, March shook his head, with an unexpectedly shy smile. Damn, Masaharu's mom knew how to tame men!

"This is March. He's—" I hesitated for a few seconds. What was he, to me? No longer a threat, not really a friend, not a lover either—although that particular point was rapidly becoming ambiguous. "He's . . . an acquaintance."

As I said this, I felt March's gaze on me. I peeked up to find the faintest trace of disappointment in his eyes, as if he had expected a better answer. I looked away to focus on Haru, who was still ogling him like a succulent piece of meat. "Haru-san, do you know where we can find Masaharu-kun?" I asked between two sips of the sweet, cold coffee.

"Oh, he's found a job. He distributes tissue packs in Shibuya," she said, checking a delicate golden bracelet watch on her wrist. "He's still on Hachikō Crossing at this hour."

I translated her explanations for March, and he gave me a look that prompted me to bring our little visit to an end. "Thank you so much for everything, Haru-san. I'm sorry we have to leave so early. We're in a bit of a hurry, and I'd like to see Masaharu before we leave Tokyo." A half lie . . . always better than a full-blown one, I guess.

She nodded her understanding and walked us to the door, all the while smoothing nonexistent wrinkles on the back of March's jacket. As we were about to pass the door, I decided to leave Haru a little souvenir I knew would make her happy. "Let's say good-bye the French way, with a kiss on each cheek!" I suggested enthusiastically.

Haru clasped her hands in delight, and I kissed her on both cheeks, encouraging March to do the same.

There are looks you can't forget, such as the look of pure gratitude in Haru's eyes when I gave her a naughty wink and allowed March to bend down to kiss her in turn. She let go of him with flushed cheeks, bliss clouding her dark eyes, and I stifled a laugh at March's obvious discomfort. He would make me pay dearly for this, but Haru was happy, and that was all that mattered.

Outside, the rain had stopped, and after she had closed the door behind us, he finally spoke, his voice uncertain. "Masaharu's father—"

I giggled. "Don't be so conservative! If Haru wants to live her life as a woman, you shouldn't judge!"

"I'm not judging—" he muttered as he unlocked the passenger door for me.

"Then stop calling her Masaharu's father." I shrugged, fastening my belt as the engine started.

TWENTY-FOUR

The Tissues

"Lady Maythorn had to choose between two men: Barnaby, the dark, mysterious rake, and Georges, the stern officer whose cold facade concealed a burning passion."

—Christina Thorbrad, *Regency Hearts #3: Two Earls for the Virgin*

March had parked the SUV a few minutes north of Hachikō Crossing, and we were strolling down the Inokashira Dori, determined to find Masaharu somewhere within the crowd. March looked down at me as we passed building after building, all covered in colorful ads. "So, why did your mother refer to Masaharu as 'the man you loved'? Was it a crush?"

I sighed. "Yeah, big-time. I was sort of stalking him a little. I went to his house a few times to watch him from the street, or I'd hide in the aisles to spy on him when he went to Life with his mom."

"Life?"

"The supermarket," I clarified.

He grimaced. "You stalked him when he was at the supermarket with his mother . . . That's—"

"Pathetic, I know. I was *fifteen*!" I groaned, remembering that I'd done the same thing with Ethan-the-Gorgeous-Law-Student. Then twenty-three, though, I had been fully accountable for my laughable attempts at finding true love.

"What was so special about him?" March asked, genuine curiosity filling his voice.

I tucked a strand of hair behind my ear. "He was kind of badass. Not great-looking, but he was an aspiring *bōsōzoku*."

His mouth twitched as he had been stifling a laugh. "*Bōsōzoku* . . . What does that mean?"

"The tough biker type . . . Well, actually he had a scooter, but you get the idea," I mumbled.

This time March laughed in earnest, the corner of his eyes crinkling. "Unrequited love for an aspiring tough biker riding a scooter?"

"Hey! A girl can dream! I eventually mustered the courage to talk to him, and he took me to see a movie in Kinshichō with his friends. I framed the ticket and hung it on my bedroom wall," I concluded, smiling at the memory of my mother helping me choose the frame at a nearby mall.

March chuckled one last time and casually ruffled my hair as we walked, raising my body temperature slightly above Mercury's—that's seven hundred degrees Kelvin, for those of you who skipped physics to have a life. "Do you plan on framing the underwear I bought you as well?"

I shook my head. Unlike Mercury, I wasn't gravitating too close to the sun, but rather to a tactless jerk, and I had a tendency to forget it too easily. "Get over yourself . . . You're nothing special, and we haven't even dated yet."

"Really? What's so special about my ears, by the way?"

Lord, why do you never let me get away with these things?

"Nothing," I huffed in embarrassment.

"Oh. Nothing at all?"

I balled my fists in aggravation as Hachikō Crossing came in sight. "Okay, they're soft. You have soft, fuzzy ears. Happy?"

"More like disconcerted, but I'll take it as a compliment."

I was about to tell him that his ears weren't that cool, anyway, when I stopped dead in my tracks. In front of the Tsutaya Music Store was a lean, lanky silhouette I had dreamed of often enough as a teen to recognize when I saw it. March's posture changed, and the relaxed guy I had been joking with seconds before vanished before my eyes, leaving in his place the guarded professional. For the first time since I had met him, I realized how much younger March seemed when he wasn't "working."

Haru had been right. Masaharu was here, distributing advertising tissue packs in front of the buzzing store. He hadn't changed much. He looked a little older, maybe a little tired too. His dark eyes had lost most of their badass spark, and his hair, while still long enough to reach his shoulders, didn't shine like it had in my memories. There was an expression of utter boredom on his angular face, and I could tell that the black suit pants, white shirt, and colorful apron he was wearing were a necessity rather than a choice. Masaharu had become a grown-up.

Gesturing for March to follow me, I crossed the street along with hundreds of hurried salarymen, confused tourists, and tanned, giggling girls skipping school to go buy makeup at the 109 department store.

It felt weird because at first he didn't look at me. I was just another shadow in the crowd to him, and he mechanically handed me one of those tissue packs, claiming my life would never be the same after I had tasted HotHotHot Donuts. I took the tissues under March's attentive gaze and smiled at Masaharu. "Thanks. I just went to see your mom. How are you, Masaharu-kun?"

There was a fleeting moment during which I saw that old spark light up in his eyes, and a heartwarming smile spread on his lips, revealing a row of misaligned teeth that I had always found adorable.

"Island . . . san, is it you?" He had seemed to hesitate before placing the polite suffix after my name. I was now a grown-up too, after all.

Trampling most basic Japanese courtesy rules, I reached up to wrap my arms around Masaharu's bony shoulders and pulled him in for a hug. I didn't miss March's stiffening behind me as I did so, but I thought nothing of it. No better way to assert I was *totally* immune to his teasing than hugging another man in front of him.

"It's been ages! I'm so glad to see you! Haru told me you were doing great!" I cooed. We both knew he wasn't really doing so great, distributing tissues at thirty-three in a ruthlessly stratified society such as Japan, but he still mattered enough for me to want to make him happy, even at the cost of a lie.

My old flame welcomed the attention with obvious embarrassment, averting his eyes, and I thought it was cute. "I'm happy to see you too, Island-san. How long will you be staying in Japan? How is Léa-san?"

He had said my mother's name almost reverently, and it hurt to give him the bad news. "She's dead. She died shortly before I left Japan."

His lips pressed in a pained expression, and I was almost tempted to hug him again, but behind me March placed a hand on my shoulder in a silent reminder that we hadn't come here to cuddle with Masaharu on the street.

"Masaharu-kun, my friend and I need to talk to you. Can we go somewhere quiet, please?" I asked, gesturing to March.

Masaharu winced, his bag of tissue packs still in hand. His eyes darted to a young girl enthusiastically promoting HotHotHot Donuts in front of a nearby store, and I figured he couldn't leave his spot without asking a supervisor first. I joined my hands in a praying gesture. "Please!"

He swallowed and laid his bag on the ground before raising his palms up to indicate we needed to wait. We watched him run toward the bubbly girl with silly pigtails, bowing at her over and over. She seemed to accept his request, and as soon as he had left, the girl resumed hopping up and down and yelling HotHotHot's slogan in a shrill voice. Masaharu went back to us, and he seemed relieved, but also a little sad.

"It's okay. I'm free for the day," he told us with a weak nod.

I guess March was a better judge of people and characters than I was, because, as we walked away with Masaharu, he figured out something I hadn't.

"She fired him," he whispered to me.

———

We were all sitting in Tsutaya's Starbucks Coffee, waiting for our drinks. A cute waitress walked to our table and checked the names on the cups before giving me my mango passion tea, Masaharu his mocha espresso, and . . . Mr. July his simple brewed coffee.

For a minute or so, all that could be heard were low sipping sounds, until March broke the silence, looking at me as he spoke. "What did Léa tell him? Does he know where the stone is?"

I translated, and Masaharu started nodding over and over again, his eyes widening. Near me, I felt March tense in anticipation, waiting for my mother's messenger to talk. "I still have it! I still have your box. Léa made me swear to keep it. I still have it!" he said, his hands gripping his cup tightly.

"My box?"

"She gave it to me a few days before you two disappeared. She told me she would be leaving soon and that she wanted me to keep the box for her. She said you might come back for it someday. I didn't understand, but I owed her so much, I had to."

I translated again for March, who leaned forward across the table, scaring the shit out of Masaharu with one of his icy bad-guy looks. "Did he open it? What's inside?"

I translated the question, and Masaharu stared at March as if he had grown a second head. "Léa-san saved my life! I would have never betrayed her!" he roared, all traces of fear and embarrassment gone.

I took it as a confirmation that Masaharu hadn't opened the box and resumed questioning him, eager to discover yet another side of my mom which I had never known existed until now. "What do you mean she saved you? What happened?"

He bowed his head, averting his eyes. "When I was young . . . I wanted to become someone, to be respected. I started doing favors for the wrong people . . . I made mistakes."

"You mean the yakuza . . . real criminals?" I prodded.

He nodded with a grimace. "I was hoping I'd be admitted to the Inagawa-kai, that I'd have a clan, a family. But one night a club that belonged to my protector got raided, and they thought I had talked to the police."

March's lips thinned, and I swallowed. Masaharu had no doubt narrowly escaped disaster. He went on in a tight voice. "Three men from the family came to look for me at home, but I was out. Mama Haru called me, and she was crying. I couldn't go home, so I hid under the tunnel, in Kinshichō."

"Where the Korean prostitutes work?" I asked, remembering the poorly lit area and those skimpily dressed girls leaning against the wall while they waited for potential customers.

He nodded again. "They found me, and they started beating me. It was already late. I think Léa-san was coming back from some shopping at Marui. She saw us and came to help me," he recounted.

"What did she do? Did she call the police?" I felt bitter that my mom had never told me this. She had saved the former love of my life, dammit!

"No. She dropped her bag, and she ordered the man who was beating me to stop. She called him a fat pig."

My mouth fell open, and I noticed March's eyebrows arching in curiosity.

Masaharu went on. "He told her to go away, and she walked up to him. She said she was going to fuck him up because he was a nutless piece of shit."

My eyes wide like saucers, I kept translating, and near me, I heard March clear his throat. I leaned toward him and whispered, "My mom wasn't that rude. I'm sure he's exaggerating."

March nodded in agreement as Masaharu finished his tale. "I didn't see everything, but she fought with them. She was much faster than these guys. She kicked two of them to the ground, and I think she pulled on the fat yakuza's testicles really hard through his pants. He was screaming in pain. After it was over, she told them that if they touched me again, she'd tell their boss that they were violating rule number one and that they had been beaten by a woman. She said they'd surely undergo *yubitsume* over that."

An expert at all things criminal, March, once I had translated the ending of Masaharu's story, proceeded to give me some additional insight. "Rule number one is a traditional rule stating a yakuza shouldn't harm a good citizen. I don't think it entirely applied to Masaharu, though, and *yubitsume*—"

"I know." I chuckled, wiggling my left hand's little finger and mimicking scissors cutting it with my right one.

"Precisely." March smiled as he finished his coffee.

Masaharu saw my gesture and nodded, as if to confirm that we had understood his tale right.

Satisfied with these explanations, March pulled a few bills from his wallet to pay for our drinks and clasped his hands with a determined look. "Excellent. Why don't we go fetch that box now?"

We drove back to Kōtōbashi with Masaharu so he could give me the box my mother had entrusted him with. Needless to say, Haru was delighted to see March return, and she kept stealing burning glances at him through her lashes while we all waited in the living room for Masaharu to come back with the precious box—which he had kept hidden in his bedroom for all these years, and from what I gathered, the area didn't exactly comply with March's or Haru's high cleaning standards.

When Masaharu reappeared holding a small black lacquered box, I felt my heart rate increase. The box wasn't anywhere near big enough to contain the Ghost Cullinan, but it didn't matter. It was a secret my mother had left for me, and this alone was worth all the diamonds in the world.

He handed me the object reverently. It had been sealed with a thin green ribbon, and Masaharu had told the truth: It didn't appear anyone had ever undone the delicate tie. I pulled on the crumpled satin with trembling fingers and lifted the shiny black lid with the utmost care. Behind me, I could feel March and Haru bend over my shoulders to look inside as well.

I heard a long sigh—Haru's—and a tongue smacking in irritation—March's. They were disappointed, and rightly so. All that box contained was a thin square of white rice paper with a word and a number on it.

Miyamoto

2120

I let out a dejected sigh, and honestly, I was on the verge of giving up, but Masaharu came to the rescue. "Miyamoto is a bank, and 2120 is the safe number. Léa said you'd know the combination."

After I had translated this to March, I gave him a desperate look. "We can always check, but frankly, I have no idea what this means, or why Masaharu thinks I know that safe's combination."

He gave me one of those coy little winks I liked so much. "Let's give it a try anyway."

I nodded and proceeded to ask Masaharu about Miyamoto Bank.

He explained to me that it was a small private bank with only one branch on the Harumi Dori in Kōtō-ku, which doubled as its head-quarters. As we discussed the best way to drive there, I seized the oppor-tunity to ask for his cell phone number and e-mail address. I intended to add him to my Facebook contacts if I survived this hunt for the Cullinan. He scribbled them on a piece of paper, which I tucked in my pocket, and I was good to go.

March wasn't.

Haru had found a way to catch his attention. Smiling at him and dusting his jacket hadn't worked. This, however . . . I watched in fas-cinated horror as she demonstrated to him a new type of remote-con-trolled mop that you could either pilot yourself or program to roam around your house during the day, so that your floor always remained sparkling clean. March's gaze was locked on the plastic robot and the bright yellow mop attached underneath. His breath was a little short, and he was completely oblivious to Haru caressing his arm as he wit-nessed the miracle of a wooden floor mopping itself.

I had to call his name twice, and when he responded, his poker smile immediately fell in place to conceal any interest in the object.

March was in love.

With Haru's remote-controlled mop.

We said our good-byes, and I plotted once again for March to kiss Haru on both cheeks, but this time he seemed happy to do so. The remote-controlled mop had obviously helped him see beyond any gender-related issues.

TWENTY-FIVE
Stars & Satellites

"Here's one secret no one will tell you about getting laid after a date. DON'T TALK. Most girls blame either their looks or excessive timidity for their virginity. This is only true to an extent. These girls are also horribly annoying."

—Aurelia Nichols & Jillie Bean, *101 Tips to Lose Your Virginity after 25*

Once we were back in the car, a quick glance at the dashboard clock made it clear that we weren't going to accomplish much more until morning. It was almost six p.m., and according to their website, Miyamoto Bank's offices had closed half an hour ago.

"How about we get some rest tonight?" March asked as he started the engine, voicing my thoughts.

"Okay. It's been a few crazy days . . . You need to slow down too, right?"

He gave me a surprised look as we waited at a red light. "Do I look tired to you?"

"You told that old prune of a doctor that you hadn't slept much since we left the United States, and those bruises you got at the Rose

Paradise probably aren't healed yet," I explained, resting a tentative hand on his right forearm.

"Don't worry. I've been through much worse." He laughed, but I didn't find that particularly funny.

March drove us through large streets, and as we progressed the surroundings started to feel colder—tall buildings, concrete and glass everywhere, and no one in sight. After a few minutes we passed a parking lot and a black sign that read Hotel Entrance, and I figured we had used some sort of shortcut.

A room at Tokyo's Ritz-Carlton. I could live with that.

After he had parked, we made our way through a huge lobby that had me wondering if the floor was real marble and whether someone would throw me out if I touched those pretty Japanese paintings on the walls, or even the graceful cherry blossom branches sticking out of that big bowl-like flowerpot. Figuring that the chances were pretty high, I decided against it and watched as March leaned against a lacquered black counter and offered an impeccably dressed receptionist his most charming dimpled smile. He leaned forward to whisper in her ear—maybe he was asking for another room with bulletproof windows?

She responded with an excited grin. "Welcome back, Mr. June. I'll see what I can do!"

Her bubbly voice and the usual lame alias snapped me back to attention. I gave March a questioning look. "What's going on?"

He gave me a reassuring pat on the shoulder and glanced at the woman, who was busy explaining his request to a short guy with slicked-back raven hair. She came back a few seconds later, and this time she looked flushed. What the hell had he asked from her?

"Arrangements will made in the suite immediately, and—" More blushing if possible. "I would be delighted to assist you personally!"

That last line had come out in a near squeal, and my eyes narrowed in suspicion. Had March been . . . hitting on her? A lump formed in my throat, which I deemed best ignored. We weren't even together to begin with, so no need to get jealous. As I brooded silently, I realized she was staring at me. She was no longer smiling, more like . . . well, staring. Up and down.

I shifted under the pressure of her appraising gaze and cleared my throat uncomfortably. "I . . . do we get a room or something? I think I need some rest."

"Can we expect you in two hours, Fubuki?" March asked her.

She nodded enthusiastically. "Yes, Mr. June! Anything else? A spa appointment for the lady, perhaps? We can offer a skin-brightening facial—"

He laid a hand on my shoulder and flashed Fubuki a bright smile. "Excellent idea! Island, why don't you get pampered before we go?"

"Before we go? Where?"

"Well, on our date. Fubuki will find a dress for you. In the meantime, you can rest and get a facial . . . skinning," he concluded, visibly unfamiliar with spa treatments terminology.

I didn't care about that last point, though. My brain was stuck a little farther back in his sentence, unable to process its meaning. "We . . . uh . . . We're going on a date?"

"Yes, one I believe I promised you." He nodded with a smug expression.

I turned to Fubuki for some sort of confirmation, but she was already gone. He *had* indeed voiced his intent to fulfill his end of our bargain back in the plane, but in all honesty, I hadn't really believed it would happen. I had filed it as little more than a pleasant fantasy, one that would keep me warm next time I'd see other people kissing.

Except it was happening, and he had asked Fubuki to find a dress for me. Like in *Accidentally Married to the Billionaire Sheikh*. I took a deep breath, trying to calm my fluttering heart. "Is this real, or are you going to laugh in my face in ten seconds and say that I got punked?"

He blinked. "Why would I do such a thing? Now run to that spa. You have one hour and fifty-five minutes left to look your best before Fubuki comes back with clothes for you."

With this, a young bellhop I hadn't noticed approaching popped at my side. Casting March one last befuddled glance, I followed the guy, my mind completely blown.

———

By the time I returned to the hotel's fifty-third floor, I had been Brazilian waxed, cleaned, scrubbed, reenergized with vitamin C and aloe vera extracts, and the blazing agony between my legs had decreased to tolerable levels. When I entered our suite, still followed by that young bellhop whom I now understood to be in charge of watching me, the first thing I noticed was that March had already changed. The slight stubble of the last twenty-four hours had been replaced by a close shave, his usual jacket and jeans by what looked a lot like a tux—no tie or bow, though, and . . .

"Are you . . . Is that *cologne* I smell on you?"

I know it's no way to greet someone, especially if you scrunch your nose while saying this, but I had gotten used to him never wearing any perfume. I suspected it had to do with his job: makes it easier to go unnoticed when people can't smell you coming for them. I can even say I liked it. At any rate, he was dashing—the incarnation of a dream date.

A dimpled grin answered my question, and past the initial shock of standing face-to-face with the closest thing I had ever seen to Prince Charming, my eyes darted around, taking in our surroundings. Now, *that* was one damn cool suite. It wasn't the size. It was a bit bigger than the one we had stayed in at the Bristol, but nothing insane. It wasn't the elegant, modern furniture with a palette of soft creamy hues, or even the bottle of champagne resting in a tall, silvery bucket filled with ice cubes.

It was the fricking view.

The bedroom possessed large windows offering a panoramic view of the city, and I ran past March to lean against one of them, squishing my nose against the thick glass as I stared at the fiery gold of Tokyo Tower shimmering in the distance.

Taking a quick tour of my new kingdom, I couldn't repress a victorious squeak when I realized that the bathroom boasted the same type of bay window, and that a smart architect had placed the tub right in front of it, lodged in an alcove.

"Aren't you going to get changed?"

March's tranquil voice hauled me back to reality, and as I returned to the living room, I finally noticed the three white bags sitting on a long beige sofa. "Fubuki picked a few things for you. She has an excellent eye for style. I trust you'll be pleased with her purchases," he said with a little wink.

I nodded and crossed the room to pick up the bags. "I'll go get ready in the bathroom."

He moved to go sit in a cream armchair facing the bay window, and I flew more than I walked to said bathroom, locking the door behind me and placing the bags on the floor. Opening the first one, I felt my cheeks flush and wondered if he had anything to do with . . . whatever I was holding between two fingers at a safe distance, like I would have a dead sea cucumber. Pink silk, frilly black Chantilly lace, ribbons everywhere . . . The lingerie set Fubuki had provided me with was simply outrageous. For God's sake, I had never even *touched* a garter belt before!

I silently praised her for the push-up bra—a nice fit with some subtle padding—but I ditched the garter belt, since my stockings appeared to hold well enough on their own. Opening the second, much larger bag, I pulled out a sleeveless LBD that had me yet again wondering if March had given Fubuki any specific instructions. Much like my beloved flapper dress, it had some nice embroidery, but its cut was much more flattering, with an elegant portrait neckline and flared skirt that reached under my knees. Fifties-ish, chic, but not too daring. I loved it.

A pair of almost perfectly sized black satin pumps and a gray silk coat completed the outfit. I examined the results of my extreme make-over in the mirror for a few seconds and came to the conclusion that the contents of the third bag were going to be needed. Being dressed like a movie star and skipping the makeup part looked weird.

Damn, these things were even more complicated than third-degree equations! Should I put on the light-optimizing primer before or after the sheer matte foundation that would control my shine? After much effort, I looked in the mirror to see someone who wasn't me but didn't look too bad. I had stuck to the basics, afraid that too much fiddling with the eyeliner or the eye shadow might turn me into a raccoon, the touch of gloss being the only actual bold move, in my opinion.

I didn't bother with my hair, confident that some finger brushing was more than enough for my bob, and gave a doubtful glance at the pink bottle of perfume staring back at me on the counter. Did I really want to douse myself in an unidentified Japanese fragrance whose name was Vice and Virtue? Hell, I hadn't gone this far to lose the battle to fifty milliliters of water and ethanol. Vice and Virtue it would be.

I can truthfully report I swayed back into the bedroom, but it was because of the shoes. Those high heels were giving me a hard time. March was still waiting in his armchair, gazing at the sparkling skyline with a flute of champagne in his hand. I took a few tentative steps toward him, and he rose from his seat, appraising me silently. He did an amazing job at giving me the *Pretty Woman* look, the one that tells a girl she cleans up nice. "You look absolutely stunning."

I didn't blush, but my ears felt a little hot at his compliment. "Thank you. Where are we going?"

"I was going to ask you. This is, after all, your date. Tell me what you'd like, and Fubuki will arrange it."

Well, that was some heavy dream date scenario. Where to, indeed? Michelin stars were not hard to find in Tokyo, and a good deal of my romance books enforced the necessity for the hero to take the heroine to a super exclusive place in order to successfully seduce her. I wasn't certain that was *my* idea of a dream date, though. Tapping the tip of my nose in deep thought, I looked up at March and got a better idea. "Where do *you* want to go?"

His eyebrows rose. "Me? I'm not entirely certain I'm qualified to choose a restaurant that will meet all of your expectations—"

"No, March. Where would *you* go? What would you enjoy? Molecular stuff? Italian?" I insisted.

The cutest expression of embarrassment appeared on his usually confident face. "Well, I—"

"What?"

He fumbled in his left pocket, still looking hesitant, and showed me a couple of bright-colored coupons, the kind of overenthusiastic advertisement only Japanese businesses can come up with. "They were distributing these near the hotel. I took some because it sounded like an excellent bargain, but I'm not sure—"

I closed my eyes, trying hard not to laugh. Some *tonkatsu* joint in the area offered a free dessert with every order of a fried pork sirloin dish, along with all-you-can-eat rice. "Okay! Fried pork it is!" I proclaimed, much more comfortable with the prospect of a ten-dollar dinner than that of some overly posh and expensive restaurant.

March nodded his approval while tucking the coupons back in his inner pocket, and offered me his arm to go down to the hotel's lobby. As I rested my left hand on his forearm and leaned closer to him, I wondered if he understood that I had asked him to choose our destination because I cared more about knowing him better than I did about my dream romance date thing.

———

Everybody stared when we entered the *tonkatsu* joint. I could understand why: we looked like some sort of ridiculously jamesbondish pair in the middle of a tiny restaurant that smelled of fried food, soy sauce, and coffee. Tired salarymen ate directly on the wooden counter, sitting on high stools, downing glass after glass of cheap beer. A young waiter guided us to a small table near a window, and March handed him his two coupons with a regal gesture. I bit my lower lip not to laugh and ordered a can of C.C. Lemon soda for myself and some iced coffee for March.

While we waited for our dishes to arrive, I pulled out a crumpled advertisement for an antiaging cream, on which I had scribbled a list of questions, back at the hotel's spa. I handed it to March.

"I think you should tell me immediately which questions are unsuitable for a date," I said, producing one of the hotel's pens from my coat pocket.

He nodded and started reading. The pen went down, and I cringed as half of my list was crossed off with a steady hand. He then seemed to examine the remaining items until his brow knitted, and he crossed out yet another item. "That is totally inappropriate."

I leaned forward to look at the list. "What?"

"I'm not discussing when, or to whom, I lost my virginity!"

"It would only be fair! Joy told you about me!"

He snorted. "I'm sure you've already heard the answer to this question anyway, and in florid detail, no doubt."

I blinked. "Kalahari?" My hands flew to my mouth as I remembered her tale. "Wow, you were twenty-four? That's almost as bad as me!"

He looked offended. "Is this the sort of compliment you usually give to your partners?"

I flushed upon realizing that I had once again failed to make appropriate small talk during a date, and I was grateful for the distraction provided by the waiter arriving with our drinks. March handed me back my list, stern blue eyes observing me over his iced coffee.

I took the paper and went through his changes. Everything related to his family had been crossed off, and I wasn't allowed to ask how he had become a professional killer either. Some questions he had answered directly on paper, suggesting that this was all I would get and the topic, therefore, needn't be discussed. Indeed, near the lines where I asked if he too was South African, like Dries, and if his mentor was a Lion as well, a simple "yes" had been scribbled in poor handwriting. That left us with friends, hobbies, cleaning tips, trivia, and . . . I crossed my eyes at the single word he had written at the bottom of my list.

"Who's Gerald?"

"My orange tree," he replied, his features relaxing.

"Oh. Why does it have a name?"

Unbeknownst to me, I had just asked one loaded question, and poked at one of the most intriguing aspects of March's solitary life. A "roommate" of sorts, Gerald had been a Christmas gift from Kalahari, along with a book on plant psychology insisting that treating an orange tree as a full member of the household would dramatically improve its production. March admitted, however, that Gerald's oranges were small and bitter, and that they weren't even that round. It was actually so bad that he secretly stashed a bag of store-bought oranges in his kitchen. He mostly blamed this unfortunate predicament on the South African Eastern Cape climate—no doubt in a bid not to hurt Gerald's feelings.

I tried to comfort March, insisting that he shouldn't let some passive-aggressive orange tree bring him down like this. What I read between the lines, though, was that he guarded himself from others so well that he was terribly lonely, and confiding in Gerald sounded better than dining alone in silence, or safer than calling Kalahari, since she might—would—repeat every single confession he made.

By the time our fried pork arrived, I had managed to make him talk about Phyllis as well and their encounter in Macau six years earlier, when she had been doing accounting for a casino owner who had apparently died since. The exact terminology March used was "dissolved"; I didn't press the issue. Anyway, she had more or less become March's life support since, taking care of all the administrative aspects of his business and forwarding him good ostrich pictures whenever she stumbled on them. Eagerly digging into the juicy, crispy pieces of pork on my plate and the fresh sliced cabbage accompanying them, I tried to extort some more intel from him, this time regarding his little cubicle house facing the ocean in Cape St. Francis.

It didn't go as planned.

"What about you?" March asked between two mouthfuls of all-you-can-eat rice. "What else do you like, apart from romance books and computers?"

I stiffened. Here came the trickiest part. I knew for certain that opening my mouth and talking about myself would precipitate this date into the depths of hell, like all the previous ones. Maybe it was time to experiment with a new strategy. "Well . . . I enjoy shopping, going to the gym, and I love modern art," I replied smugly.

"Bag of lies. You rarely buy anything when you and Joy go shopping together, you don't understand modern art, and you spend more time floating around than swimming when you go to the pool," He commented with a smirk.

I felt my entire body prickle with humiliation. How the hell did he know these things? From screening my e-mails and chat logs as part of the Board's investigations, maybe? Not only this, but why did he even care about such details? God, I hoped he hadn't somehow learned that I liked to pick my nose under the shower.

In any case, I was cornered; my head hung low in defeat. "Okay, I like floating in pools, walking aimlessly in big cities, playing video games, reading Wikipedia. I like that homeless guy who's always in front of Dunkin' Donuts on Amsterdam Avenue and calls people communists, and I want to go to space." I took a big gulp of C.C. Lemon.

"To space? On which planet? The moon?"

I slammed my can back on the table. "The moon is not a planet! The moon is a *moon!*"

I was treated to the deep, warm laugh I liked so much. "My apologies, poor choice of words."

"It's okay. Anyway, I'd like to visit Europa," I muttered.

"Oh. I've never heard of this pl—" March stopped mid-sentence as he caught the look of scandal on my face.

I couldn't take it anymore and, before I could stop myself, started a heated rant about Europa—my favorite moon of Jupiter—its miles-thick ice crust, the liquid water ocean NASA suspected existed underneath, and my own theories regarding what sort of non-carbon-based life forms might be swimming in there. Somehow that led me to the controversial subject of convergent evolution and to lobsters holding the key to biological immortality because their DNA can replicate indefinitely without any loss of genetic material therein.

When I reached the part about immortal lobsters, March stared at me for several seconds, and I thought I had ruined yet another date . . . until he asked if it was true that there was ongoing research regarding the application of this "fountain of youth" to human DNA. Turned out that since Gerald had limited conversational skills, March sometimes read articles on Wikipedia too to pass time, and he had stumbled on the one dedicated to lobsters.

Sweet Raptor Jesus. I was having dinner with a man who had not only read about the specificities of lobster DNA replication, but cared enough to wonder if you could make humans immortal by tweaking with their chromosomes in a similar fashion!

When our free desserts arrived, March praised the *tonkatsu* joint for its remarkable price-to-value ratio, since we were getting not one but two scoops of squid ink ice cream. The taste was revolting, but I ate some nonetheless, to make him happy. He wasn't picky and didn't like to waste food, so he finished my ice cream on top of his.

The waiter didn't have anything to do by the time he arrived at our table. March had wiped the plates with his paper napkin, stacked them on top of each other, placed our cutlery on them, and gathered all the crumbs on the table into a neat little pile. The guy gave us a long sideways glance that we both ignored—March because he was probably used to it, me because I didn't care. He was my dream date, crumbs or not, and I floated on cloud nine as he caressed my hand and looked into my eyes while we waited for his credit card receipt. I knew this was standard date practice, but it made my entire arm tingle deliciously.

"So, was it a nice date?" March sounded perhaps a little hesitant as we left the small restaurant and made our way back to his car.

"Remarkable! I think we're pretty good at this," I said proudly.

The ride back to the hotel was just as blissful, with our fingers moving to graze each other whenever he stopped at a red light. By the time we entered the Ritz's lobby, I was pretty much flying among pink unicorns.

Call me a libidinous strumpet who surrenders on the first date, but as we stood in the elevator and I watched the floor numbers flash one after another, I started to think that maybe it was going to happen. We would be sleeping in the same room, after all, and I had sexy lingerie . . . Plus that sadistic beautician from the hotel's spa had seriously cleared the ground down there.

Or maybe I was delusional.

To my great disappointment, once we were alone in the room together, March didn't make any noticeable attempt at ravishing me, choosing to answer a series of text messages instead while I brushed my teeth. Staring at my reflection in the bathroom's large mirror, I found myself back to square one, pondering the same, eternal question: *Now what?*

Maybe I had been a little quick in my projections. The thing was, March had consecutively earned badges for best compliment ever, first toe-curling kiss, and first 100 percent successful date—a grand slam I had taken to entail that classic and non-adventurous intercourse was next on our schedule. Yet now . . . well, nothing was happening, and I had sort of counted on him to take the initiative. Should I go back to the living room and take the matter in my own hands? Did I even have it in me? What if he shared the widespread opinion that sex was illegal before the third date?

Frowning, I mentally reviewed each possible scenario until my brain paused on a particular one that I believed Joy would have approved of, along with most soap opera screenwriters. Taking a calming breath, I exited the bathroom.

March was done with his texting. He had removed the black tuxedo jacket, and the sleeves of his white shirt were rolled up on his forearms—I had come to notice he didn't like it when one wasn't exactly rolled like the other. The ever-present holster was still there, but at this point I gathered he slept with it. I approached him with cautious steps, and a fresh smell I instantly recognized greeted my nostrils. He was doing mints. Mustering my courage, I casually turned my back to him. "Could you help me with my zipper?"

"Certainly."

I struggled to stay cool as his hands made contact with my shoulders. He pulled the zipper slowly, leisurely, and when I felt the black silk part completely and expose the small of my back, I remembered that the slutty pink bra was now visible as well and felt a blistering blush spread on my cheeks and neck.

"Island—" March's voice dropped an octave, and one of his hands moved to rest on my hip. "You didn't need any help for this, right?"

"It always works in the movies," I murmured.

Behind me, I heard a soft chuckle and then nothing but a deafening silence.

March's lips made contact with my neck.

It was so light at first that I thought I had dreamt it: the ghost of a kiss on the pulse beating under my skin, then, a second, this time closer to my shoulder. Soon enough, he was pressing his body against mine, and his left arm had snuck around my waist, steadying me while he devoured the nape of my neck. When he started nibbling the area under my ear, I thought of how cats bite each other by the scruff to establish dominance on a specific area of the couch. I leaned back into him, my ability to stand apparently affected by the intense zings traveling from my scalp, through my chest, and all the way down to my toes. Was I, by any chance . . . being scruffed?

Possibly, since I heard myself mewl, and a low purr answered my vocalizations, as if we were no longer civilized enough to communicate with words. The hand holding my waist tightened while its sibling roamed across my chest, lingering on my breasts until it traveled lower and bunched the front of my skirt with the clear intent of baring my thighs. Call me old-fashioned, but this particular move scared me a bit, because I didn't like the idea of getting undressed like that, in the middle of the room, with all the lights on. If things were headed the way I thought they were, March was supposed to undress me slowly in the dark—with a saxophone solo in the background.

I stopped his hand with mine and spun in his arms to face him. I could feel an idiotic, hormone-fueled grin stretch my cheeks, which were probably red by that point. March, on the opposite, still looked cool as a cucumber. That is, if you were able to overlook the fact that there were wrinkles on his shirt and that his pupils had dilated into black pools swallowing the blue in his eyes. His fingers trailed on my cheek in a tender gesture, and he flashed me a stupid smile that mirrored mine, like we were alone on a deserted island and I was a *fraisier*.

I made up my mind. If I was going to shame my family for at least two generations by sleeping with a man on the first date, I would at least do it right. Stepping away from him, I took his hand and tugged tentatively, steering him toward the bedroom. His brows drew together for a brief instant, and I read uncertainty on his features, but he followed me anyway, his thumb tracing slow circles on my wrist as we entered the bedroom.

I didn't turn any light on; the faint bluish hue coming from the bay window seemed perfect—dark, but not too dark. I squeezed his hand once to steel my resolve, let go, and plopped myself down on the bed, arms alongside my body, still like a sacrificial lamb.

Five seconds of absolute silence ensued, during which March stared at me and blinked a few times. Then he sat on the bed by my side, the city's lights outlining a faint smile on his lips. "Island, why are you planking?"

I felt my entire face ignite with blazing shame. "I was . . . I thought we were . . . Aren't we going to have sex?"

March's Adam's apple moved a little, and I heard him swallow. I held my breath as one of his hands crept up my thigh, caressing it absently. "It wouldn't be a good idea."

I nodded, my hands rising to play with the front of his shirt, without daring to undo the first button.

Right.

Definitively not a good idea.

First date, professional killer, no saxophone. All that jazz—or so to speak.

Except March's fingers disagreed: they hooked in my stocking and started to roll it down slowly. I'm almost positive I heard him swear under his breath, but this is Mr. Clean we're talking about, so it probably never happened. I could hear my heart pounding in my ears, and I think I tugged on his shirt a little. An imperceptible pull in the right direction. Which was all he needed, really. His lips crashed on mine, and he abandoned all pretense of being a gentleman.

I tasted mints, saw stars, and as my arms wrapped around his neck—in an effort to kiss him back like Scarlett O'Hara kissed Rhett Butler in *Gone with the Wind*—I decided that every second spent waiting for Mr. Right had been worth it.

God, even that buzzing in his pants' pocket turned me on.

Wait. What?

He tore his mouth away from mine with an uncharacteristic groan of frustration, and I felt him let go of my other stocking to answer that damn phone. I curled against him and inhaled the faint sandalwood notes clinging to his shirt, my fingers still itching to undo those tantalizing buttons.

March's breath was short and his tone curt as he greeted his caller. "Good evening. You couldn't have picked a worse time to call."

On the other end of the line, whoever had called started a lengthy rant that had the frown on his face deepening by the second.

"Didn't Phyllis send you the manual? . . . Configure the app? What app? . . . Is this a joke? Do you really think it's a crucial feature? . . . No . . . No! The manual said your Twitter login should be preceded by an *underscore* . . . Yes, then the password . . . What do you mean it's not working? . . . No! Don't test it! . . . All right, I'll be there in fifteen minutes. Stop touching it. Don't even look at it!"

After he had hung up, I looked up at him with glazed eyes. "Who was that?"

"My little nephew."

I raised a skeptical eyebrow. "You have nephews?"

"Dozens of them; I love children." He sighed. "I'm sorry, biscuit. I have to—"

"Yes, I heard. You have to go. And you won't tell me where," I summarized accusingly.

A brief kiss silenced my protests. "I need you to stay here. The room is safe, and I won't be long."

"But I—"

Another kiss. Why was I getting the feeling that sweet March was the same dissimulative guy as douchey March, only with much more convincing weapons? I straightened up, a frown replacing my enamored gaze. He read me effortlessly and brushed his thumb against my lips before I could voice my discontent.

"I trust you; we've established that. Do *you* trust me?"

What was I supposed to reply? When I had not only lured the guy into bed minutes ago, but also relinquished my stockings to him!

"I trust you, March." I sighed, squeezing his hand and looking at him in the eyes. Despite my best efforts, though, it sounded more like *I want to trust you, but I'm not sure I can . . . and maybe you can't trust me either.*

March nodded and pressed one last absent kiss to my forehead before he got up from the bed. I watched him retrieve his jacket from the long wardrobe, locked the suite's door, and within seconds, he was gone.

I felt wet. And silly.

TWENTY-SIX

The Case

"Why did Tyler hide from me that he was a billionaire? Why did he pretend to be a mere cowboy? Are things ever what they seem?"

—Stacey Maverick, *Texas Billionaire in Disguise*

March eventually came back at some point during the night, but I had gone to bed and didn't hear him. So much for my glorious sexual canoodling prospects.

I woke up to the sound of his voice and the feeling of his fingers caressing my hair. He was kneeling beside my bed, already dressed, and he smelled of coffee and aftershave. As my vision cleared, I registered his face, so close to mine I could count the little crow's-feet at the corners of his eyes. I was tempted to kiss him, but fortunately, *Cosmo* had raised me well, and I knew that I was a vile creature cursed with all sorts of icky bodily manifestations, including, but not limited to, morning breath.

He rose to a standing position and leaned against the wall opposite to the bed with his arms crossed, allowing me some space to fully shake off the morning's drowsiness. "Did you sleep well?"

I let out an affirmative grunt in response, sat up, and stretched, stirred by the pleasant aroma of toast and eggs floating in the air. Once out of bed, I wobbled my way to the living room. There, on a low table facing the sofa, an appetizing breakfast tray rested. All I had on were a tank top and a pair of panties, and I realized that March was following my every move with a slight gleam in his eyes. The idea that he might be checking out my body was equal parts embarrassing and flattering: I decided that I could learn to enjoy it.

"I'm sorry for what happened last night," he said, sitting on an armchair across from me as I wolfed down my breakfast with a cup of hot cocoa.

I looked up from my cup. "You mean . . . sorry for what you did, or sorry for leaving like that?"

"A little bit of both, I suppose."

"Ah." I made no effort to conceal my disappointment. "Do you still think it's too soon? Or too fast?" I asked with a dejected sigh, pouring myself a glass of orange juice.

He leaned back in the soft leather cushions and appraised me with impish eyes. "I think we need to finish what we started . . ."

I held my breath.

"And find that diamond." He winked.

I gulped down my glass of orange juice, slammed it back on the tray like a whiskey shot, and rose from the couch to get ready. "You're awful. If Dries manages to kill me and I die a virgin, I'll come back to haunt you."

Miyamoto Bank was located on a small artificial island in the Tokyo Bay. Not my favorite area of the city, I have to say: too cold, industrial, filled with big companies' headquarters. The round glass building was sandwiched between the Sumida river—which emptied into the bay—and a large, empty square of lawn I assumed had been meant as some sort of minimalistic garden. It was an unusual choice of location for a bank, but I figured that if they welcomed clients like my mom, it was a good thing they were close to the sea. That way, if shit hit the fan, they could all jump into a boat and make their escape.

March parked in front of the building, and we were about to get inside when his phone buzzed in his pocket. He frowned at the caller ID and picked up. "Good morning . . . Again, this is not the best time . . . You know who to call for this . . . No one cares that you brought a bathing suit! This is *not* Cancun! . . . I'll keep you updated if there's any emergency." He hung up with an aggravated sigh.

"Was that your little nephew again?" I asked, my eyes narrowing in interest.

"Yes."

I shook my head as we passed the door. "Terrible liar . . ."

Once we were standing in the lobby, my eyes widened. "Wow, I bet you like it here!"

He shrugged nonchalantly, but I didn't miss the slight twitch of his lips. Of course he liked it. Everything was white and impossibly clean, like an alien spaceship. The walls, the floor, the long desk behind which an elegant lady waited for potential visitors: they were all covered with the same pristine stone-like material, the only touch of color a couple of irises in a glass vase on the counter.

Combing my hair with my nervous fingers, I smiled at the woman. "Good morning, I think my mother had a safe at Miyamoto, under the name Léa Chaptal, maybe. Could you check that? We would like to access it," I asked, praying that my mom hadn't used a stupid alias like March did all the time. If she had, we were done.

Behind me, March waited as the long-haired girl started typing on a keyboard under the counter. Her eyes skimmed through some data, and she raised her head. "Mrs. Chaptal never possessed any safe here," she announced with a slight crease of her brow.

Blood rushed to my temples. "Are you sure? I . . . It was my understanding that she did, and I was given a safe number."

An expression of shock registered on the attendant's ivory face, but she quickly schooled it into a courteous mask. "No safe was ever registered to her name. Perhaps you should discuss the issue with her account manager."

"Miss Chaptal will do so."

I looked up at the same time that I felt March's hand on my shoulder. I nodded to confirm his statement.

"Do you have an ID?" she asked curtly.

I froze.

Why, yes, of course I have an ID. I'm Mrs. May!

Before I had the time to stutter some lame excuse, I felt March push me aside and pull a passport from his inner pocket. "There it is. Thank God I think about these things. One day she'll forget her own name!"

He patted my shoulder affectionately, and I stared up at him, winded. Just how many fake passports had he purchased from Paulie? Obviously one with my real name, among others. Did I also get one for each month of the year? The young woman took "my" passport, and instructed us to wait while she made a brief call to somebody named Mr. Sakai.

A few seconds later, the doors of an elevator opened to reveal a tall, black-haired guy with a navy-blue suit and a short beard. Mr. Sakai didn't look one bit Japanese. He gave me a friendly smile and greeted us . . . in French. "Bienvenue, Mademoiselle Chaptal. Je suis Patrick Sakai, c'est moi qui m'occupe des comptes de votre maman, je vais vous accompagner à la salle des coffres." *Welcome, Miss Chaptal. My name is Patrick Sakai, and I'm in charge of your mama's accounts here. I'll take you to the vault.*

I blinked and returned his handshake. He acknowledged March with a curt bow and gestured for us to follow him into the elevator. As we did, I noticed March turning around to slant the receptionist a suspicious glance before entering the cart. She was on the phone, and when their gazes met, she seemed a little unnerved and jerked her eyes away.

As the elevator took us to the eleventh floor, I examined Sakai's round features with curiosity. "Are you Franco-Japanese?"

He nodded with a big grin. "Yes! I miss good cheese when I'm here in Tokyo!" Then he went on in an apologetic tone. "Please excuse my young colleague. Léa's safe is one of those we don't register in our database. I'm sure you understand that exclusive clients can have . . . exclusive needs."

"I guess . . ." No. I did not understand, to be honest. But the safe was here, and I could breathe again, so I just walked along.

Upon exiting the elevator, Sakai turned back to look at me. "Back when she registered the safe, Léa was still in the process of reorganizing her accounts and authorizing you to access them once you reached your majority. It's been a long time, but have you been able to read the will since? Or would you like a summary of the assets currently being held or managed?"

I shook my head, a cold sweat breaking on my skin. "No . . . I've seen the notary, but there've been . . . um . . . complications."

March came to the rescue. "M. Étienne was a little swarmed and could not find the time to complete all the necessary paperwork. His work is *killing* him. Perhaps you could provide Miss Chaptal with a written list once we're done?"

He gave a little nod. "All right, we'll stop in my office afterward to print your account statements."

I thanked Sakai, and he led us through a series of white hallways until we were standing in front of a massive circular security door equipped with a fingerprint authentication system. I watched in amazement as he pressed his hand on what looked like a glass screen that flashed with a bright green light.

The heavy door opened to a shorter corridor that led to a second door of the same type. We followed him into the small passage, and something clicked in my mind. I looked up at March, my voice down to a whisper. "There must be metal detectors in here. Aren't you worried that—"

"I know. That's why I'm not carrying any weapon, Island. Everybody knows that there are no such things as ceramic and polymer firearms," he whispered back while Sakai unlocked a second, foot-thick security door. I cast March a questioning glance, and the wink he gave me told me that there *were* such things as ceramic and polymer guns.

"On y est! Le Saint des Saints!" *Here we are! The Holy of Holies!* Sakai announced, turning to us.

All those Uncle Scrooge comics are a goddamn travesty: there was no money pool, and no complimentary towels in Miyamoto Bank's vault, only a vast circular room with a high dome ceiling, and hundreds of shiny black doors on the otherwise pristine walls.

I pulled the crumpled paper with the safe's number from my pocket and showed it to Sakai. "2120. Is it—"

March spotted the safe on the opposite wall; he pointed to it before our host had the time to answer. Sakai nodded in confirmation, and as we crossed the room to examine it, I realized that there was a tactile screen merged with the door's sleek surface. It lit up when I grazed it, revealing a row of twenty empty squares and a touch keyboard whose virtual keys glowed with a soft bluish hue.

Awesome.

Twenty-digit code, numbers and letters: only a few *billion* possible combinations. I cast a distressed look at March, shaking my head to indicate that I had no idea where to start.

"Is everything all right?"

Behind us, Sakai's gentle voice made me jump. March and I both turned to him, amicable smiles plastered on our faces. Better not let that guy guess that we didn't have the safe's combination, and in the unlikely event that we'd manage to open it, no need for him to know what was inside either. I gave him my trademark big sad eyes, those same eyes that had saved Antonio's life—although admittedly they hadn't been much use with Creepy-hat. "Yes, we're good. This is little private, though. Could you give us a moment?"

He hesitated for a moment before retreating into the short corridor leading to the vault. There, he turned his back to us, the rhythmic tapping of his foot echoing faintly in the vault.

Once we were safely out of Sakai's sight, March placed his hands on my shoulders, massaging them gently. "Relax and think, Island. She wouldn't have set a combination you couldn't figure out."

Oh God. Killing people and kissing weren't his only skills. He was also an accomplished back rubber. I closed my eyes, feeling the tension in my shoulders ebb under the pressure of his talented fingers. I just hoped he wouldn't send me the bill.

Now, if you had to pick a twenty-digit code that would be both incredibly hard and incredibly easy to guess, what would you pick? Perhaps something involving the position of each letter of the alphabet? No, twenty-six letters, too many possibilities. I racked my brains for things that could be associated with the number. Fingers and toes? It could be, but how would that translate into a code? Dammit, I couldn't think, even with the help of March's backrub.

Even years after her death, my mother was still challenging me. I sighed at the memory of our games together, and how she would teach me how to play Find the Lady and bend the cards right, or napalm me at chess but always explain all her moves afterward so I could learn them. I hadn't discovered Nutella until the age of thirteen because she had decreed I would only be allowed to have some if I could reproduce her favorite trick—solving a Rubik's Cube with my hands behind my back.

So little Nutella, so many tears, so much frustration, and years later, I was exactly in the same place, except this was no Rubik's Cube, just a fricking twenty-digit number.

A twenty-digit number . . .

A huge-ass number. One that conjured hours spent in the kitchen moping as I watched my mom eat Nutella spread on a slice of bread with a smug look on her face.

I raised my hand to type the first digit. Even if my guess was wrong, I had no other idea anyway. With a long exhale, I started filling the empty fields one by one.

43252003274489856500

When the safe's door clicked, I nearly had a heart attack, and I felt March's grip on my shoulders tighten. I craned my neck to look up at him over my shoulder, both terrified and excited.

"What is that number?" The astonishment was clear in his voice.

"The number of possible permutations for a classic Rubik's Cube: forty-three quintillion or so."

March let out a whistle of admiration as I pulled the heavy black door. There was a big metal case in the safe, which he took out carefully. I noticed the way he used both hands to support the case while carrying it to a small desk that stood against the room's wall: whatever rested in there was heavy. He undid the clasps sealing the case and opened it. My heart skipped a beat. There it was. Uncut, but still shiny, with a few well-defined angles and looking every bit like a rough block of glass.

March and I were looking at four billion dollars.

Yes, four. You read that right.

There were two identical Cullinans in my mother's case.

TWENTY-SEVEN

The Flowers

"An army of a thousand men couldna stop me if I'm fighting for ye, my love. I swear on my kilt that I'll return to ye!"

—Diane MacRoth, *Claimed by the Impetuous Highlander*

So. As I was saying, two Cullinans, and hopefully, at least one genuine diamond among them. I leaned conspiringly toward March, my voice down to a whisper. "That knife, the one you have on your leg, what is it made of?"

"Ceramic."

"Wow, I thought they only made those for cooking!"

"Very resistant, won't trigger metal detectors." He shrugged.

"Good." I nodded. "Then if one of these diamonds is fake, there's a good chance we'll know."

"Scratch test?"

"Yup, go for it."

Within seconds, March had bent to his side and produced that small incurved knife with the black blade—which reminded me of that poor guy at the Rose Paradise, and I cringed a little. He grabbed one of the stones, steadied it with his left hand, and proceeded to scrape the knife's blade against the smooth surface. There was no suspense. A visible scratch mark immediately appeared, like a white wound on the translucent material.

"Glass, very likely," I concluded.

Taking the second stone, he carefully repeated the same experiment, except this time the shiny material resisted the blade admirably. We exchanged knowing looks. Two billion dollars' worth of flawless natural diamond. That Queen person March worked for was going to be happy. "Well, that was an easy shell game!"

"No. The rules specify that you need three shells to make it a shell game," March observed.

I shook my head with a smile as he concealed the knife back under his pants leg. Sakai turned to check on us; March slammed the case shut before our host could see what was inside and took it with him. I pushed the safe's door closed.

Sakai led us out of the vault, and we were almost at the elevator when March stopped in front of one of the hallway's windows to look down at the street. On the Harumi Dori, two black cars and a white van had stopped, the sleek black surface of their tinted windows reflecting the building's glass facade. Several men jumped out of the vehicles. Black jackets, sunglasses. Those were *not* Jehovah's Witnesses touring the neighborhood. I watched them stride toward the bank, and one of them gestured to the others to separate into two groups. March's eyes narrowed, and he stopped me before I could enter the elevator. "We'll take the stairs."

Sakai shot us a suspicious look. "What's going on?"

"Ring the alarm, order everyone to go to the top floors and stay there. Don't follow us."

I think our host was about to protest and say something like, "Who died and made you my boss?" but seeing March fish several dark gray objects from his pockets and start to assemble a gun before our eyes,

Sakai closed his mouth, nodded, and then ran down the white hallway before disappearing behind a set of French doors. A few seconds later, the shrill sound of the alarm started echoing rhythmically in the building.

I looked at March, panic rising in my chest. "Do you think they're here for the Cullinan? Did they follow us?"

"I didn't think I had been tailed, but I'm willing to bet that young lady downstairs is the one who called them."

He took my hand and dragged me down the hallway. I couldn't keep up with his pace, and most of the time, it felt like my feet were hovering over the floor. We passed a few worried employees whispering to one another while hurrying in the direction of the elevator. Once the floor appeared to be deserted, March pushed open the heavy door leading to an emergency staircase.

As soon as the door had slammed behind us, he handed me the case. "I'm going to need you to carry this." Then, he removed his bulletproof jacket and offered it to me.

I tried to push it away and back into his hands. "March, it's a bad idea—"

Ignoring my plea, he retrieved his cell phone from the jacket's inner pocket, slid it into his own jeans' back pocket, and helped me put the oversized garment on. He then placed a hand on my shoulder, locking his blue gaze with mine. "Listen to me, Island. We *have* to exit this building. We don't have much time, and the men in those cars are going to shoot at us. Do you trust me?"

I nodded, my throat tight.

"Good. You stay behind me, move only when I tell you to, and hold on to that case. I'll take care of the rest."

I wanted to nod again but, instead, gasped when I heard the sound of a door blasting open eleven floors below. Those guys weren't stupid. They were going to check the stairs first. March flattened against the concrete wall while climbing footsteps echoed all the way up to our floor. "Stay here and wait."

I fought tears of anguish when I watched him proceed downward until I couldn't see him anymore. For a while, all I could hear were those men's footsteps getting closer and closer . . .

Until there was a loud thud. I registered swearing in English and Japanese, and I heard gunshots two, maybe three floors below. I covered my ears in terror and huddled against the wall, trembling like a leaf. Growls and brief screams echoed as someone got slammed several times against the staircase's railing, sending ominous vibrations through the cheap metal all the way to where I stood.

The footsteps resumed, except this time it seemed to be only one pair of feet. Terrified by the prospect that they might not be March's, I flattened myself against the wall and raised the case above my head with trembling hands. Whoever was coming up would get a two-billion-dollar nose job if he tried to get me.

A tall silhouette emerged from the staircase. I lunged forward, but the case was stopped by a steady hand before it could do any damage.

"Come here, biscuit."

My heart skipped a beat. March flashed me a reassuring smile and extended his hand to me.

I couldn't help but steal a worried glance at the blood on his shirt. He caught the direction of my gaze as we ran down the stairs and said, "Not mine."

Not his, indeed. Two floors below, we passed the bodies of three men. Two Asian-looking guys lying on the floor with their necks twisted at an odd angle, and a third one whose short blond hair was covered in blood—probably the same blood that was smeared on the railing's metal and all over March's shirt. I gathered that those terrible vibrations I had heard were the product of his skull hitting the railing over and over . . .

When we reached the second floor, March stopped me and leaned against the heavy fire door connecting the staircase to the rest of the floor, whispering to me. "They're all waiting on the first floor for their reconnaissance team to return." He checked his watch. "It's been almost five minutes. They're going to send more men in less than a minute. For a couple of seconds, they'll be entirely focused on the first floor door. That's when we'll go."

I gasped. "But how will we leave the second floor?" I asked, my hands tightening on the metal case I needed to hold on to at any cost.

"Did you notice the mezzanine when we entered?"

To be honest, I hadn't taken the time to scan for all possible exits when we had first entered the building—which is probably why March was a professional killer and I wasn't—but as he mentioned it, I pictured that huge spaceship lobby again. I nodded, remembering a long mezzanine with a nice glass floor that overlooked the hall and allowed direct access to the building's second floor via a spiral staircase.

"This emergency exit opens on the mezzanine. On my signal, you go in and run to the spiral staircase on your left. Don't go down into the lobby. Hide behind the coffee machine near the stairs until I'm done."

Damn, I hadn't noticed the coffee machine either. March got up, squeezed my shoulders, and racked the slide of his gun, the sharp clicking sound causing a painful shiver to course down my back.

His guess had been correct.

Beneath our feet, the first floor lobby's fire door slammed open with a loud noise, and March shoved me through the second floor door at the same time. I landed on the glass mezzanine, but I was too petrified to run as he had ordered me to. He dragged me across the translucent floor and sent me sliding across the mezzanine and toward the coffee machine like a hockey puck, before the remaining men in the lobby realized we were no longer in the stairs and started shooting at us.

I screamed as several bullets hit the glass structure. It didn't break, but delicate flowers made of cracked glass appeared on the underside of the thick transparent slabs. Under any other circumstances I would have found them beautiful, but people were shooting at me, and one such flower had just bloomed a few feet away from the coffee machine with a sinister cracking sound.

I could see everything through the mezzanine, and it made the ordeal much worse than it had been back in the stairs. Their priority appeared to be killing March—something easier said than done, as our assailants soon discovered. He had shot two guys while running down the spiral staircase, and below me, I could see that he was now hiding behind the white desk. Three men remained, along with that treacherous receptionist, who was cowering in a corner of the hall, much like me. Near the elevator, the bodies of two security guards lay still. I gathered that Sakai had tried to call them, only to have those poor guys killed upon reaching the lobby.

I looked down to see that one of the three men, a bald Japanese guy, was holding an automatic rifle. He aimed at the desk and fired several rounds, perhaps in hope that a few bullets would make it through. I closed my eyes and begged Murphy's law to cut March some slack, because I was wearing the bulletproof jacket and he wasn't. March seemed to be still alive, waiting for an opening, but I was getting worried that the damn desk wouldn't resist much longer.

I came up with an idea.

Opening the case with trembling fingers, I grabbed the fake Cullinan and started crawling away from the vending machine. I kept whispering to myself that I was going to be okay: The bullets those guys had fired obviously couldn't make it through those thick glass slabs, and as long as I stayed close to the wall, they wouldn't have the right angle to fire at me with a direct shot.

Except I was already halfway across the mezzanine, now perfectly visible to all of our friends, when I started to rethink the shortcomings of my plan to throw the fake stone at them so they would try to catch it and leave March alone.

"Island, go back and do *not* move from there!" March's roar was answered by another round of bullets in the white material of the desk. Another guy moved under the mezzanine to fire a few more bullets at the glass, creating ominous flowers underneath my hands and knees. My legs were trembling so badly I could hardly move, be it either to go ahead with my crappy plan or back the hell away as March had ordered me to.

I recoiled in horror as the young black-haired man who had just shot into the mezzanine's glass ran up the flight of stairs and toward me. March seized a moment of inattention from the man's colleagues as they watched me crawl backward frantically through the glass, and moved away from the desk to shoot one of them. The bald guy with the automatic rifle was still standing, however, and March had to run for cover again behind a pillar as yet another round was fired in his direction.

Despite the situation, I still trusted we would somehow manage to escape, since March was now closer to the spiral staircase than ever. All that was left to do was to take on these two guys, and perhaps bitch-slap that receptionist who was still whimpering in fear behind another white pillar at the other end of the lobby.

I heard more gunshots, and I realized that March was trying to stop the asshole coming for me from reaching the top of the stairs, but he couldn't get any closer because that Cue Ball guy with the rifle was still waiting for an opportunity to kill him.

I thought that young man with the gun was my biggest problem . . . until it became clear that even though the glass I was crawling on was super thick, too many flowers had bloomed across it already, and they were too close to each other. *Way too close.* That flower under my right hand and the ones near my feet were already spreading, and sharp cracking sounds announced that the glass mezzanine had taken all the shooting it could.

Crack.

Crack . . .

Fuck.

I felt several tiles of the transparent floor give way under me with a terrible noise, and I fell through the mezzanine. Brilliant shards were flying around me, and for a fleeting second, I anticipated the contact of my body with the white tiling of the ground floor, pictured my bones shattering in the fall. Panic raced through my veins, but the pain itself never came: that Cue Ball guy momentarily abandoned his quest to kill March and lunged to catch me—and what he believed to be the real Ghost Cullinan—in his arms.

I crashed face-first into his gray jacket, smelling tobacco and detergent in the fabric. There was glass in my hair, some minor cuts on my hands and on my neck, and a bloody gash on Cue Ball's forehead—which I assumed was the result of a bigger shard of glass cutting him. I was in a state of shock, still clutching the fake stone, and I saw March running toward us in the debris of the half-destroyed mezzanine. Cue Ball dropped me like a rag doll to fire at him again, and all the sounds around me were replaced by a loud buzzing in my ears. It was all too much: too much noise, too much fear. My chest constricted violently as I saw March dive to the floor just in time to avoid ending his career right there and then, a few feet away from me.

I gathered March had to be out of ammo, since he hadn't fired his gun in a while and seemed to be looking for cover instead. The young Asian guy who had been trying to catch me had joined us, and he dragged me kicking and screaming toward the white van while Cue Ball finished emptying his magazine in an attempt to kill March, or at least keep him at bay. I screamed my lungs out as the younger man threw me brutally into the back of the van, and the last thing I saw before the door slammed shut was March running toward us.

As soon as the van had started, that young guy gave me a resounding slap before tearing the stone from my hands. Dizzy from the blow, I scrambled away, and he watched me as we drove through Tokyo in the dark, cramped space.

The vehicle appeared to be moving fast, and it shook a lot, as if the driver were being chased. I had nothing to steady myself and kept rolling from one side of van to the other every time we turned. Meanwhile, the young guy's smooth features contorted in an anxious snarl as he leaned against the van's back door, gun still in hand. There, he moved one of the black plastic panels covering the doors' windows to look at the street.

I focused on the way his bony fingers tightened around the handle of his gun, the sweat on his temple, the deep frown wrinkling his brow, and assumed that whatever he was looking at displeased him. The vehicle took a series of violent turns at some point, which sent my head slamming against the van's metallic wall so hard that I nearly passed out, until it seemed to slow down somewhat: we now seemed to be driving smoothly to wherever these guys were taking me.

That bitchy youth with the frown relaxed; his fingers loosened their iron grip on his gun. We were no longer being followed . . . and, dammit, I had just been kidnapped for the third time in four days!

TWENTY-EIGHT

The Master

"Dayne was so powerful, so perfect and intimidating, Chelsee
thought as she was led through his humongous mansion, entirely
decorated with black marble."

—Muffin Thorpe, *Slave to the Rich and Sexy Vampire*

The van eventually stopped and my captors dragged me out, but I
lost my balance and fell to the ground. The feeling of the hard pave-
ment under my palms and the sight of blood on my fingers helped me
focus. I had earned a few cuts during the mezzanine's collapse, but I
was otherwise okay. The glass skyscrapers and the cold atmosphere of
the street felt familiar. We were somewhere in Tokyo's business district,
Ōtemachi, probably on the Eita Dori. Still carrying the stone, Cue Ball
hauled me back up, and I noticed for the first time that he shaved his
head to conceal a receding hairline. Bitchy-youth seemed to be more
fortunate, with his mop of thick black hair, but those angular features
were anything but inviting.

We entered an impressive stone building that was a strange mix of
modern and gothic architecture. The first floors seemed rather ancient,

with a sculpted facade that reminded me a little of the Doge's Palace in Venice, and a pair of nineteenth-century-style lanterns flanking a wide entrance. The rest of the structure, however, was more recent, made up of pure, straight lines and a sea of glass that reached too high for me to make out the top of the building from where I stood. We made our way across what looked more like a stone-and-glass cathedral than a lobby, and once in the elevator, the youngest of my captors used a key to lift us to the twenty-sixth and last floor. The elevator's steel doors opened to reveal a dozen tough-looking guys guarding a long hallway.

Cue Ball shoved me forward as one the guards opened a set of large doors, revealing a double staircase plunging down into a bright and vast living room. I realized that there was, in fact, no twenty-fifth floor. It had been merged with the twenty-sixth to create a penthouse of epic proportions. The windows I had seen from outside formed an invisible wall that gave me the impression I was standing inside a giant cube, one side of which showcased a breathtaking view of the city. I was led down the minimalist black staircase and into the room, where more guards awaited.

There, waiting for us near a white sofa that seemed straight out of *Star Trek*, was a tall man in an elegant gray suit. He walked to me, his lips stretching to reveal a carnivorous grin. Now, I know it's a stupid idea, but I've always assumed that everyone who possesses the same type of gap-tooth I have is a nice person, like we all belonged to a secret gap-tooth club presided over by Lauren Hutton. That guy's smile, however, was challenging this theory. I recoiled, but Cue Ball stood behind me, blocking any possible escape.

"Pleased to meet you again, Island. People call me—"

"Dries," I murmured before he had the time to serve me the same introduction March had days ago, down to the intonation.

His deep voice petrified me. For a moment I was fifteen again, huddled under the covers of my bed while he left my mom's room, bidding her goodnight with the same posh accent that spoke of a privileged Afrikaner background.

"You're the man from Pretoria . . . the one who used to visit at night," I said, suddenly struggling for air.

He let out a dry laugh. "I see you remember me. We're practically family after all."

I stared at him, my mind conjuring memories of a broad-shouldered shadow. He was still buff, and his sharp features were easy enough on the eyes, but his brown hair was graying, and the lines on his tanned face and hands were proof that even powerful assholes couldn't cheat time. Now a grown woman myself, I could see what my mother had found so attractive, but those eyes . . . How had she ever been able to trust them? They were almost the same hazel as mine, but the golden flecks in their center made them seem yellow, and somehow, they made me physically ill.

"Are you going to kill me?" I was amazed at how calm I sounded, given the situation.

My host took a few steps forward until he was standing too close. He smelled spicy, like sandalwood maybe. His scent stirred the same kind of unpleasant feeling inside me that his eyes did, so I tried to focus on his hands instead and counted the tiny moles there. Much like me, Dries was probably constantly wondering if—or when—he would develop skin cancer.

"I was in fact hoping to have a pleasant meal and, who knows, perhaps get to know you better." He had tucked a strand of hair behind my ear as he said this. I felt a chill travel from the nape of my neck all the way down to my back.

"I doubt you really want to spend quality time with me," I muttered, squirming away from his touch.

A deep baritone laugh filled the room. "God, you're exactly like your dear mother. Why wouldn't I enjoy your company?"

I pointed my chin in Cue Ball's direction. "Tell him to give me the bag. I'm gonna show you why."

Raising an eyebrow, he nodded for his henchman to hand me the black satchel he had been carrying. As I pulled out the heavy stone from the bag, I wondered if it was the same feeling people got before jumping in front of a train—the feeling that it's game over anyway, that it no longer matters if they live or die.

I looked at Dries as I raised the Cullinan over my head. His eyes lit up, and he moved to stop me, but I jumped back before he could touch me and hurled the fake diamond to the ground with all my strength. It hit the smooth concrete with a loud crash, shattering in thousands of shimmering shards.

I saw the bare hate in his eyes.

"Checkmate. Looks like she didn't want anyone to have it, not even me!"

He might have been an asshole, but he did possess some serious self-control, I had to give him that. He didn't even blink. He merely took a deep breath and let out a low chuckle. "Oh . . . you're quite something, little Miss Chaptal."

As he said this, he cracked his knuckles, and I thought he was getting ready to beat the crap out of me—I mostly worried about my teeth—but he didn't. He pulled out a phone from his pocket and dialed a number. Someone answered, and he spoke in an icy voice. "Transfer me to him. No questions. *Now*." Whoever was on the other end of the line seemed unimpressed by Dries's display of virile authority, which prompted him to switch to hateful baboon mode. "Listen to me, bitch, pass him to me *immediately* if you don't want to find your son's heart on your doorstep tomorrow."

I shuddered at the explicit threat and listened, stiff, as he greeted his interlocutor in Afrikaans. "Goeie môre, broer." *Good morning, brother.* Brother? March? If so, the woman he had called a bitch must be Phyllis. "I give you thirty minutes to bring me the real diamond. I'll send you my instructions. Try not to run away this time . . . *of ek gee haar 'n forty-five."*

I frowned as Dries hung up. There was a part he didn't want me to understand. Too bad for him that the sticky gruel of Dutch, Flemish, and Afrikaans I had stored somewhere in my brain as a child was enough to get the general idea. Said idea being that if March didn't bring him the Ghost Cullinan, he intended to give me a . . .

"What's a forty-five?" I tried to sound badass and almost uninterested, but believe me, it wasn't easy.

"I thought you already knew." He smirked, pulling me into a loose embrace and tracing the nape of my neck with his thumb. "We cut between the fourth and fifth vertebras. You'll keep the ability to breathe on your own. Everything else is lost."

As he said this, I thought of Rislow, who had called Dries March's master before getting forty-fived himself. Nice. I can't say I looked forward to becoming quadriplegic, but I couldn't stand the idea of cowering in front of this bastard, so I summoned what little courage I had left.

"You're wasting your time. He's gonna give the real Cullinan to the Queen. Then she'll pay him to forty-five *you*, asshole!"

Damn, Rislow had made me tough. Not super tough like March, but enough to face my demise with some semblance of dignity . . . I hoped. Dries laughed again and pressed me closer, his lips grazing my earlobe. "Perhaps. You'll be my consolation prize then, little Island. I've never fucked both a mother and her daughter."

I'm not sure what happened to me . . . I flung my hand at his face, clawing at his cheek and hair. I didn't want to slap him; I wanted to hurt him, to fucking destroy him. It was like a bomb had exploded inside me and shards of pain, hate, and horror were scattering throughout my body in the same way the glass replica had disintegrated itself upon hitting the floor. For all my rage, I didn't accomplish much: only a couple of faint scratch marks on his cheekbone. His hair got tousled too, so that was something.

I quickly regretted my move, however, as he grabbed my throat, applying sufficient pressure to remind me who was gonna destroy whom in this evil lair. "Careful, Island . . . You won't like me when I'm angry."

Again, he wasted no time in regaining his composure. Shaking his head in a way that reminded me of March, he directed his gaze to a pair of open French doors that led to a dining room. "Would you like to join me for lunch while we wait for our friend?"

TWENTY-NINE

The Puppet

"No, Ramirez! I'll never be your sex doll! I'd rather die than belong to you."

—Kerry-Lee Storm, *The Cost of Rica*

Dries cultivated a sense of aristocratic entitlement and profound douchebaggery that had me wondering how a "Jesuit" like March had ever been able to look up to a guy like him. The mile-long glass table and the huge black Renaissance dining chairs already hinted at a seriously inflated ego, but the crystal tableware was the finishing touch. All he needed was a fat white Persian cat, and I would have been eating lunch with Ernst Blofeld. A silent and uptight Japanese butler crossed the room and served each of us a glass of what I assumed to be some super expensive wine. I didn't touch mine because I feared I had the one with grape juice and polonium.

With a ferocious smile, Dries cradled his glass in his upturned hand and caressed the long stem. "So, how do you like my creation?"

I frowned. "Your creation? Are you talking about March?"

"Straight from Cape Town's gutter . . . and look where he is now."

I forced myself to look into his hazel eyes. "You're the one who taught him how to kill people?"

He raised his glass, toasting me. "I taught him much more than that. When I met March, he was a nobody, a small-time thug breaking into houses for a little cash. His father was a British dealer who sold mandrax in the slums of Lavender Hill . . . and his mother was dead, I believe."

As I processed his words, a few pieces of the puzzle that was March came together. March was of British descent, so my guess about his accent had been half correct. Now, mandrax . . . I frowned, scraping at the memories of my brief stay in Pretoria. It was a popular drug, some kind of barbiturate equivalent that made people all squishy and stupid, like pot. So March was basically the son of a small-time British drug dealer and had grown up without a mother. Not much of a fairytale.

March's words when we had discussed his educational background—or lack thereof—rang in my ears. "He mentioned he went to jail. Is it because of the housebreaking?"

Dries smelled the wine in his glass and closed his eyes in apparent delight. "I'm surprised he told you about that. He served nine months at Pollsmoor when he was seventeen. Did he tell you how he got caught? I love this story!"

I shook my head, glancing at the Japanese butler from the corner of my eye. He was waiting with two plates covered with ornate silver domes.

Dries took a swig and went on. "One of the prize idiots he worked with tipped a jar of marbles in a child's bedroom. They scattered all over the place, and March lost it. When the cops picked him up, he was still crawling on all fours to put them back in the jar!"

I pictured March as a young boy growing up in poverty and left to cope alone with his disorder. My chest tightened. It wasn't funny at all; it was fricking sad. "Did you meet him in prison?"

"No, shortly after he got out. I heard about him from a 28 who had met him in jail . . . I thought that a piece of white trash who had spent nearly a year in Pollsmoor and had not only made it out alive but AIDS-free might have some sort of potential."

My eyebrows shot up. "AIDS-free . . . ?"

After his butler was done serving the two plates, revealing a small pile of caviar and a couple of mini-blinis, Dries resumed his explanations. "The 28s are a gang infiltrating pretty much every single prison in South Africa. Those gentlemen's specialty is 'slow puncture,' which consists in having a man raped by AIDS-infected inmates. It was the new hype back then."

My breath hitched in my throat. "What the . . . thank God, March didn't—"

He topped a blini with some caviar and went on. "I never cared much about that part of his life. He was obedient and fit for training. Nothing else mattered."

I hated the way Dries talked about March, like he had been nothing but a dog, a blank canvas rather than an actual human being. My fingers itched with the need to stab him with my fork. Staring down at the glistening caviar that looked like a heap of boogers on my plate, I squeezed my eyes shut and slammed my palms hard against the cold glass. Dries was trying to mess with me. And it was working.

Glancing at my untouched food, he gave me a knowing smile. "Am I unsettling you? Are you worried that March won't come for you?"

I pushed the plate away and got up from my chair under the wary scrutiny of his guards at the other end of the room. "He won't. There's no point."

He shook his head, leaving the table as well. "No. Trust an old Lion. March will answer my invitation, and he will show up with the diamond. Aren't you hungry anymore?"

"No, I'm not! And you shouldn't be either. If March comes here, it will be to kill you and all these guys!"

Dries flashed me a confident grin and gestured to the *Star Trek* couch. "He's never going to betray me. I'm the one who carved him."

I sat on the white cushions and looked up at him. "You mean that lion? Do you have one too?"

"Yes," he confirmed as he sat near me again.

I inched away. "You say he'll never go against you, but he left the Lions."

Dries stayed silent for a few seconds until he pulled me toward him, forcing us into a fake embrace that made me want to scream. "He did . . . because of you," he murmured, taking one of my hands in his larger one and leaning even closer to smell my hair.

Creep factor at being petted by Dries, on a scale of one to ten: twenty.

Shock factor at hearing that March had supposedly left the Lions because of me, on a scale of one to ten: *forty*.

I jumped on the soft cushions, pulling the hand he had touched as if I had been burned. "What?"

Dries leaned back on the comfortable sofa, looking at me from the corner of his eye. "After Léa's death . . . after you, he decided to fly solo."

My chest exploded with pain at Dries's words, and my scalp prickled in growing panic. "What do you mean? Did March . . . *No!* He didn't kill my mother! He didn't!"

"Who said he did?"

A wave of incredible relief washed over me.

March hadn't killed her. Yet he had been there; he had been involved. In truth, I had suspected he was hiding something for a while—felt it when I looked into his eyes, when he touched me as if committing a sin he was powerless to resist. There was this bond between us, which I didn't fully understand, but I knew it went far beyond our non-encounter at my dad's Christmas party.

Confident that he had my full attention, Dries scooted closer again and wrapped an arm around my shoulder, which I tried my best to ignore. "I was in the ideal position. The Lions and the Board have a long history together, and when the Queen realized that Léa had fled South Africa with the Cullinan, she called me immediately."

"But you were also the one who had arranged her escape," I murmured, remembering how fast we had packed and flown to Tokyo in first class back then.

"Yes. I believe I should also be credited for the idea of creating a replica of the Cullinan to help her create a diversion. I have to admit I never thought I'd fall prey to my own tactic or watch you destroy this little souvenir before my eyes, for that matter." He laughed bitterly. "Regardless, Léa betrayed me as well. As soon as you two had landed, she went off the grid. She never showed up at the apartment I had arranged for her in Roppongi." His hand squeezed my shoulder as he said this, and I wasn't sure whether it was intentional or not.

"You found us anyway," I said in a brittle voice. For the first time, everything was clear. We should have lived in a *Star Trek* apartment with Dries in Tokyo, but my mother had fled from him, hiding in our little house in the modest area of Sumiyoshi, where she thought a posh asswipe like him would never think to look.

"Of course I did. Léa was good, but not *that* good." He chuckled. "So I came here with March to get her and the Cullinan back, all with the Board's blessing."

"So why did you kill her instead?" I snapped. I felt mad, mad at Dries, mad at March, but the tears wouldn't come.

Dries rolled his eyes. "Have you lost your mind, little Island? Léa was the only one to know where the Cullinan was. I was going to take you both and make her talk."

I shoved him away. I couldn't stand that fucking arm around me anymore. "But someone shot her! I remembered on Rislow's table. She was shot in the head!" I shouted.

"Yes one of my men," he said coldly. "March and I were watching you two, along with a third Lion, who was supposed to cover us during the operation. We were about to intercept Léa, and I gave the sniper orders to stop the car. According to him, he merely meant to blast her shoulder so she would drop the wheel, but he shot her in the head."

Dries caressed his chin. "I wasn't entirely convinced by his explanation, but he was a Lion and he had disobeyed my orders, so I executed him."

There had been little doubt in my mind after remembering the circumstances of my mother's death on Creepy-hat's table, but hearing it suddenly made it real. It was like a burn that would have been numbed by the initial adrenaline rush, only to start hurting afterward. Now the flames were real, perhaps even more so than ten years prior. One of Dries's men had murdered my mother in cold blood.

I felt my jaw trembling and struggled to regain control of my emotions. "Victor Koerand said that she was afraid, that she knew she was going to die. And here you are, with a dead scapegoat ready for use. Isn't that convenient?"

His nostrils flared, and a flash of anger darkened his golden eyes. "Rather than making pathetic accusations, you should thank me. You would be dead as well if I hadn't brought March here to Tokyo with me."

My spine turned to ice. "What are you talking about? What happened?"

"After the shooting, Léa's car kept speeding down the avenue with you inside. You already know that."

I nodded weakly.

"Since the operation was a complete failure I ordered fallback, but March ran down the street after the car. You might not want to believe it, but each professional has his soft spot: mine is armadillos. I'd never kill an armadillo." Dries sighed. "March's . . . I suppose it's little girls. Poor fucker made it just in time to pull you out of the wreckage. He left the Lions shortly after that, a matter of guilt and misplaced pride, I believe."

I think Dries said something else after that, about how he had sent a cleaning team for March at the time, so he wouldn't appear too lenient to the rest of their "brothers." I wasn't listening. My ears were buzzing, and my heart was beating so loud, too loud. I thought of the dream I had experienced on Creepy-hat's table and tried hard to remember. My mother's still figure, the fear, the pain, and then him. His face, the blue eyes, the smell of the mints, and the black knife, the relief when my body was picked up from the seat, the way I had wanted to hold on to him, but my limbs hadn't been able to respond. March had intended to kidnap my mother and me for Dries, but ultimately he had saved me from that burning car. For no reason, no reward. Just because it had been the right thing to do.

A tear I hadn't felt roll onto my cheek fell on my lap as Dries spoke again. "I suspected he wouldn't have the courage to tell you."

"For all I know, you still might be the one who shot her." I sniffed, looking away to regain my composure.

"I'm not. Believe me, I wanted Léa alive."

"Whatever you say . . . Who got the idea to keep the diamond instead of giving it to the Board? You?"

"Léa shared my views. She never did anything she didn't want to."

"Is that what you tell yourself to feel better about what happened to her? She was blinded by her feelings, and you used that against her, you vile piece of *shit*!" I yelled. I couldn't believe my mother had died for this asshole.

"A feeling I'm sure you can relate to . . . History has a way of repeating itself, or so it seems."

Leave it to an arrogant turd like Dries to imagine that March was manipulating me to keep the stone for himself. No. March had been part of all this, done terrible things, and chosen to leave Dries and the Lions afterward because of it, but he wasn't greedy. As he had told me in his car, back in Paris, this was *not* the way he did things. "You're wrong. March has many flaws, but he isn't trying to keep the diamond. He's completely anal about his moral code."

"You seem to admire him," Dries mused.

"More than I admire you, obviously. What happened? Why didn't Mom give you the Cullinan in the end? Her notary told me that in her letter, she said she had made a mistake, that she wanted to make things right."

A flicker of sadness shimmered in his eyes, and for a moment Dries seemed almost human. "I'm going to disappoint you. I'm not entirely sure. I thought Léa and I were working toward the same goal, building the same dreams, but she grew distant, and by the time we left Pretoria she seemed to have stopped trusting me entirely. She even tried to talk me into returning the Cullinan to the Board, to smooth things over with them. I think . . . I think she believed the Board would kill you too if she was caught, and she didn't trust that I would protect you," he recalled, his gaze a little unfocused, as if my mother's distrust still gnawed at him more than a decade later.

"She was right."

He nodded. "Indeed. There's business, there's pleasure, and you were none of those. I wouldn't have risked losing the Cullinan for your sake."

I fought the lump in my throat. "I think she really loved you, you know. Did you ever—"

"Love her back?" Dries's lips moved, as if he had been about to say something else, but then he seemed to think better of it and paused. "No. She knew that, and she never expected me to. I doubt you can understand this, but I was offering more than love."

"Power?"

"You understand, after all."

Oh yes, I understood . . . I understood everything. I looked at his hazel eyes, mirrors of mine, the little moles here and there on his face and hands, the slight gap-tooth. I closed my eyes and remembered his shadow, standing in my doorway, mere feet away from my bed.

The scent of sandalwood, floating in the bedroom.

"Are you my father?"

"No. Simon Halder is the father Léa chose for you."

I felt a prickling sensation in my rib cage upon hearing his words. I pondered their meaning as he left the sofa to answer a phone call.

The father Léa chose . . .

Was Dries implying that he would have preferred being chosen over my dad? I didn't want to ask him that. I wasn't certain I could handle the answer to that question.

Meanwhile, he had hung up and turned to me with a predatory smile. "Dear little Miss Chaptal, didn't I tell you that you could trust the instinct of an old Lion?"

THIRTY

The Toy

"Destiny knew that Colt would take his revenge against the cartel when they expected it the least, and he would leave nothing but ruins in his wake."

—Natasha Onyx, *Muscled Passion of the SEAL*

Let me tell you this. I had no idea what the expression "conflicting emotions" truly meant until after that disastrous first lunch with my biological father. Did I hate Dries? Yes. Did I wish that, in another life, he had been a real father to me and loved my mom? Sadly, yes. Was I mad at March for having concealed the truth about his involvement in the Cullinan affair? Yes. Was my unhealthy crush on him getting worse now that I knew he had been my mysterious rescuer? God, *yes*.

I was in shambles.

Dries's guards and Cue Ball started exchanging little hand signals and gripped their guns in anticipation. With good reason: March was coming up. He had called Dries back to accept his deal—me, with all four limbs in working order, against the genuine Cullinan—and every single pair of eyes in the room was locked on the penthouse's entrance.

There was a faint click, and the doors opened. March was here, flanked by two guards on each side, with a third one following him for good measure. Over his bloody shirt the navy-blue jacket I was still wearing had been replaced by a black corduroy one, which I assumed possessed the same properties. I felt myself melt a little at the thought that even with his badass bulletproof jackets, March still managed to dress with a flair that rivaled only my grandpa's.

He walked down the stairs and into Dries's living room with a non-chalant, confident stride, his poker smile in place as if the men pointing their guns at him weren't there. In his right hand, my mom's metal case swung with each of his tranquil steps. On March's right, a burly man with dark skin nodded at Dries. "He's clean. No weapons."

I cast March a worried glance. Did this mean no weapons that these guys had been able to detect or no weapons at all and butt-naked?

Dries opened his arms wide and walked to March with a warm smile on his face. He then pulled him into a heartfelt bro hug, the kind that had me wondering if I was going to discover these two had been working together from the start. God, I hoped not.

After March had returned Dries's embrace, they broke the contact, and Dries patted him on the shoulder affectionately. "It's been too long! My best disciple, my *brother*."

"Far too long, indeed—" March smiled, but there was no joy in his eyes. Then he finally looked at me. "Are you all right, Island?"

"Yeah . . . great," I murmured.

"Good." His eyes traveled back to Dries, a hard gleam in their depths. "Brother, I take it this is what you were looking for."

With this, March handed the case to Dries, who walked with it to the glass table we had lunched on, laid it down, and opened it. As Dries stared at "his" Cullinan the way a pedophile stares at a five-year-old,

March took a few steps forward until he was standing by my side. I looked up at him, trying to decipher his expression, to no avail. A leather-gloved hand crept around my waist, and he glanced at his watch. As he did so, his grip tightened a little.

Then a little more.

Until it almost hurt.

Across the room, I saw Dries freeze and straighten slowly. His eyes met March's, his brow twitched, and something changed in his expression, like a sense of realization. I barely had the time to see him move away from the table: I remember a deafening noise and flying behind the *Star Trek* couch in March's arms, shielded by his body as Dries's living room was blown to bits.

Men were moaning somewhere amid the dust and smoke surrounding us. The *Star Trek* couch had protected us well, but it was ruined, and one of the armrests was on fire. I couldn't see much, but most of the area where Dries's glass table had once been seemed completely destroyed. Since he was nowhere to be seen, I assumed he had been blown to bits. Still intact, the Cullinan was sitting in the debris, a few feet away from us.

I could tell my shoulder had been bruised upon my landing on the concrete floor, but the most difficult part was remembering how to breathe. I realized I was gripping March's jacket manically, and he was trying to unclasp my fingers, one by one, so he could move. I had no idea what he planned on doing next, but he was indeed going to need both his hands. Around us, Dries's men were recovering—well, the ones who were still alive, anyway, since I could make out several still figures resting on the floor. Ominous clicking sounds suggested that they were arming their weapons as they struggled to find their bearings in the smoke.

"Take a deep breath and relax. Everything is going to be all right."

I cast a frightened look at March, who seemed entirely focused on his watch and kept pressing the chronograph buttons quickly. I realized that the glass had in fact lit up and turned into a small LCD screen. I managed to make out the word "GO" before March tapped on the screen once, apparently sending his laconic message. Why—or more exactly *who*—was he texting in a moment like this? Placing one of his hands on my head, he forced me farther down. "Thirty seconds, biscuit."

Thirty seconds to what? God, not *another* bomb!

I heard gunshots coming from the hallway that led to the penthouse, and a new explosion made the living room tremble again, prompting me to hold on to March as small pieces of plaster and glass fell on our heads. He threaded his fingers into my hair, caressing it as he kept my head down. "Fifteen seconds. We're going to be fine."

Dries's remaining men seemed to have taken cover, and we all waited—for different reasons, I suspected.

"Now."

My head jerked at March's confident whisper, and before I could ask what we were waiting for, something big flew across the living room in our direction that one of the men tried to shoot at. It landed behind the couch and into March's welcoming hands. My immediate thought was that it was a grenade, and that I was going to be horribly maimed and die; I screamed. March's black-gloved hand covered my mouth, and he pointed at the object.

His magic suitcase.

Someone had blasted Dries's living room twice and thrown March his magic suitcase.

"I'll let you take care of the rest, *Sudafricano*!" a cheerful voice called from the hallway.

A voice I knew. Against every single safety instruction March had ever given me, I raised my head from his chest where it had been buried and took a quick peek at the smoky hallway. My initiative was met by a round of bullets fired into the couch by Cue Ball, who was still standing near the French doors. March's strong hands pulled me down again, and before he could complain that I needed to stay still, I beamed at him. "Antonio! Antonio is here!" I hissed excitedly at the memory of the killer who had almost taught me how to steal a Lexus.

Indeed, in the destroyed door frame stood Antonio, clad in a classy black suit, his sharp, tattooed features contorted in a sneer, and carrying a . . . bazooka. At least that explained why Dries's living room looked like Ground Zero, and I was pretty sure that this was in fact the mysterious purchase March had made in Minas's shop. More gunshots echoed in the hallway, and I gathered Antonio was making his escape. A new round of bullets was fired into the couch, and hurried footsteps could be heard around us. Now freed from the bazooka's threat, Dries's remaining men intended to take care of us.

Allow me to turn what will follow into a cautionary tale: if you're pursuing a successful criminal career, and one day you find yourself aiming your M16 at a mints-munching guy who looks super pissed and has a magic suitcase, run away. Fast.

March opened the case and retrieved two scary-looking, suppressed black guns from the top layer, armed them, gobbled a mint, got up from behind the couch . . . and taught Cue Ball and his rifle a lesson about never hesitating before pulling the trigger. I covered my ears with my hands as bullets flew in all directions, some right over my head and into what was left of the penthouse's tall bay windows. I popped my head once or twice to check March's cleaning progress. Four . . . three . . . two guys still standing. One of them seemed more skilled than the others, forcing March to take cover because he couldn't use his favorite hey-you're-slow-I-shot-first technique.

They dueled for a good minute until March seemed to grow tired of wasting bullets and used his little black knife, throwing it between the guy's eyes when he moved to shoot again. I winced as I caught sight of the dead man's reflection in one of the last windows that were still intact. His eyes were wide open, as if he hadn't expected it, which I suspect was precisely the reason March's approach had worked. The last man standing was a young Japanese guy whose aim wasn't so great, and he ran toward March in desperation, firing haphazardly until his magazine was empty.

I'll never forget the look on that young guy's face when he kept pulling the trigger and all that echoed in response were faint clicks indicating there was nothing left to fire. I squeezed my eyes when March shot. The idea of him killing a helpless guy made my chest heave unpleasantly, even if part of me knew that, had the tables turned, that man would have killed him without hesitation.

The Japanese guy fell, and I knew it was over. March walked back to the couch and helped me get up. I thought I had been pretty relaxed throughout this new gunfight, but in truth, I hadn't. Once I stood up, I realized my legs were trembling so badly I couldn't walk. We stood in front of each other for a few seconds in complete silence, surrounded by broken glass and destroyed furniture, still bodies, and the unmistakable smell of gunpowder. I was still a little shaken, and I could read in March's eyes a mixture of tenderness and guilt. He couldn't know what Dries had told me, but he must've gathered that the lies had come to an end.

"You and I . . . are gonna have to *talk*," I gritted out. "But not now."

He nodded once as the poker smile returned to his lips. "Understood. Are you good to go?"

"Yes."

With this, we turned to the area where Antonio's first rocket had struck, scanning for Dries and the Cullinan among the wreckage. It was a strange sensation: I expected to see his body, and at the same time, I wasn't sure I wanted to. After a few seconds spent inspecting the half-burned, empty case and the various debris surrounding it, I turned to March, a cold sweat dampening my back.

"March . . . I can't see—"

His eyes narrowed. There were bodies, there was glass . . . but two things were missing from the ruins of that Blofeld-style living room: Dries and the diamond.

THIRTY-ONE

Like Lions

"Kusukela Kudala Kuloku Kuthiwa Uyimbube."

—Solomon Linda, *Mbube*

Antonio had done a number on the long hallway before retreating. Those bulky guys I had seen guarding the penthouse's entrance were all dead, and half of the elegant crystal wall lamps had been shot. Dries was looking at a huge quote from his contractor to fix up his crib.

For all their differences, March seemed to respect Antonio's skills, and appeared convinced that his mentor wouldn't have been able to make it past the bazooka and into the elevator. A brief text on March's watch confirmed this, along with the fact that Antonio had made it safely out of the building and to March's car. Barely ten seconds after this, the LCD screen lit up again, indicating that another text had arrived. I wasn't able to read it, but I think I know what Antonio asked. We made our way back to the living room to start searching the place, I managed to peek just long enough to see March's answer scroll on his watch: "NO U CAN'T KEEP IT."

We checked the evil lair's rooms one by one, and I followed March around, freezing whenever he gestured for me to do so. We found nothing in that cathedral of a kitchen, and those spaceship-like bathrooms were clear as well—we even checked the toilets. Soon the only room left to explore was Dries's bedroom, whose French doors were ajar.

March approached the doors in silence before he slammed them open with his foot, gun in hand. The room was just as empty as the rest of apartment. A massive four-poster bed with gorgeous white silk sheets stood in the center—I gathered thread count was of great importance to Dries—and the only piece of furniture that really stood out was a big golden Napoleon III mirror against the wall opposite to the door. It looked even taller than March, and I stared at our reflection in the cool glass for a few seconds—at him, bruised, with his bloody shirt and wrinkled black jacket, and me, disheveled, covered in plaster, floating in his navy-blue jacket so deep that my hands weren't visible and my jeans-clad legs looked like sticks.

We were about to leave when a detail caught my attention on the smooth concrete floor on which the mirror rested. There were faint scrape marks on the surface. Pursing my lips, I walked to the antique. It was a truly remarkable piece, with its intricate golden leaves twirling around the frame.

"Can you help me move it?" I asked March, who took hold of the frame while I pulled on it as well.

That thing was heavy! Even March seemed to struggle a little at first, but soon the elegant mirror had moved enough to reveal a locked door. He took a few steps back, pushing me aside. Before I could blink, he casually fired a few shots into the lock. The gray metal door gave way, revealing a narrow security staircase that I figured led to the building's roof.

"Wait for me here, biscuit. If you hear gunshots, run away," March said as he started climbing the stairs.

Struggling to keep calm, I watched him disappear up the staircase.

How long had it been? Seconds? Minutes already? I waited and waited. There weren't any sounds coming from the stairs, but March wasn't coming down either. I turned my head to the bedroom's bay windows. A light October drizzle had started to fall, covering the translucent surface with thousands of shiny drops. Soon it intensified into rain, but there was still no sight of March.

Unable to resist any longer, I took a series of tentative steps toward the security door until I was almost on the stairs. March had said to wait, and, according to the rules of our arrangement, I had to comply. But what if he was . . . dead? I couldn't stand here like this. I *needed* to know what was going on up there. I entered the concrete spiral staircase and made my way up.

When I reached the last step, I found myself standing in front of a roof door that looked a lot like the previous one, except March hadn't needed to shoot this one. It was ajar already. I flattened my body against a cold and humid wall, trying my best to peek through the door without risking being seen. Through the rain, I could hear voices. March and Dries. He was still alive.

I pressed a hand on my chest in an attempt to calm my racing heart, and I strained my ears.

"I have no idea why Léa suddenly decided to try to return the stone to the Board. She wrote she didn't want me to have it no matter what . . . I thought she understood what kind of power we could become. Our strength, our honor, imagine these at the scale of a country, perhaps even several! Millions of men like you, men we could train and educate!" Dries was evidently trying to make a point, talking heatedly to his former disciple.

"Our *honor*? Really, Dries?" March spat.

Undeterred, Dries went on, and I risked a peek. They were standing in front of each other under the rain, March less than a dozen feet away from the door I was leaning against, Dries much farther to the right, golden eyes boring into blue ones, guns lowered in rigid hands, so engrossed in their exchange that neither of them had noticed me yet. Dries had the Cullinan in his left hand, holding it with an iron grip. "Don't you want to be *more* than this? I see you teaming up with a piece of trash like Antonio Romos, risking everything to fix old mistakes . . . and it breaks my heart, March. This"—Dries pointed at him—"is not the man I *carved*!"

"Then so be it! You betrayed the Board, nearly got your own daughter killed—she is, am I right? I can't believe I didn't realize it ten years ago when I first looked at her! All this for some insane dream!" March shouted.

Dries seemed to choke in astonishment. "A *dream*? Can't you see this is so much more?"

"Yes, a dream! The Lions are a necessary evil, nothing else. We feed on beasts worse than ourselves because someone has to; we're never going to rule anything, Dries!" March roared.

"We *already* are! And the Cullinan is just another resource for this dream to come true! Come back with me, let me show you what we've accomplished. Don't go wasting your talent when there's so much to fight for, March."

Okay. Dries believed that he and his pals—whoever they might be—were God's gift to the world, and March thought he was just a beast meant to clean up after other beasts: that broke *my* heart.

"You're the one who taught me that Lions didn't need a cause because their honor mattered more than any sort of creed," March told Dries through gritted teeth as he started circling away slowly, his index finger tightening on the trigger of his gun. "I don't care about your dream. My honor is to *always* finish the job."

With this, Dries seemed to figure he was going nowhere fast with his former protégé, and he raised his gun. March plunged to his side in time, shooting back at his old mentor as he did so. The man had indeed taught him everything: I did see March's first shot impact Dries's gray jacket before he took refuge behind one of the roof's vents, but the projectile accomplished nothing otherwise. Did these two share the same tailor for bulletproof jackets on top of the rest?

After the first two bullets had been fired, both men managed to establish sufficient distance between each other, March having disappeared behind a roof vent as well. I couldn't see them anymore; I only heard occasional gunshots that seemed to be getting closer. Footsteps resounded to my right. One of them had, in fact, moved and taken cover against one of the sides of the roof exit. My lungs contracted in my chest when that someone took a few cautious steps forward, and I realized it was Dries. He was now inches from me, just outside the door I was hiding behind.

I took a chance.

My shoulder hit the metal hard as I rammed into the door with all my strength, slamming it against Dries's back. Taken aback—quite literally so—he dropped the Cullinan, which landed a few feet away from me. March ran toward the source of the noise, and there was a moment of confusion during which both men froze, registering my presence. I ignored them to lunge for the stone, grab it, and curl my body around it protectively.

I heard two more gunshots, a clicking sound, and I peeked up to see that the game was over. March was pointing his gun at Dries, whose own weapon was empty. I cast a pleading look in March's direction, begging him not to end my father like this.

He seemed to understand.

But not in the way I thought.

Slowly, March lowered his gun. He then removed his jacket and folded it carefully before kneeling to place the garment and the gun on the ground. When he got up, there was an intensity in his eyes that gave me chills. Locking his gaze with Dries, his nostrils flaring, March said only three words.

"Soos Leeus, Dries." *Like Lions, Dries.*

Dries smirked and shook his head. "As you like. Let's end this like Lions."

Oh God. Was this the best time for a bare-hands fight? I could understand March's point. He had a history with Dries and didn't want to kill him like some mere client, but I didn't like the glint in Dries's eyes. This was a terrible idea. Neither of them cared to consult me, though, and all I could do was watch as they prepared to fight.

I'm not a sports commenter, and I was on the ground, fingers still curled around the Cullinan, so I guess I won't be able to explain what happened all that well, but I'll try anyway. One might think that it wasn't such a fair fight, since Dries seemed to be pushing fifty while March was thirty-two and in great physical condition—regardless of what the old prune had said back in Paris. Much like Madonna, however, Dries was still kicking. Not only that, but he had taught March his moves, and it showed.

I watched in fascinated horror as the men lunged at each other under the rain—a puppet braving its maker. Animalistic growls rose from their throats with each brutal strike, muscles rippling under the drenched fabric of their shirts, feet slamming against the concrete in an effort to brace themselves for the next hit. I understood then what March had tried to tell Dries, that the Lions were better left in the shadows to do the dirty work. In that moment, he and Dries hardly seemed human anymore.

When the first drops of blood splattered on the wet ground—March's? Dries's? I had no idea—I felt my stomach heave in fear and disgust. Part of me wanted to stop this, but I was petrified, too damn weak to do anything.

Strength-wise, March was a notch above Dries, and he landed a few nasty hits, especially one elbow kick that managed to make me feel bad for Dries. I think most of my internal organs would have burst like water balloons if I had been on the receiving end of that one. It wasn't enough, though: unlike me, Dries could take a serious beating and remain standing. Once he was fully reacquainted with March's style, it became easier for him to dodge each attack, his broad frame bending every time a leg or a fist threatened to ram into his flesh.

The rain helped Dries too, I think. March's white shirt was drenched, exposing the bandages covering his bruises from the club, white areas on his stomach, side, and back that Dries started aiming at in priority. March sustained a few vicious blows, and I thought he could win until I realized that one swift jab aimed by Dries at the center of March's chest had made him spit a little blood. For some reason, I thought of that horrible sorcerer in *Indiana Jones and the Temple of Doom*, the one who removes people's hearts with his bare hand. I got scared that Dries was going to try that jab thing again and pull March's heart out. My own heart jounced inside my rib cage as if it was going to burst out, and my breath started coming in short pants.

I didn't think.

I know I should have, but I just didn't think.

I got on my feet and took a few steps toward them, one of my hands still hugging the Cullinan against my chest, and the other raised defensively in front of me. As if I could break their fight by crabbing my way in between them.

March's worried eyes darted to check on me, and the swift punch he had thrown missed Dries's face. Carried by a powerful momentum, March's entire body tilted forward, and before he could regain his balance, Dries grabbed his neck and held him in a headlock as he struck the large bandage on his stomach with his knee repeatedly.

March fell to the ground with a strangled groan, and I nearly cried when our eyes met. Was he even seeing me through all this rage? I could read the agony and determination distorting his features, the will to stand up and keep fighting, and the frustration that his body wouldn't follow.

After a few seconds, he found the strength to overcome the pain and started to get up. Dries didn't move at first, and I thought he was waiting for March to stand so he could finish him honorably, "like a Lion." Instead, he took a step toward March, and his right leg flew to throw another vicious kick in his adversary's stomach, to ensure March wouldn't get up.

There was the rain, its scent in the air, the blood on the humid concrete, Dries's long, black, pointy oxfords, but all I really focused on, all I can still see before my eyes when I close them are March's teeth. Gritted so hard I thought they would shatter, red trickles staining the white enamel. In that instant, I remember thinking that this was it; he had reached his limit. No matter how tenacious March was, Curly-prune had been right. He didn't heal miraculously, and he couldn't take any more hits on those horrible bruises, even less so if the ribs underneath had been cracked.

Taking in the sight of his former student kneeling on the ground and gasping for air, Dries shook his head, strode to where March had previously laid his gun and jacket, and took the black semiautomatic. March was still struggling to recover by the time Dries went back to his crouching form. I remembered Rislow and his men in the woods, the small brown gun, and the blood.

All the blood.

"Please stop! Please . . . please!" I screamed, my voice cracking into a sob.

Dries cast me a strange, sad look as he aimed at his "brother."

I heard March's voice, hoarse, almost pleading. "Island . . . don't—"

Don't—what, exactly? Don't step in? It was already too late, and it was my fault if Dries had been given an opening to beat him anyway. Don't give that evil douche the diamond? With March dead, I wouldn't stand a chance against Dries. He wanted the stone? Let him have it. I lunged toward Dries, placing myself in front of the gun. It had worked for Antonio. Why wouldn't it work again? Truth is, I could see many reasons why it wouldn't, but I figured once Dries held the stone, he would forget about everything else, us included. I handed him the precious cargo, my gaze locked on his. A sun ray tore briefly between two dark clouds, casting the golden light of the late afternoon on me and the Cullinan. For an instant, soft colors reflected on the ground as light passed through the stone, creating faint rainbow-colored spots on the wet concrete. I ignored them to focus on Dries, who took the stone with his left hand, without ever detaching his gaze from March. Once he had the Cullinan, Dries flashed me a satisfied smile before looking at March over my shoulder. "I'm pleased to discover that she's more reasonable than you or Léa."

Behind me, March had managed to stand up, and he muttered a couple of words in Afrikaans between his teeth that I bet were anything but polite. Dries was still aiming the gun at me and March when a faint murmur echoed in the distance. Dries started backing away, and March tensed.

So that's what Dries had been waiting for on that roof. Above our heads a big gray helicopter was approaching, preparing to land on top of the building. I had never seen a helicopter up close and was surprised by how much wind that rotor could create. Combined with the rain still pouring, it felt like we were standing in the middle of a hurricane.

I felt March move behind me and turned my back to Dries to face him instead. "It'll be okay. I need you to trust me. Let him go," I whispered, looking into his angry eyes. I hoped I was getting through to him, since March didn't give up easily; if my hunch was correct, what we needed the most at the moment was for Dries to take off with his damn stone. As the helicopter slowly landed a few meters behind Dries, I wrapped my arms cautiously around March's drenched torso in an effort to hold him back. I couldn't imagine a worse ending to our adventure than for him to be shot by his mentor.

I looked at said mentor, who was backing toward the helicopter with the Cullinan, gun still aimed at us. Through the aircraft's tinted windows I could make out more men, probably armed as well, and I prayed that my fricking asshole of a father felt safe and confident enough to make his escape without shooting us. My fingers fisted the wet material of March's shirt, his warmth easing my fears. "Let him go. Please, please don't move, March," I begged.

I felt one of his arms drape over my shoulders and pull me close. I could feel how mad, how frustrated he was. With each strong beat of March's heart, I could tell how much he wanted to lunge at Dries and kill him or die trying.

Dries reached the helicopter, and its side door opened to reveal several men clad in black military attire and carrying rifles. I shifted even closer to March. Dries climbed in while one of his men aimed at us. Before the door slid shut, Dries's gaze met mine, and I caught that same flicker of sadness I had seen there before.

I figured he wasn't going to kill us.

Call it intuition, or maybe a leap of faith, but I had the feeling that seeing me face-to-face had affected an itsy bitsy chunk of his rotten soul. Throwing me into Creepy-hat's claws when I had been nothing but a memory? He could do that. Kill the man he had trained himself, for the sake of fulfilling a greater goal? He could do that too. But killing his own child standing in front of him? Now, that might be where a guy like him drew the line. Despite all that had happened, even if he had never been there for me, Dries *was* my father.

He wouldn't shoot me, and wouldn't order someone else to do it either.

With this certainty, I pressed myself closer to March, shielding his body with my own. I turned my head to look at the helicopter as it slowly took off, watching Dries through the dark glass. I felt March's arms squeeze me a little harder in response, his presence soothing me amid the chaos of the rain, the wind, and the roar of the aircraft's rotor.

The helicopter flew away into the darkening sky until all that was left of it was a distant buzz.

THIRTY-TWO
The Kimchi

"Angelihannah tore Rick's boxer shorts with desperate moans, eager to feel all of him. He was the condiment without which her life had no taste, no meaning."

—Madelline Chandelier, *Captive Enchantress*

I looked at March, at the bruises, the blood on his shirt, the water running in rivulets all over his body, washing away more blood from a wound on his brow. Part of me wanted to yell that he would have caught Dries if he had been less of a testosterone-stuffed idiot and handled the situation in a calm and responsible manner, instead of trying to kill his father figure in a fistfight. But *I* had been the one to distract him, nearly getting him killed in the process.

We had both acted like idiots, and I realized it didn't matter. In that moment, only one thing mattered.

"I'm glad you're alive," I said, lacing my fingers with his.

"Thank you," he murmured, avoiding my eyes. Then he seemed to remember something, and life returned to those weary sapphires, along with an accusing gleam. "I told you not to come up. You could have gotten yourself killed."

I stiffened. "Seriously? I saved *your* ass, and here I am, trying to cheer you up, about to tell you that you didn't need to prove anything to Dries, that you're in a league of your own, and you're going all nit-picky-rule-bookey on me?"

His dimples creased, an impish smile replacing his stern expression. "In a league of my own?"

I looked away to conceal my embarrassment at having unconsciously returned the sweet compliment he had given me in Paris. "Slip of the tongue."

His right hand rose to cup my cheek, wiping the dirt there. "I'll find him, and I'll get that diamond back. Not for myself or the Board, but for *you*."

I felt an uncontrollable grin spread on my lips and lift my cheeks up. "Maybe you won't have to—but I need to call Masaharu!"

March gave me a surprised look but walked to his jacket, retrieved his smartphone from his inner pocket, and handed me the device.

The former love of my life picked up after a few rings, and when he heard my voice, he sounded relieved. Skipping small talk, I jumped to the point. "Masaharu-kun, is our old house in Sumiyoshi still there?"

He answered with an uncertain voice. "Yes, but it's been turned into a co-rental for Korean students."

"Did they modify the building?"

"No, you know how Watanabe-san is. He doesn't spend much on his properties."

"Okay! Thank you so much, for everything. I've always loved you!" After I had hung up before leaving Masaharu a chance to confirm that we weren't meant to be, I raised a victorious fist to the sky.

Upon witnessing my joy, March turned all business. "Island . . . what's going on?"

"Okay, the good news first. I think the Cullinan Dries took off with was a decoy too. I noticed the way it reflected the light when the clouds dissipated: a real diamond wouldn't allow that kind of refraction," I explained.

March's brow furrowed. "We did a scratch test, back at the bank."

"It could be moissanite, synthetic corundum, or even cubic zirconia. All these could beat your ceramic knife on the Mohs scale of hardness, and you didn't press the blade very hard." I shrugged.

"So there's a third stone? The real one?"

"I think so. You said it yourself. It's not really a shell game if there are only two shells," I reminded him.

"Where do you think it is?"

I hopped on my feet, electrified. "At first, I really thought my mom had meant to leave me that book as a souvenir, but then I connected the dots."

"And?"

"Have you ever heard of nightingale flooring?"

March scratched his head. "It's an ancient Japanese defensive device, a wooden flooring that produces a specific whistling sound when you walk on it."

"Exactly. In our house in Sumiyoshi, there was an area in my bedroom where the floorboard had moved a little, and it would squeak whenever I walked on it. My mom said that it was like having nightingale flooring."

"You think the diamond might be there?"

"I can't guarantee anything, but one thing is certain: she went through the trouble of hiding two decoys, and it fits the way she did things. My mom didn't like simple."

He flashed me a dimpled grin as he picked up his jacket. "Neither do you. Let's check this."

When we left the building, two police cars were already in front of the main entrance, and firemen could be heard coming in the distance, thanks to Antonio's little stunt with the bazooka. We had to escape through a small window on the ground-floor ladies' room—where a young woman drying her hands looked at March as if he were a rapist and scurried away in a panic.

We eventually made it out into a narrow back street, and from the looks of it, we weren't the only ones to have risked sexual harassment charges in the restrooms. Down the street, Antonio had been patiently waiting for March, our brown SUV parked just far enough away to avoid raising any suspicion. When he saw us, he dangled the car keys with a smug grin.

"Your stuff is packed inside. Now that I'm done, Okinawa's bikini babes are about to get a piece of . . . *Antonio*."

He slicked his wavy black hair back, struck his little gun pose again, and I couldn't help but applaud: Antonio was the epitome of badass.

March, however, seemed a little surprised by his colleague's over-zealous car valeting, and perhaps Antonio noticed it, because he deemed it necessary to justify himself. "When I do things, I do them well. Even for a *psicópato* like you."

I snickered. "He called you a psychopath."

March let out a long-suffering sigh. "I know what it means, Island, thank you."

A deep laugh rose from Antonio's throat as he threw the SUV's keys to March. "My debt is paid. Next time you go after me, I kill you and feed your balls to my dogs, *Sudafricano*."

March nodded with a faint smile and walked to the back of the car, opening the trunk to put away his magic suitcase that we had retrieved from the ruins of Dries's living room. He was about to close the trunk, but seemed to hesitate. I watched as he pressed his thumb against one of the case's sides for a couple of seconds, and a faint click resounded. Fingerprint lock. Pretty cool. He picked up a tiny syringe from a perfectly organized first-aid kit, opened his dirty shirt, and casually stabbed his bruised stomach with the needle. Catching the look of horror on my face, he gave me a reassuring smile. "Light painkiller."

I nodded and averted my eyes, feeling queasy. March cast Antonio a questioning glance, holding out the small plastic box where the syringe had been for him to see. It dawned on me that, while Antonio didn't seem to be wounded, his suit was a little torn and crumpled, and there was a possibility that he had been hurt during their vigorous cleaning of Dries's lair.

Antonio shook his head. "I have my own painkillers." He then pulled out an elegant golden case from his pocket and opened it to reveal a row of red cigarettes. He took one and lit it up under March's disapproving gaze.

"A very unhealthy habit," March commented.

Antonio didn't reply. He just glared at his "colleague" as the first curls of smoke escaped his lips before evaporating in the air. I guess it had to do with the fact that he had visited March's trunk and therefore knew there are worse things for your health than weed. I watched him take a few steps to lean against the SUV, surrounded by his cigarette's pungent fumes. He pulled it away from his lips and held it out for me with a smile.

My eyes darted to March. His eyebrows drew together. Nope. No pot for you, Island. I shook my head. "Thank you, I'm good."

Antonio muttered something under his breath about March's latent homosexuality and urgent need to loosen up. Behind me, I heard an aggravated huff, and I think March was about to give him a taste of the volcanic temper I had witnessed back on the roof, but he was interrupted by the faint tint of a bell, coming from Antonio's front pocket.

Several bells tinted again, and the culprit pulled out a black smartphone, before checking it with a prideful smile. I couldn't resist the temptation to glimpse at the screen and tilted my head to better see it. Antonio wrapped an arm around my shoulder, pulling me toward him, and showed me the source of his contentment.

"What is it?"

March sighed.

Antonio laughed, and then proceeded to explain to me that March's little shopping spree in Minas's shop had resulted in his acquiring the latest trend in real toys for real boys. Coming straight from Ukraine, the AZ 504 was some huge high-tech bazooka with a digital aim, complete with real-time detection of your targets, and a cool app that posted a status update on your Twitter account, saying "BOOM!" every time you fired it. March wasn't on Twitter, but Antonio was, and the souvenir of the two rockets that destroyed Dries's living room probably still rest among billions of other tweets.

There were a ton of questions I wanted to ask, starting with who was "ViktorDasButcher53," but March reminded me that we were on a "tight schedule," as he liked to say, and we hastily said our good-byes.

No, Antonio still didn't get to keep the bazooka, even after he begged.

———

With March momentarily defaulting on his principles and allowing himself to drive like Steve McQueen, we reached Kōtō-ku in record time. We both agreed that while my dear daddy was neutralized for now, it was preferable that we find the real Cullinan and deliver it to the Queen *before* Dries tested his own stone and discovered he had a promising future in budget jewelry. March did stop at a few red lights, though, perhaps to comfort himself a little.

Nostalgia started swelling in my chest when I looked through the window to see that we had passed the Sumiyoshi station's entrance. The bright yellow signs, the escalators, everything was the same as I remembered. Once we were out of the car and walking down the Yotsume Dori, surrounded by low buildings, colorful shops, and the peaceful hum of the city, I contemplated forgetting about the Cullinan to just take a stroll down memory lane. I felt March's hand on my shoulder, and I wondered if being here brought some memories of his own.

The tiny, tree-lined street where my mom and I had spent our last months together came into view. People still parked their bicycles wherever they could, and air-conditioning units disfigured every single house. I guess that, much like the Lions, those were a "necessary evil." Fall in Tokyo was rainy, but okay; by July, however, the heat and humidity would become stifling. We strolled up the alley leading to the house's entrance, sandwiched between two brick buildings, and I squeezed March's arm. There's only so much doubt and stress a girl can take; I needed him and his calming presence.

Masaharu had been right: Watanabe-san needed to take better care of his properties. The house was even more dilapidated than the last time I had been there. The brown tiling protecting its facade was half gone, the garage's doors seemed to have disappeared at some point, and the wooden stairs leading to the first floor looked like they might collapse any second. We made our way up, each step creaking ominously under our weight, or maybe mostly March's.

It feels a little weird to knock on the door of a place you've lived in before, realizing that now you're a stranger, and you don't have the keys, boo! That feeling was only exacerbated by the fact that no one was answering. March picked the lock—well, technically, he broke the door. It was made of light, cheap plywood, with a low-grade lock that the right amount of upward pressure destroyed completely.

I still believe that the disaster awaiting us inside this house was a sign of Raptor Jesus trying to tell March that he needed to go easy on Joy and me because there were worse dumps on earth than our apartment. My nostrils flared as I scanned the place and tried to find my old bearings. Kimchi doesn't lie. Korean students definitively lived there, as evidenced by the strong smell of cabbage and garlic permeating the air. I feared I would lose March if someone opened that vintage green fridge.

He seemed pretty rattled already, standing in the middle of that forsaken living room, his fists clenched so hard the knuckles had turned white. I observed him as his gaze traveled from the old stove covered with a thick layer of black and brown grease to the overflowing trash can, before lingering on the dried lettuce leaves and the corn flakes scattered at the feet of a dusty dining table.

I was worried, terribly worried.

A faint rustling sound came from what had once been my room, and March reacted instantly, storming into the small space, gun in hand. There, on a camp bed, a young Asian guy appeared to be waking up. His face was covered in zits, and his tangled hair was dyed green and blue. He gave us a bleak stare through heavy-lidded eyes until he registered the gun. Then he screamed, raising his hands in surrender.

March glared at the devastation that most people would otherwise refer to as a male student's room, and his eyes fell on a crumpled schedule pinned to the wall. Half of the annotations were either in Japanese or in Korean, but the ones in English were pretty explicit. It was 5:35, and that guy should have been in English class. His lips pursed in aggravation, March aimed his gun at the Korean. "Go to class. Now!"

God, it still made me shiver when he raised his voice, even if it wasn't me who had scattered lettuce everywhere and skipped English. It might be too much information, but when the guy scrambled to grab his Converse and backpack before dashing out of the room in tears, I noticed he had pissed himself a little. We heard him wail all the way down the stairs, and after he was gone, I started searching around the room for my nightingale flooring. When a faint whistle under the bed answered my efforts, I struck a little victory pose and smiled at March.

"Can you remove it?"

He knelt by my side and produced the incurved knife he had concealed under his pant leg. My heart raced as I watched him work on freeing the incriminated floorboard. It came loose with a cracking sound, and I think we both experienced the same kind of epic disappointment when the missing floorboard revealed . . . nothing. Just smooth concrete. Had I been wrong? My brain was running wild while March stared at me, his blue eyes begging me to come up with a new idea.

I couldn't find any. It made perfect sense for the stone not to be hidden here. After all, had Watanabe-san decided to change the flooring, the Cullinan would have immediately been discovered.

My neurons were stalling.

Thank God March's weren't. I could tell the difference between real and fake diamonds. *He* could tell the difference between concrete and well-disguised plaster.

I watched as he used his knife to stab the smooth gray surface and created a deep dent. He let out a little huff of satisfaction and set about destroying what was, in fact, a thick layer of plaster mixed with some fine gravel to imitate the surrounding concrete. After a few minutes, the black blade of his knife hit a hard obstacle, which nearly caused him to lose his grip on the weapon. I knelt by his side to get a better view of his little excavation job, and soon March held in his left hand some kind of ugly, plaster-covered rock that seemed a little bigger than my fist.

I'll tell you what: I had no regrets at the idea of surrendering it to the Queen. The real Ghost Cullinan was even less sexy than its replicas. I thought of Dries. What was it he had called March, back in Ōtemachi? "Poor fucker . . ." How fitting. Dries was a poor fucker who had risked everything for one big chunk of what was likely synthetic corundum.

March put the floorboard in place, wiped all the dust with one of the Korean student's pairs of freshly laundered boxer shorts before throwing them in the guy's laundry basket, and insisted that we clean the Cullinan in the sink before leaving.

I sat on a chair in the living room and watched him scrub off the plaster under a trickle of hot water. He had requisitioned the Korean student's toothbrush for the job, and the sight of the clean and shiny stone seemed to progressively relax him, a peaceful smile creasing his dimples. Once he was done, I brought him another pair of boxer shorts from the Korean student's chest of drawers to dry the Cullinan with, since my cleaning expert deemed those rags lying near the sink too dirty for the job—even I agreed that he was right on this.

We used a third and last pair of underwear—pink kitten-printed—to wrap the stone in and left the house. On our way down the narrow alley leading to the street, I saw March fish for his cell phone in his pocket—to inform the Queen his mission was a success, I guessed.

He never made that phone call.

When we reached the sidewalk, there was a monstrous black Bentley limo blocking the road and attracting curious glances from the passersby on the Yotsume Dori. A group of awestruck schoolgirls tried to stop to take some pictures, but they were politely invited to get lost by a row of suits-clad gorillas barring the small street's entrance with two black Mercedes sedans.

They didn't seem to pose an immediate threat, and March showed no sign of tensing: I made a silent guess that I was about to make the acquaintance of his mysterious employer. I held on to his arm as one of the Bentley's rear doors opened in a silent invitation.

"Is it gonna be okay?" I whispered as he helped me inside.

"Yes."

I climbed in and sat on one of the black leather couch-like seats with March, still gripping his arm. On the other side of the car, sitting on a similar seat, was a woman in a gray dress, deeply engrossed in an issue of *Elle*. She was flanked by two guys wearing expensive-looking dark suits who were staring at us. Our host closed her magazine with slow, deliberate movements, placed it on her lap, and when she raised her head to look at us, my breath caught in my throat. I knew those red lips. I knew that single pearl and the long black curls framing it.

Guita. The nice cat-lady from the Bristol was the Queen.

And she read *Elle*!

She tucked a strand of shiny hair behind her ear and gave us a warm smile. "Good evening, Island. I'm happy to see you again. How have you been?"

Kidnapped by a professional killer, tied to an operating table by a creep you hired, put in the trunk, handcuffed, shot at . . . Why do you ask? That's what I wanted to say, but my balls of steel appeared to be unavailable at the moment. "Great . . . thanks," I said lamely.

She responded with a satisfied nod. "Glad to hear that. You'll have to excuse me for imposing. I was getting a little impatient."

"We can perfectly understand." March nodded with a courteous smile before extending the underwear-clad diamond for one of her bodyguards to take. The burly blond guy leaned forward and grabbed the stone before passing it to the Queen. She unwrapped the Cullinan and pinched the pair of pink boxer shorts between two delicate fingers, holding them in front of us questioningly. I averted my eyes, and March had the good grace to clear his throat in mild embarrassment.

"Logistics issues."

Guita gave the garment to the blond man and inspected the stone, caressing its cool surface slowly. "Dearest March . . . do you ever disappoint?" she asked in a velvety voice.

March answered her compliment with a cocky smile. "I try my best not to."

"Seems like you're even better when I don't pay you."

I jumped a little at her words and stole a glance at March. He looked uneasy. "Wait a minute! You get a *two-pound* diamond, and you're not gonna give him his paycheck? What the—"

His hand covered my mouth before I could call her a cheap bitch, and she broke into a crystalline laugh, revealing sharp incisors. "What paycheck are you talking about, darling? March collected a favor from me. There's no way I'm paying him a single cent for this. It's entirely his loss."

I felt March's hand leave my mouth, and I looked back and forth between him and Guita. "You . . . didn't hire him?"

March looked like he wanted her to leave it at that, but from what I gathered, no one was supposed to snap at the Queen or, worse, interrupt her when she spoke.

She shrugged. "Not exactly. He heard through the grapevine that the Board was interested in you, but I already had Rislow—still can't believe that pathetic skunk betrayed me, mind you. Oh, well, it doesn't matter! Anyway, guess who contacted me to ask that I let him 'assist' Rislow?"

I didn't answer her riddle, because there was no need to. March had requested from Guita the right to get involved. In his own clumsy way, he had been trying to help me from the start, to fix the mistakes of the past, knowing he wouldn't make a dime. The sheer enormity of the news hit me like a punch in the face. Paulie, Kalahari, Ilan . . . I now understood their behavior, all those little remarks.

I wasn't March's client.

I had never been.

My eyes bored into his, trying to read him. He seemed unhappy that Guita had revealed his dirty little secret, almost like he was ashamed of it himself. Part of me wanted to claw at his face for having scared the living shit out of me, for having first chosen fear and confrontation as a means to obtain the truth.

I had trusted him so much.

Goddammit, I *still* trusted him, even after yet another lie. I looked down and balled my fists until my knuckles hurt. I couldn't meet his eyes yet.

"Are you gonna kill Dries?" I asked Guita.

"Do you even have to ask?" She looked at March as she said this, and I shivered. I wasn't certain I could handle the idea of March being sent to kill my father . . . kill his own mentor.

He gave me a comforting smile. "Don't worry about that. I pick my clients wisely."

I wanted to lose my temper and ask if that rule applied to me as well, but I figured Guita's car wasn't the place to rip his head off. Ostensibly bored with our exchange, our host picked the magazine from her lap and instructed the driver to start the car with a little flick of her wrist. "Well, that will be all for today. Until next time, March."

March took my hand, helped me out of the Bentley, and we watched the car drive away. We walked back to the SUV that he had parked on the Shin-Ohashi Dori, and once the car started moving, I managed to relax a little. Night was starting to fall over the city, bright lights dancing around us like fireflies and gliding across the windows. As we reached Roppongi Hills, I stirred, watching the luxury store displays, the elegant Tokyoites carrying large shopping bags, and almost always a little drink: milk teas, ice coffees, strange sodas . . .

"Stop the car," I told him, straightening in my seat.

"Why?"

"Because you don't want to have this conversation while driving," I said, intentionally using those same words he had pronounced back in Paris.

The peaceful smile that had been dancing on March's lips until now vanished. "All right."

THIRTY-THREE

The Voice of Reason

"Destiny tore Colt's shirt passionately, revealing his huge, hard SEAL muscles. 'I will never be afraid of death as long as I am with you!' she moaned passionately."

—Natasha Onyx, *Muscled Passion of the SEAL*

March parked the car in a vast underground garage under the Ritz-Carlton. We both got out, and he stood in front of me on the concrete floor, waiting for the words to come.

I tried hard to sort my feelings and find the right way to tell him how mad I was that he had kissed me, swept me off of my feet like Ryker, the billionaire werewolf . . . and lied, lied like my parents, lied from the moment we had met in my apartment.

Too many thoughts were colliding inside my head—good and bad memories, the temptation to forget it all and jump into his arms, or, on the contrary, to yell at him until my voice was raw. All these boiled and merged until they were concentrated in one single response. Without thinking, I closed my eyes and gave him a violent slap. I slapped him so hard I hurt my own hand, the sound of my palm against his cheek resounding with a loud smack in the deserted garage.

Of course, March could have dodged; I'm not Jet Li. Yet he didn't, and kept looking at me calmly, the imprint of my fingers reddening his skin.

"You *lied* to me! About everything! I wasn't your client . . . and you were there, the day she died! I remember you now!"

He remained silent, gazing at me with a saddened expression, and I almost wanted to slap him again for shutting down on me like this. How could he not see that he was messing with my heart? That said heart was beating like never before, for him, despite all that cleaning and folding!

Of course, I could have told him those things, but I wasn't sure I could handle hearing him say out loud that we weren't on the same page. I didn't want to end up cast in the role of those pathetic spinsters who fall for the first guy who shows some modicum of interest. So I swallowed back the words and sought a dignified way out, my eyes intently studying the white lines painted on the floor. "Never mind . . . You saved me from the car. So thank you for that, I guess."

A gentle smile tugged at the corners of his lips, and he finally spoke. "No, *you* saved *me*."

I blinked. "Why do you say that?"

His hand rose to caress my hair, and I struggled to control the blush I could feel coming to my cheeks. "Pulling you out of that car . . . was the first good thing I ever did in my life. It made me realize that if killing was all I'd ever be good for, I had to at least do it on my own terms, with my own code. You're the reason I left the Lions." March paused, before concluding in a hesitant voice. "And when I saw you again last year, saw the woman you had become . . . I felt a little at peace with myself."

Okay, he was obviously trying to make sure that I'd never get over him. My heart was racing in my chest, blood hammering in my temples, and that damn blush was probably long since out of control. I'm not gonna lie, for a moment, there, in that garage, I pictured the kind of happy ending that only happened in my books: he'd say he was sorry, that I was awesome and he wanted no one else, and I'd burst into tears, and we'd kiss . . .

You can't blame me for trying: I took a step forward, grabbed the front of his jacket, stood on tiptoes, and pressed my mouth to his. For all my inexperience, I didn't miss the way his lips first parted, almost like a reflex, only to close. I kept kissing him anyway, because love makes you a little stupid and very selfish, I guess. His hands eventually moved to rest on my shoulders and push me away delicately.

Believe me, that single gesture hurt much more than not getting called back by my past dates. I looked up into March's eyes, and in all that blue, in that sad and gentle smile, I saw everything that would never be.

I remember that I felt a little dizzy.

I remember realizing that neither Masaharu nor Ethan the gorgeous law student had truly broken my heart, but March was. And that just like the day my mother had died, I was powerless to stop the crash: all I could do was watch and count the seconds until it was over for good.

I took a deep breath to fight the strange metallic taste in mouth, the prickling sensation in my nose and in my eyes. "Sorry about that. I guess I kinda . . . I imagined things."

March's eyes widened, and once the flash of surprise was gone, all I could find was guilt and regret. We both knew that I hadn't imagined anything, that something had been there, at hand's reach, that neither of us were apparently ready for—or more exactly that *he* wasn't ready for, because, frankly, if he had offered, I would have gladly become his bitch for all eternity.

In any case, it didn't work like that.

Life didn't work like that.

After all, even if it had been possible for us to stay together, would I have been able to live surrounded by lies, wondering if I'd ever see him again every time he left?

His hand moved to take mine, warm and tentative. "Island—"

I shook my head. "In *Muscled Passion of the SEAL*, in the end, Colt Brannigan tells Destiny that he has to go, because she'll never be safe around him since the FBI and the CIA are after him for a murder he didn't commit."

His fingers' grip around mine tightened a little, and a line creased his brow. "He's a very reasonable man. But then again, SEALs often are."

I couldn't repress a small smile. "They don't get eaten by Lions much?"

"They do swim quite fast," March conceded with a nod, before pursing his lips in apparent respect.

I nodded in my turn, throat tight. "When will you go?"

"I'll leave Tokyo once I've arranged a flight back to New York for you."

"Tonight?"

He glanced at his watch. "I suppose it's a little late for this. I'll ask Phyllis to book a seat for tomorrow morning."

"Okay," I rasped out.

He took my hand again as we made our way to the elevator, and I found myself wondering if I should tell him that after Colt has informed Destiny of his intention to leave, she fights him and decides to abandon her entire life to follow him in the shadows.

When we made it back to the Ritz's lobby, no one dared to comment on our disheveled state, but Fubuki offered to send a doctor to check on us, to which March agreed.

I assume that this doctor too encouraged March to take it easy on the bazooka business, but I was in the living room chatting with Joy over the phone, so I didn't listen this time. There was, in fact, a crisis brewing. My dad was getting suspicious of the way I hadn't been answering my phone since the "pocket call" incident, and he had called

Joy, only to hear her explain that I had suddenly embarked for a romantic weekend in Paris—no, wait, in Tokyo!—with some forty-something limp-dicked guy who delved into bondage. Joy's claims that March was reportedly a good kisser had done little to appease my father's wrath, especially after she had confessed that she had no phone number where she could reach me.

Once I had raided the minibar for snacks and taken a quick shower, I decided to be brave. I called my dad while March soaked in the tub in his turn and watched a BBC documentary about star-nosed moles on the bathroom's wall-mounted TV—a bit of luck, since these repulsive creatures were March's second favorite animal after ostriches.

As expected, that was one tough phone call, filled with many occurrences of the words "immature" and "unacceptable" . . . that is until I cut into my dad's tirade to mention my mother's will. I asked him if he had ever planned on telling me about my inheritance, and his tone immediately changed. For once, the great Simon Halder didn't sound so confident; he sounded like a father afraid of losing his only child to long-buried secrets.

I listened as his voice broke, and the tension between us dissipated. "Honey . . . When I arrived in Tokyo, Léa's apartment had been searched, everything had been wrecked, and then there was that notary, all that money . . . You were so young, and I was afraid . . . afraid of what M. Étienne might tell you about Léa's life, and about—"

"Dries."

Panic gripped his voice. "You know about him?"

"Barely," I lied. It was better this way. My dad seemed to gather Dries was bad company anyway. "It doesn't change anything. You're my father. No one can ever replace you," I murmured.

"Honey, same goes for me. I never cared about him! I was so proud that Léa had chosen *me* to help her raise you. You bet no one will ever replace your daddy," he chuckled anxiously, as if he didn't believe it himself.

"I love you." I pretty much never said things like this—my dad and I weren't too good with big displays of affection—but that night, I felt like it was the only thing he needed to hear.

He breathed a sigh of relief. "I love you too, honey. When are you coming back? Joy scared me out my mind. We'll find you a good, decent boyfriend when you get home. I recruited this young analyst, and I was thinking—"

"Dad."

"A Harvard graduate . . . and, hear this, his mother is in the same yoga class as Janice!"

"Dad!"

On the other end of the line, a curt huff indicated that my dad was willing to grant me a five-second slot to speak. Which was all I needed, really.

"It's over. I don't want to discuss this," I mumbled.

A silence; an embarrassed sigh. Did I sound that gloomy? "I understand. When are you back in New York?"

"Tomorrow, I think."

"Call me as soon as you land. Goodnight, honey," he said before hanging up.

As I was about to get up and place the phone back in March's pocket, I realized he had gotten out of the tub and was standing in the bedroom's doorway, wearing a clean white shirt that wasn't entirely buttoned, revealing fresh bandages around his torso, a pair of jeans as usual, and, of course, the hotel's complimentary slippers.

"How bad?" he asked, walking to my bed and sitting by my side.

"Not that bad. He just got scared." I sighed.

March draped an arm around my shoulders. I shivered. "Rightly so. I'm sorry . . . for everything that you've been through," he said. Then, that gentle smile again that made my chest tighten. "Would you like to get some rest?"

I really missed my smartphone in that moment: had it still been with me, I would have been able to pull together a playlist of super sad Italian songs and cried myself to sleep while listening to Riccardo Cocciante sobbing that he loved me more with every day that passed. I pondered over my state of exhaustion: would I perhaps be able to stay awake until dawn? That would amount to what, ten, eleven hours left to spend with him? The tears I had successfully held back in the garage bubbled back with a vengeance, blurring my vision. I swallowed and squirmed away from him. "I'll watch some TV."

THIRTY-FOUR

Good-bye Time

"Shy girls don't get laid. The solution? I-NI-TIA-TIVE. Remember, though: the line between initiative and rape can sometime thread thin (see our table on p. 78 on what qualifies as either initiative, sexual assault, or rape)."

—Aurelia Nichols & Jillie Bean, *101 Tips to Lose Your Virginity after 25*

I still don't understand: How did I manage to fall asleep in front of a Japanese game show where the contestants get smacked in the balls if they fail to answer the host's questions?

Fact is, I woke up with a start around one a.m. I was still in my bed, wearing my underwear and a tank top under the hotel's terry robe, as I had been when my eyes had started to close a few hours earlier. The TV had been turned off. My heart sped up when I realized I was alone in the room. Was March gone already? Without a word? The worst part was that I wasn't really surprised, just hurt and strangely panicked, as if I had just lost a little chunk of myself—yes, kinda like a Potato Head if you will.

I sat up in my bed and squinted in the dark, until I noticed something that made my heart leap again, but for entirely different reasons: the light in the hallway had been turned on, allowing a thin bright ray to filter inside the room from under the set of double doors. Soon dark shapes cut through the light; someone was standing behind the door.

When the lock's click broke the silence, I lay back in bed and pretended to be asleep. March walked into the suite carefully, making me wonder if he could tell when someone wasn't really sleeping: if he could, he didn't seem to mind that I was quietly spying on him the dark. I caught a faint whiff of something sour and smoky. Alcohol. Dammit, here I thought I had been kidnapped by the perfect citizen, and that idiot had gone drinking while I had been asleep.

He went to the bathroom, and I suppose he splashed some water on his face—that's what it sounded like—and brushed his teeth. After that, the light in the bathroom remained on for a few seconds, but there were only very faint sounds: I assumed he was wiping the sink and cleaning after himself.

I'm not sure what I had expected: maybe that he'd rest on the couch with his clothes on, like he had in Paris . . . Certainly not for him to actually follow Curly-prune's advice and get some actual sleep. My eyes widened as I watched him undress, his silhouette outlined by the faint glow that penetrated the room, the product of Tokyo's millions of lights. He folded every single item of clothing neatly on the back of a chair, until all that was left was a pair of dark boxer briefs clinging to his skin.

From what I could make out, the rest of March's body lived up to my first impressions: he didn't just have a fine chest, he had fine everything, and I couldn't remember having ever entertained that sort of thoughts about a man's butt before, not even Masaharu's. He walked to the second twin bed and lay down, sliding silently under the covers and rolling on his side so all I could see was a dark lump I gathered was his back.

His breathing slowed down until I figured he was either asleep or doing a great job at pretending to be. I, however, was nowhere near following suit. This was one of those moments where you know what you have to do—sleep—and all you can think about is doing something stupid instead—like sneaking into his bed and snuggling against that broad, inviting back. Of course, after he had made it clear that he didn't want to take things any further between us, that would have been inappropriate.

No doubt about that.

Don't judge me, I was a victim! I was traumatized and stuff. I crept out of bed like a shadow, scared that the mere sound of my hand pushing the sheets away might wake him up, and tiptoed to his bed, the air coming to my lungs in short, trembling breaths.

He didn't move. Not a single muscle. Not when I lifted his covers, not when I lay close to him in the bed, not even when I covered us both with those same covers, still warm from his heat. I molded my body against his still one, pressed my stomach against that wonderful butt, brushed his legs with my feet: it was pure heaven. Resting my cheek against the skin of his shoulder blade, I couldn't resist the temptation to cop a feel too: I traced the valley of his spine and explored the firm flesh surrounding it, careful to avoid his bruises. Dents, ridges: each scar was like Braille under my fingertips, telling the story of his body. Traveling higher and higher, my palms eventually met the rough, tormented lines of the lion on his shoulder, losing themselves in the maze of thin and blistered scars. As my thumb lingered on the threatening jaw and the perfect circle encasing the design, a powerful emotion washed over me, like my chest was being crushed, but I didn't want it to stop. Before I could think, my lips made contact with the lion's cheek.

I breathed in March deeply, his scent a combination of many ordinary and wonderful things: the alcohol he had been drinking, soap, skin, a little sweat—which, oddly enough, I found incredibly erotic. My mouth resumed planting soft kisses all across the scar, as if that might somehow heal it, make it disappear. I was unconsciously massaging his arm with my right hand, and when his triceps contracted under my fingertips, it dawned on me that his breathing had changed.

March was awake—well, had likely never been asleep in the first place.

Like all those people who show up at the ER in the middle of the night with strange things stuck up their butt, I had a thousand of good excuses ready—most of which sounded nearly as convincing as *I was cooking soup naked at two a.m., tripped in my kitchen, and fell back on a butternut that had been standing on the floor all along.*

I never had the time to test any of these on him, though.

"Island—" His voice was quiet. He sounded exhausted.

Like I said, don't judge me. I lost whatever was left of my dignity.

My voice cracked. "Please . . . I don't want to spend the rest of my life wondering—"

"How it would have felt?"

I swallowed and nodded, even though March couldn't see that. Maybe he just felt it against his back. With a single, fluid movement, he rolled around to face me and pinned me under him, his hands closing around my wrists. A hot flush spread throughout my body that only got worse when I felt his knee force mine apart, settling between my legs.

"I'm drunk. Is this what you want?"

This near-growl was a far shot from the kind of tender intonation I had envisioned for my first time. I nodded again, almost mechanically.

The fingers around my wrists tightened, and the corners of his lips trembled with what appeared to be barely repressed anger. "Is *this* what you want, Island?"

Just a drunken mercy fuck, huh? He was right. I didn't want that. "No."

March released his grip and shifted away. "Good. I can't think of a worse scenario for a first time."

A little part of me wanted to punch him for ending our time together with the same words with which it had begun. I sighed and

Camilla Monk

snuggled against him—yes, I did seize the opportunity to caress that wonderful chest hair: it was at least something, and God, it was even silkier than I had dreamed.

One of the hands that had been pinning me seconds earlier rose to wrap around the base of my neck and force my head up. I remember thinking that it had to be true love, because when March kissed me, I didn't even care that he was still reeking of alcohol.

"Good-bye, Island."

Oh.

I processed his words, my lips searching for his clumsily in the dark.

I felt his fingers squeeze my neck.

And that douche choked me out.

THIRTY-FIVE

The Vanilla Jumbo

"Lucy, I'm your father."

—Dyanna Carlyle, *War in the Stars*

That sneaky bastard had packed sometime during the night, and when reception called to wake me up at seven sharp, I was alone. There was no note, nothing that would have served to at least make a clean cut, just his scent lingering on the sheets and a faint imprint on the pillow suggesting he had spent a few hours in the bed by my side. As usual, there was no questioning his organizational skills: a one-way ticket for JFK and some cash was waiting for me on the nightstand; room service showed up with breakfast at seven thirty.

I didn't touch anything on the lavish tray that little spy groom brought me; I was too brokenhearted. Around eight, I had already showered and packed everything March had bought me in the precious Monoprix bag, fake passport included. My flight would take off at eleven: I had more than enough time to find a cab and head to Narita Airport. I checked out, said good-bye to Fubuki, and my chest heaved a tiny bit when she called me Mrs. June.

After I had taken my first steps alone in the open, I was submerged by an incredible sense of freedom, which seemed to momentarily soothe my heartache. I had spent almost five days as March's "prisoner," depending entirely on him, watching my world shrink until it consisted of only him and the deep bond forming between us, and, as intense, as life-changing as these days had been, I had felt smothered, caged like a bird.

I missed him badly already, almost like he had always been there. But at least I was now free to wander in Roppongi's streets among salarymen and tourists. Inhaling the cool morning air, I looked around until I spotted a Lawson convenience store across the street. Maybe it was time for some self-medication.

Ice cream, here I come!

Dammit, so many brands, so little time! I hummed the tune coming from the shop's speaker, some happy, catchy J-pop hit, as I tried to make a decision: Vanilla Jumbo or Giant Chocolate Cone?

"Make your choice, it's my treat."

Oh.

Fuck.

I didn't turn, in hopes that the deep masculine voice that had offered to buy me ice cream was, in fact, a figment of my imagination, much like the whiff of spicy sandalwood cologne and the presence I could feel behind me. If I didn't see him, he didn't exist, right? A long arm, covered with a dark gray fabric that suggested an expensive suit, a tanned hand grabbing two Vanilla Jumbo ice-cream sandwiches from the freezer. So many little moles. *Dries.*

Straightening my back, I tried to act natural as I turned to face him. I doubt that really worked, though, since a sheen of sweat was already threatening to form on my brow. I looked into his golden hazel eyes, taking in the transparent strips and bruises on his face. He responded with a sardonic smile and greeted me with a curt bow of his head, barely cocking it. "Shall we?" he said, gesturing to the combini register.

"If you try to kidnap me again, I'll scream for help, and I swear you'll have to tear the whole place down to catch me," I hissed, baring my teeth. I thought maybe this was what I needed to look like a bad guy too.

My threat was answered by a surprisingly gentle laugh. "Don't be so dramatic, little Island. Can't a father buy his daughter ice cream and chat for a while?"

I followed him to the register, wondering if the young girl processing Dries's credit card could tell I wanted to bolt. Apparently not, judging by her vacant stare. Now or never, two choices: follow him outside as if everything was all right or jump away from him and alert the people around me. Would he perhaps pull out a gun and kill everyone? For two Vanilla Jumbos he had already paid for anyway and my sorry ass?

In all fairness, I had the intuition that Dries wasn't here for that. Playing along seemed like the best and only way to learn the reason behind his presence. Taking a deep breath, I walked toward the exit with him. "I give you ten minutes. I say where we go, and I'm not following you inside a car or anywhere else secluded. If you try something funny, I'll cry rape in the middle of the street."

"You are in no position to name your terms, but I'll humor you, little Island."

Once outside the Lawson, I guided us toward a small street on the left, which I knew would be a shortcut back to the hotel. Dries followed me, and as Hinokicho Park came in view, he pointed at the peaceful and well-lit alleys bordered by cypresses and cherry trees. "Why don't we sit?"

I gave him a wary look and walked to the bench nearest to the park's entrance, unwilling to wander too far from the hotel. We both settled on the smooth wooden surface—I was careful not to sit too close to him—and for a while, the only sounds were those of paper tearing and teeth biting into crisp waffle before sinking into cheap industrial ice cream.

He eventually stopped eating to speak in a calm, almost subdued voice. "You don't have to worry. Being a good strategist is also knowing when a battle has been lost and cannot be fought again."

"Is that your way of saying you're not going to hurt me this time?"

He nodded. "Yes. I did lose to both your and Léa's games. I made the same mistake with you that I did with her. I believed you could be trusted."

My chest heaved in indignation. "You make me sound like the villain here."

"Receiving and possessing stolen property, use of a false passport, association with criminals, illegal use of a firearm, aggravated assault, attempted murder . . . Should I go on?" he asked, gulping down the last bite of his ice cream sandwich.

I imitated him, looking away to conceal at least part of my embarrassment. He was right. Over the past few days, I had turned from March's captive to his accomplice, and well, I *had* shot one of Dries's henchmen. "You didn't leave me much of a choice. Do you want to discuss what happened at the Rose Paradise, or even with Rislow?"

"March and his friend *chose* to offer resistance at the club." Dries sighed. "And I took care of Mr. Rislow personally."

"What? You're the one who shot him?"

He turned to look at me, and the hard gleam was back in those golden eyes. "I ordered him to bring you to me. He disobeyed that order."

My thoughts raced at the implication of Dries's words. "You mean . . . you didn't ask him to do the . . . table thing?" I asked hesitantly.

His expression darkened. "No."

I stared down at the crumpled paper in my hands. This warm feeling in my chest was, in fact, worse than the sort of Stockholm syndrome I had experienced with March. He, at least, had possessed some redeeming qualities, and his moral compass, while customized to accommodate the demands of his job, made a surprising amount of sense. Dries . . . Dries was *Satan*, the man I held responsible for my mother's death. And my father . . . who had executed Creepy-hat as a punishment for trying to dismember me in his own special way.

In other words, Dries *cared*, to some limited extent.

"Thank you," I murmured.

He gave me a surprised look. "What for?"

I shrugged. "Buying me ice cream and telling me this. Maybe you could have been a decent father . . . in another life."

Dries laughed. "I doubt so."

"Why did you really come back?"

The last of his laughter died, and he tilted his head, examining me with piercing eyes. "There was something I wanted to give you. It's only fair you should have it, now that it's no longer of any use to me."

I stiffened reflexively as he reached inside his jacket, but all he pulled out was a folded sheet of paper, which he handed to me. It was a little crumpled, and when I opened it, the logo of Paris's Hôtel de Crillon decorating its header seemed to have partly faded over the years.

The start of everything. My mother's letter.

The one Dries's men had stolen from M. Étienne's office after spying on us at the Rose Paradise. The one I should have received ten years ago, if my father hadn't told Étienne's assistant to leave us alone.

It was in French, but at first I couldn't really focus on the words. I kept caressing the paper, tracing her round, ample handwriting.

Island,

If you are reading this, I can only hope that you will forgive me for all the lies, for everything I couldn't give you because of the choices I made. I leave it to Simon and Étienne to tell you who I was, what I've done. My only regret is that I won't be able to do it myself.

By now, Simon probably told you that he is not your biological father. I would have wanted for you to meet that man, to see him in the same light I have, but it's better you don't. He's not ready, and may never be. Unfair as it may sound, keeping him away from you was perhaps the only good decision I ever made as your mother.

It's a little ironic that at thirty-eight, I'm finally beginning to understand that for everything we do in this job, for every tip of the balance, there are large-scale consequences. Yet it's too late, the clock only ticks forward, and my time is running out. I won't be there to see you become a woman, I made a terrible mistake, and all I can do now is try to make things right before I go.

If I fail, and people ever come to you or Simon asking for a little trinket I once borrowed, go see that young man you love in Tokyo, he has what you'll need. Do not let your father have it, no matter what. Do not trust him. He's a dangerous man, one who'll choose his brotherhood over you in a heartbeat. Go to the police if you must, but don't trust them either. Use them to shield yourself, that's all they're good for anyway.

I'm sorry, I know this is a lot to take in. I never wanted for you to grow up so fast, like I once had to. I wanted a different life for you. I still do. I know you'll be happy with Simon, he's a great dad, and you're everything to him. Go to school, make new friends, I don't want you to become like me. I've sometimes felt all-powerful, your father made me feel like that, but in the end, it wasn't worth all the things I had to sacrifice.

I love you,
Mom

As I finished reading, I wondered how Dries had felt when going through those same lines. Had it been like looking at himself naked in a mirror? Had it hurt? There was nothing in there he didn't already know: my mother had chosen to escape him because she no longer wanted the Lions to have the Cullinan, and she had been convinced he would never choose us over his "brothers."

I gazed at him and recognized that look, one I had seen in March's eyes. A sense of emptiness, of loss, too deep to even allow for regrets. There was a strange ache in my mouth, a prickling in my eyes. "Was she right about you?"

A familiar poker smile stretched his lips, the very same one he had taught March, I assumed. "You've already asked me this, little Island. If I remember well, I told you that—"

"Dries, *was she right?*" I felt so stupid for crying in front of him, but I couldn't help it.

Now, I'd like to state that if anyone ever confronts me regarding what happened next, I'll deny everything.

He hugged me.

Yes, with his arms.

No, there was no knife, no gun.

I'll never forget the way I froze, the chill I felt course down my back at first. I'm a little ashamed of my reaction, but hey, Dries was no father of the year. Once I had processed that he wasn't going to crush my vertebrae or kidnap me again, I relaxed in his arms, and the smoky scent of the sandalwood seemed warmer than it had once been. My arms found their way around his torso, burying themselves under his jacket, and I rested my head on his broad chest, listening to his heartbeat.

Above me, I registered his voice, low, almost strangled. "I'll never know if she was right, little Island . . . Maybe . . . But I wish she had given me the choice."

Hearing this only made me cry harder. My fists bunched in his shirt, and all the pain, all the anger that had been bottled inside me found their way out, drenching the blue cotton my cheek was pressed against. We both let go after perhaps a minute, and to my amazement, he looked almost as embarrassed as I did. He recovered quickly, though, a calm mask falling on his features again, leaving nothing but an enigmatic smile.

I grinned back, almost in spite of myself.

I think he was about to say something when something changed in his expression. A frown deepened the lines on his forehead, and his index finger rose to trace a tender spot on my neck, making me shiver. "Interesting."

I took me a couple seconds to figure out what he was talking about. When I did, my cheeks heated up, and I thought of the hero of *Scorching Passion of the Billionaire Werewolf* marking his lover. A love bite. Somewhere along the way, March had given me a fricking *love bite*!

Dries probably sensed my distress. His eyes narrowed and took on a devilish expression. "Am I mistaken in presuming that my favorite disciple defiled my own daughter?"

I did feel my lower lip quiver at the memory of my last moments with March, but dissolving into tears again in front of Dries would have been the worst possible response. I straightened my back, steeled my jaw, and jerked one of my shoulders in a badass shrug. "Indeed, you are. He's gone."

"I see . . . Well, I suppose it's better this way. I certainly wouldn't have given my blessing," he noted with a little judgmental pout that reminded me of my dad.

I couldn't suppress a chortle. "I wouldn't have asked . . . Dries, what are you going to do now?"

He leaned back on the bench, placing his hands behind his head and casually crossing his legs. "Do you mean in the next five minutes, or are we having a more general philosophical debate here?"

"Very funny. You know what I mean: the Queen wants your head. Badly. She asked March to do it, but he refused, so I guess she'll send someone else after you," I said, imitating Dries's virile posture.

He stretched nonchalantly. "I wish them the best of luck!"

I winced at the memory of how he had beaten March, back on the roof; the best of luck, indeed . . .

He rose from the bench, towering over me with a mysterious smile. "I suppose it's time for me to say good-bye, little Island."

I gave an affirmative nod and watched him walk away in the direction of the narrow street we had arrived on. After his tall silhouette had faded in the crowd, I got up to head to Narita Airport. This moment might have been all he and I would ever have—*could* ever have—but it was a tiny, precious memory I would cherish. For the record, however, the official version remains that Dries was a soulless turd.

———

I think I floated through the huge, half-empty halls of Narita: I can't remember much until that moment where I was sitting in the boarding area, struggling to concentrate on an issue of *Hanako* while a toddler was throwing a tantrum a few feet away.

Outside the terminal, a light rain started to fall on the tarmac.

Should have I told Dries?

My mother said in her letter that I shouldn't trust him, so I had chosen not to say anything.

What about March?

I felt my cheeks flush with guilt. Ultimately, I had been just as unworthy of March's trust as he had been of mine. I wasn't sure why I hadn't told him. Probably because it had made no sense at the time. Then people had started shooting at us in the club, so it wasn't the best time. Then . . . then it had just become my secret, something warm that I cherished and kept jealously because it came from my mother, and it was only for me, even if I had no idea what it meant.

The little secret Mr. Étienne had whispered in my ear at the club.

I2000009.

I two million nine.

ISLAND AND MARCH RETURN IN *BEATING RUBY*,
THE SECOND NOVEL IN THE SPOTLESS SERIES
BY CAMILLA MONK.

ACKNOWLEDGMENTS

Many thanks to Sharon Belcastro and JoVon Sotak for giving me my shot, to Tiffany Yates Martin for educating a clueless grasshopper in the mystic art of editing, and most of all, to Katerina Baker—my friend and crit partner—without whom I wouldn't have submitted in the first place.

Last but not least, I'd like to thank you, dear reader, for either buying, receiving, borrowing, or stealing this book—no, it did *not* "fall from that truck." Jesus *saw* what you did. In any case, it means a lot to me, and I hope you had some modicum of fun reading *Spotless*!

ABOUT THE AUTHOR

 Camilla Monk is a French native who grew up in a Franco-American family. After finishing her studies, she taught English and French in Tokyo before returning to France to work in advertising. Today, she's a managing partner in a small ad agency, where her job is to handle all things web-related and make silly drawings on the white board when no one is looking. Her writing credits include the English resumes and cover letters of a great many French friends, and some essays as well. She's also the critically acclaimed author of a few passive aggressive notes pasted in her building's elevator.